Blackmoore

A
Novel

MARCUS JAMES

CANDIANO BOOKS

Blackmoore

A
Novel

MARCUS JAMES

Also by Marcus James

Following the Kaehees
In God's Eyes
Bloodlines
Symphony for the Devil

Featured short story anthologies

Ulitmate Undies: Erotic Stories About Underwear and Lingerie
Best Gay Love Stories: New York City
Ultimate Gay Erotica 2007
Dorm Porn 2
Travelrotica 2
Best Gay Love Stories: Summer Flings
Island Boys
Frat Sex 2
Best Gay Love Stories 2009

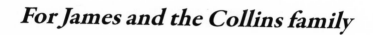

For James and the Collins family

Blackmoore

A

Novel

There are spirits that are created for vengeance,

And in their fury they lay on grievous torments

Ecclesiasticus, 39.33.

ONE

The sounds of slamming locker doors painted green and yellow and the inaudible conversation of teenagers filled the afternoon hall, reveling in the freedom of the weekend. More than a two-day break, it was a chance to escape pre-described rules and dictated behavior. It was a moment when kids could party; it was the marker of rebellion. The time of the week all teenagers waited for in anxious attention: it was finally Friday, and what was more, in two hours it would officially be Friday night.

Trevor Blackmoore made his way in awkward silence, moving between loitering bodies, trying desperately to avoid the snide glares from his peers, praying to make it to his bus before it left the school's property.

The hall was littered with self-proclaimed Goths decked out in black velvet and leather, painted in gaudy eyeshadow and black lipstick. There were neo-hippies and new-ageists, clad in corduroy and Birkenstocks and smelling of patchouli oil. The butt-rockers in their jeans and band t-shirts, not caring about Pacific Northwest weather, glorifying in their long hair, seemingly stuck in the 1980s, though they were all just beginning to fill out their Huggies and Pampers back then.

All of these groups primarily associated together, taking up a series of round, dirt-brown lunch tables in the cafeteria, protecting and teasing one another, guarding against the socially elite and labeled conformists. Trevor knew which group he belonged to. He was aware of his status at Mariner High School; he knew what crowd took him in with open arms and which ones pushed him into the proverbial wayside, and it wasn't the elitists.

They called him names like 'fag' and 'butt-rider', not caring that under his skin and beyond his silence there was feeling, raw teenage emotions just as validated and real as theirs –but in truth, why would they need to know that? When they were who they were, and Trevor was who he was.

He kept his fair hands tucked in the front pockets of his faded sandblast American Eagle jeans. A studded belt of black leather fit loosely around his waist, and a pair of chunky black and red Pumas on his feet, the laces tied sparingly; his feet shuffling along the floor and scratching on the linoleum, the sound almost deafened entirely by the voices of teenagers.

His body was fit, muscles visible through his small navy polo, a patch reading "GAP" was stitched in red just above the left breast, his jaw well-defined, and a pair of dimples became visible whenever he smiled—and that smile of his was perfection. A scattering of dim freckles ran across the bridge of his nose and under large hazel eyes, seemingly able to absorb the world and swallow everything in it whole. It was these eyes and sweet face that made him seem too soft. His hair, short and spiked, seemed to have the glow of a halo under the white luminescence of fluorescent light, the dark red still as sheer as it was in childhood.

Have to get back to Jonathan.

He was so close to the doors, the windows in the middle revealing the weather. It was cloudy, filled with hues of gray, but light from an invisible sun pierced through the clouds, casting bright golden light like showers on the brick of the school and the wet pavement. The grass was mucky and damp, covering a courtyard hosting a wet and rusted anchor, salvaged from an old fishing boat back in Bellingham's glorious cannery days.

The last hurdle for Trevor before reaching the outside was making it past the A-listers of Mariner High School, crowded around the locker of Christian Vasquez, the central god of Mariner. He played all of the sports available and won championship after championship for the school; he'd been Homecoming king every year for the past three years, and Trevor knew that if you were allowed to be in the Homecoming court your freshman year, Christian would have won it then too.

Trevor hated passing these people, hated that every time he came into their galaxy his stomach turned, hated how Christian made his palms sweat and his eyes weak, darting this way and that, unable to focus on one thing—hated it, but couldn't control it.

Christian was gorgeous. One of only two Hispanics at Mariner, standing at a perfect six feet, large almond shaped black eyes contrasting with immaculate mocha flesh, a sheen of barely visible black hairs lining his arms. His lips were dark and like cushions, a patch of black hairs tucked under his bottom lip, trimmed with care, exemplifying his sexual luster.

He looked as if he had stepped right off the cover of an Abercrombie & Fitch catalogue, a nearly impossible feat for most teenage boys, but here Christian was, being just that. In fact, Abercrombie was pretty much the only thing you could find clothing his body; his sly grin made Trevor's knees buckle.

There were others as he passed Christian's throng, all of them looking like models. There was Cheri Hannifin, a perfect size two, standing at five feet six inches, her brown hair wrapped up in a bun, loose strands hanging down selectively in curly tendrils, a set of black chopsticks holding it in place.

Her petite body was clothed in a white dress shirt, the collar large and folded down, resting atop a tight black cardigan, the buttons just reaching to her chest, cupping her breasts. She wore a plaid skirt—the colors charcoal, red, and white—and a pair of black-and-gray diamond patterned knee-high socks, her feet encased in high-heeled Mary Janes, the black of the leather buffed and polished. She was maybe the most vicious person Trevor had ever known, though she hadn't started out that way.

As he passed them, he watched the popular throng turn and look at him. Christian leaned against his locker, his right foot propped up behind him, a wry smile on his face, revealing perfect white teeth, his black eyes like two pools of dark waters, and it sent chills down Trevor's spine.

"What are you looking at, fag?"

Trevor met with the cold gaze of Cheri's brown eyes, standing out against perfect milk skin, her black brows thin and plucked, her lids colored in black powder, her lips rouged in a red-brown. It was a color that made Trevor think of dried blood, and her cheeks were lightly pink with blush. But her voice was harsh and like a knife, not soft like one would suspect when looking at her.

"Nothing, I'm just going...."

He bowed his head and made his way to the doors, the crowd around him in perfect unison, matching their pitches of laughter. Trevor looked behind him, his eyes catching with Christian, a soft smile resting on his face. He was not laughing; he never really did, but he still created an unease inside of Trevor Blackmoore, an unease that pushed him to nausea.

The school bus was packed with noisy high school students, all of them taking up the seats in the back, forcing Trevor to the front of the bus. He hated the front of the bus, hated it because freshmen sat up there, hated it because it meant less of a chance of sitting on your own, and it meant possibly being spoken to by the bus driver.

The winter air made the stainless steel interior of the bus as cold as ice and the brown vinyl of the seats were almost equally as chilling, forcing Trevor to reach for the black hooded sweatshirt inside of his book bag, pulling it over his head quickly, shivering as soon as his body began to make its transition from cold to warm. He just wanted to get home.

As the bus made its way out of the school's cul-de-sac drive, pulling onto Bill McDonald Parkway, Trevor spied Christian

Vasquez, Cheri Hannifin, and others in their group make their way to the parking lots, moving as if they owned the world, and standing out like they were glowing gods, gracing the world with their ethereal light.

He lost sight of them as the bus made its way up towards Western, driving by crap-brown portables and the music hall, as well as the usual evergreens, so common to the Pacific Northwest. He gained sight of them once more pulling out of the parking lot, pissed that they had to let the bus pass by before they could pull out.

Christian, Cheri, and another girl were sitting in Christian's blue Mustang convertible. Despite the cold the top was down, and behind them was the silver Camry of Greg Sheer, another member of the A-list and competitor/friend of Christian. They were friends because they had to be, but truly enemies underneath.

The worst of it for Trevor was that he had grown up with all of them. Gone to the same elementary school, the same middle school, and now the same high school as the rest of them. In kindergarten they had all played together, gone to one another's birthday parties, and played in each other's yards. That was the world of South Hill, the eldest and most elitist part of Bellingham, where old money families fought to keep their standing against the new money invasion that bought land and built modern mansions in the cliff-side properties of Edgemoor, overlooking Bellingham Bay and parts of Fairhaven.

Fairhaven was the original town, founded by new arrivals, making a profit from their designed fishing port, not officially joining the town of Bellingham until the near end of the nineteenth century, though Bellingham had grown out of this little village.

Overlooking it all were the dominant Victorians, vestiges of what once was, and a perfect postcard of what it was still trying to be. The school bus turned up Knox Street and made its way up the winding hill past the Society for Photo-Optical Instrumentation Engineers: a building made up of perfectly formed geometric shapes, dominating a grassy knoll, made of a combination of stone and brown siding, the building itself conjuring all sorts of ideas in the deep recesses of a persons fevered imagination.

As Trevor neared his stop, positioned in front of the alley separating his home from the one next door, he could feel a soft murmur, like a mild vibration funneling in his body, stirring his soul and awakening him from his droll day. It pulled him from his lazy slouch and towards the bus door before it had even come to a halt; Jonathan was waiting for him.

"You have a good day!" the bus driver shouted out to him as he stepped off the bus, his feet tapping the wet pavement.

The alley before him was long and silent, cast in blue shadow, the sun slowly setting beyond the bay. Its orange, red, and pink light lit the sky ablaze, though the clouds were still prominent, as if waiting for the sun to extinguish before it could take over the city completely and envelop it in its dark-puff arms, preparing to let down a shower of rain or possibly snow.

Poking out above the homes down the alley was the triangular arch of a large Queen Anne Victorian with wood siding painted plum, accentuated with powder-pink trim. Two large, red-bricked chimneys were visible, reaching out like a pair of lightning rods, their patches and crevices filled with rich green moss—the same state as every other chimney in coastal Washington.

To the right of the lane was his home, its front lined by dominating maples, the yard groomed into perfect green. A dark flagstone path led to a mammoth, two-story federal-style manor, its siding as white as fresh clouds, the multi-frame windows accentuated with royal green shutters.

Protecting the rooms from curious onlookers were rich green satin drapes, and the front door was accentuated with a pristine molding. Carved against the wood of the house were two faux columns, seemingly to hold up an ornate decorative portico, and a set of four topiaries decorated the front of the house.

Trevor felt that familiar pull and looked up, his eyes meeting with the second floor's hall window, directly above the front door. He watched as the curtain parted and spied a faint male form blurring, staring down at him, coming in and out of visibility. Jonathan was calling.

Inhaling a deep breath and drinking up the crisp, clean winter air tinged with sea salt from the nearby bay, Trevor closed his eyes for just a moment, extinguishing the thought of school and Christian. Allowing it to pass him as the air passed through his lungs and back out, exhaling through his passages and recycling into the atmosphere.

Another tremor.

Trevor Blackmoore made his way to the front door, inserting his key into the matching hole on the left, grasping the wrought-iron handle, and stared at his reflection in the window pane. He pushed the door open and stepped inside his home, looking behind him once more, looking upon the grim afternoon before turning and closing the door.

He was home.

The hall smelled of chrysanthemums and fresh juniper, most likely purchased down at the little garden shop in Fairhaven, a favorite place of his mother's, who delighted in those brief moments when she could go out into the world and still keep in her seclusion.

To his left was the formal living room, filled with sleek French and English furniture, many pieces formed from black leather or satin, sitting atop red and green antique rugs with ornate patterns over aged hardwood floors, the large space permeating with old world sophistication. It was suffocating in its own right.

Just beyond the room's entrance was a sun room, added to the home in 1920, completed eight months later. This room was the entire length of the home—not a particularly spacious room, but due to its length it could fit as many as thirty people at one time. Its floor was made of brick, furniture of white wicker occupying the space. The large drawing room doors that separated this room from the living room were pushed wide open most of the time, only closing when his mother entered into one of her suffocating bouts of depression, forcing herself into such a state that it bordered on catatonic. Many people were afraid of her; not Trevor.

He knew his mother and understood her, understood her suffocation, suffocation brought on by strict religious fervor. She was in a chain of Irish Catholicism, unable to break free from it, though she hadn't gone to church regularly in years. It seemed to Trevor that even though she was a devoted wife to his jerk of a stepfather, she truly was detached and cold, sometimes even unable to communicate with her own son.

To his right was the media room, filled with relaxed couches, a large television set hidden inside a chest made of cherry-wood, and with the simple press of a remote control the set would rise up from its secret compartment, ready to be viewed. Both of these rooms led to others within the house. To the back of the sitting room was a large office, occupied by his stepfather—though before his arrival it had been his mother's ball room; in fact, it was constructed as such back in the 1880s.

When his stepfather moved in, the room was changed, truly killing his mother on the inside, but as with most things she kept quiet, opting rather for peace than for selfish banter of wants and haves.

Beyond the media room was a formal dining room dominated by a grand cherry-wood table, the chairs large and ornate, the table-top itself always decorated with polished china and silver basins. The walls in the rest of the home were striped in red-and-white paper. It was like this even in the sun room, even in the office, but in the dining room the walls were covered in red satin, translucent patterns of moons and planets visible only in light.

Just beyond the swinging wood door was a large gourmet kitchen, updated with modern utilities of stainless steel and a large island-combination-stove, with the trash dispenser hidden discreetly within. Before Trevor now was the long narrow hall, paved in hardwood, draped by a long, green rug. Down the hall to his right was the stairwell, facing a narrow bookcase, spiralling its way up to the second floor where Jonathan waited.

Trevor spied a wiry shadow move along the top floor, silently beckoning for him. He made his way to this now, though he was brought to a halt by the sudden call of his mother.

"Trevor!"

Her voice was smoky and seductive; it was the voice of the great Kathryn Blackmoore.

He pulled the doors open.

"Yes?"

He found her in there, a Screwdriver held secure in her strong, pale hands—her midday drink of choice—and her long arms were folded around her thin waist. Her five-foot-nine body was clothed in a sleek, black spaghetti-strapped dress which was tight around her full breasts; a three-tiered pearl necklace rested in her cleavage.

Her features were sharp and her eyes as pale blue as humanly possible, looking like ice. Her hair reached to her shoulders, a rich auburn layered by expensive hairdressers. Her entire form breathed sexuality, and this was further complimented by long legs strapped in a pair of Bellemar black stilettos by Michael Kors, spiking the floorboards; this was what made Kathryn Blackmoore Kathryn Blackmoore.

"How was your day?"

There it was, that voice, sultry and somewhat masculine; Trevor wished he sounded like that.

"Uneventful as usual...."

She nodded and smirked, taking another drink from her glass.

"Let's go out for dinner tonight!"

"Is Tom coming with us?"

Kathryn shook her head and made her way towards him, placing her soft hands on his shirt, smoothing it out.

"Tom is in Virginia; he left thirty minutes ago."

He felt the pull within him, felt it as always.

"Now, go change; someone's been expecting you...."

He looked at her, startled, but Kathryn Blackmoore only winked. She always knew so much, but how could she know of his friend upstairs? Trevor walked towards the living room, trying to shake off the strangeness of his mother.

"And Trevor!"

"Uh-huh?"

"Close the door behind you."

He did.

Trevor bound the wood steps, winding up to the second floor, brushing past the large fern on the landing, hearing the house moan with life.

TWO

The last rays of light pierced through those familiar parted drapes, rich and green, the light like a beam, piercing the air of a particularly dim room, particles of dust visible in the bright intrusion, causing Trevor's eyes to squint closed, the corners of the lids creased, lines running together. He hated reflecting on the school day, hated having to reflect on the people there—the same people that had played in his backyard all throughout childhood, those same people who now looked down on him and considered him to be nothing more than an infringement on their privileged world.

He closed his eyes, ignoring the gentle brush of vibrating air, hot and somewhat moist, caressing his forehead. It was simply Jonathan, his childhood friend, the only one who continued to stay by his side, the only one to truly know Trevor inside and out. Like all things in one's secret world, everything breathes the air of your own life.

He drifted back into dreams: dreams made of memories, dreams of a time when Trevor belonged, dreams made strictly for childhood.

"...Three, two, one, ready or not, here I come!" Little Trevor Black-moore opened his tiny lids, his delicate lashes fluttering like moths' wings, adjusting to the bright summer light, standing in his back courtyard, the red brick reaching from one end to the other, leaving no room for grass. On the brick were two black wrought-iron benches and three sets of black wrought-iron tables, with four chairs each, decorated with tiny white candles inside little glass votives, the Fourth of July party was preparing to start.

Kathryn was inside of the house, most likely in the sun room chatting with friends, all of them with drinks in hand, laughing and speaking of adult things while their children played hide-and-seek in the back. Four maple trees reached out strategically in the back, no more than twenty feet in height, and strung about with Chinese lanterns; no doubt someone was hiding behind the trees.

Trevor was determined to catch one person in particular: Christian Vasquez, who always made it to home base, which was the carriage house along the road, now his mother's secret place, a place that was secured with three padlocks, a place that Trevor had only seen once and could only vaguely remember.

It was a place that had smelled wonderfully and sat illuminated with firelight. A place of plaster eyes, a place that filled him with fear and peace all at the same time. A strange combination that was often confusing, even now, even though he at this point was intimately aware of the mirrored world: the place of trance-words and things named Jonathan—the most familiar place in all the world.

'I know where they are...' he said to Trevor in the secret language of the mind, in the voice that only Trevor could hear, touching him with the flesh that only he could feel.

"Where's Christian?" Trevor was scanning the courtyard, trying not to look conspicuous, wanting to be as nonchalant as possible, well aware of the danger of people knowing too much of him.

He felt that vibratory hand graze his shoulder and grasp his arm, directing it to the appointed area just behind the drapery of Virginia creeper along the thin wood fence, slowly rotting away with erosion and the growing weight of the plant.

'There....'

Trevor nodded casually and made his way between the trees, running lightly along the flagstone, his little tennis shoes tapping on the brick, seeing the others pop out of hiding.

Cheri Hannifin brushed past him in her blue jumper and brown pigtails, giggling inanely to herself.

Little Greg Sheer was not far behind, wearing a pair of jean shorts and a black t-shirt with the Batman emblem on the chest, his golden hair bright like the sun, and his blue eyes were not unlike his mother's: steely and cool.

But he could care less about either one of them. Trevor only wanted Christian, and with his specter's help he was going to get him.

The air smelled of the sea and barbequed meat from the back kitchen, as well as from the fire pits in the surrounding yards. The collective clouds of smoke and the fragrance of charred flesh filled the warm summer air and carried itself on the cool breeze.

Trevor crept behind the carriage house.

"I found you, I found you!" he called repeatedly, his little index finger pointing at the little boy crouched behind the green and rope-like plant. A smirk spread across his face, followed by a wink, and then he was off, both boys laughing as Christian made his way to home base, confident in his success and spotless hide-and-seek record.

Trevor watched as the vibratory form of Jonathan moved in front of the little boy and stood his spectral ground, pulling energy from Trevor as well as the earth, making himself as firm as possible, causing Christian to run right into his phantom gut, bringing the little boy to a halt and not allowing him to move.

For a brief moment Trevor just stared, fearing that Jonathan would become visible to the others. Normally he looked like nothing more than the heat that vibrates from metal, looking wavy and somewhat like gas, but in this new solidity Trevor feared discovery. He realized rather quickly that no one could see him, so Trevor ran.

"You're it!" Trevor declared, placing his hand on Christian's shoulder, causing the boy to look at him in brief disappointment, but like all things with children, this disappointment was passing. The four children continued to play, as other kids began to arrive.

Trevor's cousins and fellow classmates from Lowell Elementary arrived, ready to join the existing game or form a new one altogether. Trevor was wary of Jonathan's presence, knowing that he wasn't the only one who knew about spirits. In fact, it was a well-known thing in his family, and his cousins had their own strange secrets much like Trevor, but completely individual in their form.

The soft whisper of his name forced Trevor back into the present. The light of day was fading fast, and his room was becoming darker by the minute, and Jonathan was growing desperate, commanding attention. The curtains were pushed open by male hands, visible in the dark; in fact, all of Jonathan was visible in the dark.

Standing at a steady six feet and three inches, dressed in a tweed suit made of shadow, a strong face with prominent cheekbones stared out on the front lawn. Translucent white skin, like well-polished marble, big oval black eyes deep and endless, absorbing all of the light, his dark hair well-groomed, styled much like Trevor's and making this specter—this familiar—look incredibly beautiful, sharing secret desires with Trevor Blackmoore, desires named sinful by any God-fearing human being. Thankfully Trevor had no fear of God; in fact, God was a foreign concept to Trevor.

'*You need to be dressed for dinner....*'

His voice always seemed like a whisper, trailing off, and never with question. That was one of the things Trevor adored about Jonathan.

"I know."

Jonathan nodded and went to Trevor's closet, pulling it open and removing a crisp white shirt and fine black slacks draped over a wood hanger, laying it before Trevor on his bed. The spirit went to his chest of drawers and pulled out a pair of white briefs and his black dress socks, laying them out atop the shirt and slacks.

Trevor stood and lifted his shirt from off his head, his nipples becoming erect at the moment of Jonathan's touch, those spectral hands moving along his body, those ghost-lips upon his flesh, slowly moving down his chest, trailing along defined abs and pulling open his jeans. Trevor's eyes rolled into the back of his head as his exposed body found its way back onto the mattress, indulging in the familiar routine.

THREE

The Vasquez residence sat atop an almost football-sized grassy knoll on South Hill. A long concrete path led from the sidewalk and up to the front door, rising just a little as the front sloped just a bit. The original house had been torn down eight years previous, and a new two-story home was constructed in its place, the Vasquez family taking temporary residence in a large condo while the two-year construction took place.

The house was simple in shape: an intricate square, painted in white maple, the front patio extended far on the left. One large picture window looked out onto the yard, and to the right were a set of French doors, the frames made of rich redwood. In the middle was the front door, made of the same redwood, a sleek glass pane adorning the center.

Jutting out at the left was the dining room with its two picture windows; the first looked directly out onto the front of the house, and the second was around the corner, overlooking the side. Illuminating the property were modern flood lights.

The second floor was just as simple. A square roof sat atop a series of French doors overlooking the front yard and the bay. Directly above the front door were another set of French doors, which opened up to a gallery which wrapped around the front of the house, supported by three redwood posts fixed to the ground by stone columns. Around the corner was another, more defined balcony, with an enclosed corner.

There were another set of doors which led into Christian's room, which hosted a fireplace. The roof was adorned by four discreet cylinder chimneys, and at night the second floor lit up with the same flood lights as below. Though magnificent and obvious in showing wealth, for Christian the size of his home was nothing more than a passing thought. In his world, this wasn't privilege; it was simply a way of life.

A polished white pine floor led from the front door into the large, open foyer, and a matching pine stairwell reached up from the center of the foyer, opening on a landing. To the left and right of the landing were two staircases leading up to the second floor, which hosted the Master bedroom, a library, three guest rooms, two guest baths, and Christian's bedroom, which had its own granite-covered bathroom and spacious walk-in closet.

To the right of the front door was the entertainment room, which was filled with large Italian leather sofas and matching arm chairs, as well as a large plasma television set which was positioned discreetly behind a large Monet which, when commanded by a remote, lifted up, revealing the hidden television. Stored in the ceiling just above this was a large film screen which spanned the thirty-five foot room, coming down at the simple press of a button.

To the left of the front door was the formal living room, filled with soft furniture made of rich fabrics, such as velvet and satin, the focal point being the granite fireplace mantle—five feet in height and carved with two mermaids, not unlike the trademark seal of Starbucks. Just beyond the formal living room was the large dining room. The long oak table sat in the center of the room, dressed with sheer white fabric, further accentuated with clean white china and crystal wine glasses, the room itself almost always empty.

Through the swinging door was the large show kitchen, complete with two islands and three stoves, each with its own oven, and in the corner of the kitchen in an out-cove lined with a wrap of bay windows overlooking the back garden was a small breakfast table made of oak and clear of any dishware. The only thing decorating the table was a crystal vase filled with fresh-cut white oleanders.

All of the walls in the home were cream in color and neatly supported one-of-a-kind originals painted from all over the world.

Christian's mother Lila was an art and antiques dealer, and she took many works home with her. Tract lighting lined the ceilings, making it feel as if you were in a gallery. Down the hall behind the stairwell was a set of steps that led out onto a spa with walls of glass, complete with an enormous lap pool, Jacuzzi, and sauna: a favorite spot of his mother's—as well as his father's—when he would fuck around with a female client during the day.

Directly across the pool was a large door which led out onto the two-acre back garden, filled with rose bushes and lilac trees, as well as carnations and cherry blossoms, which were so common in the Pacific Northwest. To the right of the spa entrance was a set of pocket doors, which were pushed back into the slits in the wall, where a series of steps led down into the game room.

The game room was the size of a classroom: filled with two pool tables, an air hockey machine, eight couches—all strategically placed—and twelve pinball machines, some dating back to the late Seventies.

"God, can you believe him?" Cheri Hannifin said, following it with a laugh and looking at Teri Jules, who rolled her eyes and turned her attention to the boys playing pool. Teri's intoxicated gray irises watched as the balls clanked around, some rolling into the corner and side pockets, others just rolling on the surface of the green fabric.

Teri wrapped her finger around a strand of blonde curl slightly dry and crunchy with hairspray, her khaki capris feeling soft on her now touch-sensitive hands. The spring pink of her polo seemed to glow under the bright lights of the game room. She wanted Greg badly, and truly could not care about anything else.

"He's just a stupid faggot, so what?" Greg shrugged his shoulders, wearing a blue tee and flexing hard biceps just past the sleeves, looking with steely blue eyes.

He waited for Christian to take his shot, upset that he missed the pocket by less than an inch.

"So?" Cheri arched one sharp eyebrow, looking to Christian for support; he said nothing. "He was also one of us, and now he walks around school as if he doesn't know who we are, hanging around with that less-deserving crowd of misfits, like that fucking Braxton Volaverunt!"

She took a swig from her drink.

"He just threw us aside as if we never existed!"

They all watched as one red solid rolled into the side pocket, circling around a little in the plastic basket.

Christian looked up at all of them for the first time since coming into the game room.

"If I remember correctly *we* threw him aside, not him. I mean, who cares what he does, or who he hangs out with for that matter? I know I don't give a fuck...."

Christian finished his bottle of hard cola, letting the slightly bitter syrupy liquid ride down his throat, burning slightly.

He cast the bottle aside and went to the large fridge, removing another brown bottle and popping the cap, consuming most of it in the first swig. He looked outside, out on the nighttime garden, the spotlights turning on as timed, the green of the lawn brightly lit. He tried to forget the intruding memories of his childhood.

"That's not the point. Besides, you threw him aside; we just followed suit because that little freak's a fag. Whether he admits it or not, that's what he is. He betrayed us, but how dare he disrespect us or how we've all grown up by associating with *those* people!"

Cheri was in a rage; everyone could see it. She perhaps had been the closest to Trevor Blackmoore, next to Christian, but he broke all of that trust by being something else—something other than them, and he acted as if it had never mattered, as if he had not disrupted the social order of their prestigious neighborhood.

"What did you want him to do, Cheri? Did you want him to spend every day alone, unable to have any friends?"

They all looked at him now, a sick smile on Greg Sheer, venom in Cheri's eyes; it was as if she was about to consume him.

"Are you defending him now?" Cheri fired back.

It was more of an accusation than a question, and there was no way Christian was going to lose control over the pack that he led.

"Look, I think that he is a worthless faggot just like you guys do, and we were right in getting rid of him, but I don't think that he should not be entitled to a life.

"We got rid of him; we let go of our control, so as of now it is none of our business!"

He took his pool stick and leaned down over the table, placing the cue just behind the white ball, focusing on the left hole in the corner pocket—trying to forget Trevor Blackmoore, trying to get his sullen image from off of his brain, wanting nothing else than to get that ball in the pocket.

"You know he has a crush on you?"

He let go of the pool stick, losing his shot, scratching on the green fabric; Cheri's words had summoned something buried deep.

"Really, and how do you know this?"

Teri Jules stood at one of the pinball machines, trying in her drunken haze to actually see the round metal ball and not just hallucinate it; she let out a slight giggle at her best friend's comment.

"That's easy, it's in his eyes whenever he looks at you. It's so easy to read on his face, but then again you've always done that to him...."

She looked over his shoulder and locked eyes with Greg, who nodded cautiously.

"Done what?"

He looked down at her, casting her entire body in his shadow, her breasts plump and heaving up and down with each breath.

"Made him blush."

Christian's mind was beginning to race.

"It's true, you make his cheeks turn as red as your mom's convertible; Trevor adores you."

The realization struck him like a baseball strikes a gloved hand, drilling into it with professional heat.

"I think you should do something with that."

His black eyes grew large with wonder before his lids came down and forced him to look at her with obvious suspicion.

"Why?"

Cheri Hannifin stood up and looked at him, a sinister grin on her face, her brown eyes sharp, not caring about her skirt, which had ridden up just a little in the front, revealing black silk panties.

"Because it might be fun, and who knows? Maybe, just maybe, he'll realize how much he betrayed us...."

She knew that Christian did not get off on the same kind of mind games that she did—or Greg, for that matter. They all knew that they were going to have to rope him in, just as Christian would have to rope in Trevor.

"Well, I think he would be suspicious of that. Besides it's not like my sexual history isn't known throughout Mariner—"

"Don't worry about that; you can just make up some bullshit like, well, your sex life is bullshit—a cover up. I'm sure he'd buy it!"

Christian shook his head, not really wanting to know what he could or could not do to Trevor Blackmoore. After all, that entire family was strangely iffy.

"I don't think that this is a good idea. It doesn't make any sense; I'm not set out to ruin his life, I'm really not—"

Greg cut him off.

"Dude, he started airing out our dirty laundry with all of his friends, including stuff about your dad."

That was the ticket and Greg knew it; they all knew it. It was no secret that Christian's dad was screwing every other woman in Bellingham and abroad, but Christian wouldn't want it announced to the entire world. If telling him that Trevor was doing this would get him in the game, then so be it.

"All right! All right... I'll do it; I'll do it."

Christian tried to push away this mix of anger and regret, focusing only on his plan of attack. Cheri kissed him on the cheek and he and Greg high-fived, all of them stumbling in a drunken haze.

"I say we all go swimming!" Teri Jules shouted, running up the steps and towards the spa door, throwing off her polo and kicking off her shoes.

Greg was in hot pursuit after her, taking off his clothes, revealing a soft tan on a sculpted frame, removing his jeans—now in nothing more than plaid boxers, ready to screw Teri in the sauna.

Christian and Cheri stayed behind, watching the spectacle. Both feeling the freedom of wealth, knowing that no one could truly live this kind of sexually and socially libertine life without money and power.

It left him feeling hollow inside.

Cheri reached down and squeezed one firm cheek, laughing in Christian's ear before joining the other two in the spa. He thought he was going to vomit.

FOUR

They sat in the black Lexus in silence, no one really sharing what was on their mind; neither one could care less.

Downtown was bright in the winter night. The orange light of the street posts caused the thick clouds to look as if they were on fire; the usual throng of hippies and artists and those who liked to think of themselves as such were gathered outside of Stuart's Coffee Shop, the two-story bricked piece of Bellingham Americana. They drove past the corner bank and the vehicle took a left on Commercial Avenue, parking across from the Mt. Baker Theater.

The driver, who was an aged man in his early seventies, walked over to Kathryn's door and opened it, taking her hand gently as she stepped out, clothed in an iridescent red dress stopping just past her knee, a matching pair of Manolo Blahniks on her feet, the thin heel spiking the cement of the sidewalk. Trevor climbed out behind his mother, desperate to get inside and protect himself against the crisp winter air. It was dropping to seventeen degrees rather quickly, and the threat of snow was eminent.

"Have your cell phone on; I'll call you when we're ready to leave," she said to the driver.

"Yes, Mrs. Blackmoore."

They exchanged nods and he climbed back into the driver's seat, pulling out and moving out of sight.

"Ready?" she asked her son, the usual string of pearls around her neck, her eyes sharp and attentive. They walked to the looming Bellingham Towers, a fourteen-story building which used to be a hotel, but was now inhabited by a slew of corporate offices. The very last floor was the Nimbus Bar and Grill.

Trevor grasped the iron handle and pulled the door open, allowing his mother to go in first before following. The lobby was lit but quiet, all of the offices closed up for the evening, and Trevor imagined that a few scattered lawyers were still in their offices, working till the late hours of the night.

In silence they walked to the wall of elevators, pressing the button marked with the 'up' arrow, waiting several seconds for the door to open. Trevor thought his mother stoic and regal in her Prada dress and designer heels, a woman who commanded attention from the people of Bellingham, and with just a look she could instill life-altering fear inside a person without giving them a second thought.

Kathryn's gaze was killer.

"Ahem...."

They both heard the purposeful clearing of a male throat, and Kathryn and Trevor turned, acknowledging the familiar face of Emanuel Vasquez. He stood behind them, staring, a smile like his son's on his face: grinning with something more despicable behind it.

He continued to look Kathryn up and down, taking all of her in, not the least bit ashamed of his thoughts. His salt-and-pepper hair dipped in a widow's peak and his skin was glossy and dark, so much darker than his son's. Trevor guessed that he had just returned from a warmer climate.

His simple black suit made him look powerful, which he was, but Trevor also knew that he was afraid of his mother.

"Emanuel..." Kathryn smiled, and gave a slight nod.

"Kathryn, how are you?" He seemed so fake and Trevor wished nothing more than to drive his knee into the man's crotch.

"I'm fine, and you?"

He nodded and began to go on and on about his trip to Belize; it felt as if it had lasted for twenty minutes.

"That's wonderful," his mother interjected.

Emanuel Vasquez looked at Trevor, taking him in, straining to recall the last time that he had seen the young Blackmoore.

"And Trevor—my, how you've grown; are you enjoying school?"

He did not want to speak with this man about Mariner High School or anything else that involved his son.

"Fine."

He made it well-known by the tone of his voice that he did not wish to speak of the matter any further.

"So, Emanuel, how's Lila?"

The question seemed to make his blood run cold, and he looked at Kathryn with brief contempt, but in fear of it coming off too obvious he calmed his sneer and chuckled.

"Oh, you know Lila, always finding some rare piece of art. Would you excuse me?"

Kathryn nodded and Trevor just stared, snickering as Emanuel made his escape down the hall and into the junction of offices.

"Well, that went well...." Kathryn placed her hand on the small of her son's back and guided him into the open elevator.

"They're all pompous assholes, him and his son!"

He could not keep his anger at bay; the very thought of the Vasquez men made him sick to his stomach. Kathryn only nodded casually. Trevor stared at their hazy reflections in the steel doors of the lift, wishing that he had the courage to tell all of his former friends what he truly thought of them, but he feared the kind of control that they could exude on the rest of the student body.

The restaurant had most likely been the penthouse suite when the building was a hotel, and it was made up of large windows which gave patrons a 180-degree panoramic view of the entire city of Bellingham and beyond it, into future development sites. This was the tallest building in the city, and nothing seemed to matter up here, nothing at all.

"Two?" a young woman asked, no more than twenty-three years of age. Her skin was milk-white and her hair was long and brown and kept in loose tendrils.

She wore powder-pink lipstick, light blush, and soft lilac eyeshadow. She was dressed in a simple white shirt, a black skirt, black tights, and black heels. A little diamond necklace was hanging in her cleavage, and her entire demeanor was bright.

"Yes."

The hostess nodded and led mother and son through the restaurant.

The table was lit by a single candle, a bottle of wine sitting against the window sill with the salt and pepper, draped with a thick white cloth. Fine napkins of cloth were rolled up and pulled through a sterling silver ring, and there were two wine glasses.

Trevor and Kathryn took their seats and the young girl sat the wine list down in front of her, ready for her discriminate viewing.

"Your server will be with you shortly," she said before departing, his mother smiling and nodding her away, ready to intoxicate herself even more.

Trevor could not help but think about his former friends. Memories were playing with him, pulling on the chords of his brain, massaging his flesh with thoughts, thoughts of happier times. He needed to forget them.

"Tell me about Catholic school?"

The question seemed to take his mother by surprise, and in fact it seemed as if her blood had run cold, looking up from the wine list, staring at her son for a moment before setting it down and flipping back her auburn hair.

"What should I tell you?" Her voice, so rich, so controlled, appeared now to give way to a terrifying weakness.

"I don't know, anything; anything at all."

His curiosity acted like a knife, cutting his mother deeply, exposing an infected wound not yet healed.

"Well,"—another deep breath—"the nuns were cruel. So cruel, in fact, that many people left there thinking that they should've all been arrested and given the death penalty. It was an awful place, a place where you left afraid to challenge even the idea of God because you feared what might have happened.

"My mother Annaline did not want me to go. In fact, she could not come and see me during the week, but my father Trevor—for whom you are named –thought that it would be good for me.

"He also feared the 'radical' influence my mother was having on me, and he feared our family, feared the name Blackmoore. I think that fear started when he married my mother and she refused to take on his last name."

It looked to Trevor that his mother was not with him anymore, her eyes placid and looking out over the city, lit with sparkling lights; he felt so confused.

"But I thought you loved Grandpa?"

She looked at him for a moment and smiled softly, letting it die from her face before continuing.

"Oh, I adored my father, but he was so scared, so scared of Queen Mab; hated that my mother and I spent so much time over at her house, and he would frequently walk down the alley and demand for us to come back home, making up some terrible excuse."

Queen Mab.

He had not seen his great-aunt in almost a week, though she only lived four houses down the alley. School had just taken up too much time, and stories of ghosts and other things, though wonderful, were not at the forefront of his brain.

"Did you ever tell Grandma about what happened?" His mother never really ever spoke of Catholic school, and yet it still affected her, dictating her very own comfort in being out in public alone.

"It wasn't until a priest's unfortunate accident that she learned of what truly happened."

"Were your parents mad?"

He felt as if it would only take the simple act of closing his eyes to see what had happened to his mother, as if he could travel back into her past and discover what had hurt his mother in such a way that it shaped her into the secluded person that she had become.

"They were upset with what happened—though my mother was simply happy to have me home, and she threw a big party in the old ballroom and celebrated for days. My father, on the other hand, seemed quite upset, though he died only a week later."

"All of the men and women not born into this family die early." She averted her gaze. "I think all of the Blackmoores have learned that if you marry someone, death will take them shortly thereafter ... like your father."

It was true. When Trevor was only eleven years old, his father died of a sudden brain tumor. No amount of chemotherapy could have helped; he died within an hour of discovery. His mother had known, had been prepared, and so for many years—in fact, as long as Trevor could remember—she had been somewhat cold, even to him.

"That's why most of the women have one-night stands or lovers on the side. Until the Sixties the only way a man could respectably have a kid was by marrying—well, same with a woman—but no matter how much they loved their wives, they all knew that the women would die and there was nothing that they could do about it.

"Like I said, if you're not born into this family, you're going to die."

"So we're just a family of widows...."

Kathryn nodded.

"And if any one of them is getting married or planning to marry, then they are well aware that they will be burying soon and are most likely putting money aside for the funeral."

"How are you both this evening?" The waiter looked no more than nineteen years of age—not very tall, perhaps five feet five inches at the most, but he looked wonderful: a true American beauty.

He had a soft-structured face, short dishwater blond hair, bright blue eyes, and a winning smile—a smile that ignited Trevor in the most secret of ways, similar to the shock that was Christian but so very individual from it.

This waiter (whose name tag read *Parker)* seemed to be unconscious of the effect his smile had on people, which made him pure—unlike Christian, who knew exactly what his looks could do, and knew exactly when to use them and when not to.

Parker was beautiful and Trevor wished to have him, wished to keep him tucked away in his pocket, accessible whenever desired. Instead Trevor chose to allow this boy's face to burn itself onto the surface of his brain, where he could then look on it whenever he chose; it was the next best thing.

"Wonderful," Kathryn said, catching her breath.

Trevor could see by the reaction on his mother's face that she was also taken by this young man, but like always, she regained her composure quickly.

"Have you decided on what you would like to drink?"

Parker's eyes sparkled in the candlelight.

"Yes, I think we are. I'll have a Screwdriver and Trevor will have a Coke, please."

Parker's face tightened slightly with a grin before heading over to the bar to put in the order.

"What happens to Blackmoores when we die?"

He tried to remember his father's funeral, but could not; he had tried so hard to block it out of memory that it had worked. The most he could remember was the coffin being pushed into one of the slots inside the mausoleum and the fount of tears.

"Well, that's a complex question which merits two answers. First, those married into the family are interred in the Blackmoore mausoleum in New Orleans, which is where the family emigrated to from Ireland. But for the actual Blackmoores, well, we are returned to Ireland to be buried in the family cemetery.

"It's been that way since 1788."

Parker returned, halting Trevor from saying more. The round tray was resting on his hand and two glasses filled with their drinks of choice sat atop of it, glasses sweating, waiting to be consumed by Trevor and his mother.

"Here you go...."

Parker smiled that wonderful smile and sat the glasses down before the two Blackmoores, seeming to do this with a bit of caution. After all, everyone in Whatcom County knew who the Blackmoores were, and everyone took to them with caution.

"Thank you, Parker," Kathryn said, looking at him with those ice eyes, causing the waiter to blush despite himself.

Trevor had to suppress a laugh.

"Have you two decided on what you want?"

Parker the waiter pulled a little black leather book out of his apron, removing a pen from his ear and preparing to take down their orders. The very presence of Parker was making Trevor's heart race.

"Yes, I'll have the bacon-wrapped filet mignon with demi-glace and fresh crab potatoes."

He nodded and turned his attentions to Trevor, winking at him casually; Trevor felt himself begin to harden.

"Um, I'll have the pomegranate-balsamic half-duck with fingerling potatoes." Another wink. "Yeah, the duck...."

Trevor blushed and looked away, turning his attention to the city below and beyond, taking in the sparkling lights over the land. The world looked like a giant Christmas tree, all lit up for the holiday season.

When he turned back around Parker had already gone with their orders, and his mother was staring at him knowingly.

"Any more questions?" Kathryn asked her son, taking her glass to her lips and drinking it down, the vodka warming her and burning her throat despite its dilution.

"Why do people die?"

She looked at her son as if he were stupid.

"You know why people die; what do you mean by asking that?"

Trevor looked away for a moment, thinking of his father Sheffield Burges and his all-too-sudden tumor.

"I mean, why do people who marry into this family die?"

Kathryn nodded in understanding, silently telling her son that she had spent many a night pondering the same question.

"Sex with a Blackmoore kills. If you want the truth, we contaminate people. Our genes are poison and we kill, and that's how it's always been!"

Kathryn spoke this matter-of-factly, as if there was no questioning it.

"Do you know why?" He realized almost instantly that this was a stupid question, but he missed his father and wished to understand.

"Who knows, but it's not important anyways. All you need to know is that our DNA is poison to anyone who is not a Blackmoore.

"That is why I have never let you donate blood. That is why I have told you never to let someone touch you if you were bleeding, in case they had an open wound.

"You don't want to be responsible for anyone's death; it is a strong burden to bear."

Trevor felt sick, as if he were going to throw up. He knew that there must be a scientific explanation for this, but his mother would never let him get away with getting his blood tested. In fact, she had forbidden it on more than one occasion, saying that Blackmoore business was just that.

"Well, what are we supposed to do?"

He had no real plans of having sex, but he did not want to think that the possibility of it was forever out of his reach.

"If you truly love someone then you will never have sex with them, not unprotected; never. Not unless you want to live with the fact that they will die!"

He wanted so desperately to chalk up his mother's warning to the paranoid delusions of a grieving widow, but he knew better.

Parker the waiter returned with their meals, setting the plates down before them and smiling, telling them to enjoy their dinner and throwing a wink once again in Trevor's direction, but Trevor was too sad to notice or even care.

He looked at his plate of roasted duck with its sauce of fresh pomegranate juice and balsamic vinegar, with its side of roasted yellow fingerling potatoes and seasonal vegetables, giving the dish a sweet and aromatic flavor; he only wished that he was in the mood to eat.

Kathryn, too, felt little hunger. Though her beef tenderloin wrapped in bacon looked beautiful, seared and served over the whipped potatoes with Dungeness crab and the side of sautéed patty pan squash, and topped with a truffle-infused demi-glace, it was still too hard to think of food, too difficult to eat.

The knowledge of death was fermenting in the air, mixing with the smells of food, and now even the meat was enhancing this thought. Both of them were aware that they would be taking their meals home with them, and for now they would sit in silent melancholy, contemplating the thick isolation of their family.

FIVE

It was cold outside, almost unbearable, but Christian forced himself to ignore it. He leaned up against his Mustang on Knox Street, looking at the darkened home of Trevor and his mother. The white Federal looked mysterious against the backdrop of nighttime clouds. The naked limbs of the maples that lined the sidewalk swayed in invisible wind—wind that was not felt, a wind that hovered over the Blackmoore home and no other.

It was a phenomenon not unknown to the people of South Hill; it was a breeze that forced pedestrians to suddenly cross the street and walk away from the house, staring.

It was a force that they called: *ghost wind*.

He had thought about knocking on the door but was suddenly afraid to do so. He could not explain the fear, and knew that if Greg had been with him he would have accused Christian of being a pussy—but luckily for him Greg Sheer was not with him, therefore he could dwell in his fear without the threat of having to prove his masculinity.

He tried so hard to forget the flood of memories that were washing to the surface of his brain, tried to ignore the regret in his heart, weighing on his conscience, and this was a terrible task.

He had to tell himself over and over again that Trevor Blackmoore deserved this. He was advertising secrets that were not his to advertise, and if he had just left well enough alone, then he wouldn't be subjected to the punishment that was going to be dealt.

The memories were forcing their way onto the surface of his brain, and Christian had no choice but to give in, to allow the thoughts to come, like a movie on television during sweeps week: it's the only thing on, these phantoms of childhood.

The house was dark and creaked with age, despite the fact that it was bright outside and all of the curtains had been pushed open. It was still grim, and playing hide-and-seek inside was more difficult due to the fact that there were too many rooms to look through.

Ten year-old Christian walked down the dark hall, passing the staircase and making his way to the back door directly in front of him, ignoring the scary daguerreotypes, faces of Blackmoores long since dead, with eyes that seemed alive due to the image printed on the silver-resin paper.

The house smelled old. It was a faintly putrid smell amongst heavy floral, the smell of antiquity, not unlike the smell of the local second-hand store. To his left was the ballroom, hidden away by French doors with ornate brass handles: a convenient hiding place.

Christian wiped his sweaty palms on the blue of his little jean shorts. His white polo seemed to be collecting dust from the air and looked dirty even in the dimly-lit hall. He took a deep breath and grasped the handle, turning it and pushing the door open expecting to find Trevor hiding within, but it seemed to be empty.

His large black eyes darted around the room with its long, bare hardwood floors, wood-paneled walls painted white and reaching twelve feet. Two crystal chandeliers hung from the ceiling lined with three-tiered crown molding. One large window sat directly across from him. The midday sun filtered through thin curtains and the light was reflecting off of the crystal drops, casting rainbows formed to look like rain drops.

As he walked through the large room, his shoes tapping lightly on the wood, he heard muffled laughter coming from outside and what appeared to be a male voice, an adult male voice—and this scared Christian. He knew that neither Trevor's dad or his mom were home, and he feared that Trevor might have been hiding out in the back courtyard and a man walking down the alley, a stranger, had spotted little Trevor and began to speak to him.

With his heart pounding in his eardrums, Christian Vasquez ran out of the ballroom and turned the corner, racing to the back door. He clasped the handle and looked out of the glass pane, realizing his fears to be true.

Out there, sitting against one of the tall maple trees was Trevor, dressed in a blue t-shirt and khaki shorts, looking up with innocent hazel eyes at a man in a black jacket and pants telling something to Trevor and laughing, leaning down to whisper in his ear and placing his hand on the boy's shoulder.

The fear inside of him grew. He was afraid that this man might be a kidnapper, a pedophile, looking to take Trevor away. It was not uncommon for people to come into South Hill and kidnap children, knowing that they could get a ransom out of the unfortunate child's grief-stricken parents.

"Trevor!" Christian yelled.

He threw open the door and was ready to rescue him from the man, but as soon as he opened the door the stranger was gone, as if he had never been there. This was confusing to Christian, who stood on the flagstone, bright red with sun. A few scattered robins chirped in the trees, hidden from sight, revelling in the summer.

"Hi, Christian!"

He looked at Trevor, who was staring at him as if there had been no man, no strange adult speaking to him amongst the maples. Christian tried to make sense out of confusion, knew that no one could just disappear from a backyard in two seconds; it wasn't humanly possible. The man had been there, and in the swing of a door was now gone.

"Who was that?" he asked him, his voice looming on the edge of puberty, slowly deepening with each passing day.

"Who was who?" Trevor asked back, looking at Christian in dumb confusion.

After a second of thinking on it, Christian waved his hand in dismissal and walked back into the house, trying to think of a logical explanation for what he had seen.

"You want a peanut butter and jelly sandwich?" Trevor called after him, running in behind and throwing open the door to the kitchen.

"Yeah," Christian responded, following him inside, forgetting to close the back door behind him.

They quickly got to making their sandwiches and popping open a couple of cans of root beer. Birds continued to chirp outside and the boys felt calm, only sharing a few one syllable words, the laziness of the summer day working itself over their mood, making them serene and comfortable even in the large and silent house.

And then the door slammed shut.

"What was that?" Christian asked, jumping with a start, unable to contain his alarm.

"It was just the back door," Trevor responded, shrugging it off as if it were nothing, and it might have worked if it wasn't for the fact that the wind could not have blown a door shut when it opens outside in, and not inside out.

"This is weird...." Christian suddenly wanted to go home, or just ride his bike as far away from the Blackmoore home as possible.

"Well, don't go home; let's just ride our bikes down to Fairhaven!"

Trevor consumed his peanut butter and jelly and neglected his soda on the island, taking Christian's hand and leading him to the front of the house, where their BMX bikes rested atop the manicured green lawn.

It seemed to Christian that Trevor had read his mind, but like all things in the excitement of childhood, it was washed away, pushed back into the file cabinets of his mind.

He shuddered. Ashamed in his fear of the house, but what he remembered was real and had happened, and now here he was again—after five years of being so apart from Trevor Blackmoore and his world, staring at the two story Federal across the street, holding almost every secret of Christian's adolescence.

"Fuck this!" he said aloud, flexing his biceps under his warm black fleece, trying to pump his own ego, eager to not let his childhood fears of ghosts and goblins rob him of his power and sex.

He chuckled slightly and made his way across the street with subconscious caution; in the back of his mind he was unsure of what was lurking in the yard or just around the corner. This was a world so mysterious to him, so unknown that he was uncertain of how to approach it.

The maples slammed against each other as the ghost wind picked up in strength, as if testing Christian's resolve. Was this truly what he meant to do? Go over to the Blackmoore home and silently challenge all of the secrets which it held inside? All of its insane power, power made of mysterious deaths, witchcraft, spiritualism, and Vodou—Vodou that Kathryn was known for, magic that Queen Mab was famous for concocting?

In Christian's opinion, it took more nerve to approach the darkened Blackmoore home than it did to sit down with a serial murderer who was not bound by chains or confined by bars.

No, this was much worse and required a lot more courage and validity.

As he made his way up the path that the oxygen was suddenly evaporating from the air, making his lugs hurt as they squeezed closed and then contracted, the atmosphere becoming cold and bitter—much more so than in the rest of the neighborhood.

Whatever it was that existed with this family was aware of Christian, and it appeared to want him gone.

He forced himself against the glass of the door and peered inside, trying to make out the interior through the thick darkness, his sight adjusting slowly. The sting of the December night felt like needles in his eyes, and he had to clench his teeth from calling out in pain.

It was then that something stirred, as if the shadows could actually move and take command of the world around them.

Christian tried in desperation to convince himself that it was just his mind creating shapes out of nothing, trying to make sense out of something that had no form. It was natural for the brain to do this; if it is unable to see in darkness, it might sometimes form something on its own in order to reconcile for not being able to decipher the surroundings.

"Jesus!" he exclaimed, his breath taking form in front of him, hitting the glass and fogging it up, forcing Christian to wipe it away with his sleeve. He squinted and tried to cancel out the lights from the street and the unit just above the door. He had thought that he was ready for anything, but in truth was prepared for nothing.

A lanky black figure moved from the formal sitting room and into the television room, passing by the door, taking no notice of Christian's face peering in the window. Christian shook his head and rubbed his eyes, pressing his face against the glass and looking again, unsure if he had really seen the silhouette of an actual person.

As his eyes searched, he heard what seemed to be a hardening—a cracking making its way across the glass, and it seemed cold and hard like ice. When he looked he observed in astonishment that the windows on the door as well as the house were frosting up, freezing right there before him.

Christian fell back to the grass, watching the strange phenomenon with awe-struck eyes.

"Fuck!" Christian yelled, jumping to his feet and running to the sidewalk, daring himself to turn around and take just one more look.

He did.

The windows were normal; no frost to speak of. The air was calm and lacking in its strange wind.

Christian scratched his head in confusion before letting out a nervous chuckle, convincing himself that he knew all along that it had been an illusion; his mind had just been playing tricks on him. He had scared himself so much with memories that he had gone up to the house subconsciously expecting something weird to happen.

"Christian, you pussy, get it together!"

Once again Christian Vasquez flexed himself and walked back to his car across the street, strutting as he went along.

SIX

They each held onto their little Styrofoam boxes of food, the complete vestiges of an expensive meal gone to waste by the truths of family life. Kathryn hated when these conversations occurred, hated that all it did was make her think of her deceased husband, the only man that she had truly ever loved, and who had truly loved her. She knew why Tom was with her, and she knew that it was anything but love.

It was sex.

He liked to fuck her and he expected to do it three times a day. He loved having her suck his cock, and he liked fucking her in the ass. He screwed Kathryn like one would screw a man, and yet he experienced women. When Kathryn had told him that perhaps he would be happier with some gay boy, he slapped her hard across the face, attempting to bring her to her knees but failing miserably.

After the nuns, a little slap across the face did about as much harm as poking yourself in the arm with your own finger. She had fixed him them, giving him a giant scare. After Kathryn had finished with her husband, he was afraid to go anywhere in the house alone at night, and that was exactly how Kathryn wanted it.

She looked at her son with heartbreak. He had hardly known his father Sheffield and she feared every day that her son would forget him, confusing memories of his natural father with Tom, and therefore seeing his real father as an asshole or not seeing him at all—other than in the pictures in the living room. The city lights raced over the car, passing over their faces with orange light. Both of their eyes seemed distant, away from the truth of the world around them.

The Lexus moved up Harris Street and took a left on Fifteenth, making its way past the Larrabee home. It was a large, two-story Queen Anne painted in forest green and decorated with an ornate

46

balcony, the rail made of wood and cut-out shapes of suns, moons, and stars. The home was built by the Larrabee family in the nineteenth century. They were one of the most influential families in the birth of the city of Bellingham, and a school as well as a park was given their name sake.

When the car reached Knox on the top of the hill, Kathryn looked on Dianaca Castle with disdain: the large, three-story Victorian painted in royal purple and fashioned as the most haunted home in Bellingham. It was surrounded by a large, spiked, black wrought-iron fence and its numerous Grecian statues, the most notable being the two Poseidons wrapped in ivy and guarding the front steps.

The mansion was famed for witchcraft and murder. It was a home made up of legend, some of which was true. Kathryn had known the family growing up, had known them and hated them, as they hated her and every other Blackmoore; but in the end the Blackmoores imposed their will and the family left. Two rivals with dark secrets, and they wound up fleeing away in the night, leaving the home available for occupation.

As they approached their house, Kathryn took notice of the young man standing across the street, staring at the great house, looking from the structure to the car. The face was as familiar as her own child: it was Christian Vasquez.

"What is he doing here?" she asked, rolling her eyes.

Trevor only shrugged, his young face pressed against the cool glass of the car window. She didn't like the look of longing on her son's face. It was a longing for a life that he no longer lived, inhabited by friends he no longer had, and it seemed to her that Trevor was lighting up at the simple promise of what this could mean.

The car came to a halt along the curb in front of the house. This rich fuck coming in and playing with her son was the last thing that she needed, but she had never stepped in and dominated over his life, and she wasn't about to start now. Besides, she had other ways of keeping a protective eye over her son.

"I'm going to see what he wants."

Trevor reached out for the door's handle, not choosing to wait for the driver, but instead acting in desperation to see his former friend.

"Wait!" cried Kathryn, grasping her son's arm and forcing him to look at her, his eyes displaying a mix of fear and wanting. "Be careful; he's not the same boy you knew."

"I know that—a"

"No! No, he's different now; he's a man. A man who understands the kind of power that he can have over people, including you. Please be wary of him, Trevor, please."

Her eyes were soulful and blue, like liquid, and Trevor did not know how to respond except by nodding and gently placing a kiss on her cheek, his soft lips gracing her gentle flesh. She could not help but close her eyes and release the tears that were resting along the rim of her sockets.

"I will, Mother; I will."

He opened his door and stepped outside.

Kathryn watched as he made his way across the street, mindful of cars that would never come and childhood familiarity that he could no longer know. The old driver in the black suit opened the door and assisted Kathryn outside, looking on her gently, Kathryn doing the same.

She looked over at her son interacting with Christian Vasquez and wondered what she could do to protect him tonight from whatever business it was that Christian was trying to involve Trevor with. She knew instantly what her only option was, and she looked on it with sullen regard.

"Thank you," she said to the old man, placing a kiss on his lips, gentle and sweet. It was as if the death of dreams was coming on the

Blackmoore home, and she could feel it like she could feel so many other things in this place, seen and unseen.

She wished with all her heart that it would go away, back into the deep dark depths of the world, returning to the land of shadows.

She handed him a check and placed her key into the brass lock, the door jutting open as she pressed on, allowing a sigh of despair to pass her lips, the house alive with age.

She walked inside and stood in the darkened home, trying to resist the urge to look on her son but unable to deny curiosity's pull. In reluctance she went to the window and parted the green drapes, the orange light from the lamp post illuminating the left side of her face, the ice of her eye glittering in the glow.

Kathryn held her breath as she saw these two teenage men standing together and conversing, this image an echo from the past, two ghosts of childhood resurrected by invisible kinetics. She prayed that she could choke on her tears until there was nothing left but a wisp of decay in the passing wind.

"I hope that you don't mind my coming over..." Christian said to him, shuffling his sneakers against the pavement, refusing to look directly at Trevor, who shook his head in mild amusement and titillation.

"Not at all."

Trevor smiled and looked past his former friend and figured enemy. The sky was black and the streets deserted. The naked trees were now alive with fury, a fury understood by Trevor; it was a fury created by the dead and the lost. The air smelled of burning wood and leaves, and almost every home had a cyclone of bluish smoke rising from their brick chimneys, curling in the wind.

As they stood outside, Trevor could feel others around them, watching—not the eyes of the living, but the awareness of the deceased. He looked at Dianaca Castle and took notice of the faint orange light coming from the window, the glass made exquisite by English latticed frames. The eeriness of the glow and the thick inky blue of night filled him with distinct unease.

"That's good. Um, could we talk?" Christian asked him, looking at Trevor and flashing that classic smile, his deep sensuality prevailing over Trevor even in this thick December darkness. The patch of hair under that full bottom lip was tempting to him and Trevor wished only to reach out and touch it, experiencing its soft delicacy.

"Yeah, but let's go someplace else; I'm feeling a little weird out here."

Christian looked from him to the Blackmoore residence and back at Trevor, nodding vigorously in agreement.

Trevor wondered what it could have been that caused Christian to look at the house with such fear in his eyes. Was it the memories of their youth, or was it something else, something made of Bellingham folklore?

The two boys went to his Mustang, the black top now brought up on the car—unlike earlier in the day, when it had been pulled down into the vehicle, the two female passengers with Christian screaming out in the Friday afternoon air. Trevor left with his pain and his ghosts, all of this inside the confines of a yellow school bus.

"Where do you want to go?" Christian asked him, turning the ignition and starting the vehicle, allowing the heater to warm up and bring comfort to the inside of the sports car.

Trevor shrugged his shoulders.

"I don't care."

"Well, I could just drive and see where we end up...."

The world was dark and the hour was late. There was not much of an option in where they could go, and that was all right with both boys, who only wished to fill the empty air of five years and come to some sort of understanding.

The car was brought around in a U-turn and made its way down Knox Street, passing the infamous mansion.

Trevor looked out through the window and spied a woman in illuminated white standing on the large wood balcony, her face appeared sullen and distant, and it was as if the light of the moon shone down upon her in cursed witness. There was an air to this woman that bothered him; her presence seemed to disturb the natural world and part the veil of reality.

As they drove a tree moved quickly into his view, blocking the woman in white, and in a second the scene was cleared again and the woman was gone. She was the grieving mother, the spirit in search of her baby. She was the one who cried out through the ether, and Trevor knew her and knew her heart; he wanted to cry.

They sat in silence. The desolate cold began to weigh itself upon the quiet town, the frost already developing on the lawns and mute automobiles. Trevor looked at Sacred Heart Cathedral in silent contempt; this was the place that had broken his mother those many years ago. Priests and nuns inflicting their harm, people who violated Kathryn Blackmoore and reduced her to a shell, an empty shell created long before his birth but only strengthened in cold after his conception.

The cathedral made of wood and painted white, with its spire steeple and windows of stained glass, the entire structure lit by orange coming from the posts along the street, and connected to the side of the church.

Trevor felt strange in this car with Christian Vasquez, and the symbolism of his shame in puberty began to surface, working itself on his conscious.

"So, um, how's school?" Christian asked him, keeping his eyes steady on the road. The car turned on Fourteenth Street and made a second turn on Harris, passing Sycamore Square, one of the few original buildings left in Fairhaven, which was constantly being updated and expanded. The community suddenly seemed to Trevor as if it was unable to appreciate its past.

"I'm sure it's the same for me as it is for you. After all, we go to the same place." Trevor's voice was tinged with annoyance and Christian could feel it, looking at him nervously.

"Yeah, you're right; sorry."

His face looked pained, forcing Trevor to instantly regret his harsh response.

"No, I'm sorry; it was a fine question. School is school. I have a few good friends—none as close as ... well, nevermind; it's just not the same."

Trevor remembered eager laughter, four children running around the busy fishing port during Ski to Sea, the annual festival of the city, the Northwest's answer to the Olympics. He hated memories.

"I know what you mean."

Trevor looked at Christian. His large black eyes were absorbent of every possible source of light in the world, and his short black hair was glossy in the street light. But it was that smile, that killer smile of his, that could melt away the coldest demeanor; it was something Trevor did not like but was finding so hard to resist.

"Really?" He rolled his eyes and looked away, not wanting to stare at that deceptively sweet face for another moment. He only wished to move on from the subject.

"I think about it every day. I wonder about what things would have been like if—"

"If what, we'd stayed friends? That's something I can't answer."

Trevor's tone was unusually calm, and the fact that he hadn't taken the opportunity to say what he had wanted to say for the past five years was confusing to him, but he continued to hold his tongue.

"I know, and I know I fucked up royally, and I'm sorry."

The car came to a halt.

They were in the parking lot of Marine Park, the little patch of acre lawn along the shores of Bellingham Bay, lined with large stones and broken concrete, the slow moving waves lapped against the rocks. The only light was coming from the covered picnic area with its two bathrooms and large fireplace.

To the left were the train tracks, wrapping along the coastal line and disappearing around the bend of rocks and trees. The *dong* of a lone buoy echoed in the distance and the shadowed islands of the San Juans mirrored the distant shores of the land of the dead.

Neither one spoke for several moments, both boys walking towards the tracks and following its forever path.

The air smelled of salt and smoke from the newer mansions of Edgemoor: the community of new money, many homes built like castles, extravagant in a way that differed from South Hill—which, though it hosted many amazing homes, was still somewhat modest in its old and gentile way.

Many people went through South Hill looking on the mansions and commenting on their beauty, but none felt the urge to stop in their tracks and gawk at the Victorians, Tudors, Craftsmens, Federals, Colonials, Cape Cods, and aging neo-classicals of lumber and stone—unlike Edgemoor, which was filled with curious people who would simply stop what they were doing and stare at the homes in dumb wonder.

"Do you ever think about me?" Christian asked suddenly, breaking their silence. His taut body was defined even under the pull-over fleece, the water crashing under the tracks beneath their feet.

"Sure, I think about all of you; how can I not—"

"No! No, do you ever think about *me*?" Christian interjected, a sudden look of desperation on his face, his body closing in on the short distance between them.

"How could I not? I spent the most time with you growing up; we were inseparable. You were always overprotective of me growing up, and whenever I was teased, you would step in and fight them to the ground.

"Of course I think about you. There were times that I needed a protector, someone to chase the bullies away; it had just never occurred to me growing up that I would need protection from my own friends."

Trevor swallowed hard, looking on into the silent night.

"But I'm much better now, and I've gotten to a point where I can protect myself—at least I like to think that I can."

"If it's any consolation, I tell Greg and Cheri to leave you alone."

Trevor looked at him and cocked his head, giving his only acknowledgement.

"I know it's not the same; I hate what happened, but things change, don't they? I mean, we couldn't stay friends forever—could we?"

It was a painful declaration, one that he could not bear to hear. Christian's words were like acid to his ears, eating away at his drums and causing him to bleed a thin trail down the side of his neck.

Trevor shuddered.

"I don't know the answer to anything, and I choose not to care. I quit trying to figure it out a long time ago."

Trevor had his memories, and that was enough. He had them and they were pure, and the last thing he needed was some explanation to why it all came to an end, and why he was left with Jonathan.

The winds had suddenly come in, causing the air to howl and the trees to convulse. Trevor knew it to be his invisible familiar, keeping his guard over his teenage partner.

"I'm such a shit!" Christian let out a bitter laugh, a chuckle of condemnation, a laugh that was probably supposed to go unnoticed by Trevor.

"Not in the way—"

Christian raised a hand in protest, stopping Trevor from finishing his remark.

"I was always there, always the one to protect you from the world. I was there with you when your father died; I took care of you while your mom lost it...."

When his father had died so suddenly of his tumor, Christian had been there, over at his house. They had been playing checkers when it happened, and Christian alone stayed with Trevor while the ambulance rushed Sheffield Burges and his mother to the hospital, screaming at him to hold on, just hold on until they got to the emergency room; he didn't.

Kathryn had become void then, walking in the world made by her brain, a world where a boy named Trevor did not exist, a world where the only inhabitants were she and Sheffield. Christian had slept over every other night for six months, helping Trevor make breakfast, lunch, and dinner. Christian came by every day, walking with Trevor to and from school, staying into the late hours of the evening on nights he did not sleep over, always in the same bed as Trevor and always ready to embrace Trevor and allow him to cry against his body. At that point, the only solid thing in Trevor's life had been Christian Vasquez, and now it had come to this.

"I abandoned you. I never teased you, but I wasn't there for you either. I left you along with Cheri and Greg; it was a dick thing to do and I'm sorry."

His voice was breaking and his eyes were welling, ready to spring with tears.

"Why now?" Trevor responded, his voice without a hint of malice.

"What?"

"Why are you making contact with me now? I don't understand; it's been five years. We see each other in the hallways. We acknowledge each other; we're civil, so why now?"

Christian was obviously stung and searching in desperation for a response. The cold was biting at Trevor, and he tried desperately to keep from shivering.

"I miss you, okay? I miss you. I miss being with you every day; I miss being with someone who knows me inside and out, someone who doesn't look on me as some rich kid poster boy. I miss having contact with someone...."

Trevor was unsure if he should laugh or nod his head in sympathetic understanding.

"From what I understand, you have *tons* of contact."

It wasn't a question, it was a known fact. Christian was famous for his sexual conquests, and apparently bragged about every single one of them.

"It's all a lie. The pressure Greg and the other guys on the team put on me is suffocating; I just make up the shit so they could leave me alone. Besides, I can't really make it with anyone when I'm always wondering about you."

Trevor looked up at him, his hazel eyes large and full of question. He felt himself light up inside, something secret that he had desperately wished for. It seemed as if through some trick worked on the universe it was finally coming into shape.

Jonathan became upset, hurling the wind at them in record speed, the air suddenly beginning to scream through the wisps of leaves. The calm waters of the bay became wild, crashing against the shoreline and bringing a wet mist to the air. Trevor began to shiver despite himself, screaming in his mind for Jonathan to stop, to just rest himself, but he would not; Jonathan was furious and would have none of it.

"Here...."

Christian grabbed the hem of his fleece and pulled it up over his head, wearing a white tee. His dark skin stood out against the shirt, and his toned and defined body became enticing to Trevor, who quickly looked away in embarrassment.

Christian slipped the fleece over Trevor's head before he could utter a rejection in taking it. "That'll keep you warm!"

Christian was smiling, stepping behind Trevor and placing both hands on his shoulders, guiding him back gently to the car, while Jonathan was refusing to settle.

"I should give this back to you," Trevor was saying, standing in front of his house, the porch light seeming to burn in the black night.

Christian was looking down at him and grinning.

"Why don't you hang on to it for a while?"

He placed his hand on Trevor's waist, letting that familiar intimacy pass between them.

"Are you sure?"

Trevor felt strange, not knowing exactly how he felt with keeping his fleece, not sure how he felt about all of this. In truth, he was scared, and to Trevor, Christian was the most terrifying force in the world right now.

"Positive!"

He took Trevor's hand and squeezed it before walking back to his car, silently moving in the midnight world.

As Christian drove down the road, back in the direction of his house, Jonathan became roused with anger and directed all of his concentrated will at a branch, ripping it from off one of the maples that lined the sidewalk, tossing it across the street, and hitting the pavement with a loud crack.

Trevor rolled his eyes and went into his house, not caring about anything but Christian Vasquez and the promise of something new and familiar, and the anticipation of Monday morning. This sweater was tangible and real—unlike Jonathan, who was nothing more than a well-skilled spook.

Trevor knew that was what bothered Jonathan the most—for how could he compete with flesh and blood, when he hadn't been such in over a hundred years?

SEVEN

Braxton Volaverunt made his way through the conclave of students, filling the halls of Mariner High School, wasting time with one another until the bell sounded, officially announcing the start of yet another Wednesday.

He stood at a height of six foot two—not towering, but far from short. His skin was soft and olive, and his cheeks were naturally blushed with soft pink. A single tiny mole rested above the right side of his lip, just below the nose, and his brown eyes were large. His thin brows and short mess of hair was deep and black, darker than even Christian Vasquez.

He wore a pair of baggy jeans with a long silver chain running from his front belt-loop to his wallet in the back pocket, a tight black tee snug against his chest. Hanging close to his neck were two chains, one longer than the other, and his nails were painted midnight blue, accentuated by a studded leather cuff around his right wrist. Sheltering him from the cold was a small jean jacket, the blue as dark as could be without being black.

Braxton was considered by most to be as hot as Christian, perhaps hotter, and he played soccer right along with the school god and his minion Greg Sheer. He was the bassist for his band, *The Spit Monkeys*, who were a school favorite and played at almost every pep assembly that Mariner put on—and the school put on many, reveling in their achievements in sports and a favorite for state championships.

He made his way through the halls and towards the cafeteria, cocking his head at various people who waved to him as he made his way through the teenage throng. He was eager to see Trevor Blackmoore, who he hadn't seen since the previous Friday. Trevor, who he had befriended in the seventh grade and nurtured up until now.

At eighteen, Braxton felt that he knew everything that he need-ed to in order to survive in the world. Braxton afforded the ability to travel to various countries growing up, his parents wealthy and old money. His mother Tammy was like a gypsy until the day she died when Braxton was just eleven years old. She had developed an untreatable tumor, which had come about suddenly and claimed her life without the chance for chemotherapy. It killed him to think of her, and therefore he tried to avoid it as much as possible.

He had loved the bohemian life that they had lived. Always traveling, never staying in one place—and now that she was gone, it was as if they never left. Braxton's father Eric kept himself oc-cupied with work and misery, hardly ever leaving his room. He walked between worlds—the land of the dead and the place of the living—and it seemed that everyday Eric Volaverunt was making a choice as to which one he would reside in.

He thanked the universe every day of his life for Trevor Black-moore, who had also lost his father. Though Braxton was unsure as to how the man had died, it was still comforting to have him there to always know and understand without either one of them having to say a word. Though, Trevor was so much more guarded; he had a wall, a wall that Braxton was desperate to break down.

He pushed open the double doors and walked up the concrete path to the cafeteria, sheltered by a canopy of steel. The cafeteria was a large rectangular structure made of brick, the first doors en-tering into a large lobby lined with soda machines and bathrooms. The next set of brown doors led into the cafetorium with a large stage to the left of the building's entrance, and straight across from the entrance were the various food areas. Between this and the en-trance were a littering of tables: all brown, all big, and all segregated by the various groups and cliques in the social hierarchy.

"Yo, Brax!" He turned around to see his friend and band mate, J.T. Oliver, waving at him from a nearby table dominated by kids clad in black shirts and jeans. A couple of the girls were dressed as gothic Catholic school nymphets with red-and-black plaid skirts and fishnet stockings, as well as platforms and black collared shirts, their lips painted black and their hair streaked with black and purple. Not exactly attractive for Braxton, who only had eyes for a quick-witted, cocky seventeen-year-old who seemed to be nowhere in sight.

"What's up?" he replied, giving his friend a high five and taking a seat next to him, forcing one of the gothic twins to end her flirting with J.T.

"Nothing much, you ready for practice tonight?"

J.T. wore a blue tee that strapped tightly around his barrel chest, a pair of khakis hanging halfway off his ass, the bottoms frayed, and his mess of shaggy brown hair was covered by a knit ski-cap. His voice was deep, so much deeper than Braxton, whose voice resounded with a slight tenor.

"Yeah." Truth was, he had only half-heard his friend's question, his eyes searching the cafeteria desperately for Trevor Blackmoore. "Have... have you seen Trevor?"

J.T. laughed and shook his head, knowing about his friend's provocations towards the young Blackmoore but refusing to bring it up, due to the lengthy vow of silence that Braxton had put him through.

"Why don't you just tell him? It's not like the kid hides being gay."

Braxton looked at J.T. and rolled his eyes, knowing he could never do it.

"He's also never flat-out admitted to it."

His friend nodded in defeated agreement. He was going to say more, when J.T. cocked his head and directed his eyes towards the cafeteria entrance, silently telling Braxton to turn around.

It was as if the world had slowed up or stopped altogether, and the only person to exist in real-time was Trevor Blackmoore, who walked in with a bright smile on his face, his eyes locking with Braxton. It felt as if his heart were going to rupture.

Trevor was dressed in a pair of blue jeans hugging his ass, his upper-half clothed in a V-neck black sweater, the deep red of his shirt collar poking out and folded over, and a single chain was fastened tightly around his neck. It was a chain that Braxton recognized almost instantly as the chain he had given Trevor a year ago.

"Hey, guys!" Trevor said. His voice was unusually perky; his hazel eyes sharper than usual and his entire demeanor appeared different.

Braxton hoped that maybe today would be the day that Trevor confessed his love for him—or so he always fantasized.

"What's up, Trev?" J.T. said, yawning and using his elbow to nudge Braxton in the back.

"Yeah, what's going on?"

Braxton felt like such an idiot, asking the same question again.

"Not much. Um, Braxton?"

His palms began to sweat as he looked at Trevor, who stared back at him with imploring eyes, eyes that would have made Braxton do anything.

"Yeah?"

J.T. snickered and Braxton shot a quick glare his way, telling him without words to shut up.

"Can I talk to you?"

The question seemed like a request from God; how could he say no?

"Sure, what's—a"

"Not here, in private."

Braxton's jaw hung open and he nodded. His entire reaction was dumbfounded; J.T. pushed him up out of his chair, as if saying *"go get him."*

They stood out in the foyer next to the Coke machine, the little red light requesting a dollar for a twenty-ounce bottle of soda.

"What's going on? You know that you can tell me anything, right?"

It was as if the both of them were holding their breaths and one of them would collapse from suffocation at any moment.

"There's someone that I like, and I don't want it to weird you out!"

Braxton nodded vigorously, silently urging him to go on.

"Well, it's a guy, and I've known him for a really long time and ... oh, God, this is so hard to say...."

It was coming: the moment that Braxton had been anticipating for the past three years.

"Who is it?"

Heartbeats, mind swimming, pulse racing, palms damp with sweat.

"Christian Vasquez."

It was as if a plane had lost fuel and descended fast from the sky, colliding with the earth below.

"That's great.... Um... um, does he feel the same way?"

He couldn't, it wasn't possible.

"Yes, he told me so the other night; can you believe it? I never thought!"

Nothing was real at this point—not the school, not the people who moved past them, not even Trevor.

"That's really great; I'm happy for you."

Trevor hugged him fast and fierce, whispering something inaudible and unimportant, letting Braxton go and walking away, disappearing into the cold morning air.

Everything began boiling inside of him, all of those seasons, all of those moments with Trevor for the past five years, elevating to what he thought was something wonderful, now nothing more than shit.

He clenched his fist.

"Braxton?" J.T. asked, walking out.

CRACK.

Braxton slammed his fist into the glass of the Coke machine, the shards splintered and jagged now, dripping with crimson, his knuckles cut up by the impact. He could hardly feel the pain or care less.

The lobby was now filled with students, all of them looking at the scene with a mix of humor and fear. Most people thought it to be the warnings of a school shooting or gang violence—though not much worry for gang violence in a city like Bellingham which, had an enormously low percentage of gang activity when compared with other cities in the state.

"Jesus, man, what happened?" J.T. asked, staring at his bloodied friend in confusion.

"Christian Vasquez!"

J.T. Oliver knew what he meant, but could not believe it. Christian got almost as much pussy as J.T., the only difference being the fact that the lead singer of a band was always more appealing than a Varsity achiever.

"You should get out of here before you get—"

"Mr. Volaverunt!"

The squealy voice of Assistant Principal Austin rang over his shoulder. She was dressed in a pair of white pants and a blue-and-white horizontal striped sweater, her hair big and copper in color, completely unflattered by an outdated perm.

"I'll save you the trouble, Miss. I did this. I got pissed and so I immaturely shoved my fist into the soda machine. I'm sorry."

He could tell that the tone of his voice and his words softened her, working on her crude features and perhaps saving him from suspension.

"Well, I'm sorry for that, but you need to come with me. We'll fix you up and then we'll figure out what we're going to have to do with you."

Braxton nodded and followed her out.

He sat in Principal Austin's office, staring at his bandaged hand, and contemplated all of the ways that he could kill Christian Vasquez. First period was coming to a close and then he would have to go to second, which was soccer practice, a class that Braxton was now unsure of due to the company it kept.

He thought of the chain that he had given Trevor a little over a year ago, began to remember the day and the incident involving the chain. It was a memory of happier times, times when Christian was the enemy and he was the saint.

"I just don't understand why they do it," Trevor was sobbing, sitting on the wood bench on Braxton's front deck, which extended ten feet over Lake Samish. The sun was setting and the pink-orange light was dancing on the water, his tears like glitter in the fading glimmer.

"It's not about you, okay? You need to know that right off the bat. It has nothing to do with you. It's because they're rich assholes who think of no one but themselves and you are the only link to a life in which they were different, where they were normal and kind.

"But the truth is, Trevor, they don't want to be that anymore. They want to be these hardcore gods of the halls, and in order to do that they need to wipe you out of the picture, and the only way to do that is by ripping you to shreds everyday.

"When they break your spirit, then they break away from their past; it's as simple as that!"

He had hoped that the warmth of the Southern Comfort would ease his cries, but after one swig Trevor was brushing the bottle away.

"I just wish they would stop. I wish I wasn't always alone when they do it...."

He wiped his nose on his sleeve before the snot could drip down, and his face was stained red by his tears.

"Well, here." Braxton reached behind his neck and unhooked the smallest of the three chains, pulling it off slowly, running completely on spontaneity. "Wear this. Whenever you feel that you need me, no matter when it is, you feel alone and I'm nowhere in sight, just put it on and think about me."

Trevor nodded and smiled, allowing Braxton to place it around his neck. A strange wave of electrical warmth passed between them, and their noses grazed gently; Braxton was suffering from the beginnings of a hard-on.

He could feel his heart for the first time, and it seemed to be breaking. He stifled the urge to cry and thought again on the situation that landed him in here. It was the revelation that Trevor did not see him, did not even recognize his existence beyond friendship, and Braxton was going to have to accept that—for now. What he would not accept was the idea that Christian Vasquez was genuinely interested in Trevor, at least in the way that he had presented.

This was some sick game; it had to be, and Braxton was going to find out, even if it ruined his relationship with Trevor or killed the chance for it to be something more.

He rested his chin on his upturned palm, his elbow propped up on the wood desk, the light of day fighting to break through the thick of blue-grey clouds. The bell sounded, and soon the halls were busy with kids making their way slowly to their next class, thanks to the ten-minute passing period. He had just begun to stand and look out for Principal Austin when a familiar chuckle could be heard resonating through the hallway, coming in his general direction.

"Fuck me!" Quickly Braxton stood at guarded attention, waiting to see the intended target of his hatred. Christian Vasquez and Greg Sheer were walking down the hall past the office, oblivious to the intense gaze of Braxton Volaverunt, his blood pumping fast in his veins.

It hit him hard and fast as he looked at Christian, dressed in his usual designer jeans and flannel shirt, the checkered pattern green and white, a starched tee underneath, laughing his confident and pompous laugh.

The headache—the throbbing sensation attacked the back of his neck, sharp and quick, and Braxton felt his body begin to convulse mildly, used to the act but never quite prepared for it.

He hated the visions.

They came on fast and wild, like a silent film in black-and-white, cut up and out of order, each flash of images like pricks on his brain—stabbing, stabbing, stabbing; moving like a tattoo needle.

There stood Trevor, lost and alone, the pain on his face intense, the chain nowhere in sight. Christian was standing next to him, standing next to him and laughing. Greg was there and Greg was laughing, Cheri Hannifin resting her arms on his shoulder—all of them pointing at Trevor and laughing.

The image changed, and Trevor and Christian were sitting in Trevor's backyard, sitting on the bench and looking at one another, Christian leaning in, Trevor doing the same. They were kissing. They were kissing, and the leaves were being ripped off of the maples and fluttering like snow. It changed again, and Trevor was walking in an arched room, illuminated by candles and filled with plaster saints, all of them seemingly alive and real, all of them seeming to know of Trevor's presence.

Trevor was not wearing a shirt and he suddenly began to call out wildly as blood started to bead out of his chest. Strange markings, almost tribal—religious—began to take shape on his skin.

Another shift, and Cheri Hannifin was on a large dark table, her eyes wide with fear and dripping tears. There was a man above her, grinning. He lifted his arm and curled his fingers into his palm, making a fist, and without warning the man shoved his fist through her chest and ripped out her heart.

Cheri convulsed throughout the violation before going limp, blood pooling out of her. The man smiled, looking down at her lifeless body.

It ended.

"Shit!" Braxton wiped away the beads of sweat that soaked his hair and dripped off his nose.

His heart was pounding in his ears, and his hands were shaking, desperate to catch his breath. The force of the visions caused him to take off his jacket and drop it on the floor, his mind frantic to piece the images together, desperate to get to Trevor and stop it all from happening—but he could do nothing in the office.

As his mind rolled it around, he figured that what took place in Trevor's yard happened first, followed by the scene in the hallway, the scene where Trevor was humiliated in front of the entire school. Why wasn't he wearing the chain? What Braxton could not place were the last two images. What was their order; what was going on in them, and who was that man?

Those were things he could not answer, but what Braxton Volaverunt was certain of was that it all had to do with Christian Vasquez and his posse of South Hill degenerates who wanted to rip Trevor apart and keep a piece of the broken boy as a trophy.

"All right, Braxton, here's the deal. I told security that it was an accident and that you were trying to force a soda out that had jammed in the machine and you just hit it too hard—besides, I think you learned your lesson well enough with the damage you did to your hand."

Principal Austin looked down at his bandaged knuckles; Braxton only nodded.

"You're just lucky that soccer doesn't involve hands. Now, you're a good student and a wonderful player; don't screw it up by getting yourself suspended from school or the team."

Braxton nodded in understanding, though he was more concerned with the recent onslaught of visions.

"Now, get to class; you can still make it if you hurry."

The old woman smiled at him and Braxton returned it, grabbing his jacket from off the floor, departing into the cold morning air, his feet now bounding down the concrete path to the gymnasium, desperate to get changed and make roll call.

The locker room smelled of sweat and was damp with humidity created by the showers. High school boys were standing around in different stages of dress: some missing shirts but wearing their uniform gold-and-green shorts, others fully clothed in their jerseys and shorts, while a few were covered in nothing more than white jock straps, their cocks concealed by the fabric pouch and cup.

It was loud and guys were laughing and horsing around, talking up their exploits of the past weekend, trying to outdo each other in worthy "pimpness."

Braxton normally rolled his eyes to this, but upon spotting Christian and Greg amidst their lockers he chose to keep his ears open, unable to shake off the series of visions that had consumed him not ten minutes earlier.

Carefully he opened his locker and threw his jacket inside, followed with his shoes. Braxton curled his fingers under the bottom of his tee and pulled it up off his head, revealing a smooth muscular body. His nipples were dark and the size of quarters; a tiny trail of thin black hairs ran from under his navel to the hidden area under his pants, the mix of cool air and hot moisture making his nipples erect and his hairs stand at attention.

From the corner of his eye he kept watch on the two jocks, both of them pulling on their shorts over their nakedness, the two of them speaking crudely. Braxton tried to ignore the urge to punch his locker, and instead focused on getting ready, removing black American Apparel boxer-briefs and revealing a thick eight inch organ, perfect in form, the black hairs trimmed and his balls shaved smooth—all of this grooming done in the hopes that if he and Trevor were ever caught up in the heat of the moment, then he would be as perfect as possible.

Again, the reality of his conversation with Trevor earlier that morning slashed that dream into nothing more than hopeless longing.

He pulled a fresh white jock from his gym bag and slipped it on, disliking the elastic straps that rode up on his ass; no matter how long you wore one, it never got any better.

Finally he was dressed and ready to go, wearing forest green socks with gold bands and his cleats, the tiny spikes making the tiled floor of the locker room feel strange beneath his feet. Christian and Greg were already out on the field, most likely flexing their authority; after all, Christian was team captain.

The air was crisp and bitter, and despite its fight the sun had lost its battle with the clouds, keeping the world in dark winter-gray. The grass was wet with dew, and beneath it the brown earth was becoming loose and slightly muddy, easily kicked up by the directness of the cleats.

"Nice to see you join us, Braxton," Coach Peters said snidely, causing a flurry of mocking chuckles to erupt around him.

Braxton waved it away and got in line. Perhaps as a mixed blessing, Braxton was lined up next to Christian and beyond him stood Greg, who looked hard and vicious.

The coach went on talking about practice and game plans. His skin was obviously self-tanned, but he was fit and his hair similar in copper color to the principal, and his face was lined in a thin beard. Braxton could care less about game plans; his only interest was the conversation between Greg and Christian.

"So the fucker bought it?" Greg asked. His arms were folded across his chest, his blue eyes quick and clean like ice, his voice deep, reminding Braxton of J.T.

"Well, you know how it is," Christian began, stretching his arms. "I know how to work my shit. Hell, I even gave him my fleece, which he was probably jerking off on the entire weekend!"

Both guys began to laugh. Braxton could feel his heart begin to pound, and his hand was beginning to throb, drawing attention to his wound.

"So, how far are you actually going to go with this shit?"

Braxton was awaiting this answer as eagerly as Greg, and he allowed the rage to boil to the surface.

"Until I get the fag willing to suck my dick. Who knows, maybe I'll even let him do it. Ain't nothing wrong with getting a free blowjob out of it! I can just close my eyes and think of some bitch like Paris Hilton!"

Greg hit Christian in the shoulder and they went on laughing, not caring that they might be tearing Trevor up in front of someone who might know him and care about his interests. It was a stupid and arrogant thing to do, but then again these people were stupid and arrogant, and usually assumed that no one would ever challenge them. This was perfect for Braxton, who was feeling the air of anger fill his space, breathing it in and out.

Who gave a fuck about his hand? This was not going to pass without incident.

Braxton spun round, pivoting on his heel and clasping his fingers on Christian's jersey, feeling the cool of the material against his skin. Christian looked at him, dumbfounded. In a moment of blind fury Braxton hurled Christian Vasquez to the wet field beneath them, the grass squeaking underneath his body. Braxton was on top of him, knocking his head repeatedly against the earth, everyone else too stunned to try and stop him.

"What the fuck is your problem, man?" Christian asked him, his black eyes large with fear but slowly washing over with rage.

Braxton was aware that Greg Sheer was standing on top of him, prepared to assist his friend at the drop of a hat; he could try, anyways.

"You, you piece of shit! You hurt him and I'll kill you."

Without a clear thought Braxton lifted his hand and curled it into a fist, preparing to drill it into his face. What he was unaware of was the fact that it was the same hand that he had injured earlier by pulling a similar stunt on the Coke machine.

"Who are you talking about?"

Braxton chuckled and felt himself give way to a great sigh of release, trying to keep a level head on the situation. Though the coach was barking at him to get off of Christian, Braxton did not move.

"Trevor Blackmoore, that's who I'm talking about. Whatever this sick game is, I suggest you end it and end it fast!"

A cynical laugh came from Christian, who waved his hand and attempted to throw Braxton off of him, but he realized very quickly that moving him was not going to be an option.

"Look, don't worry about Trevor or what is going on between us; we got something special."

He and Greg laughed in unison, and Braxton reached up under with his knee and drilled it into Christian's crotch, forcing the school god to wince in momentary pain.

"Fuck you!" Braxton yelled, using every ounce of will power to keep his fist from connecting with the young Vasquez's face.

"I was there before you, and I'll be there long after you're gone. That's how it works with our families. Our parents knew each other, and our parents' parents knew each other, and it'll always be that way."

Christian began to laugh, but once again Braxton lifted his head and dropped it on the wet grass.

Braxton was sure that he had heard a dull *thud* come from his skull.

"Not anymore. You forfeited any claim on Trevor as soon as you and your little shit friends tossed him aside and made it a point to try and ruin his life every single fucking day for the past five years.

"Now Trevor is under the impression that you never actually had anything to do with the bullying, but you and I both know that that's wrong. We both know that you were as much behind it as these other sorry excuses for human beings, and if you don't end this little game, I will make your life a living hell until the day *you* die!"

With his point made and his anger like fuel now running on low, Braxton Volaverunt stood up and walked back to the locker room, ignoring the protests coming from the coach, who called at him to come back, that they weren't finished yet.

The sweat slipped down his face and hair, distorting Braxton's vision slightly. A few lengthy strands of hair were now hanging in his eyes; his hand throbbed and his knees ached from being on the ground like that. He could not see how this day could possibly get any worse.

The locker room was best when it was empty, not a soul in sight except for Braxton. He opened his locker and sat on the long wood bench, which was worn through with age. Behind him was the great row of showers, all of them blessedly empty of students and tempting—even for Braxton, who hated school showers.

He had just slipped on his underwear when he heard the steel door to the changing room click open and cautious footsteps approach. Braxton was prepared for it to be Greg and Christian, looking to settle the score.

He turned around.

"Trevor!"

There he was, not ten feet away, an anxious look was worked into the features of his face. He had a sudden air of innocence that was refreshing to Braxton, who felt for a brief moment that he was in the presence of a lost little boy.

"Hi...."

His voice was meek and his stance seemed a little off, making him wonder if anything was wrong. Both boys walked towards each other smoothly, as if the locker room and the benches did not exist, as if they were in a private field where the air was open and nothing was in their way.

His eyes were so big that Braxton felt that they would swallow him whole and leave nothing left except for an empty shell. The deep red of Trevor's hair was glossy under the light, and radiated like a halo; an angel descending from heaven to fill Braxton's world.

"What are you doing here?" Braxton's voice was almost a whisper, and he could not suppress the grin that had taken over his solemn face.

He caught Trevor staring at his bare chest for just a moment, and that moment alone was enough to fill him with all kinds of ideas, ideas that tried to work their magic between his legs and caused his nipples to become erect, and for the gooseflesh to cover his arms and torso.

"J.T. came into the business office and told me that you were really upset and that you had punched a hole into the Coke machine in the cafeteria."

Trevor looked down at his bandaged hand and sighed.

"So I told Ms. May that I would go and pick up the attendance sheets, and from there I went to the cafeteria and sure enough, I see broken glass and dried blood everywhere and all I could think was, 'Braxton, what happened to make you do this?' And then I thought that I should come here and find you."

He lit up inside. It wasn't some fluke; Trevor had come here looking specifically for him and him alone.

"You were worried about me?"

Trevor nodded and laughed, his face like a cherubim, soft and warming.

"Of course I was; why wouldn't I be? If something's wrong, you need to tell me."

Braxton shook his head. How could he say what he really wanted to say, when it meant telling him to stay away from Christian? It was a no-win situation.

"Sit down for a moment."

Braxton took a hold of Trevor's hand and led him down to the wood bench; it felt like electricity when he touched the soft of Trevor's skin.

"I need you to do a favor for me, and it's very important, and I need you to do this no matter what—all right?"

Trevor nodded, his eyes full of questioning. Braxton could tell that he was uncertain of what it was that he was agreeing to.

"Be careful with Christian. I know you don't want to hear anything like that, and you want me to be happy for you... which I am, but I still want you to be careful."

"Remember, he's not the same person you grew up with, and you don't know how his brain works anymore."

Trevor nodded and stood up, trying to fight the mist of tears that was welling in his eyes.

Daring so much, Braxton stepped forward and wrapped his arms around Trevor, crushing him to his bare flesh, feeling the wet of his tears on his shoulders, trying to be mindful of the erection that was growing, trying to tent his boxer-briefs. Trevor's fingers on his bare back were like a working of needles, each one unique and electrifying.

"Thank you for always looking after me," he sniffled, and Braxton rocked him gently, his eyes closed and his mind wandering. He had never felt this much peace inside of himself.

"And I always will...."

He ran his fingers through the tiny shaved hairs on the back of Trevor's head. He smelled sweet, like salt and honey. Braxton wished to breathe it in forever, losing himself for eternity in this moment.

"Promise?"

Braxton chuckled slightly and then felt his heart stop for just a second as Trevor's fingers found their way momentarily to the elastic band of his underwear, gently grazing the upper half of his buttocks before moving away just as quickly.

"Promise."

The moment seemed to go on forever, sweet and eternal, like a scene in a movie that had no end, lingering between life and death, fantasy and reality, a terrifying dance of dreams made flesh and lust turned to nightmares. The two of them were intimate in a way that they had never, and now seemed had always been. The rules of friendship and sex appeared tethered to a pole, a pole that allowed them to swing in constant disarray.

EIGHT

The house was quiet, filled with cold noon gray. The rain had subsided, but its touch on the world still lingered, even inside the great manor. In silent contemplation, Kathryn Blackmoore moved within its walls, ignoring the dull wails of the only other occupant of Trevor's bedroom.

Dressed in a black-and-white pinstriped pantsuit, with her usual pair of black Manolo Blahniks strapped to her feet Kathryn moved into the office, prepared to follow through with her usual weekday routine. She would begin with calling her husband's cell, knowing that she would most likely be interrupting him in his infidelity, but that was just a fleeting disgust. She could care less who Tom was fucking; after all, she had married him to fill the void of Sheffield, not because she actually needed him in her life.

Kathryn sat down in the large Italian leather chair. The ornate desk, mammoth in size, made her feel small and weak, which she could not abide, always tempted to have the thing picked up and dropped off at the city dump—but it made Tom happy, and to appease him she tolerated the damn thing. She picked up the black cordless and dialed the number to his cellular phone, assured that he would pick up the line.

"Hello?"

It was a woman's voice, deep, but unlike Kathryn it was not smokey. On the contrary, it was rather flat and unappealing, but this was not the problem; the problem was that it was this stranger answering the phone, and not her husband.

"May I speak to Tom?"

The girl gave a sigh and called out Tom's name. She could hear that Virginia dialect instantly and distinctly, as well as the grunt of annoyance from her wandering husband.

"This is Tom."

Kathryn twirled a manicured finger around a strand of auburn hair, feeling the sharp stab of rage puncture her stoic demeanor.

"What is some slut doing answering your phone?"

She could feel him choking on his saliva following it up with a rough cough.

"Kathryn, hello."

"Don't give me that shit! I give you free rein to stick your cock in whatever hole you want, when you want, but all I ask is that you keep some things between us—like phone calls! It's one thing to fuck some slut, but it's quite another having her answer your phone!"

The anonymous tramp in the background kept asking over and over again who it was that Tom was speaking to.

"Kathryn, can we talk about this later?"

Calmly she closed her eyes, feeling her mind clear and a throbbing heat buzz inside of her body, doing what she had done so often before in her life—reaching outside of herself and merging with Tom's brain, connecting with each nerve and registering everything that he saw.

The girl was young, perhaps twenty or less: a very skinny body, the kind of body made popular by drug addicts, and her hair was platinum and fried, her hands slowly removing her clothes, performing a sloppy striptease for her husband.

She returned to herself.

"That bitch is stripping for you!"

Her cold demeanor was all but gone, taken over by blind and uncontrollable fury.

"How did you...? Never mind."

Suddenly the girl called out to Tom, coaxing him to get off the phone—and like most men, her husband thought with his dick, and the dick always won out in the end.

Before Kathryn could say another word, he hung up the line, leaving Kathryn to the automotive voice asking her to hang up and try again if she wanted to make a call.

"Fuck!"

Kathryn pitched the phone across the room, watching it hit the hardwood floor and break in half, the wires and chips littering the wood like glass. She threw her head into her hands and cried, letting out a great flood of tears. She could not understand why she had ever put herself into this position, giving herself over to a man she could not love, a man who had never loved her.

The Blackmoores had money, and Tom had wanted it. In the end he got it, moving up quickly in the social ladder, joining a country club that Kathryn had refused to join, and associating with people that she had never wanted to associate with.

Kathryn had abandoned the world of the privileged as soon as Trevor had entered the seventh grade—when she realized how different her son was and how those who had grown up with him and loved him had so suddenly abandoned him and brought him to tears. His saving grace had been Braxton Volaverunt, a saving grace that Queen Mab had told her about long before he had arrived.

She had been humiliated by her husband and had been ignored for a young piece of anorexic ass, and that was unforgivable. If she could command the forces of hell itself, she would do it, but fortunately she had the next best thing hiding itself in her son's bedroom.

"Jonathan, come!"

The fragile windowpanes began to rattle, as well as the glass doors of the various cabinets. The force of the spirit made the air heavy and the world now seemed condensed.

'*Yes?*' the voice asked, speaking to her on the inside like a soothing murmur within her heart.

"Work your will, spirit. Work your will for me like you used to do when I was a child. Work it for me and do my bidding, or I'll cast you into the walls once again, as I did when I became pregnant!"

The glass cabinetry cracked, splitting apart and yet not enough to make the pieces fall to the floor.

The truth made the specter angry.

Kathryn had been the first to bring him life when she was no more than nine. Like he was with Trevor now, he had been her ever-vigilant companion, protecting her and loving her. It was not until she became pregnant and saw his esteem for the not-yet-born Trevor that she had worked her will to bind him back into the very walls, the place he had been before she had called him out with her spirit board.

'What would you will of me?' he asked, his voice filling her with sweetness, fresh and enticing, luring Kathryn towards a sense of lethargy.

"Go to my fuck of a husband and scare the shit out of him! Make him fear you and make him wary. I want him alert and I want him paranoid, but do not cause any kind of harm to him, none at all.

"Just scare him; I'll take care of the rest."

The final rope had been cut, and there was no choice of possibility. She would do to Tom what she did to Father Magnus those many years ago, and she would enjoy it; she would savor it and examine it like a glass of exquisite wine.

'And what of Christian?'

The spirit had filled her in on the events of Friday night, had told her of the conversation and his distrust of the privileged child. The older he got, the more like his father Emanuel he became, though Trevor refused to see it.

She hated the idea of keeping some kind of happiness away from her son, but Christian was not such a thing. He was smooth, charming, and clever, but he would bring anything but happiness to her son. Kathryn knew this; she knew this like she had known so many other things in life. But like her, Trevor would have to learn on his own, would have to understand his own personal legacy, like the overall puppet-master that was the entire family's Legacy. It was a destiny unavoidable, no matter how hard any of them tried to escape it.

"I will do what I can in the situation, but you, Jonathan, you just do what I ask of you, and nothing else!"

The air stirred and the curtains on the French doors gave way to a slight ripple, signaling to Kathryn that the spirit had parted, passing through the ether on invisible lines, taking him to the target.

Her mind was wrought with agitation, upset by her son's desperation and his sudden disregard for anyone else that was not Christian Vasquez. Throughout the course of the weekend he had hardly spoken of anything else—as if even when Christian was not around, Trevor was still obligated to worship him and sing the young man's praises.

What was Kathryn going to do: lose her son to an evil that wore a teenage face, or lose him to her interference and objection? Her aunt had told her it would be so easy, that the universe would work everything out. Trevor was where he needed to be, and all those around him were where they needed to be because of that—but what now?

That was before Christian Vasquez came into her son's life. Now it seemed Braxton did not matter—the boy who had guided her son for the past five years, the boy who had been courteous and polite, and who fixed into Trevor's life in a way that he may never know, and a way that Kathryn herself vaguely understood.

So many questions and guidance seemed out of reach, lost in a world abandoned by her a long time ago. A world filled with pews and women dressed in black and white, a world where you sat in a box and confessed your soul amidst the scents of antiquity. Her faith had mixed with it so well, and it was still a blending—an orgy of deities, copulating and creating a bastardization of religion—but even to that she felt distant.

Sheffield had been her saving grace, and in the end her love for him had ended his life, had created a monstrous mutation inside of his head, attaching to his brain. It had been so sudden then: his convulsions, his sweats, and the blood that had seeped from his nose. Trevor had stood at the top of the stairs screaming, dressed in a pair of khaki shorts and tennis shoes, calling for his daddy.

Kathryn had told him to shut up then. She hadn't meant it, but she could not think and the ambulance seemed to take an eternity to arrive, and though the lethality of it was quick, the actual dying was slow and torturous for both persons.

She had done whatever she could to slow the process.

She had invoked every god that she had known and loved throughout childhood.

She had tried so hard to envision the structure of his brain and the tumor that lay attached. She had tried to use her mind to stop it, to slow down its hostile takeover, but nothing had worked. She had thought on the death of her own father when she was only eleven years old, the same age as Trevor had been when his father died.

It was the Legacy of the family, her mother Annaline had told her in a dream, trying to ease her tears, and now the words of her mother had penetrated her once again.

You cannot stop what is happening to your husband; it is the will of the Legacy, and the Legacy always wins.

Kathryn Blackmoore wiped her tears away, realizing that she had never explained it to her son—not in those words, not in that way. The other night she had explained it to him in distant and technical terms, not going into it personally, not describing what it felt like. In the end it had seemed that it had become nothing more than a passing notion, a waking theory, a theory that would not touch her son.

Kathryn tried to shake it off, tried not to think of her son just pushing away those warnings. Not her little boy, the child who had laughed and giggled, who had loved his friends and loved the holidays. Her little Trevor who had loved his daddy more than he had loved his own mother, the little boy who had watched the Legacy work its will and kill his father.

But he was not that little boy anymore.

He knew sex, knew it intimately because Jonathan had most likely shown it to him when he was coming of age. No, the little boy was gone, replaced with a cunning and guarded young man.

"Enough of this," Kathryn growled under her breath, dismissing all of it like she dismissed so many things around her in the world.

She grabbed her purse and her umbrella, taking it in case the rain chose to come once again, laying its usual claim on the Pacific Northwest. She opened the front door and took a deep breath before stepping outside, allowing the smell of moss and ocean to fill her senses and calm her conscious.

Kathryn thought of Sheffield once again and said a little prayer, blessing his name and asking for solace, hoping to get through the day. She closed the door and locked it, making her way down Knox Street and towards Fairhaven, forming a mental list of the things she needed to do and what it was she needed to achieve in terms of her husband, her son, and the rest of her soul.

The village of Fairhaven was buzzing with life, despite the cold. Old lamp posts wrapped with rich green fir boughs and wreaths with red ribbon seemed like precious jewels. The rich nineteenth-century buildings were lined with white lights, as well as the naked limbs of the trees that lined the streets.

Holiday tunes trickled from many speakers connected to the shops and the restaurants, which were permeating with the filling scents of bread and spices—all of these reminders to Kathryn that Christmas was less than a month away.

She was going to kill him.

She knew it, had known it from the very moment that she had been hung up on. The abuse and anguish that Tom put her through was not worth it, and it was in her power to deliver death. It always had been, whether deliberate or accidental; death was her gift, and she would exercise that gift like the ability to inhale and exhale.

She made her way down Harris Street, nearing the little herb and flower shop next to Village Books, eager for some nightshade and roses, content with the knowledge that she could do this all from memory, and not by the assistance of a how-to book of Afro-Anglo faith.

She was taught by her mother and her aunt, and she knew that eventually she would have to introduce Trevor to the truth of the Blackmoores and what they could do—but for now she would allow him to linger in ignorance with his willful spirit.

Abigail's Garden sat on the corner of the street: a little brown, shed-style shop with its own private garden in the back where they fertilized their own herbs and flora. They sold garden décor, herbs, and candles, which Kathryn already had an abundance of, but it couldn't hurt to stock up on a few more.

Her fingers felt brittle and numb, the color an off-purple, her veins as visible as the faces around her. She walked slowly across the white gravel of Abigail's, cringing at the sound the stones made under her feet. She hoped that no one would speak to her; the last thing she needed was to feel that sense of fear and abandon that a child could feel around faces and bodies that it did not know.

The church had taught her to fear the world around her and the strangers who inhabited it: people who were prone to murder, sex, drugs, and many other forms of corruption. Because of the church she feared the human heart and the tales it could tell. She could not conceive of allowing herself to rely on pure instinct and abandon looking at the mortal mind altogether; she knew that she did not trust others enough to let go of that upper-hand. The human mind was always open to her; though memories changed and ideas faded, the true psychological nature of a person was always mapped out along the great tundra of the moist and fleshy brain.

Kathryn placed her hands on the wood gate that led to the back garden, wrapping her chilled fingers around the wood fence-posts, the wood straining to stay strong in spite of the damp of the world. Before her now was a graveled garden, rich in botanic and flora. The only flowers that could survive in the death that winter brought bloomed, and the heads of many rose bushes and styled flower beds laid vacant or decapitated.

The scent of death was strong, and drifted along the brittle breeze, carried to the clairvoyant senses and lingered there, fermenting with the thoughts and voices of those long passed who still existed in cohabitation with the living and the breathing.

Upon clutching the ends of her long, black velvet jacket, she closed her eyes and opened herself up to those who seemed like her: invisible and forever stuck in the in-between, unable to go backwards but hindered in moving forward. Slowly she inhaled with her nose and exhaled through her mouth, letting the air pass through her and cast itself back out into the winter world in a coating of visible breath.

She could hear the distant sound of laughter coming towards her. It was sharp and beautiful, the laugh of a child, the kind of laugh the was purely subconscious in form, the kind of laugh a child can only make when they are completely consumed with indescribable joy and exhilaration: a laugh that made Kathryn think of her own son.

Kathryn fought with herself to stay inside, to keep focused on this laughter and the feelings and smells that were trying to develop because of this. She smelled lilacs and lilies, roses and tulips, and a foundation of carnations—all of this enriching the air with its touch and expression. The air itself became warm and fresh, the atmosphere smelling of the bay and the sky thick with the sounds of seagulls and conversation.

It seemed to Kathryn that someone quite suddenly brushed passed her, knocking against her flesh. At first she was scared, fearing what it could be and the contact that developed between her and someone that she did not know, but then it quickly became something else, forcing her to smile and giggle slightly despite herself. The ideas that plagued her conscious before this moment had amounted to nothing, and Kathryn opened her eyes.

The garden and the shop were gone, nothing of it left for the eyes.

Kathryn stood atop a grassy knoll, staring at the red-bricked side of what would be Village Books, but was for now some other shop or apartments. The manner of the building was unimportant, especially since Kathryn would not be approaching it. Before her the sun was bright on the emerald field, and children clothed in garments of long since past played with one another in careless thought.

The girls dressed in white and pink dresses of cotton reaching to their knees, their legs covered in tights of black and white, and little black boots and Mary Janes adorned their feet. Some of their hair was long and lush, twisted in curls; others had hair that bobbed at their chins. Their faces were beautiful and their eyes brilliant, though they moved apart from Kathryn. The entire world was separate from her, as if she were standing within a silent film reel and the film was dyed so the characters had color.

She looked to see a sparse scattering of Model Ts along the paved road of Harris Avenue. A rich oak trolley made its way up along the tracks and stopped just short of the intersection to allow passengers to get on and off the machine. In silent wonder Kathryn watched this world and understood its decade. It was sometime in the Twenties, though as to the actual date and season she was unsure—but it felt to be spring, or possibly even summer. The look and feeling of the city had very little difference between these two seasons.

"Mabel!" Kathryn heard the name called out—Mabel like her aunt, Mabel like the matriarch of the Blackmoore family. She heard the name called out once again and this time she searched with her eyes, searched the field looking for the source of the call; she found it.

Not ten feet away from her was a woman, clothed in a long white dress with tiny sleeves that cut off at her shoulders and a long three-tiered necklace strung with amber around her neck. Her skin was fair and lightly pinked; her face was soft and oval in shape. Her lips were without rouge, her eyes like a set of bright emeralds, and her hair was flaxen and red, draping down her back and stopping just short of her buttocks.

"Mabel Blackmoore, you come here right now, darling; we need to go!"

Mabel Blackmoore.

It struck Kathryn hard and forced her to look desperately for the child, her eyes scouring the field for this little girl who would become the great leader of the family.

"Coming, Mommy!"

A little girl with dirty blonde hair that fell to her shoulders came running across the rich grass, her little body clothed in a dress of lavender and black tights, her shoes missing from off her feet and held in her little fingers. She laughed erratically and her eyes were deep and blue like nighttime waters, so unlike the gray that they were now.

She appeared to notice nothing, nothing until she came upon her mother—who was none other than Fiona, her grandmother, her grandmother who now resided in New Orleans, the start of the Blackmoores in America, and where she was being looked after by Queen Mab's daughter and Kathryn's younger cousin, Magdalene.

The child who would become Queen Mab stopped just short of her mother and turned in Kathryn's direction, locking eyes with the woman who was out of place and supposedly invisible—but, like Kathryn, if she could tap into their world then they could tap into hers.

They stared at one another for a long time, the little girl ignoring the calls of her mother, not caring to respond to her pleas. Kathryn was now an interest to the little girl with the dirty blonde hair and large eyes. They could feel the ethereal air between them thinning, and eventually they would be in one mutual world, something that could not be.

"Mabel, dearest what are you—"

Fiona looked up from her daughter and towards the direction of her gaze, either seeing or sensing Kathryn. She wasn't certain, but the look in Fiona's eyes sent chills through her body.

"Depart!" Fiona yelled, raising her hand towards Kathryn, who only watched on in awe.

Her mind and vision shook, unable to keep steady, and her eyes were forced shut by the jarring pain; she could hear only a howling wind and a cold and empty atmosphere, a world frozen by death and ice.

She opened her eyes.

Kathryn was once again in the present, standing in the dead garden of Abigail's, unable to get her mind into focus. The jarring pain of the moment had taken her and now she was forced to gather her wits and remember what it was that she had to do in the present.

"Mrs. Blackmoore, are you all right?" Kathryn looked up to see Betty staring at her—the young college girl with the soft white skin, mop of brown hair, and usual green sweater and blue jeans. She was the only other person besides Miranda—who was the shop owner, having named the place after her mother—who worked at the garden store.

Betty was a sweet girl who loved to assist people and who seemed to be the only other person aside from her son that Kathryn communicated with, and now this gentle girl seemed worried for her customer's well-being.

"Oh, Betty, sweetie, I'm fine. I just got shocked by the cold, that's all. Trust me, I'm wonderful; I just need to pick up a few things and I'll go to the tea house or something."

Kathryn placed a cold, brittle hand on the young girl and smiled gently, silently assuring the girl that she had no reason to worry for the forty-one-year-old woman.

"All right; I'm sorry, what is it that you need?"

Good question, Kathryn thought to herself, trying to recall what it was that she had come for. The time was pushing 12:30, and she needed to do what she planned before her son came home and forced her to avoid her task.

"I need Nightshade, Black Snake Root, Devil's Shoestring, Tonka beans, and a bag of dried rose petals. And I think a few candles: two whites, three reds, and four blacks."

Betty nodded and made her way up through the garden and disappeared inside the little wood shack that was Abigail's, leaving Kathryn alone in the dead winter world, drifting in her mind, trying to understand the reason for the time slip and what it could mean in the entirety of the Blackmoore family.

It smelled to Kathryn as if it would snow.

NINE

The first thing to hit him was the air, which smelled crisp and clean, yet lined with a preverbal moisture that seemed to touch just beneath the surface.

Braxton knew it would snow.

The bell had rung not a minute earlier, and already the entire campus was littered with the South End's population of teenagers; all of them making their way to the cafeteria or to their vehicles to get lunch and consume it within their forty-five-minute time frame.

Braxton Volaverunt made his way under the metal breezeway towards the cafeteria, his hands tucked in the front pockets of his jeans. The chain felt like ice, as if it had been kept in a freezer and not removed until just before lunch. His clunky black boots shuffled along the concrete. His large brown eyes were averted to the walkway and his entire demeanor seemed closed off, his mind unable to shake off the visions of earlier or the contact with Trevor in the locker room.

"Shit..." he said under his breath, trying to muffle the sudden onslaught of tears that had begun to stream down his face.

The last thing he needed to do was cry in front of the entire school, especially when they all had a certain image of him—one that was raw, tough, and rebellious. Out of all the words that described his image, a crier was not one of them.

Braxton had to squint his eyes upon opening the large fire doors, protecting his vision from the harsh light of the white fluorescents, which seemed to illuminate with intensity when looked at against the clouded darkness of the freezing afternoon.

The cafeteria was loud, and words were undistinguishable in the inaudible noise. Students moved like vultures circling their prey on desolate desert tundra, the carcass being the many tables inside the large building, and the exposed insides being the many teens that filled its seats.

He stood in the doorway for several moments searching the cafeteria for Trevor Blackmoore, desperate to see him once again and perhaps finally confess all of that which had been tormenting his brain and panging his heart.

He looked over at his usual table and saw Trevor's book-bag resting on top of the solid surface, the wear and tear of the year already visible on the black material, the zipper opened and his school supplies exposed and tempting to any delinquent who felt like stealing someone's school books just for the hell of it, the boredom of the city giving them no other entertainment.

Quickly Braxton made his way to the table and pulled out the chair next to the book-bag, taking a seat and waiting anxiously for Trevor to return, thankful that Christian did not have the same lunch period.

His palms began to sweat and his heart pounded as he spied Trevor coming towards him, a tray in his hand and a sub sandwich wrapped in white parchment lying atop the brown plastic tray.

The young man's face lit up at the sight of Braxton sitting at the table waiting for him patiently.

"Hey," he said, not the least bit surprised when Braxton stood and pulled out the green plastic chair for him and pushed it back in as soon as he took his seat. The smell of his cologne filled Trevor's senses and forced him to think back on the locker room, his heart breaking slightly at the thought that everything between he and Braxton would be perfect if only his best friend was gay and not just this sensitive and overly protective straight boy.

"Wassup?" Braxton replied. Trevor smiled at him and Braxton returned it, unable to think of what to say next.

"About earlier..." Trevor began, picking up his sandwich but setting it back down without taking a bite. "I'm sorry to have barged in on you like that in the locker room; it wasn't exactly appropriate."

Memories of a wonderfully soft and sculpted body clothed in black boxer-briefs, dark nipples erect and tantalizing, torturous sex with masculine air, lust heavy and humid.

"No, not at all; I'm glad you came. It really made my morning a lot better...."

Trevor blushed and looked away, unable to hide his smile.

"Still, I shouldn't have done it."

Braxton shook his head and chuckled, placing his hand on Trevor's leg, but retracting it as soon as he looked at Braxton with large, wondrous forest eyes.

"Hey, come walk with me," he suggested suddenly.

Trevor nodded in confusion, unsure of what this walk was about. They both stood up and collected their book-bags, Trevor wrapping up his sandwich and placing it inside, both boys making their way out of the cafeteria with anxious strides, each of them thinking the same thing but not knowing how to express it.

The air outside was chilled and Braxton wasn't certain of what it was that he was hoping to accomplish by coming outside, except possibly frostbite.

Trevor brought his arms around his chest and folded them, attempting to circulate his body heat and keep himself warm. The December air was freezing and biting his flesh. His nipples became hard and felt like ice, and there was actual pain when they came into contact with the fabric of his red shirt underneath the black sweater.

"I've never known things to be so hard before... I have so many things that I want to say, and now it seems like have no words with which to say them with."

Braxton was getting sidetracked, stalling, trying to gauge what it was exactly that he was going to say, and how he was going to confess all of that which had been plaguing him these past three long years.

"What is it?" Trevor asked with slight trepidation.

They were standing close now, huddled together, their bodies being used to block against the slight breeze.

"I've needed to say this for a long while now, and—"

A cold fluff tapped the surface of Braxton's nose, bringing him to a halt and causing he and Trevor to look at one another, wide-eyed and full of curiosity.

It started out sparse and slow. Tiny white specks gliding down gently, landing on their clothes and hair, dotting them with white for a few seconds before melting away into wet. Other students who were also outside for one reason or another began to stop and gawk, dumbfounded at the December miracle.

Within several moments it began to pick up in pace, cascading down from the gray thick in the sky and obscuring the vision of the people outside.

"It's snow!" Trevor exclaimed. By now the entire conclave of students had departed the cafeteria, choosing to neglect their food and even their book bags for the opportunity to revel in the falling white.

Some students twirled about, others were playfully pushing each other. A throng of girls stood with their tongues hanging out of their mouths, trying to catch the soft flakes. But all of the students, no matter what, moving or just standing, were all laughing and allowing themselves to experience the pure and simple joys that that first snowfall could bring, allowing them for a brief moment to forget that they were simply children masquerading as adults.

"I can't believe this; can you believe this?" Trevor asked him, becoming increasingly neglectful of their purpose for being outside.

"No, it's... its great."

His head fell and his lids lowered, his brown eyes misting slightly, his entire demeanor becoming sullen. Braxton knew that once again he was going to have to bow out of the notion of confessing his secret to the fragile teen.

"Well, it looks like someone's having fun!"

Braxton lifted his head to see Christian Vasquez open his arms and wrap them around Trevor, closing his eyes and smiling. When Christian opened his lids and looked at Braxton, it was as if tiny knives were being hurled at him, sticking firmly into his flesh, tearing the skin and causing the blood to flow, to ooze out of the thin infliction.

"What are you doing out here?" Trevor asked him, his face consumed by a dumb grin.

"Yeah, shouldn't you be in *class*?" Braxton glared at him, embittered by the presence of the jock and now wishing that they had remained in the cafeteria—though Christian would have found them in there, no doubt.

"I should be but I'm not; I wanted to spend the afternoon with my boy."

This statement was thrown at Braxton with sharp resolve, both boys trying to outdo each other in the most subtle of ways. Braxton figured that Trevor was too enamored to pay any notice—and if he did notice, he wasn't caring.

"Really?" Trevor asked, only half-believing, Braxton not believing at all.

Christian nodded, and in a move that shocked him and even Trevor, Christian planted a soft kiss on his forehead and lightly ran his fingers through Trevor's mess of wine-red hair.

"Yeah... now, what do you say to getting out of here?"

Braxton seemed to fade in this instant, becoming nothing more than part of the background, his presence unimportant to the one person that he loved more than the entire world.

"I don't know...."

The doubt on Trevor's face was genuine, and at the moment he cocked his head and looked at Braxton, silently asking for advice, but as he went to open his mouth and protest Christian placed his hand on Trevor's face and turned his head back in his direction.

"C'mon, it'll be good for you to do something spontaneous and crazy. We could go for a walk through Whatcom Falls, go get an early dinner... how about it?"

He pouted his cushion lips and looked at Trevor with pleading black eyes. Braxton could see Trevor's reserve fading, washing away with sick flirtation; Christian was going to get his way.

"All right... but I can't be out too late; my mother and I need to go pick up our Christmas tree."

Christian nodded and watched in silent gloating as Trevor turned to say goodbye to Braxton.

The rage began to boil to the surface, and Braxton hoped that they both could feel it. He knew what was coming; the visions were never wrong, and all he could see in the future was humiliation and death, and a world in which Trevor was coming back from neither.

"Thank you, I'll call you tonight!"

Braxton nodded and Trevor ran into him, wrapping his arms around Braxton's waist and keeping him in a tight embrace. To Braxton it felt as if the universe had caved in on itself, spilling into planet earth and crashing into Braxton's body; the anguish was wretched.

"I'll be waiting...."

In a move that was equally as surprising, Braxton closed his eyes and kissed Trevor on the cheek, allowed his lips to linger there for several seconds. Braxton knew when looking at Trevor's face that he felt automatic shame, telling the young Volaverunt that there was something so much more than feelings of friendship that rested behind Trevor's eyes.

"Bye."

Braxton watched as Christian placed his hand on the small of Trevor's back and led him through the parking lot and towards his car, the snow flurries growing thick, distorting his vision and causing Trevor Blackmoore and Christian Vasquez to disappear in the haze.

As he turned to head back towards the school, his emotions in mourning, he spied Cheri Hannifin staring at him with a triumphant smile on her face.

She was dressed in tight, boot-cut jeans, a tight black turtle neck fit snug around her breasts, her hair hanging loosely over her shoulders, a pair of open-toed, lime green heeled sandals on her feet, and a white Louis Vuitton handbag at her side.

Her eyes were like poison, poison meant for Braxton, and she was secretly devouring him and drinking up his disappointment.

In this moment he cared for nothing: not for the magic of snow fall, not for school, not even for his own self-preservation. If in the end he was going to lose Trevor, then so be it, but he could not allow Trevor to walk into some sort of trap; at least, not any more than he already had.

As Braxton made his way to his car he resolved that on the phone he would say all that he needed to say, and he accepted the fact that he was risking everything in the process. He knew that to protect the ones you love, sacrifices had to be made, and sometimes that meant sacrificing those very people that you choose to keep safe.

Greg's cock felt like fire inside of her. Despite the flesh that lined her vagina, she could still feel the exact form of his mushroom-shaped cock-head grinding against her. She could feel very little difference between the condom and a bare organ, and had told Greg that when he complained about having to use one.

They were lying out in the back garden outside of her house, a large two-story Victorian mansion that had been built by James Hannifin back in 1887—as soon as he and his family had arrived from Dublin, Ireland. The garden had been created and loved by his wife Alexandra, the lawn tended and raised by her hands, and now it had become a perfectly soft bed for fucking.

She was naked, and lay out spread-eagle. Her jeans and thong were missing, her knees up in the air, and her sweater still covering her breasts. With his massive hands Greg was cupping them underneath and holding them like the handles of a bicycle.

He was so much bulkier than Christian, though he was just as fit, his skin soft and fair. His nipples were pink, the nest of blond hair between his legs was trimmed, and his thick member drilled into her, the sweat glistening off of his naked backside. Cheri placed her hands on his smooth, sculpted buttocks and squeezed, invigorating Greg Sheer and driving him to pump harder.

Though he growled, Cheri made no sound and she chose to ignore his, looking up into the sky and counting the flakes that fell. A soft coating of white formed around them, and in her mind she was constantly plotting and forming, deciding every course of action with snake-like precision. She would never be taken unawares.

She became increasingly wet and her eyes found themselves rolled up inside of her head, the clear juices spilling out of her entrance, her body floating between consciousness and euphoria. She was so hot that she could not feel the icy breath of winter upon her.

"Fuck..." Greg moaned, spilling himself inside of the condom.

She could feel its liquid warmth and prayed that it would not slip off, risking pregnancy.

"Oh, Jesus..." he exclaimed once again, pulling himself out and lying next to her, his cock falling to the side and resting on his thigh, the milky semen slipping out of the condom and oozing over his flesh, caking the trimmed nest of pubic hair, his body covered in gooseflesh.

They both laid there inside of themselves: the couple no one was to know about, and the sex that was kept secret. Though Greg could care less, Cheri had a reputation, one of purity and maturity. She could not be seen as a slut, or even something as simple as a sexually-active youth. In South Hill, you were either a daddy's girl or a whore, and being known as a whore was not an option.

Braxton's black Acura sped down Chuckanut Drive, the highway now sleek and black with the wet of the snow, and the earth and firs were becoming thick and white. The lake rocked with gentle waves, and the many boats that lined the shore were now in motion with the water.

He took a sharp right and drove down a path made of brick, stopping along the side of a large, single-level, lakefront home, a third of a block long and made with a combination of stone and cedar, the front of the house lined with trees and bushes, most of which were now missing their foliage.

A narrow white stone path led under a white veranda made of wood and covered in ivy. A stone pedestal birdbath stood nestled in the corner, the water already beginning to freeze. He walked along this now, passing the row of large picture windows with white frames which lined the long hallway. The wood walls were painted in a light cream and decorated with paintings of colonial New England and turn-of-the-century Bellingham, his father finding the most ordinary of things to be extraordinary and worth collecting.

The front door was cedar-framed with double-paned glass in the center, entering straight into the formal sitting area, which extended forward and had an arched canopy attached to it, held secure by two thirteen foot cedar posts, fastened to the large deck which moved over the lake.

Braxton pulled out his key and stuck it in the lock, waiting for the familiar click before twisting the steel handle and walking inside, ready to immediately switch on the heater. The formal sitting room was furnished with two black couches made of Italian leather. A rich mahogany coffee table filled the space between them, and on opposite ends of the table were matching arm chairs made of the same leather as the couches.

The walls were painted in a rich caramel wash and a large cedar mantled fireplace loomed across from the front door. A set of two mammoth picture windows looked out on the expansive deck, and between these two frames of glass were a set of French doors made of wood and glass paneling.

Braxton stood and watched as the snow fall faded on the lake but made some impact on the white ash that extended over the water and its stainless steel rail that lined the deck's edge.

Cautiously he searched the home with his ears, trying to pick up any indication that his father Eric might be home. Silently he moved towards the back of the house on the opposite end of the formal room, slipping between numerous pieces of furniture from around the world. A matching set of French doors like those that led outside were open, and marked the entrance into the dining room.

A picture window looked out on the thick evergreens at the back of the house, the table made of mahogany and lined with a set of ten slender leather-back chairs, the table decorated with dishes never used and candles never lit.

All of them were reminders of his mother, who used to throw several parties and informal get-togethers, always making use of the table in one way or another—whether it was to have a place to set the food or to sit the people who were there to enjoy it. All of it was a painful memory of a life that no longer existed, and a father that was alive, not the empty shell of a man that roamed the halls of this great house.

"Dad?" Braxton called out, finding no response except for that of his own echo bouncing off the walls.

He closed his eyes and shook his head briefly, dismissing his mother Tammy and his zombie father. There was no reason to mourn for those that would not be coming back—whether they were dead or alive.

Braxton pushed himself against the stainless-steel swinging door that led into the kitchen, made with industrial materials and too sleek to actually be enjoyed. Braxton hardly ever found himself going in here, opting instead to eat out most of the time.

Cold, gray light shone through the windows and onto cold steel materials. The distant phantoms of laughter and his mother could be heard just beyond the spiritual horizon, Braxton trying to block out the ghost of dreams from tormenting his brain and pulling on his heart.

He thought of Trevor and that naïve smile that rested on his face when he looked upon Christian, remembered his laughter and Christian's arms holding Trevor, Braxton knowing what truly lay behind the jock's grin.

The anger inside him was once again becoming fever-pitched, trying to break out and pour over the surface. Braxton knew that there was no controlling it, so he let it out, screaming over and over again and punching the steel island just as many times, not caring that he was wearing down the tissue in his hands, and ignoring the jarring pain that was shocking his bones.

He could not understand why Trevor was falling into Christian's trap so easily, the young Blackmoore completely disregarding the five years of pain that Christian and his friends put him through, completely ignoring all of the tears that he had shed on Braxton's shoulder on their behalf. Why was he giving in, and why was he not seeing Braxton and the feelings that gnawed within him?

After getting the aggression out of his system, Braxton adjusted the heat and went to the fridge, removing a bottle of Budweiser from the shelf against the door and maneuvering back out into the dining room and back through the formal sitting room, taking a moment to twist off the metal bottle cap.

He felt the slightest sorrow begin to build inside of him, just as his rage had done, and now Braxton chose to be alone with it. He pulled open the French doors and stepped outside, walking slowly towards the edge of the deck. The expanse of the cold lake was before him, the trees seeming to part and make way for him, framing the edge of both worlds: the earth and the sea.

The snow fell about him and his breath was visible, moving in and out of his open mouth, his fingers becoming numb and completely unfeeling, and the glass of the bottle felt as if it were chiseled from ice.

By this time the entirety of Whatcom Falls Park was covered in a soft, thin blanket of snow, sticking to dry grass and hard earth, refusing to go away with the wind. The thick branches of evergreens were now weighed by the heaviness that was building, and the naked oaks and maple trees were now made beautiful by the white that clung to the limbs. The rushing and rolling of the numerous waterfalls made the entire park seem like another world, a world that was unchanged and uncorrupted by man.

They hadn't said much, really, Christian passing along dismal remarks and mediocre questions, trying to charm his way with Trevor through a few smiles and absorbent glances.

Trevor hadn't really considered the dullness of the moment; something within him seemed off, and he guessed that it had more to do with his interaction with Braxton than it had to do with his interest in this childhood lust, now made real and tangible right before his eyes.

The closer they came to the park the nearer they were to Bayview Cemetery, which was the park's neighbor. From this land Trevor felt the pulse, the drone, the inhaling and exhaling of the souls that existed within.

He didn't like it.

Cemeteries sickened him, usually forcing nausea and severe migraines, not to mention the pleas and self-loathing from those departed. They always seemed to scream or say nothing at all, walking around blindly and confused.

Trevor did not like them because they knew him, knew that he could see them and understand them all of the time. The dead always looked for those that could see them, hear them, or at the very least, sense them.

It was an opportunity to convince that living soul to help them in their embittered endeavors upon this living plane, and upon those people that were still here.

"You okay?" Christian asked him.

He knew that Christian had spotted the distressed look on his face, but he could not worry about that now.

The dead were calling and they needed to get away.

"Huh? Oh, yeah, I'm fine; it's just ... well, I don't like cemeteries."

He thought that it was an answer that would sustain Christian, but Christian only laughed and shook his head, appearing to doubt Trevor's words.

"Oh, please; you used to tell me when we were kids that you were going to build a house inside a cemetery and you would live there all the time, making friends with the ghosts –"

"Well, I'm not a kid anymore!"

Trevor's tone was sharp, and his disdain for Christian and their former life was returning to him. For a brief instant he was wishing Christian dead, but he knew the power of his thoughts and emotions, and he knew that if not careful it could be directed on the young Vasquez and wreak its havoc on his life.

"Sorry, it's just ... well, a lot has happened since we last knew each other. I'm different, and the realities of death have kinda made themselves a lot more prevalent in my life.

"I'm not so sure that I'm willing to take the risk in flirting with it again."

He knew that his words were hinting at something more, and if he wasn't careful Christian would start inquiring as to their meaning.

"No; no, it's my fault. I'm the one that fucked up; I shouldn't have brought up the past, but it's just that it hasn't completely left me."

He broke away for a moment and then stopped, gently placing his hands on Trevor's shoulders, and forced the young man to face him.

They were standing on a bridge under naked limbs and thick evergreens, the cool mist of the rushing falls moving below them. The snow fell from the heavens, littering the earth and spotting the wine-red of Trevor's hair. His cheeks were flushed pink from the cold, and his large hazel eyes looked into Christian with curiosity.

"Let's face it..." Christian went on, staring into Trevor. "You've taken me over. I can't think of anything other than you and when I try, it only tears me up inside."

His voice was soft now, nothing more than a whisper, and on this bridge they came together, with their eyes closed and their lips parted, allowing them to connect and their tongues to slip through, the heat of their breath shocking their mouths and warming their cheeks.

It was the sweetest and most dangerous kiss. A kiss that Trevor had wanted for most of his life.

At first it was slow: the moving of their tongues, massaging one another with wet roughness. Then it moved into something more fevered, something that was acting as a murmur of something else, something hidden deep inside.

It passed through them both, making them think of their childhood games and sleepovers, of haunted houses and peanut butter and grape jelly sandwiches, of sun-drenched floors and expanded porches.

The both of them were someplace other than the park, and it scared them. It scared Christian most of all because he was realizing one very important and damaging detail: he was liking it.

"Wow..." Trevor exclaimed, unable to prevent it from leaving his lips, and immediately embarrassed. He had just made out with another guy for the first time in his life and he was treating it as if it were the hand of God healing his wounds.

"You can say that again!"

They looked at one another and laughed. It was thrilling, this erratic kissing, this coming together. They had broken the rules of gender, giving up that power that a man is supposed to have, and allowed one another to dominate.

Not only that, but they had done it in public, at risk of being seen by the entire world, and yet it did not matter. They were both experiencing something amazingly brilliant and sacred, and it seemed that no one on earth could ever know what it was like to feel that kind of physical, emotional, and psychological pull.

It started out in pieces: the sound and the picture were running against one another, not in sync with their components, but Trevor was still able to make them out.

He saw a scared woman with blonde hair and a rail-thin body, wearing nothing but her bra and panties, running out screaming from what appeared to be a hotel room. Objects were flying around, and a scared middle-aged man was curled up on the large bed, hanging onto the wood post for his life. It was like listening to things when you have your head under water; it's muffled and resonates in a different way, in a different frequency.

As his mind came closer to the man's face, he saw who it was, saw that familiar mouth, those steely eyes and rigid facial structure, recognized the chiseled chest with the salt-and-pepper hairs. He knew that it was his step-father Tom and understood instinctively who it was that was creating the assault.

"Jesus..." he let out, grasping the edge of the bridge with his hand, ignoring the painful freeze that was biting him, not caring that he looked like someone having a heat stroke.

Christian looked at him, confused, scared, worried that this mysterious boy somehow caught something from their kiss—that the true details of the plan were now revealed and Christian would be exposed.

"Are you okay?" he asked him.

He was genuinely concerned, but also fearful, gauging Trevor's body language in response to him.

"Yeah," he said, raising his hand in protest. "I just need to go to the bathroom."

Christian nodded and assisted Trevor across the bridge, gently guiding him to one of the facilities.

As they walked, Trevor had to continuously swallow his own vomit. The fear that Tom felt was excruciating, and it was wreaking havoc on his body. The visions would not stop. His stepfather continued to hug the wood bedpost as an ash tray went flying at him, missing him by less than an inch and crashing against the wall. The glass stained with ashen flecks broke, shattering into little tiny shards and littering the bed, falling like glitter. He understood the psychic connection with his spirit, his spirit that had somehow developed the strength to leave Bellingham and travel across the country to Virginia to punish a cheating husband.

He heard Tom scream for help. Understood his fear and the sickness that was existing within him, unable to comprehend what it was exactly that was happening to him, could not properly define the phenomenon that had sparked in his hotel room—just as he understood that if he did not pull Jonathan away now, he would most likely kill the wandering Tom Preston. Leaving his body to rot in that hotel room, leaving everyone unawares, until the stench became too awful and unavoidable.

"Excuse me," Trevor said, placing his open palm lightly on Christian's stomach before stepping into restroom.

It smelled like piss. That was one of the first things he noticed, and the fact that most of the porcelain urinals had not been flushed in weeks—perhaps years. The white was permanently stained a disgusting dark yellow, and the pink urinal cakes were mostly eaten away by the acid of human waste. There were five sinks, and all but two were either missing handles or faucets, and the stalls reeked.

The walls of the bathroom stalls were all covered in graffiti: things like 'For a good time, call...,' 'Satan rules,' and 'Suck this shit,' followed by a pathetic sketch of a dick, were all over the place. These basic messages, written and re-written in different ways but meaning the same thing, were the only reading material one would have inside of this place, and a child having to use the bathroom would come out with a few more choice words added to his vocabulary.

It made Trevor laugh and roll his eyes in disgust all at the same time.

"Okay..." he said to himself, closing his eyes and beginning to inhale through his nose and exhale out his mouth, focusing on what he was seeing in the visions and allowing his mind to reach out and grab the far-off spirit.

"Jonathan, come here!" he said aloud, but not loud enough for anyone to hear.

"Jonathan, now!" he said again, reaching with all of his might, seeing the vision slowing down, knowing that he had been heard and the spirit was now paying attention.

"Right now, Jonathan!"

He felt the ghost's resistance, but knew in the end that he would not be ignored.

Within seconds the vision had faded completely, and when he opened his eyes he could see the reflection of the back of the spirit's head in the mirror, though in front of him he could see nothing. He looked at the mirror once again, and sure enough it still showed that Jonathan was standing in front of him, blocking the sink, just a few inches taller than he was.

'Yes?' the voice asked him, vibrating inside his chest.

"What were you doing?"

The sickness was subsiding and he could feel the fever breaking.

'What Kathryn would want me to do....'

"No matter what Tom was doing, you don't kill him; that's not your call. Besides, you don't do anything unless I ask you to!"

He could feel the pulsating effigy of the familiar filling the bathroom and taking over his senses.

His head was throbbing.

'And what are you doing? Spending time with Christian, perhaps?'

There was anger in Jonathan's voice. It seemed to be dropping to a strong vibratory bass, and the glass of the mirrors seemed to pulse as if alive, as if they had a heartbeat hiding just beyond the reflective surface.

"You listen! It doesn't matter what I do or who I'm with; if I want you to know I'll tell you. Now, please...

"Go home."

The vents howled with air and the mirrors pulsated even more, the glass ready to give way. Trevor closed his eyes and turned away just as the row of mirrors split and the shards blew out, falling around Trevor like reflective snowflakes.

"What the...?"

Trevor opened his eyes to see Christian running in, looking around the bathroom in horror, the glass reflecting in his pools of black. His mouth hung open and he looked up to Trevor for answers, but he had none that he could give. Christian was going to decide his explanations for himself, and in the end the young man would make this explanation work for his brain and put the terror behind him.

Trevor shook his head and clasped Christian's hand, curling his fair fingers around the dark of Christian's, smiling warmly and leading him back out into the open, the world now blanketed in cold white.

TEN

Their imprint on the wet grass had only just begun to disappear under the snow, and the yellow of the porch light made it glisten. Alexandra Hannifin's garden could not have looked more beautiful than if it were in the fresh bloom of spring.

They stood in the kitchen made of wood paneling and painted a gorgeous cream. Though an old home, the kitchen had been remodeled and now looked fresh, with granite countertops and birch-wood cabinetry, and the tract lighting above the island created the room's only illumination.

Cheri looked out upon their secret bed and laughed to herself, knowing that she had so much control over all of those that orbited within her universe, and a prime example was her dumb-witted Greg Sheer. She looked over at him, sitting on a white wood stool, a glass of wine in his hand, staring back at her with drowsy hunger and drunken humor.

To tease him, Cheri reached back and curled her fingers under the hem of her Guess skirt, having opted to put that on versus the wet jeans. She began to raise it slightly, feeling Greg's eyes on her flesh, knowing that at the very moment that he would begin to act on his desires, she would drop it back down and squash his hopes.

She did this to him all the time. It was a game for her amusement. In fact, Greg was only amusement, and yet she knew that without him she would have no one—and in a world like this, governed with rules like hers, you needed as many people on your side as you could get. After all, they were the ones who could get you out of any situation if you were in danger of being caught.

"Greg?" she said. He was still disappointed from her little tease just a few moments earlier, though he was prepared to cast that aside and give her his undivided attention. The sharp glow of the tract light danced on tiny golden hairs, nearly shaved completely off; his blue eyes docile and his jaw lax.

"Yeah?" he asked her, as if drifting in and out of dreams.

"What do you think Christian and Trevor are doing right now?"

She had wondered about this for so long. Was he still the same; did he still have that innocent desperation that he had had when he was a child? Fearing that if they did not do everything in the moment, then the world might end and nothing would ever get done.

Her heart broke just a little, wishing that she could have those days back, wishing that they did not have to mature and put away childhood dreams, wishing in a way that they were still permitted to laugh. It felt to her that as soon as you became a teenager the world grows so much bleaker.

It was a harsh reality, one that no child would believe possible, and no reality that a parent would wish to tell. As a child, you are never told that it's going to be hard on you—emotionally or mentally. You wait impatiently to get older, to be able to do older things, but as soon as it happens, as soon as your body matures and innocence fades, you can't help but wish for those years back—years when the world was good and there were no voids in your life. Years, Cheri reflected, that Trevor still had, perhaps through his friendship with Braxton Volaverunt.

She shook the thought from her mind.

"They're probably sucking each other's dicks!"

Greg's voice brought her back, though it took her a moment to remember what it was that they were talking about, and what it was that she had asked him.

"You really think so? You think Christian would do that?"

It was no secret to her that Greg disliked Christian, though that would be different if it were Greg on the top of the Mariner High School food chain. But to hear his conviction in the actions of Christian with Trevor Blackmoore was something else, something that she herself had contemplated from the very beginning, but had not shared with Teri or even her own diary.

"The fucker loves Trevor. He claims that he despises him, and maybe on one level he does...."

Greg consumed the rest of the wine in his glass, and this time he took the bottle and removed the cork, preparing to chug the rest straight from its source.

"...But that's only because what he sees in Trevor, he sees in himself."

Cheri nodded in understanding and obvious agreement. The thoughts began to turn inside of her brain: always thinking, always plotting.

She knew that Greg wanted to be where Christian was, and now it seemed that they were armed with the tools needed to get him there.

In a way this had been the plan all along: to drag Christian through the mud just as he was doing it to Trevor, but the likelihood of him going through with it was doubtful. But now, perhaps, if they sought it out they would be able to find exactly what they needed.

"How would you like to take him down?" She walked over to her boyfriend and wrapped her petite arms around the bulk of his shoulders, placing her head on them and kissing his ear.

"I want that more than anything." His eyes seemed to light up, the ice of them cold enough to chill one's pulse or stop one's heart. His skin was warm from the wine and Cheri reached down and took the bottle from him, taking a swig of the pungent liquor herself.

"Then listen to me. We need to collect proof of he and Trevor together; we need to follow him, see where he goes, and somehow get what we need."

His attention was waning, the alcohol taking its effect on the young man's body.

"How do we do that?"

Cheri watched as his eyes prepared to roll up inside of his head; his voice was slurred and his breath hot and reeking of wine.

"Just leave that to me...."

On the other side of the window was the water. The wash of the coming dark began to make it look black and dirty, as if it were filled with awful and unnatural things, things that might reach out and grab you at the very moment that you thought that you were safe and alone.

Splayed out on his queen-size bed with the black comforter and sheets, resting on a mahogany four-post frame and strung with black lights, was Braxton: shirtless and wearing a pair of blue flannel pajama pants, his head curled in his arms and his backside soft and defined, the contour of his muscles formed like art from clay.

Possession by Sarah McLachlan blared from the speakers, forever on repeat, causing him to think on horrid visions, his mind creating twenty thousand different possibilities of what Trevor and Christian were doing at that very moment.

He thought of his mother Tammy, thought of her warm smile and seemingly perfect demeanor, thought about her large grey eyes and black hair, her curved body, those wonderful hips, hips that his dad used to hold her by and dance with her around the house, with jazz on the stereo and candles glowing throughout the house.

Now, no one danced.

The floors were never noisy and the house was either dark by night or lit by day, but no candles were ever touched and jazz was never played, and worst of all Eric did not move unless it was to work or to the kitchen. He was always in his bed or at his desk. Like a ghost, his sighting was rare and disturbing—though Braxton always felt a slight joy within him, like one would feel after seeing something so unbelievable as an apparition.

The clock read 5:15. He was going to call Trevor at seven and hope that he would be home. He knew that he was with Christian Vasquez; that was the horrible truth of it all, and he hadn't the slightest idea of how he would reveal what he knew through the visions of the morning.

He knew Trevor would not want to hear any of it, and he would shoot Braxton down the minute he even tried to say what he needed to say. Trevor did not like doubt, he liked to give people the benefit of such a thing. Whenever he began to doubt the sincerity of someone's convictions he shut it down, choosing to believe that everyone is undeniably good inside, whether they showed it to others or not.

The truth was that that was what Braxton liked the most about Trevor. When they had met, it had just been a year since his mother's death and he was still reeling from it. No one liked him, except for J.T. Oliver, who had known Braxton before Tammy's passing and therefore stuck with him.

He did not like people and was prone to teasing them. He teased people in a way that was very similar to the way in which Christian, Greg, and Cheri teased Trevor, and by all logical purposes, Braxton should have disregarded Trevor when he first spotted him in their math class—but he didn't, and he knew why.

Trevor had been familiar. He had been as familiar to Braxton as J.T., perhaps even more. It was as if Braxton had known Trevor his entire life and was just now revealing himself. To Braxton, Trevor had also been beautiful, beautiful in a way that he had never seen another person be, and he knew that he needed to be around that all of the time.

It was as if their first encounter had just happened yesterday, as if time was so easy to cross, and the gulf of years did not intervene.

He had been sitting at his desk, just three chairs back from the front of the classroom. Mr. Kingstrom had been a tall and rather gaunt man with broad shoulders, uncombed silver hair, a thick silver mustache, and a pair of aviator glasses—the style made famous by sheriffs in the South and Southwest.

His voice was a steady monotone and often cast many students into slumber, and he was without notice. As a result, he often told his class that he could not comprehend why it was that they had such poor grades under his tutelage.

There had been a knock on the large cedar door, and instantly all eyes went to the frame: some giggling, others looking on in confusion, as they spied the young man in the khakis and black polo standing somewhat bewildered, his eyes large and green.

He appeared extremely shy, refusing to look up from the floor—even when he handed his pink slip to Mr. Kingstrom, informing the dull man that Trevor Blackmoore was having to transfer math classes due to a schedule conflict, and the boy was now in his room.

The man nodded and sternly pointed to the desk behind Braxton. Returning the nod slightly, Trevor moved down the aisle quietly taking a seat, mindful not to bump his desk against the back of Braxton's.

The truth was that he had been silently hoping that the insecure boy would do such a thing; that way, he would have an excuse to talk to him.

The phone rang.

He wiped the tears from his eyes and rolled over, hoping that it would be Trevor on the other end, hoping that perhaps the boy had come to his senses, and was ready to leave Christian and be with him.

"Hello?" he said into the receiver, choking back the rest of his tears, trying to sound as if nothing had been wrong.

"Dude, what's up?"

It wasn't Trevor, it was J.T.

"Nothing much, just sitting here."

He could have told him the truth, could have told his friend that he was sitting in his room wasting the evening, dwelling in memories and hoping that perhaps things would get better, and it would all make sense. Christian would go back to his world of sports, popularity and student council priorities, instead of involving himself with Trevor and whatever scheme it was that he was trying to pull off.

"Cool, cool. Yeah, I'm just chillin' in my kitchen; my mom's out and all."

"Oh, yeah; where'd she go?"

He would have asked him anything to avoid talking about his problems.

"I dunno. I think she had said something about going to L.A. for the week, but whatever. I'm just trying to figure out what I'm gonna do in this house for the entire week—"

"Throw a party...."

He could tell by the pause in J.T.'s voice that he was actually considering it.

"That's not a bad idea; thanks, dude. Hey, I know; we could play!"

His voice was reaching a fevered pitch of excitement.

"Why, so you can get a lot of pussy?"

He wondered if J.T. could hear the sarcasm in his voice.

"Exactly!"

"Well, maybe."

"Sure, dude. Hey, we can invite our number one fan."

"You mean Trevor?"

The idea of it was turning the tide of his stomach with a sickness.

"Yeah; you wanna get with the kid, right? Well, of course you do; you have for the past three years!"

"Well, I don't know about Trevor. He seems rather busy with Christian Vasquez...."

"Fuck that Enrique Iglesias wannabe. Trevor wants you, dude."

"Yeah...right."

He was growing even more embittered than he had previously been. Sluggishly, Braxton ran his hand through his hair, letting out a great yawn at the same time. The night was growing and he was drifting into sleep from lack of food.

"Nah, dude, don't be like that about it. You don't see the way he looks at you, but I do. I notice it, and trust me, Trevor's convincing himself that he wants Christian, but he really wants you!"

This information helped to lift him, but he was wary of false hope. All of this was just so confusing for him and a part of Braxton wished that he could feel nothing—like it was after his mother died, like it was until Trevor Blackmoore came into his life five years previous.

"Well, I guess...." The uncertainty was real, and he was unsure of how he would go about inviting Trevor to the party—not without inviting Christian along as well.

"What if we surprise him? I mean, his birthday is coming up on Christmas Eve; why not throw him an early birthday party?"

Trevor was going to be turning eighteen, the youngest senior at Mariner High School and yet he seemed to be the oldest. It had always been like that: age resting in the back of his eyes, hidden just beneath the surface, breathing below the concealment of liquid green and brown.

"I'll see, but I don't know."

Again he was thinking of Christian and his smug grin, his air of superiority; it made Braxton sick.

"Don't worry about his so-called boyfriend. I'll just tell him that it's a private party, for him—well, him and personal fans of The Spit Monkeys, that is."

"So *you're* going to invite him?"

He was taken aback by this, as if he would somehow get it wrong or screw it up.

"Of course, dude, and I'll tell you why:

"We need him to want you, to get rid of that fuck-face and have Trevor all to yourself. And the only way to do that is to have the person throwing the party give the invite and the specific instructions—that way, I'm the asshole and you're not, get it?"

It was a great plan in theory, but that was the problem: it was in theory. They had no idea how Trevor would react if he was told that Christian could not come along, by any means.

"Look, I don't know...."

"Hey, just leave everything to me, okay?"

Though he was uncertain about the whole thing, he decided to give in. Perhaps J.T. knew what he was doing, or perhaps he hadn't the faintest idea and this whole plan was going to crash and burn.

Either way, it was better than lying around and mourning for the entire night.

"So when do you want to do this?"

"How about tomorrow night?"

"It's Thursday. You can't throw a party on Thursday; no one will come!"

"Dude, just leave it to me, all right? I can handle it, and *every-one* will want to come!"

Though he was strongly opposed, he could not argue with J.T.'s one-way logic, and he'd be stupid to try. So he just let it be and continued on, J.T. changing the conversation from Trevor Blackmoore to what they were going to play at the party.

ELEVEN

The smells of burning candle-wax and patchouli filled the air with thier noxious scent, hovering like a cloud within the room, the rafters and wood-beams laid firm across the room, stretching from one post to the other, garlands of foxglove and wolfsbane streaming from one to the other, hanging above her, ready for use.

In the center of the space was a thick wood post of palm, positioned in the flagstone and reaching to the very roof of the structure—the potomitan—the vessel of the gods, from which they traveled from the heavens to ride the faithful.

About this now were many white candles and flowers, all of which were laid out in a specific position. Rings of red and black were painted on the wood, like that of a snake, as if in life it had not been wood at all but a giant python, gutted and made hollow for a more sacred cause.

Beyond the post and its paraphernalia was Kathryn, standing before a large table pushed up against the wall directly across the entrance. Amongst candles and the eyes of plastered saints she prayed, kneeling on a low bench and looking to these faces for comfort and strength, requesting in silence for their guidance and direction.

But for her these were not saints, but gods masquerading as Catholic deities, as if in mocking drag. Before her was Papa Legba, Keeper of Keys, the one who granted permission to speak with the rest of the *Loas*.

There was Damballah and Ezili, as well as Ogu-Badagri and Baron-Samedi, all hidden in the faces of saints and awaiting bequeathment and instruction. Tonight she was going to need Baron-Samedi, god of the underworld. He would exact her revenge and accept the offering of the black chicken which squawked within a cage of chicken wire.

She lit the candles, paying special mind to the red and black ones, centering herself and beginning to make the call in silence.

Kathryn reached for a large basin filled with cornmeal and threw handfuls of it to the ground. It was cool and grainy, finding its way beneath her nails and in the microscopic pores of her flesh. She took a thin stick and placed it in the pile of sand, tracing two elaborate designs: the *Vèvè* of the chosen deities—Legba and the Baron—reaching out in a trance-like state, knowing that they would hear and answer to her call.

"*Papa Legba, ouvriez le barrier por moi passer ....*"

Already there was a buzzing in the air, a soft static that licked her flesh.

She knew that he was hearing her, this wonderful and important of all gods—the granter of worlds and the bridges that united them, the great communicator and sacred interpreter, the one who knew the languages and interpreted each to the gods of the Afro-Haitian pantheon.

"On this night I seek your most divine aid; hear me and answer me, Legba!"

Her entire body began to tingle, to electrify and ignite from within—stirring all of that which was her own.

She hadn't heard the steps just outside the door, moving cautiously, as if knowing that she was kept within.

"Mom?"

It was Trevor.

"Don't you remember? We're supposed to get our Christmas tree tonight!"

Her first instinct was to call out to him, to let him know that she was home and that she could hear him, but upon looking around the carriage-house she remembered that this world before her was a world that she did not want Trevor knowing, not ever—not under any circumstances. Even though it seemed all

Blackmoores knew the mysteries, she did not want to pass that on to him.

It was a world and a power that you could never truly abandon once a relationship was begun, and the fact that he had Jonathan, that infernal spirit, was enough of this world for him to know. It was upon the death of her husband, upon the dreaded Legacy, that Jonathan was able to come through in the first place, able to reach out to her son and draw on the power of his blood—a dark inheritance which claimed a Blackmoore's life from birth and determined how they would live out their years.

"Shit...." she said under her breath, the flames of the candles beginning to flicker and lose strength.

The sacredness of the moment had been lost on her son's tongue, and now that he was home there was no chance of continuing with her self-appointed mission.

She bent down and ran her hand through the elaborate designs in the sand, smearing them around and distorting their image, letting the bits of ground corn to fall into the cervices of the ground. Kathryn blew out the candles and watched through the bottom of the door as Trevor turned and left, his shadow vanishing into the dark.

She found Trevor in the formal living room, sitting in the dark and appearing as if he were in a trance: unmoving, unblinking, refusing to acknowledge Kathryn's presence. His eyes, though large, looked like nothing more than pools of black, the color of his irises completely indistinct in the darkness.

The light from the lamps outside were the only indication of life in his face.

The shadows on the wall once again appeared to move, as they had always seemed to do, and she wondered if her father and his family still lingered here, too weak to communicate or unwilling to try.

Her father Trevor had grown up in this house, and in fact it had been in his family from the beginning; he and her mother Annaline growing up together as neighbors and coming together as lovers.

The image of South Hill being littered with old families that have always known each other was not a false image at all, but an underlining truth that embedded itself within the very streets and harbored within the oaks and maples that to collected around the neighborhood amongst the ever-present pine trees.

"Trevor, honey, you okay?"

He turned and looked at her, as if seeing Kathryn for the first time, and for a moment it seemed as if he didn't even recognize her.

"Mom, hi. Sorry, I was just... thinking."

She nodded and smiled compassionately, making her way to him now in the dark. His slender frame seemed all the more tiny as he sat unmoving on the large sofa.

"What about?"

She sat next to him and placed her arm around his shoulder, ignoring the presence of Jonathan hovering in the corner, staring at her as if she were the enemy.

"People." He looked up at his mother and sighed. His eyes looked into hers as if searching for the answer to all of life's problems.

This was innate in every child, this compulsion. Growing up it would seem that a mother could make everything okay and make all of a child's troubles disappear, and no matter how old that child became, a mother still seemed to always have the answers.

"Oh...." She nodded at him slowly.

"Yeah."

"Well, what kind of people?"

He looked away from her for a moment, as if ashamed of his thoughts. Kathryn knew all about her son and his convictions, and it all seemed to make up the kaleidoscope that was her child, her Trevor.

"Christian Vasquez and Braxton Volaverunt...."

Kathryn nodded, urging him to continue.

"Mom, I'm dating Christian!"

Her ice eyes grew large, but quickly Kathryn gathered her composure.

"Okay; well, that's what I thought, go on."

Trevor looked to his feet and concluded.

"It's like, this is what I secretly have wanted since I became aware of sexuality. It seems like I finally have what I want, and yet something's off. Though I'm not quite sure, but it does seem that something is out of place, or not as it should be...."

He stood and began pacing in a tiny semi-circle, his silhouette constantly interrupting the light from outside.

"And then there's Braxton! God, Mom, I care about him so much, and secretly I've wanted nothing more than to be with him, to be around him all of the time. But it seems like, I don't know, he and I have somehow known one another our entire lives, and yet we haven't.

"I guess this quickness with Christian is coming from the fact that Braxton is straight. He likes girls, not boys, especially not fucked-up boys who belong to the most talked about family in the city!"

This was true. Ever since the Blackmoore clan had moved to Fairhaven, first: in the large bungalow that used to occupy the now-vacant lot next to Dianaca Castle that "mysteriously" burnt down in 1909, then into the sprawling Victorian down the alley back in 1910, the one now occupied by Queen Mab only—the home which was built by the Donovans and occupied by Jasper Donovan and his wife, Claudette, along with their young and tragic son Michael.

The home which they had abandoned and sold to Tristan Blackmoore of New Orleans at the age of one hundred and twenty, the place where he was taken care of by his grandson Jeremiah and his wife Sarah, along with Jeremiah's sister, Aria.

The family was a hotbed of rumors, love affairs, and supposed secret meetings with the devil: a family of great power, a family that was like a plague.

This air of disgust and fear hung over the Blackmoore name until the family split and members moved away, or by the passing of time. In fact, it was not until Kathryn was a sophomore at Mariner High School back in 1977 that the rumors had finally died away and people had started treating her like a real person.

She had met Sheffield in her freshmen year, and he was the first to look at the gossip as nothing more than that. Though he was new to the city of Bellingham, people still tried to warn him away from anything which bore the Blackmoore name. People still talked about the family, but only in passing, and it was always very brief. No one really wanted to test the limits of a Blackmoore's patience, especially if it seemed to be wearing thin.

Trevor stood before his mother and stared. She had drifted into other thoughts and she knew that her son was demanding her attention, and so along with other things she pushed these thoughts aside and let young Trevor continue with his rant.

"This is just so hard, Mom!"

His voice was full of desperation, and she wished so much to take all of his troubles and send them away, and in truth she knew how. But it was not her place to do so; Trevor had to learn from doing, not by her control and cushioning of his life.

"Well, how do you know that Braxton doesn't feel that way about you? I've seen the way that he looks at you, always with such compassion. It's like his heart breaks every time he's around you.

"I think he may very well love you."

She watched as Trevor's jaw seemed to hit the floor; his eyes began to search the room franticly, attempting to piece together his mother's theory and somehow fit it into his mindscape.

"And even if that was true—which I highly doubt, but let's just say it is...."

"Uh-huh?"

"What about this fucking Legacy; what am I supposed to do about that? This plague, this... this thing inside of me, these poisonous cells waiting for me to pass them along to someone else, someone unsuspecting, waiting to kill? Kill like it has done to anyone that a person in this family has ever loved.

"kill like it did your father and my father and all of those unknown people who have slept with Blackmoores, not knowing that they would die from the encounter years later.

"What do I do about that?"

Kathryn shook her head, not in disagreement but in understanding of his distress, his pain. She knew the answers, but they were vague. She could not share them and explain their logic like others could do.

"Baby, you need to talk to Queen Mab about that. She has the answers you're looking for, not me."

It broke her heart to see her son suffer, but worse yet, it pained her to know that he could very well walk the path that so many other Blackmoores took: the path that ultimately led to death. The feeling of being like a cancer ended up weighing too heavily on the heart, and therefore pushed them to suicide.

"All right." Trevor nodded, and Kathryn stood to face him, opening her arms and wrapping him tightly, trying to bring a comfort that would never be.

"Now, why don't we see about that tree?"

He nodded and Kathryn went into the office, calling Sam, who was her landscaper and who had brought them their tree every year since her husband died.

When she came out of the office she saw Trevor whispering to the shadows, shadows that she knew to be Jonathan and his hellish aura.

She rolled her eyes and deliberately slammed the office doors, causing her son to jump with a start.

"Oh, Mom. Hey, um what's up?"

She made it seem as if she had not seen him.

"Oh, nothing; I was just wondering if you were hungry."

"Yeah, but for something small; I don't think I can handle eating some big meal."

Kathryn felt the same way, and the despair in her son's eyes seemed to be eating through her flesh. She wanted so much for him to be happy, and yet it seemed he never would be—and like all Blackmoores, he may just fade into the darkness of human existence, snuffed out like a candle's flame.

Quietly they opened the door and stepped out into the white nighttime streets. The glittering lights of Fairhaven and the bay looked like many Christmas trees, and the powder-white blanket crunched beneath them and fireplaces burned, giving texture to the winter sky. The clouds above them looked to be on fire in a soft velvet haze.

All about them the snow kept falling.

The fire from that kiss still burned on his lips, tinged with what felt like a mild abrasion, peeling the delicate flesh, leaving him with a metallic taste much like blood from an open wound.

Christian Vasquez sat parked outside of the Hannifin home. The light from the kitchen windows was the only thing visible in the jungle of skeleton oaks that encased her yard.

He knew that he needed to dismiss the presence of Trevor from his brain, knew that he had to push their latest encounter to the deepest recesses of his mind, and that was not an easy thing to do.

He hadn't expected to kiss him, and for a while he had tried to convince himself that he had only done it for the sake of the plan, that the kiss had meant nothing, that Trevor was just another lowly fag ripe for the picking. But he knew that this was just another bedtime story that he was telling himself to keep away the big bad things of the world: namely his own homosexuality, and his secret lust for the young man from the mysterious and dangerous family.

It had really been something else; a kiss that was filled with a kind of electricity that he had never known before, and which he had never experienced with any girl. He had fucked so many over the years, mostly at parties in a drunken stupor or at the end of soccer matches. Letting off some end-of-the-game steam that had built up and needed to be released. But with Trevor Blackmoore it was different; it was a call to his soul, telling him without words that it was time to wake up and understand what it was that was his truth, and his truth was becoming too scary to deal with.

"What's going on?" he asked in a whisper, as if speaking aloud—even in the shelter of his Mustang—words would somehow reach his friends ears and reveal his image as a lie.

After taking a few moments to regain his composure, Christian popped open the car door and stepped outside, allowing the bitter and sharp winter air to lick his skin and open his black eyes wide, as if awakening from a half-sleep.

He could hear laughter from within the mansion's walls, and knew that Cheri was with Greg, and that fact alone would make it all the more difficult to remain calm and collected.

"Well, well, if it isn't our elusive friend," Cheri smiled at him, and Greg laughed.

Their eyes had a look of hunger to them, and it seemed as if Christian was a frog and they were biology students preparing to dissect.

He didn't like it.

"Hey, you guys."

He spotted the dark green bottle of wine and immediately went to it, moving cautiously through the dimly lit kitchen, trying to avoid their gazes.

"So, where were you?" Greg asked him, running his fingers on the cool of the island's countertop.

"Out."

He put the bottle to his lips and drank it down. The flavor of fermented grapes did little to soothe his nerves, and the alcohol burned as it slid down his throat.

"Where?"

Again it was Greg Sheer who asked, his words hinting to the idea that he was digging for something deeper, sniffing out clues for Christian's dirty little secret.

"Were you out with Trevor?"

He took another swig from the bottle, knowing that Cheri's question had him stuck between a rock and a hard place.

"Yes. That's what you guys want me to do, after all."

They nodded and it seemed to Christian that the atmosphere had somehow changed—as if there were a black cloud, a cloud made up of envy and suspicion, hanging above their heads and growing bigger and blacker with each passing second.

"And how is our former?"

Cheri reached for her already-poured glass of wine and took a gentle sip, closing her eyes and savoring its flavor—that, or she was savoring the flavor of Christian's fear. Her lids opened, and with stoic brown eyes she stared at him, forcing his heart to pound.

"He's fine, I guess. I've got him nearly in the palm of my hand."

He smiled, quickly absolving himself of the guilt he felt in this game with his former best friend.

"What do you mean, *nearly*?" she asked him. Greg only snickered.

"What I mean is that he's very cautious. He has a wall up, and I think that that's our fault. I'm breaking through it, but it's going to take a little longer than I thought."

This time he finished the bottle in one swift swig.

"You sure it's that, or is it because you're enjoying the time that you're spending with him?

"Are you trying to stall the game as long as possible so you can be worshipped again?"

This time it was Greg who proposed the question, and it made his skin crawl.

"Worshipped; what are you talking about?"

The air crackled with tension and Christian took a deep breath and tried to remain calm.

"Oh, come on, now, dude; don't give me that shit. Everyone at school praises the ground you walk on and Trevor Blackmoore is no different.

"If anything, he was your first fan."

A sting of truth hit him like the blade of a knife, and Greg's words cut an invariable wound that would be slow to heal.

"Greg, you're talking bullshit. Trevor may have possibly looked up to me in the past, but now, after all of the shit we've put him through, he's more afraid of me than anything else. You can't tell me you didn't expect that."

Greg shrugged.

"Look, Christian, you've got to wrap this shit up soon, before winter break—"

"And I will; it's nearly there. A couple more days of this shit, and that little bitch will wish he never messed with us!"

They smiled, and Greg and Cheri toasted to his declaration.

Christian looked out on the snow-covered lawn and felt his insides freeze up, touched by the cool fingers of Jack Frost, icing his heart and chilling his lungs. He said a little prayer then, a silent prayer just for Trevor, requesting forgiveness in advance for what he was about to do.

"So, what's your name?"

They were walking through the crowded halls of their ancient middle school, pushing through the students and staff that filled its narrow passages. Lunchtime was everyone's favorite hour of the day.

"Trevor... and you?"

He gave a shy grin.

"Braxton. Braxton Volaverunt."

Trevor nodded and clutched his books in his arms, squeezing them against his chest. His dark red hair hung loosely in his eyes which were now hidden by its curtain.

"Braxton... I like that name; it's a normal name, but not one that is much used."

He nodded, thinking of his mother Tammy. She had named him after her younger brother, who had died of leukemia when she had only been eight. But now, like his uncle that he never had the chance to know, his mother was gone, taken by a horrible tumor. He thought that he was going to cry.

"Oh, yeah, thanks. I like yours too."

Trevor nodded and smiled once again, flashing adorable dimples.

"So, who do you normally hang out with?"

Braxton's jeans began to slide off his ass, and yet he didn't mind it. After all, he was the one who purchased the three-sizes-too-big Jnco's.

Before he got any kind of response, Trevor halted in a dead freeze and turned to face Braxton, his eyes full of fear.

"What is it?"

Trevor began to shake slightly, unable to steady himself.

"Can we go another way?"

Braxton shook his head in confusion.

"Why?"

Running on pure instinct, Braxton placed his hands on Trevor's arms, trying to ease his shaking.

"It's them."

Braxton shook his head.

"Look over my shoulder."

Braxton's large brown eyes moved from Trevor's fear-filled face and out into the hall. It took him a moment but then the realization came to him: it was Cheri Hannifin, Greg Sheer, and Christian Vasquez.

The three of them were moving through the halls like a pack of wolves. Grins on their million-dollar faces and expensive clothes on their million-dollar bodies.

Every student watched them in awe and fear; Braxton felt neither.

"Are you afraid of them?"

Trevor nodded.

"But why? They're just like you and me. The only difference is that they're from South Hill—"

"And so am I."

He broke free from Braxton's hands and made his way down the hall, moving quickly and without notice of those who moved in a slower pace.

A sharp, jarring pain attacked the back of Braxton's head and a rush of images filled his head.

"Jesus!"

He stood there in stunned silence. The fear that emanated from Trevor was incredible, and as he stood there piecing together the images that had suddenly flooded his brain, he did not know what to make of them.

He saw children laughing and running; playing in a large and manicured backyard with large maple trees that glistened in summer sunshine. Next he saw Trevor on a staircase in khaki shorts, staring at a lifeless human body. Finally, he saw a man in a tweed suit stare down at a crying Trevor, laying out on a large bed, the lightning outside illuminating his pain-stricken face.

He shuddered.

"Hey, do you know who that kid was that you were talking to?"

He turned to see Christian Vasquez staring at him. His large black eyes looked too charming to be real, and the same went with his smile.

"Yeah, his name's Trevor."

Christian shook his head.

"No, it's not. It's Trevor Blackmoore."

The name struck him like a bolt of lightning. Everyone knew the Blackmoores; they were one of the oldest families in Fairhaven and one of the most talked about.

"So?"

Again Christian shook his head.

"He's dangerous. If you know what's good for you, you'll stay away from him. That's what we did."

He looked over Christian's shoulders to see Cheri and Greg nodding in agreement.

"Oh, please; are you sure that this isn't just some South Hill thing? I mean, you cast him aside, but at the same time he still belongs to you because you all grew up on the infamous hill.

"It makes sense to me; how about you?" Braxton grinned.

"Hey, do whatever you want. But if you get involved in his world, I'm warning you, it may take you years to come back."

Once again, his entourage nodded in agreement.

"Really, and why's that?"

Christian grinned and gave him a pat on the shoulders.

"Because ... he's a witch."

They made their way down the hall, not giving Braxton another thought. Braxton, on the other hand, could not help but stare in dumbfounded silence.

Seconds passed and the students rushed by him, yet Braxton was unmoving. He had no reaction to Christian's warnings, no sense of who this kid really was, and at the moment he was beginning to wonder the same thing about himself.

A loud ringing sailed through the halls and he thought it to be the school bell, but the more he listened to it, the more distorted things became, and Braxton began to lose his grip on the world that he was now standing in.

He felt as if he were going to puke.

He opened his eyes.

It was the phone and it had only been a dream, a recollection of the past while his brain was free to think on whatever it wanted to. He had to answer the phone.

"Hello?"

The telephone's receiver was hanging loosely from between his chin and shoulder; the slightest move of his neck or his arm could send it falling to the floor.

"Braxton...."

It was Trevor; his voice sounded strange to him, as if he had either been yelling or crying—or perhaps a little of both.

"Yeah?"

Braxton took hold of the receiver and sat up in his bed. The window was misted in frost, and icicles were already forming from the gutters. Distant lights from across the lake seemed no more than little glowing fuzz balls.

"Did I wake you?"

Trevor gave a sniffle.

"Actually you did, but don't worry. I was just sitting around waiting for you to give me a call, so it's no big deal."

A slight chuckle came from Trevor's end of the line and Braxton blushed, feeling embarrassed now that he had admitted to such desperation.

"Braxton, I need to talk to you about something, and you need to understand that this is very hard for me to do."

Braxton's heart began to pound, expressing the nervousness that he was feeling, and his palms were now sweating profusely.

"What is it?"

He took a deep breath, following Trevor's lead. His brown eyes steadily focused on the flickering from a single midnight blue candle.

"Christian was a mistake."

He grinned.

"He was a very stupid mistake. I liked him once—a long time ago, actually, and part of me still does—but then there's you."

His voice broke away, and it looked as if the presence of the young Vasquez was fading instantly from their lives, returning to the position he once held.

"Me?"

Braxton thought that he was going to have a heart attack if he did not relax and remain level-headed.

"Yeah, you. See, um, I like you, Braxton. I like you so much, and I have for a few years now."

Again he stopped, as if gauging Braxton's reaction, but he gave none.

"Go on."

"I just don't know. It's like I'm stuck right now. I mean, I'm in love with you. Well, at least I'm pretty sure of it, but I do know how you make me feel, and I always want to feel like that...."

He started to sniffle even more, and slight whimpers came from his mouth. A fear was reaching out to Braxton, a fear that he understood all too well.

"Shh, don't cry, Trevor. I like you too."

It was like breathing for the first time. It was life-giving and extreme, and it was dangerous and addictive.

"I've liked you for so long now, since I first saw you in Mr. Kingstrom's class in seventh grade."

"Really?"

He could hear Trevor perking up on the other end. Finally, things were going the way that they needed to.

"Yup, I've been waiting so long to tell you. Goddamn, it's been an insane few years."

Trevor gave a slight "yeah" and then laughed—a laugh that was somewhat bitter, somewhat overjoyed; it was a laugh that was confusing to Braxton.

"Oh, shit, I've gotta go, but I'll see you tomorrow?"

Braxton grinned, feeling aglow inside.

"You can count on it."

They hung up the line and Braxton lay out in his bed, arms folded behind his head. The ceiling appeared to move, as if it were rising, moving further and further from the rest of the room. It felt as if it were going to break away and expose the night outside, letting the flakes of snow fall to him.

He thought he could stare forever.

In tired effort, Trevor opened the door to his room. The glow of the Tiffany lamp by his bedside was illuminating the aged floorboards and Trevor was unsure if he had left it on or not.

"What are you doing in here?" he questioned Jonathan.

His hazy, misted form was standing next to his bedside table, looking down at his black, 1930's rotary telephone. His tweed suit was easy to make out, despite his fading form, yet he gave Trevor no recognition.

"Answer me!"

He walked into his room and slammed the door, removing his coat and throwing it on the back of his desk chair. He looked to the window with rigid eyes, now green, the fall of fresh flakes beginning again.

'Can't I wander wherever I wish? After all, this was my home long before it was yours or any other Blackmoore's.'

Trevor curled his fingers into his palms, digging them in deep; wincing in growing pain. Tonight was not the night for fights.

"Whatever. Look, this is my room now, and I don't like you being in here without consent!"

The spirit shook his hazy head.

'It has never been a problem before, not until a few days ago ... not until Christian Vasquez.'

The spirit's words stung him, but Trevor was unwavering.

"Leave, Jonathan, please leave now!"

Without any verbal response or rebuttal, the spirit simply faded out of existence, back into other parts of the old house.

Trevor shook his head and undressed, pulling off his jeans and his red collared shirt, standing about in gray briefs, forgetting to call Braxton as he had promised—but too exhausted to care.

He crawled under his covers, moving his legs atop cool sheets, smiling in his tired state. Lazily he reached for his lamp's little chain and gave it a tug, the light shutting out quickly, leaving Trevor in comforting dark.

TWELVE

Thursdays were better than Wednesdays. Not by much, but they were still better.

Trevor felt exhausted from the lack of sleep; his brain had been troubled with too many thoughts to allow him any rest, and yet he was confident that he could make it through the day.

After their fated kiss the other day at the park overlooking the falls and snow, Trevor was anxious to get to Christian, to see him and be with him once again. To feel that for once, everything in his life was working out just as it needed to—and that for once, being himself was as normal as breathing.

He navigated through the throng of bodies with ease, relaxing for the first time in five years, no longer hindered by the expectation of vicious words from Cheri or Greg or the rest of their posse. For once, he figured, the snakes would let him be, choosing another victim to infect with their poisonous venom.

"Trevor!"

He turned around and looked, but could not see who had said his name, so he continued to walk.

"Trevor, wait up!"

Again he heard the distinctively male voice and stopped, turning a quarter of the way to spy J.T. approaching, pushing through students without the slightest apology.

"Oh, hey. Sorry, I wasn't sure who it was."

J.T. nodded. He was wearing a navy blue pea coat with a gray scarf, his usual knit cap on his head. His chunky brown boots clunked on the tiled floor. Though extremely attractive, Trevor could see J.T.'s fraternity destiny laid out in his demeanor.

Trevor found it hilarious.

"Don't worry about it."

They began to walk down the hall in a slowed pace, shuffling through teenagers too oblivious to people to care, absorbed in conversations about MTV and snowboarding on the slopes at Mt. Baker as soon as break arrived.

"So, what are you doing tonight?" J.T. asked him, briefly eyeing a young girl who skirted passed them, dressed in tight hip-huggers and a petite cashmere sweater, the color a soft pink and making J.T. think of cotton candy.

"Nothing, probably go home and watch some T.V. or read... why?"

J.T. grinned, and despite himself Trevor blushed, aware of his mild attraction to Braxton's best friend. He felt ashamed.

"Well, no you're not, you're coming over to my house tonight."

"I am?"

Again he blushed, and despite his overwhelming straightness, J.T. could not help but feel slightly flattered and worshipped by his flushed cheeks and awkward glances. He could see why Braxton loved him so much, and he also wondered if this adoration was a big draw for Christian Vasquez in the earlier years.

After all, affectionate praise and worship always meant something much more when it was coming from another guy, versus some random girl, who by society's standards is supposed to do exactly that. Boys weren't, and that's what made it mean something greater, something that bordered between the sacred and profane.

"Yup. The band's playing tonight since my mom's out, and I want you there."

"I don't know...."

"Please, I want you there. I *need* you there; what do you say? Please be my groupie?" Trevor laughed and rolled his eyes nodding.

"Well what's in it for me?"

J.T. dug into his pocket and reached out for whatever he could find.

"A shiny nickel!"

"Well, okay." He took the nickel and laughed, sticking it in his back pocket. "Can I bring Christian?"

J.T. had been expecting this and turned to face him, placing his hands on Trevor's waist, a move which drew in some gazes, but J.T. took no notice.

"I would prefer it if you didn't."

Trevor began to frown.

"Look, I know you guys got something going on and all, and that's great, but I think that it would be better if he didn't come.

"A lot of the people who are going to be there don't fit in with Christian or his crowd, and in fact, most of them have been shit on by them on more than one occasion."

Trevor nodded in understanding. It was true, and he couldn't deny those accusations, for he had suffered the same indignities from Christian and his pack.

"Besides, it would really bum Braxton if he was there. And we don't want to do that, now, do we?"

Trevor shook his head but still no smile could come. The distance between his life with Christian and his world with Braxton was really being felt, and he hated it.

"Okay...."

J.T. nodded and walked away, telling him to be there by eight—though now, after this revelation, Trevor was no longer so eager to see Christian as he had been at the beginning of his day.

"I honestly think we should ditch at lunch," Teri Jules was saying to her best friend, Cheri Hannifin.

Both girls were dressed for warmer weather: Teri in her low-cut white top covered only by her baby-blue cardigan sweater, wearing pants made of both cotton and polyester, the color a brown-green with red iridescence in the light, her feet in clear three-strapped heeled sandals with a glittered butterfly on the four bands that fell across her toes.

Her blonde hair was straightened and brushed the tip of her shoulders, her makeup soft and delicate. Light, white glitter eyeshadow brought out the blue of her eyes, and her lips were slick with clear gloss.

"I think maybe you're right; I was really thinking about those Marc Jacobs that I had seen at Gary's the other day."

Cheri wore a long-sleeved black top made of a very simple, sheer material. A tiny black slip was visible beneath it and her legs were accentuated by a thigh-length, cream-colored skirt, and a pair of sleek black heels on her feet.

Her brown hair was slightly curled on the ends and her lips were rouged in a light maroon, her nails painted the same shade.

"Oh, you mean the scallop ribbon sandals?"

Cheri smiled and nodded.

"You totally need them!"

Cheri was going to say more when she spotted Greg coming her way, eyeing her with primal hunger; it made her cringe.

"Hey, I'll catch up with you after third period, okay?"

Teri nodded and they kissed the air against their cheeks, waving as they parted.

"Damn, girl, you look good."

She rolled her eyes, not the least bit flattered because she knew it to be true.

"Did you bring it?" she asked him.

Greg nodded and revealed the video camera that he had concealed in his book bag, both of them ready to get their little show on the road. They looked ahead of them in the hall to see Trevor run up to Christian and whisper something in his ear. Whatever it was it made him alert, and they raced out of the side door, thundering down the concrete steps.

"All right, let's make our movie...."

They smiled and the two of them slipped outside in cautious pursuit, wanting to get close enough to them to see and record, but not close enough to be spotted.

"What is it?" Christian asked, watching as his breath formed in front of his face, their feet crunching on the snow-covered field beneath them, slowly making their way far from anyone's view.

"I can't do anything tonight, unfortunately."

Christian frowned.

"Why not?"

Trevor shook his head.

"Because my mom wants me to go to some stupid show with her...."

Christian nodded, and Trevor hated the lie that he was telling, but he concluded that it was a lot better than telling him the truth.

"Well, that's all right. I mean, I'm with you now and that's all I need."

Trevor smiled and Christian kissed him on the cheek, pulling him behind the gym and groping his body, his hands finding their way to Trevor's belt buckle. Their tongues moved to their own rhythm, separate from the thoughts of Trevor's brain, ignoring the red alerts that were sounding inside of his skull, blaring with a droning pain.

Christian threw off his Burberry jacket, tossing it to the snow, followed with the black turtle-neck, which he pulled off of his head, allowing it to drop to the snow with sudden neglect.

His skin was cold and covered in gooseflesh erect with titillation and chill, his navy carpenter jeans tented by a painful erection.

His heart was pounding and his breath was hot, warming Trevor's neck, his flesh grazed by his tongue.

"Jesus!" Christian let out, grinding his pelvis against Trevor, who was giving himself over to the sway of the moment. He ran his fingers down that sculpted body, sticking his right hand down his jeans and feeling Christian's hard-on, which he teased, tugging at it lightly with his fingers, getting him worked up.

"Take it out..." he whispered, and Christian obeyed, unbuttoning his jeans and pulling down the zipper.

The freezing temperature no longer mattered to them, and this moment was becoming so much more than what had been intended.

Christian slid down his jeans and stood before Trevor in black boxer-briefs, his cock throbbing to come out and Trevor more than ready to oblige.

Trevor took it out and went down on him; the moist heat of his mouth was soothing to Christian, who let out a soft moan. Christian's hands searched his head, fingers petting through deep red hair. The world had seemed to split open and fall apart, and like water, the ghosts of the past oozed out, but only Christian could see it.

"My turn...."

Christian pulled him up and threw Trevor against the wall, kissing him before descending to his knees, sliding down Trevor's jeans and removing his erect cock. He looked up and licked his lips before sliding it in his mouth, working with furious desire.

The world seemed to drift now and Christian was working him hard, trying to make him cum, trying to get him to spill inside of his mouth. The act was urgent, desperate, and yet within minutes Christian had brought him to the threshold of orgasm, and with a lapse of thought he was going to let it out.

"No... no, I can't."

Trevor took hold of Christian's head and pulled out, spilling onto the snow and on his face.

"It's okay," Christian responded, looking dumbfounded and yet exhilarated all the same.

He took the tip of his index finger and swiped the side of his face, staring at the pearly white substance, closing his eyes and bringing it to his lips, his tongue sliding out.

"Don't."

Trevor grabbed his finger and pulled it away; Christian opened his eyes and stared at him in confusion.

"You can't; it's poison... I'm poison."

Trevor pulled his underwear back up to his waist and buttoned his jeans, grabbing his book-bag and hurrying from him, the cloud of his family hanging over his head, forcing him to leave Christian there in shame, left to snow and confusion.

It was a moment with no answers.

"That fucking faggot," Greg let out in a huff, standing, prepared to knock the shit out of Christian.

Cheri reached up and grasped his arm, pulling him back down.

"No, not yet... we have what we need right here."

She shook the camcorder in his face and smiled, her mind plotting her scheme.

"All in due time, all in due time."

Greg grinned and kissed her, their breath hot, and his saliva was bitter. The taste of beer seemed to be forever prevalent in his mouth; it made Cheri nauseous.

"All right, we'll wait, and then we'll get him; we'll get him real good."

She nodded and they stood, walking back towards the school.

They looked back at Christian Vasquez once more, feeling the last shred of care for their friend leave them both: his pitiful form still resting on his knees in the snow, his jeans and boxer-briefs down at his ankles, not caring to get up fast enough, and completely unaware that he had been watched.

"So he's coming?"

J.T. looked at his best friend and nodded, seeing the excitement in his wide brown eyes.

They were sitting in their European History class, whispering cautiously in the back row, occasionally looking up to see if their overweight and elderly teacher was noticing them; he wasn't.

"That he is. Though when I told him that Christian couldn't come he got a little bummed out; but don't worry, he'll get over it."

Braxton looked away, staring at his boots with uneasy eyes. The weight of guilt that he was feeling for putting Trevor in this position was almost enough to make him back out of their plan.

He wore the same three-sizes-too-big Jnco's that he had worn when he and Trevor had first met, not growing much more than a couple of inches since that time five years previous. A black-and-white pinstriped shirt hung open, revealing his black tank top which clung to his defined frame, his chains slightly cold from the chilled air, his hair glossy in the fluorescent light.

"Well I don't think we need to worry about Christian."

J.T. looked at him inquisitively.

"What do you mean?"

Braxton shook his head, dismissing his own comment. He was still unsure if he was ready to disclose his conversation with Trevor from the night before.

"Nothing, it's not important. Let's just say that I'm confident... that's all."

J.T. shook his head and picked up his book-bag, finding the bright blue flyers that he had printed off at Kinko's that morning, prepared to pass them out at lunch to all of those who weren't members of Mariner's high society.

"Well, tonight is going to kick some major ass!"

They both nodded and grinned, deciding to return to the discussion on Nazi Germany and the gruesome genocide that it left in its wake.

The both of them sat in the television room of the Blackmoore home, two ten-year-olds trying to act brave while watching a scary movie at 1:30 in the morning. The eerie blue glow of the screen served as the only illumination in the old home, cuddling beneath a knitted throw blanket.

Cheri stared at the screen. Her brown hair in pig tails and her tiny body dressed in a pink Hello Kitty *tee with matching cotton pants, her heart was pounding deep within her chest.*

Next to her sat Trevor, his eyes reflecting the light and his tiny nose scrunched up and his lips parted, holding his breath, wearing a Teenage Mutant Ninja Turtles *tee and navy flannel pants. Their toes were curled beneath their feet and their arms wrapped around one another, while his mother hid upstairs, still grieving for her lost and beloved husband.*

They slept over at one another's homes every Friday night, pigging out on pizza and snacks, drinking tons of root beer while telling ghost stories and staying up late. Too young and too energetic to sleep.

Cheri liked Trevor's stories the best; they all seemed to deal with his family and they were all "insanely creepy," as she put it, sounding too detailed to be real. In Bellingham, everyone knew of ghosts and it wasn't a far fetched idea like in most places.

Everyone and every place had a story, and the Blackmoores were no exception.

"Cheri?"

She looked up to see Teri standing before her, holding those chosen sandals by Marc Jacobs, oblivious to the tears that rested in her eyes, the tears that she quickly wiped away and would blame on allergies if asked about them.

"Oh, sorry, I was just thinking about what I could get to wear with them."

Teri nodded in understanding, accepting her shallow response as the most obvious, and Cheri shook her head, damning herself for still caring about Trevor, and angry about the fact that she missed him. He had broken the rules of their world and he deserved whatever he got. Still; she wondered how she had ever become so cruel.

"Did you hear about the party at J.T.'s tonight?"

Cheri nodded, looking at a set of handbags, trying to get her mind off of her current thoughts, but it wasn't working.

"Yeah... why, did you want to go?"

Teri shrugged, afraid to answer truthfully.

"Because you know we're not invited."

She figured that Trevor would be there, and perhaps that meant Christian as well, and suddenly her interest was peaked.

"But since when did *we* need an invitation?"

She grinned and Teri returned it; following Cheri to the cash register with shoes in hand.

Trevor ran up Knox Street, not caring that he would possibly get in trouble for ditching, his head swimming with guilt at the thought that he almost passed on his family's curse to his boyfriend.

The snow crunched beneath him; though it had been swept away from the roads earlier that morning, the sidewalks were still polluted in white. When he came upon his house standing on that corner, his first instinct was to go inside and perhaps drop his book-bag off, but instead he went past this, turning on Sixteenth Street and walking three houses down—prepared to speak with his Aunt Mabel, who was more affectionately known as Queen Mab.

1510 Sixteenth Street dominated a hilled lot, its grassy knoll now dressed in white, glistening in the dull gray. A set of steep concrete steps led from the sidewalk to the aged wood porch of the two-story Queen Anne, the siding's color a deep plum; the trim traded off on white and pink.

The bay windows of the dining room to the left of the house were shrouded in antique white lace, concealing the view of her dominating mahogany table. Above the dining room was the turret room with somewhat gaudy pink curtains, its towered roof caked with bits of snow. From the right of this, the roof squared off, becoming rather angular and domineering; a set of gabled windows looked out on the front lawn and those who may be approaching the home without permission.

The decaying wood steps creaked beneath Trevor's feet, and he stared at his reflection in the narrow glass door with its fir frame. A set of three theater seats, purchased at auction from the Thistle Opera House upon its closing, sat nestled in the left corner of the porch.

To the right was a large wicker bench with candy-striped cushions and a matching chair, positioned beneath a large picture window.

A natural wreath made of twigs and wrapped in white lights hung in the window's center; the thing was the size of a semi's wheel. Over that was the bamboo blind that concealed the inside of the Victorian.

The right-side of the house boasted a brick garden, which bloomed with roses in the spring and summer months. An ornate three-tier fountain with a three-headed, torch and serpent-bearing goddess fount loomed over the garden; her face stoic.

He was half-tempted to open the wood gate and follow along the narrow brick path, which slipped under an arbor covered in English ivy to its stop at the back door when startled—he heard music inside, music that he had not heard since childhood.

Tchaikovsky's *Violin Concerto in D op. Thirty-Five* screamed from behind the Victorian's walls. The sharp laughter of his aunt carried on and it sent goosebumps down his arms and spine. Trevor's eyes grew wide with curiosity as he approached the little white door bell, suddenly afraid to ring it, not exactly sure of what was going on inside.

"Fuck it."

He pressed his finger in and the device gave a loud buzz. The laughter of his aunt died away, and his heart seemed to thump at an accelerated rate with each footfall from beyond the door.

"All right, Michael, stop playing."

Her voice was smoky, and the name *Michael* began an immediate swell of questions in his head. The glass knob twisted and the ancient door jutted open, skirting across dark, hardwood floorboards made of fir.

"Yes?"

Queen Mab stood before him, tall and thin, her eighty-eight year-old body dressed in a satin slip of burgundy, a long black coat made of fine velvet draped over her, and her familiar three-tiered amber necklace hung from her neck, the longest string reaching to her abdomen. The second rested under her breasts, and the shortest rested in her cleavage.

Her face was narrow and her eyes large and gray, looking on her nephew with amusement. Her thin lips were rouged in scarlet and turned in a half-sneer, and her graying blonde hair draped her shoulders. He stared at her hand, which was fair in shade and held her hip, while her right hand braced the thick door. Her plum-colored nails gleamed in the winter light.

At first he was uncertain if she even recognized him.

"Auntie, it's me."

She appeared to laugh, though he couldn't be certain, and then she nodded, stepping aside and allowing him entrance into her home.

The inside was impressive to Trevor, who was always awed by the thirteen-foot ceilings painted in a rich gold with white-painted trim moldings. The walls were lavished with old daguerreotypes of Blackmoores long since passed, as well as a collection of scattered paintings—most of which were depictions of old, decrepit Irish cemeteries, as well as the coastal lines of County Mayo and the sod house with attached farm: the place where Bernadette Blackmoore gave birth to Sarafeene back in 1769.

To his left, white pocket doors stood open, pushed into their slots, revealing the octagonal dining room with its grand ten seating mahogany table, the walls papered in various fruits. A great, brick fireplace sat burning, a collection of antique bears at its floor. A protective iron grate with gold grape leaves appeared to glow with the fire's light.

A narrow door opened to the squared kitchen with its extended ceiling papered in images of book covers; its tiny window, which rested above the sink, did little to brighten the room.

In front of the dining room's bay windows stood a ten-foot tree, illuminated by pink-and-white lights. The ornaments were distinctively Victorian, and from Jeremiah and Sarah Blackmoore's collection from 1871.

Before they had moved their family from New Orleans to Fairhaven, purchasing the Victorian from the Donovans in 1910 as well as taking over the Donovan Mill, pulp factory, and shipping yard—converting them into the Blackmoore Cannery, as well as the Blackmoore Boat Construction and Shipping Yard.

The family's stock in the city grew rapidly through these companies, and upon the slow decline of the cannery, the family had gone underway with a project to convert the three-block-long warehouse into a bayfront shopping village and eatery, his mother Kathryn taking creative control since Queen Mab's two-year lack of interest.

"If I'm not mistaken, you should be sitting in class right now, shouldn't you, Trevor?" He turned and looked at his aunt, who was standing in the front parlor, the grin still evident on her face.

"I should be, yes."

She nodded and leaned against the back of her ornate green sofa, the lengthy stained-glass windows behind her, kissed by frost. The grand fireplace with its antique fir mantelpiece dominated the space between these two windows. A mirror hung above it, the gold frame also seemed dull in the cool light despite its polish.

"Well, then, please tell me, what brings you to me this early in the morning?"

He averted his gaze to the impressive staircase with its sweeping banister. The tiny windows of the landing cast strange shadows on the walls and boards, and for a moment Trevor thought that he had seen someone in the corner before the final set of steps that led to the second floor, but he shook this away as quickly as the thought came to him.

"The Legacy...."

His voice trailed off, and he expected her to shake her head or look surprised, but the great Queen of the Blackmoores only nodded, as if expecting it.

"There is much to the Legacy, Trevor; what do you want to know?"

Again she placed her hand to her hip and looked at him in anticipation. Her aged face was unhindered by the wrinkles that made her skin tight and her throat loose. Her voice was exquisite, like his mother's; he only hoped that she would not avoid his questions.

"All of it."

His heart began to pound in his chest—a familiar reaction to his aunt, who always seemed to reveal the most of every situation, spitting out answers as if they were nothing more than chewed tobacco needing to be released.

She shook her head and turned from him, walking around the couch and towards the tiny pocket door to the left of the room opposite the large window, her hand waving slightly, beckoning for her nephew to follow her.

She pushed the white door into its slot, the music room opening up before them, its walls lined with shelves stacked with books, and its three lengthy windows, two to the left and the other directly across, both concealed with the same bamboo blinds as found in the front room.

A round cherry-wood table sat atop an antique Persian rug; a collection of candles sat on the near edge of the table, a gold case lay on the opposite end, and a black velvet pouch rested on the table's center. Two chairs sat across from one another and Mabel took a seat in the chair facing the door, watching as her nephew approached with cautious steps.

"Close the door, Trevor. As you know, a Blackmoore's home always has ears."

He did as she asked, sliding the pocket door across its runner, suddenly feeling trapped in the squared room with his aunt.

Queen Mab was a mystery to him, one that he had given up trying to figure out a long time ago, knowing that her secrets and whatever knowledge they kept would be forever owned by her until the day she died. The chance of her departing these things was as likely as the ground opening up and swallowing the city whole.

"In regards to the Legacy, I cannot tell you everything."

She reached for the gold case and opened it, revealing a collection of slim white cigarettes. She took one between her fingers and placed it to her lips, striking a match and lighting the thing, taking in one long drag before letting it go, her gray eyes watching the wisps of blue smoke.

"But I can tell you what I know. I can share with you what I understand, and I believe that I can tell you what it pertains to you."

He nodded, knowing that there would be no point in asking her questions. Those things would come in time. Through her words he would somehow find his answers, and he would make of them what he needed to.

"All right," Trevor responded. He was still so unsure, thoughts of Christian's lips on his body, on his cock. It scared him.

"As legend has it, when your *extremely* great-grandmother Sarafeene were sent to New Orleans with her husband Malachey back in 1788 as indentured servants for the cousins of their Landed Gentry—aristocrats—at the Big House, as the great plantations of the Ulster Irish were often called.

"The Irish in America had not been met with a great reception. In fact, many had to work in the fields and in the plantation houses and town houses of the wealthy. Some with a contracted end date, and others, Like Sarafeene and Malachey, had no idea if their servitude would ever end.

"The rest, those who found their way here by their own means, had to find work doing odd jobs around the different parishes, while discovering that the only place that they were permitted to live was on the banks of the Mississippi, a place wretched with cholera and yellow fever.

"Sarafeene had been a Romani or Gypsy, shunned in her own native Ireland. Things did not come much easier for her in what would become known as the Irish Channel. The immigrants there saw the mixed blood in her, and as a result she was feared and avoided; her husband Malachey suffering the same fate.

"She had found quickly that the Afro traditions of the slaves and Free People of Color reminded her much of the traditions of her own people, and when she was sold off to a home within the Quarter, she found that though she and Malachy were so far from their native home and the divinities who guided them, they were welcomed into the circles of those who they worked alongside.

"They danced in Congo Square and lit fires for an array of gods and goddesses, all of whom seemed like an extension of one's own family."

She took another drag from her cigarette before continuing.

"But there was one woman, a Marie St. Clair, who did not welcome the presence of an Irish Romani fresh off the boat in her city.

"Now, Marie St. Clair was one of the Free People of Color, and made no secret of the affair that she carried on with her white sugar plantation suitor. In fact, she bragged about it whenever she could, but her ties within the Hoodoo and Vodou communities were so tight that no one dared challenge her presence.

"*The devil keeps his witches, Sarafeene Blackmoore!*' she used to say to her, though never going any further than that. Some said that it was because she was afraid of Sarafeene, but others would shrug this notion off. After all, with her connections how could she be afraid of this frail girl who was essentially a nobody?

"Now, Malachey was also Romani. In fact, he was a cousin who came from a neighboring clan, and he and Sarafeene had been wed in their ancient traditions; but with the press of the church as well as that of England, they had learnt to hide it within those Christian rituals—just as the slaves had done in Haiti and the New World.

"Well, one evening Sarafeene came home to their little shack along the water to find Malachey in bed with Marie St. Clair. He immediately looked on her with surprise and then turned to Marie and pushed her out of the bed, revolted, screaming over and over again that he thought that it had been Sarafeene.

"As legend tells it, Sarafeene knew that Marie had bewitched her husband, enchanting him with a glamour, making him think that he had been making love to his wife when in truth it was that vile priestess.

"So do you know what Sarafeene did?"

Trevor shook his head, his brain fogging up with images of this family tale.

"Sarafeene screamed wildly, and apparently the windows began to rattle before splitting altogether as Marie gathered her things, desperate to get out.

"*May you know no peace, Sarafeene Blackmoore, and may your blood act as the poison that it is; this I bestow upon you!*' the bitter woman yelled, waving her finger at Sarafeene on her way out the door, disappearing into that tropical night.

"The next morning Marie was found dead in her lavish apartments, her neck snapped in half, a message writ in blood on her mirror, pricked from her finger. Its message was confusing to most, except those of the faith and who had known of the conflict that stirred."

"What did it say?" Trevor asked, taking a cigarette from his aunt without asking, and not really caring to, simply playing with it in his fingers.

"'The Devil will come. The Devil will come and walk amongst men, claiming souls one by one. For the Devil keeps his witches, and will always come back for them. The end of the Devil will be at the hand of his own child.'"

Trevor felt a cold chill, and then something that had sounded like shattered glass erupted from beyond the music room's doors. It made the both of them jump.

Christian Vasquez walked along the field's edge, not caring that he had now missed two classes or that he was at risk of suspension; everything was just so complicated now, and he desperately needed to make sense of it all.

He replayed the events of earlier that morning, seeing Trevor's panic-stricken face when Christian had attempted to taste him, to know him. He wondered why he had held him back—and more so, why he had referred to himself as *poison*?

It was all a complicated riddle, one that needed an answer.

The snow kicked up as he shuffled along, watching as his breath formed with every exhale; drifting into to air, just as his thoughts drifted along the surface of his brain.

He was in love with Trevor Blackmoore; he knew this and was confident in this realization. He had, in fact, loved Trevor since before that day when Sheffield Burges had died, leaving a broken and fragile child to cling to the banister of his stairwell, no longer aware of Christian's presence looming over him. He had wondered even back then how he would take care of his best friend? Imagining that he would collect Trevor and they would run away from that accursed house and the claustrophobic neighborhood known as South Hill.

What was he going to do?

He knew his mission: to track Trevor down, to win his trust, to make the young Blackmoore fall in love with him, and then to finally destroy him. Leaving him along the social wayside, fresh for the picking by any one of Mariner's population.

A car was heard down the tree-lined slope opposite the chain-link fence, slightly skidding on the snow beneath its tires. He turned his head to the sound's direction and then let it go, half-expecting someone—perhaps Trevor—to be standing there, ready to forgive him for the cruelty that he had not yet inflicted.

"Fuck me..." he let out, knowing that he was going to have to wrap up this little scheme before the end of the week. Greg and Cheri were growing restless, and people were talking—most likely Teri Jules's doing.

The girl had a tendency to run her mouth, and his social status was at risk—and if word caught his father's ears, he knew that Emanuel Vasquez would not be forgiving.

Upon return from Trevor's house years ago, his father had begun to bombard him with questions about his time spent over at the Blackmoore home, and the excuse of Sheffield's death had no longer been adequate.

"Are you a faggot?" his father asked him, standing in their former home, which, before renovation, had been a 1930s Wright-inspired house with sharp lines and detail to the windows that you did not find in the houses of today.

"No, Dad, I'm not...."

But the accusation had struck a chord within him, one that he knew could not be excused.

The next day while at Fairhaven Middle School, Christian, Greg, and Cheri had been standing outside in a completely different spot than the usual—which had been on the front steps at the entrance, where they would wait for Trevor to arrive in the morning.

They had asked him why they were hanging around at a new spot, but Christian had refused to answer, not really knowing himself. Then a young Teri Jules had approached, already known for her big mouth and her desperation to date Greg and hang out with Cheri.

"Where's Trevor?" she asked, looking immediately to Christian—who was the unspoken leader of their group—her eyes searching for an answer.

"Trevor? Trevor's a fag."

He looked to see the shock on his friends' faces, and he was certain that he had seen tears in Cheri Hannifin's eyes.

He walked away from them, disappearing into the building, the acute sense of nausea in his stomach, the acidic taste of vomit riding up his esophagus: Christian was going to throw up.

Trevor's fate had been sealed then, branding him with an invisible target. Teri had spread the word, and by the end of the week no one would talk to the young Blackmoore, the children of South Hill casting him aside, and the newer heirs and heiresses of Edgemoor trying to get a leg up on the predominantly Irish-English-Scandinavian preteen royalty came at him with blatant cruelty.

They had attacked Trevor with a colder, wilder vengeance for being different, a vengeance that did not fall short of bombarding him in the hallway and calling him names in the middle of class.

Though just as mean, the kids of South Hill had learnt from their parents that anything you did to a person had to be done in shadow, while to the rest of the world you had a drink in your hand and a smile on your face, none being the wiser. In the end it was all the same, and Trevor paid the price.

He shuddered.

"Fuck me," he sighed, and kicked up some snow, wanting so desperately to be able to tell Greg and Cheri the truth, wanting to confess his love for Trevor Blackmoore—but he knew that it could never be.

He had been the one to condemn Trevor those many years ago, and now he was going to have to own up to that condemnation. If he backed out, it could mean ruin for the both of them.

He looked to the school, seeing the world that he had created for himself, the world that he governed, and knew he could not let it go.

Students poured out of every door, some going off to lunch, others heading to their next class, and he knew that he was either revered or hated, and it was in his position to be that. Trevor had become something that jeopardized all of it, and that could not be.

"Stay right here," Mabel instructed him, rising from her chair and walking towards the music room's door. Trevor nodded and watched as his aunt slid the door open and slipped out, closing it behind her.

Trevor searched the room with weary eyes, the vast collection of books ranging between history and mythology: books on gods of old, and spines reading *The Secret History of Voodoo* and *A Treasury of Witchcraft*, as well as a host of many others. He could feel his blood pumping in his ears as he listened intently to where in the house his aunt was located.

He strained and focused, clearing his mind and tuning his ears while he concentrated, feeling his body become somewhat weightless, as if he were floating in a pool of water.

Without warning, a quick image formed along his conscious: his aunt was in the back hall directly across from the front door. A young man appearing no older than Trevor stood before her, dressed in a fine black jacket and creased black pants, his hair brown and parted at the sides, his eyes large and black, his skin white like marble and his face was as handsome as ever.

For a moment Trevor thought it to be Jonathan, but as quickly as the idea came to him, the young man came into closer focus and he realized that this was not his spirit at all. This spirit belonged to 1510 Sixteenth Street, and perhaps could not leave.

He shook the image from his head and rose from his chair, walking silently towards the bookcase. His hands shook slightly as he walked, and the bitter chill of the morning seemed to be seeping in through the window panes. He tilted his head for a moment and realized—for the first time, it seemed—that an ornate, tree-branch-designed, iron chandelier hung from the ceiling's center, connected to a pulley and attached to a brilliant gold-tasseled rope.

Trevor's eyes followed it to the far corner of the room. Nearest to the back of the house, it was looped around a brass hook, and this made him come to a realization: the chandelier had not been wired for electricity, and for some strange reason he found this chilling.

He returned his attention back to the books, and upon scanning many of the titles he finally found one that piqued his interest, and this one had no title at all.

It was thin and bound in a jacket of worn red leather: rustic ties held it closed, and it smelled of lavender. He slipped it out and stared at the thing for just a moment, unsure if he should give in and open it up, but he knew that the longer he contemplated, the sooner his aunt would be to returning.

"Screw it!" Trevor decided, pulling the leather ties loose and flipping open the front cover, staring at the first page of parchment. He read the title in complete shock, not knowing if he should proceed further.

"Revelations of Blackmoores and the Death of Man."

He flipped through the pages and scanned them briefly. Names of Blackmoores from long past came back to him in written form.

Photos and daguerreotypes on silver resin called to him with a silent hum, and things that looked like quotes but appeared to be prophecies tempted him further.

As Trevor flipped through the pages of parchment and ink, a bundle slipped out: a collection of pages neatly-folded, landing at his feet, making a tiny tap on the floorboards.

He bent down and retrieved it, running his fingers gently along its sides, his heart thundering inside of his chest. He looked to the door for a moment, weary of his aunt's return; she was still on the other side of the house. Trevor lifted the pages and began to read, knowing that this was something that he should not be doing.

"The darkest of evils will rise amongst men, and amongst these men he will walk, tempting all those and claiming their souls—feeding on their fear.

"Upon this earth he will come, seeking out the one who holds the key, searching without exhaustion till he's gone through them all, testing each until the one is found.

"Upon the tenth generation this evil will come, and the Blackmoore blood may cease to exist. The key to this evil rising will be the Blackmoores who conquer the Legacy, and it will be these same Blackmoores who can bring about evil's end.

"Of disbanded clans they'll come, sharing the same gene, they will be known by their initials, which will hold the answer to the mysteries—"

He was alerted by the sound of his aunt's footfalls approaching. Trevor quickly threw the loose pages into the notebook and slid it into the shelf, grappling for the first book his saw and opening it up, pretending to be reading and trying to stay calm.

"*Are You There, God? It's Me, Margaret* is a great book; it helped your very own mother through her first period."

Mabel smirked and Trevor blushed, immediately feeling embarrassed, wondering if his aunt knew the truth of what he had been doing while she was out.

"Sorry, it looked interesting... is everything okay?"

Mabel nodded and proceeded to sit back in her chair, waiting for her nephew to come back round and join her.

"Everything's fine... just a mouse."

Trevor nodded, though he knew that she was lying. Mabel's cold gray eyes watched him intently as he took his seat back in the chair, prepared for her to continue with what she had to reveal to him.

"The Legacy's a strange thing, Trevor, and one that should not really be explored.

"For though it did not occur as we know it until the end of 1788, it spans so much further—back to our ancestors who gathered at great standing stones and wooded hollows.

"We're so much more than is ever comprehended now."

She lit another cigarette and this time she offered one to her nephew; Trevor declined, and Mabel shrugged.

"The great evil," he said under his breath, gauging his aunt's reaction, and startled when she gave him a sharp glare, her pupils dilating just a bit.

"Yes, Trevor, the great evil." She shook her head. "You need to be careful, my young Blackmoore, for the night carries many things within it, and places which seem the scariest may just be the safest. And those who you cannot trust now may turn out to be your only savior."

He did not like this. Though she was denying nothing, she was also omitting much, and he knew that his aunt's temper would not allow him to press much more for details.

"What is the great evil, Auntie?"

He cracked his knuckles and stared at her, his mind filled with so many dreadful thoughts, wondering if she would actually confirm any of them.

"No one is certain, but it is believed that this great evil may have been some dark god of the Irish wood, revered by the tribes until the onslaught of Christianity—when those either left the old faith, or were killed for not leaving it. Either way, this dark god may have lost his power and now wishes to regain it through a powerful bloodline—"

"But why us?" he interjected, noting the slight annoyance on his aunt's face.

"You mean, when there are so many other families like ours out there?"

There was sarcasm in her tone and Trevor looked away, spying the stacks of magazines resting in the corner beside a single armchair.

"In the very beginning there were gods who existed as a primal force, gods who craved the flesh of man, and others who fed off the sheer pleasure of others.

"These gods were nice, blessing those who wanted nothing but happiness, and upon the creation of the written word most of these beings transcended, their names carrying on and their temples surviving, for these gods were the Great Ones....

"but there were the others.

"The other gods fell into forgetfulness because their names were not recorded. Their habits and rules were not notated, and therefore people forgot of their existence.

"As the world continued to grow and expand in culture, these more primal, vile gods vanished, now only regarded as the Ancient Ones, and briefly mentioned amongst superstitious persons—if brave enough to do so."

Trevor shook his head, desperately wanting his aunt to get to the point.

"But that still doesn't explain why it would come for our family."

The veins in his temple were pulsating and he put his fingers to his head now, as if attempting to slip his fingers through his flesh and massage the sticky membrane within his skull.

"We were named for a wooded hollow in the west of Ireland. It was known as The Black Moors, and it was in this hollow that our clan began, honoring the female god force.

"This energy was beautiful and loving to our clan, but then at night, as the story goes, the clan felt a dark and suffocating force take rise as soon as the sun would set.

"They would feel it in the wind, sense it pulsating within the earth, and course through the limbs of every tree that surrounded them.

"As the tale is remembered, one night the priestess of the clan began to have erroneous fits and was forced into seclusion.

"Finally all seemed to be calm; she had become complacent and all was well. And then on the night of the dark moon, everyone heard screaming but dared not emerge from their earthen huts for fear of some wild beast or raving barbarian such as a Viking—but they would regret it forever."

Trevor was now in awe.

"What happened?"

He felt like a little child on Christmas, waiting in desperation to open his gifts.

"They awoke the next morning to find their priestess lying out dead in the middle of the hollow. Her flesh had been removed and her heart had been torn out, and yet no sign of it seemed to exist.

"Well, you can imagine their fear. This entity had taken the strongest of the clan and stripped her of her skin and heart; it was awful.

"Well, to appease this being, the clan of the Black Moors began to capture weary travelers and persons of other tribes, sacrificing them on the dark night of the moon, desperate to please this being; the clan's salvation had been the introduction of written language.

"As they began to record their history and practices, they decided to omit this being's name from the records and leave the moor, taking two things with them—their goddess and their name: Blackmoore. It was so that they would never forget, and constantly pay penance for the evil that they had taken part in as a result of trying to appease this ancient god."

Mabel inhaled from her cigarette and continued.

"I suppose that's why the family took to Catholicism so well: the Goddess took the shape of Mary the Mother of God, and all of those lesser gods seemed to exist within the saints.

"But I believe most importantly it was because the Catholics had a dark god of their own—and to them, this dark god was very real, just as the one in the wood had been, and it served as a means to remember that this vile thing could take over anything, no matter how pure or strong, much like their priestess and her strange fits and eventual demise... or so the story says."

Trevor nodded, and again felt that cold chill ride up along his body. The world suddenly looked to be growing darker outside and safety was nowhere in sight; he felt like crying.

"Now, hurry and go; your mother's coming up the front steps. Here, get to the back door and pray that she does not see you."

Trevor nodded and grabbed his things, slipping out of the music room and racing down the long and narrow hall to the back door. He passed the brilliant bathroom with its clawed tub and antique barber's chair. Paintings of old Bellingham hung from the papered walls, and for a moment Trevor had spied someone's reflection in the glass frame, but he ignored it.

He turned to his aunt and saw her bring her finger to her lips, instructing him to say nothing about their conversation. He nodded and smiled, seeing his mother's silhouette behind the lace curtain on the front door, thankful that he had gotten out in time.

As he ran up the wood steps that led to the alley, Trevor tried not to think on what had happened, not on the notebook and not on his aunt's grim tale of his family's history. All of it seemed to be too much, and he was uncertain of how he was going to process all of it.

He felt as if he were going to faint.

Trevor's feet nearly slipped on the iced steps that led from the alley to his gate, grateful that he lived on the same block as his aunt. Sometimes she felt like his only refuge from the rest of the world, a world that was completely ignorant to that of the Blackmoores' reality.

THIRTEEN

"Did you see Trevor at all again today?" Braxton asked J.T., his dark eyes focused on the strings of his bass guitar, tuning them and tweaking them with his pick.

They were in the recreation room of J.T.'s house, which was in fact the basement, but had been remolded by his father when the Olivers first moved in. The white oak floors, freshly polished, gleamed with the tract lights above them, the two pool tables already set up for people to play, and the Irish pub-style bar was stacked and ready to go.

Their friend—and J.T.'s sometime fuck—Christine Bellaire would play bartender for the night, Braxton already knowing that she would spend a good portion of the time staring dreamily on J.T., desperate to take him upstairs and blow him for ten minutes.

It made Braxton laugh just thinking about it.

"Naw, dude, I didn't see him all day—well, except for in the morning when I invited him to the party... his surprise party. And don't worry, he still doesn't know."

Braxton smiled and looked over their playlist, waiting for Tim Roth to arrive. He was a freshman at Fairhaven University, and the Spit Monkeys' only drummer, though his frat boy personality made it hard to rely on him.

"Why in the hell am I so nervous?" Braxton asked, not really to anyone but himself.

J.T. turned and grinned, pulling off his knit cap and running his fingers through his shaggy mess of chestnut hair, shaking his head slightly.

"Well, gee, I don't know... uh, could it be that it's because you're about to seal the deal between you and Trevor? It's just a hunch."

Braxton tore a piece of paper from his binder and crushed it into a little ball, laughing sarcastically before hurdling it at his best friend, the waded ball hitting him on his forehead.

"Aw, thanks, I'll treasure it forever...."

They laughed and continued setting up, knowing that a little more than half the population of Mariner High School, as well as some of Fairhaven's, would soon be flooding through the front door, clamoring down the steps and into the rec room, which was the width of the mansion, and nestled along the cliff-side of Edgemoor.

Kathryn and Queen Mab sat in two armchairs across from one another, lingering in silence, their attention not at all waning from the other's gaze, neither one very anxious to speak.

The Victorian was silent. Save for the occasional creaks and ghostly disturbances, the home was peaceful and Mabel knew that if someone didn't speak soon then they would both fall asleep.

"So, how's Tom?" Mabel asked, not really caring.

She took a sip of her martini and then proceeded to take hold of the little black plastic sword with an olive impaled to it, sticking it in her mouth. The saltiness of the olive contrasted well with the sweetness of the little red pepper that was stuffed inside of its pit.

"Fine; he's coming home today."

Kathryn had some Bailey's in a scotch glass, the three ice cubes clanking around as Kathryn brought it to her lips. The sweet, milky flavor did little to sweet the sting of the alcohol.

"Oh, grand, and I'm sure he's just eager to touch the family's money."

Mabel had never liked him; in fact, she despised him and wished every day for his demise. She could never understand why her niece had married him. She knew it was in part to quell the loss of Sheffield, but the rest must have stemmed from a certain insecurity—perhaps a hole left inside of her when her father, Trevor Mayland, had passed away.

"I'm sure he is, too, but he's in for an unpleasant surprise."

Kathryn smirked and took a sip from her drink, twirling her fingers around a strand of her soft russet hair. Her icy eyes appeared to smile sinisterly, and Mabel raised an eyebrow in silent question.

"I've fazed him out. I canceled his credit cards and I cashed in his stocks and sent the money to Darbi. He'll be starting college next year, and I want him out of that Catholic boarding school that he's been in for the past eight years.

"Yes, I want him far away from that place... definitely."

Kathryn looked so distant, remembering a time of her life that she dared not recall through words; the slight truths that she had given away over the years did little to stifle her insecurity of others, or the church for that matter.

Mabel's mind began to race with the thought of her fourth-cousin.

Darbi was a smart boy. His mother Mona had passed away when he was twelve; she had been in a car accident on her way home from the Blackmoore & Morales Law Firm in El Paso, Texas.

She had been struck in the rain on the corner of Mesa and Executive; her car had flipped three times and she was killed instantly.

Kathryn had been ready to take Darbi in and raise him herself, along with Trevor, when she learned that his grandfather and her cousin, John, had paid for his full tuition at Our Lady of Guadalupe Academy, sealing his fate within the walls of Catholic suffocation.

He had grown up strong, taking part in several sports such as football and basketball, as well as soccer and lacrosse. He seemed to know nothing of the Legacy, and he was already interning at Blackmoore & Morales with his grandfather. Yet whenever he sent letters or pictures, Mabel could feel the blood growing within him.

In his pictures his eyes were distant, as if the shadow of his heritage were only a step away, and the influence of his mother's presence was taking over by the minute. In the end though, she believed that he would be all right.

"Did he tell you that he's flying in for Christmas? Though John has advised him against this."

Kathryn thought on the most recent letter from her young cousin; his words had felt mournful and cold, a demeanor that every Blackmoore knew all too well.

"Why?" Mabel asked. Her voice was sharp and irritated with her idiot cousin, whom she had not seen since his daughter's passing.

"Oh, please; you know why. It's because he thinks that as long as Darbi stays away from us he'll be safe from the Legacy and our... unique gifts."

"Yeah, because living in El Paso did him a hell of a lot of good; where's his wife, Amy? Oh, wait, that's right; she's dead and gone, just like the rest of them!"

With that she reached for a cigarette, handing one to Kathryn, both of them lighting up in silence, their minds filled with bitter thoughts—thoughts that could find their source within a warm December night back in 1788, when the vile curse of a soulless woman would affect generations to come.

Trevor sat on the edge of his bed, staring up at his specter; Jonathan was drawing strength from every electrical source in the room, desperate to keep his form.

Sugar Water by Cibo Matto flowed lightly from the speakers of his stereo, and the world beyond his green satin drapes began to grow heavy with night, and once again the snow began to fall. Trevor was wary about the party at J.T.'s, but knew that he had to go. He had made a promise and he didn't want to disappoint his friend—as well as Braxton, who no doubt would be severely hurt by his sudden refusal to show up.

'*Tom is coming...*' Jonathan said, his voice humming inside of Trevor, riding along every nerve.

Trevor stood, his heart pounding, fearful of his stepfather, fearful because his mother was not home, and whenever that was the case Tom Preston had a tendency to get forceful with Trevor. Once, he had even thrown him into the wall along the landing.

Jonathan had been eager to hurt him then, to inflict his phantasmal will on the rigid man, but Trevor had stopped him, ordering his friend to do nothing.

Trevor looked out of the window just in time to spy a taxi pull up in front of the house, far different from the limo that Tom usually arrived in whenever he left for—or returned from—one of his many trips, meeting with potential investors and clients for the family's many endeavors.

Trevor watched as Tom pulled out a wad of cash held secure in a sterling silver money clip, handing a few to the driver, who had set his suitcases on the curb, not bothering to help him bring them to the front door.

The annoyance on Tom's face was evident, and looked even worse due to the orange glow of the lamp post.

"Shit, Mom, where are you?" he let out, his hand shaking; now he was definitely certain that he would be going to that party.

He held his breath as the deadbolt unlatched and the front door swung open, creaking as it made its way across the floor, colliding with the wall.

"Motherfucking... that bitch..." Tom mumbled, setting his things down and using his foot to close the door behind him.

He immediately moved into the formal room, going for the bottle of scotch on the black, wrought-iron wet bar, showing little concern for the things that he slammed around while grabbing a glass to pour himself a drink.

Trevor played with the little chain that was around his neck; thinking of Braxton seemed to be the only thing to ease his nerves.

As he took hold of his pea coat and made his way down the steps he prayed that he would be able to slip out of the house without notice. Halfway out the foyer he had thought that his prayer had been answered, until that familiar gruff voice called out to him.

"Trevor, my boy, where do you think you're going?"

He turned to see Tom Preston sitting in one of the chairs, the Christmas tree lit behind him, already decorated; Trevor hadn't even noticed it when he came home earlier that afternoon.

"To a party at a friend's house."

His words were quivering in his throat as his stepfather waved his finger for him to come closer.

"And who said you could go? I don't recall giving you permission."

He took a final swig from the glass and stood, moving towards his stepson slowly, his hands shaking in anger.

"Did you ask your mother?"

Trevor shook his head.

"No, I don't need to. All I need to do is call in and let her know that I'm there and what time I'll be home."

Tom shook his head and the veins in his forehead seemed to throb. Trevor could feel Jonathan Marker drawing near, and was silently telling him with his thoughts that the spirit needed to back off.

"You fucking shit, you think you can just do whatever you want without permission?!"

He was knocking the glass against his leg.

"You Blackmoores just strut around like you own the fucking world... thinking you're better than everyone else—don't you? Don't you?!"

Trevor shook his head, backing slowly towards the door; it was at that moment that Tom pitched the scotch glass across the room. It sailed over Trevor's shoulder, grazing his ear before it collided with the wall and shattering into a thousand glittering pieces.

"It's time to teach you some fucking respect—"

"Tom!"

He stopped in his tracks, directing his attention to the front door; a grin spread across his face.

Trevor turned to see his mother behind him, her face blank, her eyes cold, and her gaze directed at her wandering husband.

"Trevor, honey, go to your party; stay the night if you can."

She looked from him and back to Tom; a sly grin spread across her face.

"Your stepdad and I have some things that we need to discuss."

Trevor blew past his mother, kissing her lightly on the cheek before darting out of the house. His mother's driver Miles, the kind old man who had driven them to Nimbus the week before, was waiting for him; the black Lexus was blanketed in a thin sheet of snow.

"Where to?" he asked, his body shaking lightly in the way that old people do. He grinned and Trevor returned it, turning once more, afraid for his mother and praying that Jonathan would keep her safe.

"Morris Lane, in Edgemoor."

Miles nodded and smiled once again as he shut the door to the back seat, making his way into the front and pulling out of the house. The seats warmed up and Miles slid one of Trevor's CDs into the player. The haunting words of Tori Amos drifted into his ears, the lights of the car shone on the wet road, and the tiny flakes of snow glistened like stars falling from the sky; it was brilliant.

Her words brought gooseflesh along his arms and he felt as if a dark cloud were beginning to spread over the city, as if something was going to happen, something that no one could come back from. He was suddenly aware that the world was opening up, and things like comfort and normalcy were slowly unraveling.

"Who's ready for a party?" Christine Bellaire asked, walking into the rec room. She was a petite girl of 5'4, dressed in a pair of tight blue jeans, a blue-and-pink striped rugby over her chest, stopping short of her navel, with the white collar open.

Her face was thin and her hair was a dark blonde—soft and straight. Her olive skin looked dark under the tract lights; the gloss on her lips shone, and she looked warm in the loose button-down brown sweater which reached to her knees, a matching scarf wrapped around her neck.

"Did you get the cake?" J.T. asked her.

His lack of "hello" stung a little and they both could see it, though she shrugged it off and gave them both a smile.

"Yes, I got the cake; it's in the trunk of my car. It's a little big, though, so if one of you strapping young men could help me bring it inside that would be great."

She sat a bag down on the bar and shook her head, looking at the stage that had been created by several cinder blocks and a large piece of strong sanded plywood, the instruments set up, waiting to be played with.

"I'll do it!" Braxton said, rising up and walking over to where she was standing.

Both men had dressed in suits: Braxton in black pants with white pinstripes, a matching jacket over a black oxford, with a crimson tie secure around his neck. His olive skin and dark eyes stood out even more than usual and his hair was actually worn down for once, instead of the usual spikey mess that he was accustomed to wearing it.

J.T. grinned, wearing a similar suit, but the pinstripes were blue instead of white, and the tie was also blue.

Christine noticed that he had taken a hot iron to his hair, so it was now longer than she had thought, reaching to the line of his jaw.

"Wow, calm down, Braxton. You're acting like this party is for someone you're going out with."

They both looked at her and she blushed, immediately catching on and feeling embarrassed.

"Oh, I didn't know... shit, I'm sorry."

Braxton shook his head and J.T. grinned, watching as his best friend stalked up the stairs. Christine shrugged and pouted her bottom lip.

"Don't worry about it; no one really knows... though I don't think it's too hard to figure out."

She nodded and looked back, aware that Braxton was waiting for her.

"But, Jesus, Trevor Blackmoore? I mean, shit! Isn't that like playing with Pandora's Box?"

J.T. laughed, knowing what people thought about his quiet friend and his family.

"Don't laugh! I mean, one: rumor has it that Trevor is running around with Christian Vasquez, and second: he's a fucking Blackmoore! That family has got more secrets than the government, and not only that, but everyone knows that they're...."

She hesitated for just a moment.

"That they're witches!"

J.T. managed another laugh and shook his head, dumbfounded at the superstition of his town.

"You really believe that shit? Man, you South Hill people really have some weird rumors."

She shook her head, knowing that he wouldn't understand.

"My grandmother told me all about them. His aunt or whatever, Mabel Blackmoore, she used to be known for her tarot readings and séances; the same went with Mabel's mother, Fiona Blackmoore.

"You just don't know; you aren't from our world—"

"Thank God—"

"I'm serious, they're dangerous."

J.T. walked over to Christine and wrapped his arms around her, whispering softly in her ear. She smelled of vanilla and her body was warm; that's what J.T. liked about her most of all.

"Don't worry, I know Trevor, and he's no more dangerous than you are—excluding when you're on the rag!"

She hit him playfully and they both laughed, kissing gently.

"Now, please go help Braxton get the cake out of your car."

Christine turned and walked up the steps, J.T. watching her as she left, a semi-bulge threatening to become more, thinking suddenly of Trevor; he wondered if Christine was right?

"What did you do? Did you know that I had to take a fucking cab here?"

Tom Preston locked eyes with the steely gaze of his wife, the smirk on her face twisting into a sick grin.

"Really? Well, that's too bad, now, isn't it?"

Kathryn stood before him in a crimson silk dress with a matching silk choker around her neck, her auburn hair feathered slightly, her lips rouged and her eyeshadow dark. She rested a hand on her hip and tapped her usual Manolo Blahniks on the floorboards.

"You bitch! What did you do?"

Kathryn looked away for a moment, sensing Jonathan's presence, knowing that the spirit was ready to act.

"What did I do?"

She turned to face him.

"Well, first I cancelled your credit cards and our joint bank account. Then I cashed in all of your stocks and bonds in the companies—which are under the Blackmoore name, mind you—and I gave the money to my cousin, Darbi, in El Paso."

He went rigid. His eyes shifting from side to side, tears beginning to well up at the rims of his lids.

"Why would you do that?"

She walked to him slowly, knowing that she had him by the balls.

"Because you fucked me for the last time. Because my son hates you.

"But most importantly... because you're a waste of my space."

He brought his hand up and struck her hard across the face.

Kathryn had felt the air part and make way for his open palm; she just didn't expect it to hurt as much as it did. He had split her lip open, and she turned around and gave a laugh before spitting a thin stream of it in his face—which he wiped away in disgust.

"I told you the first time that you hit me: if you do it again you better make sure that the first hit takes me down, because if it doesn't, you'll never get the chance to do it again!"

Kathryn closed her eyes for just a moment and took a deep breath, and in that moment the four lamps that lit the parlor blinked out without a flicker. It stopped Tom's heart just a little, but he shrugged it off as nerves.

Kathryn ran from the parlor and down the hall, making her way up the stairs, her heels pounding on the wood. Tom was quick to chase after her, but as he stepped out into the foyer, the chandelier above his head suddenly exploded, raining down billions of glittering shards, some of which got in his eyes, hazing his vision and causing irritation.

"When I get done with you, the only way they'll know who you are will be by your teeth!"

Tom Preston staggered up the stairwell, knocking into the framed photos and bringing them crashing to the ground. He looked from the left to the right as soon as he reached the second floor, peering down the long halls. The house now eerily dark, and it was when this house was dark that Tom knew to be the most cautious.

"Fucking bitch!"

He rubbed his eyes, which slowly began to bleed from the glass. His broad shoulders swept the dark around him, and the fog of injury that he was having to navigate through became all the more dense every time he rubbed his irritated eyes.

The French doors that led to the balcony at the back of the house were swinging open. The satin drapes flapped like the wings of birds and Tom followed the sound, figuring that if his wife was anywhere then she was outside.

"Stupid cunt, forgetting to shut the door...."

The hall was narrow and the wood creaked beneath his feet, but for the first time since moving in, Tom felt as if he were in control of this house, feeling as if those dark secrets that plagued the Blackmoore name no longer had sway over him.

He had struck the great Kathryn Blackmoore and nothing had happened; in fact, she had ran from him, hiding like a coward on the balcony.

If I kill her, he thought, *then nothing can stop me from taking her place on the Board of Directors for the West Coast companies.*

It was at that moment that Tom Preston made the decision that he would in fact kill his wife, and then he would ship that faggot son of hers to a boarding school in Switzerland—though had he actually given this plan a little more thought, he would have realized that her family would stop at nothing to ruin him, and perhaps send him off on a trip of his own ... a trip from which he would never return.

"Kathryn, honey... I think we need to talk. I'm a little tired of chasing after you and I think we need to discuss your position in this marriage."

He stepped out onto the wet wood. Snow lined the balcony's post, and the wrought-iron table and chairs were hosts to a heavy pile of the white wonder.

"You're right. We do."

Kathryn stepped out from behind the open door, the bluish light from the moon illuminated her face and glistened in her eyes. Though dressed only in her dress and heels, she appeared indifferent to the cold.

"Look at you, so helpless, up here all alone without any help... without anyone to hear you scream."

She walked towards him, unhindered by her possible demise, walking blindly into Tom Preston's arms.

"You're wrong," she whispered. "I'm not alone."

She raised her hand and quickly brought it across his face. Tom's head went to the side and he felt the immediate trickle of blood run down the side of his face, knowing that she had split his cheek open.

He took hold of her hand and looked at it, seeing that both sets of engagement rings and wedding bands were on the same finger, the multiple sets of diamonds tearing open a thin line in his flesh.

"You bitch!"

He took hold of her arms and turned her around, pushing Kathryn against the railing, unsure if he would throw her over or finish her off first, then throw her over.

"You bitch, I'm gonna kill you!"

As the winds around the house began to pick up in speed, Tom Preston moved his hands up to her throat, wrapping his fingers firmly around her neck. His grip was getting tighter and tighter, just as the wind began to kick up the snow from the table and roof, as well as the many evergreens that surrounded the house.

Kathryn coughed and her eyes began to close, a smile spread across her face which made Tom stop for a moment to contemplate its meaning, and it was that contemplation that gave Kathryn enough time to regain her senses and attack.

She took hold of his arms and brought him close, driving her knee into his crotch as hard as she could, watching him reel in pain.

"Oh, Jesus..." he moaned.

The wind swirled about them, and Tom looked up to see what appeared to be a man in silhouette come barreling towards him, though in his nearly-blind state he couldn't be certain if it wasn't any more than a hallucination.

He felt a powerful weighted mass throw itself into him and he went over, his legs catching onto the balcony before suddenly letting go, becoming weightless, and the icy air wisped at his sides and howled in his ears.

In the seconds before Tom Preston collided with the brick beneath the trees, the brick which snapped his neck in two, he thought of his first wife back in Olympia. The first wife who was six feet under the ground. The first wife who would be awaiting him in hell.

He had one more thought enter into his brain right before the world went dark. One more thought that put a bitter grin on his face:

If only Kathryn had been as easy as she had been.

"Fuck me..." Trevor said under his breath, staring at the line of cars along Morris Lane, the private drive that led to J.T.'s house.

Teenage boys and girls went about, some of them stumbling drunk, others so wrapped up in one another that they didn't seem to notice that they were at risk of getting smeared all over the pavement by a reckless driver.

The citadel-like evergreens lined the cliff-side estate, allowing only glimpses of the bay and neighboring San Juans. The moon was struggling out from behind thick, snowy clouds; dancing on black waves.

The Oliver home was like a castle: a mammoth, three-story structure made from limestone. The English latticed windows were eerie with their lamp-lit glow, strange shining beacons in the deep dark.

The house was in the shape of a slight U, and a sweep of stone banisters followed the home's path, concluding with a set of shallow steps that were accentuated at each end by ornate lamp posts.

Miles brought the car to a stop and the sound of live music could be heard, pouring out of the large, opened oak doors.

"What time do you want me to pick you up, Mr. Blackmoore?" Miles asked him, holding the door open and allowing him to step out.

Trevor remembered the words of his mother asking him to stay away for the night; he only hoped that she would be all right.

"Oh, I'm staying over tonight, but thank you."

The gentle old man nodded and went back to the driver's seat. Trevor watched as he turned the ignition and started the car, the black Lexus growing faint in the distance.

"Well, here it goes."

Trevor walked slowly up the steps, feeling as if a thousand eyes were on him; some of them were.

People he recognized and others he didn't watched as he made his way into the front foyer, the walls paneled in wood of a deep varnish. A large round table with a statue of Pan grinned at him from a seven-foot elevation, the flute held at his cloven side, his hair in curls, and his tiny horns poked out like two antennas directed towards heaven.

"Oh, excuse me," a young girl said to him, colliding with his shoulder, a plastic cup in hand and her breath reeking with alcohol.

"Don't worry about it."

Trevor looked up the grand staircase and noted how humble his aunt's home seemed when compared to this. Trevor looked down the hall to the right of the stairs, knowing that this path would lead him down into the rec room beneath the house, his heart pounding slightly at the thought of seeing Braxton. At the same time, a sense of dread began to make itself noticed in the back of his mind. Trevor had no idea where it was coming from, but he also knew that he would be a fool to ignore it.

His own thoughts seemed to become inaudible as he made his way down the steps, the sound of J.T.'s voice filling his ears, and the bass and the drums made his insides jump and his body hum; it was a feeling that he did not particularly like.

The rec room was packed almost to the point of being claustrophobic, and for a moment Trevor felt dizzy, and all he wanted to do was sit down. They were playing one of their own songs and as his eyes surfed the throng of jungle bodies he spotted Braxton, playing his bass with such ease, his eyes dark and his skin warmed in the light. His cheeks were flushed and pink and his black hair was already damp with sweat.

Trevor suddenly thought of that morning in the locker room the day before, when he had seen Braxton as a beautiful young man, and not the best friend that had walked by his side for the past five years. That morning when Trevor had stared at his friend dressed in nothing more than a pair of black boxer briefs, complimenting what it was that made Braxton a man.

His tight, sculpted chest and abs, those dark nipples which stood out amongst fair flesh, and his sudden and slightly jarring aura of domination.

Braxton looked up and their eyes met, a certain electricity surging between the two of them, riding along the currents of their ley lines.

"Fuck me..." he groaned, making his way through the dimly-lit dense, fumbling his way to the bar, desperate for a drink.

The bar was surprisingly only slightly flocked with people; the promise of alcohol to subdue his worries was sweeter than any kind of love song that the Spit Monkeys could have played. The hope of his brain becoming clouded and unfocused was like a whispered prayer coming true.

"Excuse me!" he called out to the young girl behind the bar.

She was focused on a frat reject on the other side and when she said "just a second," she appeared to be completely annoyed.

"What? Oh, hey, Trevor!"

It took him a couple of seconds to realize that it was Christine Bellaire who stared back at him. A dumb smile spread across her face, her eyes sparkling with desire for J.T. Oliver.

"Hey, um, can I get a Screwdriver, in a tall glass... with five shots of vodka, two shots orange juice, please?"

She looked at him peculiarly. "Isn't that a little too strong for your first drink?"

He shook his head; he didn't need to justify his drinking habits to a girl who was known to throw back more drinks than his mother in a single hour.

"No... it's just enough strong."

Christine shrugged and went to mixing the drink, knowing that she should really water it down, and if it had been anyone else she would have, but it wasn't anyone else; it was Trevor Blackmoore, and she was terrified by the idea of getting on his bad side.

"Here you go, Trevor: one Screwdriver."

He grinned and placed twenty dollars in the tip jar; it was the biggest tip she had received in the past two hours.

"Hey, um, can I please get everyone's attention?" J.T. Oliver raised his hand into the air, trying to silence the crowd of over one hundred and fifty; the rec room could only comfortably support one hundred and eighty-five.

Cheri Hannifin and Teri Jules strutted through the doors, leaving everyone who knew them to drop their jaws in their wake.

The Oliver home was impressive, but Cheri concluded that it lacked the grace of her South Hill neighborhood. They had just entered into the rec room when J.T. had asked for silence from the crowd. Her eyes searched through the faces until she found Trevor at the bar, sitting with a drink in hand.

Her first instinct was to run to him, to tell him hello and give him a hug, but that was over. Christian Vasquez had seen to that five years ago, and she knew that it had been better to follow along, better to act twice as vicious rather than suffer Trevor's same fate.

She really just wanted to go home.

"Everyone quiet down...."

J.T. looked over at his best friend and band-mate and winked, nodding to him and speaking in some secret, silent code.

"Now, there is a reason for this party tonight, and the reason is right over there at the bar."

He lifted his finger and pointed, everyone turning their heads with bemused grins on their faces. Trevor looked behind him and was shocked to discover that Christine Bellaire was also staring at him, her glossed lips spread in a gentle grin.

"What the hell...?" he questioned, downing the rest of his drink, his brow raised and his eyes fixed on both boys, trying to decipher their motives.

"Trevor Blackmoore is going to be turning eighteen on Christmas Eve, and though it's a little early, I thought that it would be a good time to celebrate it now!"

Trevor rolled his eyes and sighed, wishing that they hadn't done this, knowing that it was putting a certain pressure on him, one that in light of present situations was not the best pressure to be under.

"Happy birthday, Trevor...."

He turned around and felt like throwing up when he saw the extremely large chocolate cake that was being placed in front of him, eighteen candles dancing in his eyes, looking rich and green within this dense.

"Make a wish."

He turned to see Braxton standing in front of the microphone, his face lit with a grin. Trevor closed his eyes tightly and wished to be anywhere but here, and then to his disappointment he opened his eyes and the face of Cheri Hannifin stared back at him, her body positioned uncomfortably on the wood stool next to him.

"Shit!"

She smirked, her hair looking perfect as usual, and Christine looked at her with disdain.

"Happy birthday, Trevor... you deserve it."

Cheri Hannifin rose up and walked back towards the stairs, her hips swinging from side to side, and the pleats in her skirt swished gently with her movement.

"Trevor...."

He looked back to the stage, trying to shake off the feeling of discomfort and insecurity that was beginning to take over.

"This is for you."

He knew the song right away: it was his favorite song, *Keep Myself Awake* by Black Lab; and what was more, he was surprised that Braxton was the one singing. It was something that Trevor had never heard him do before.

He walked to the stage slowly, amazed that Braxton was doing this, and even more amazed at how incredible his voice was, smooth and yet gruff in the way that men's voices are. His eyes were shining and he had a smile on his face, a smile that Trevor had never seen before, and he wondered if his mother was right. Did Braxton Volaverunt really love him in a way that went beyond friendship, and if so, could he abandon everything just to go with that?

Tears were coming; he could feel them, and though Trevor tried so desperately to avoid them, he could not. Soon they were spilling down his cheeks and resting on his lips, the salty taste of his tears became an odd comfort, testifying to him that he was real, that Trevor Blackmoore did exist and that he was feeling.

"Thank you..." he said, feeling everything inside of him lift, and the lights behind Braxton made him look like an angel.

In this den of cigarette smoke and gin, he may just have been the only real thing that he had in his life.

"My pleasure," he said, leaning down.

Their eyes met, and then in an instant everything seemed to change, and a world of uncertainty opened up before them both.

Braxton placed his lips cautiously to Trevor's and the hot of their breath passed between them, followed by a slight contact of tongue—just enough to send a jolt of electricity through their bodies; the world fading at the same rate that gooseflesh began to spread across their arms.

Suddenly he thought of Christian and pulled away.

"Wait, I can't do this."

Trevor turned from him and spirited through the throng, making his way up the steps and into the front foyer of the large house, his mind swimming in an ocean of confusion. He felt as if he were drowning.

"Trevor, stop!"

Braxton took hold of his arms and spun him around, his dark chocolate eyes filled to the brim with tears.

"What do you mean, you can't do this?"

Trevor averted his gaze, not understanding how everything could be going so wrong, driving him further and further within himself. Blackmoores weren't just poison in the bedroom, they were poison to everything that they touched; no wonder no one in his family were known for their people skills.

"What do you think, Braxton? I'm with Christian, and you're not even gay!"

His declaration stung his friend; it was visible and sharp, like the blade of a slick knife.

"But you told me last night on the phone, and I thought...."

He was searching for answers, answers that he realized were not inside of Trevor Blackmoore, answers that may not even exist.

"On the phone? We didn't talk on the phone last night!"

Braxton backed away from him then, backed away from him as if he was suddenly meeting a stranger that he had mistaken for someone else.

"But I...."

Trevor shook his head in tired defeat.

"I better go."

He turned and pivoted back around on his heel, feeling himself becoming hallowed inside. He reached back around his neck and found the clasp to the chain that Braxton had given him, taking it off for the first time in several months, seeing the pain in his best friend's eyes as he curled it back into the palm of his hand.

"You should probably take this back; I don't want to hurt you anymore."

In an instant Trevor was gone, racing down Morris Lane and running out of Edgemoor, knowing that it would take him more than forty minutes to get home.

"What in the hell am I supposed to do with him?" Kathryn asked Jonathan, her cold eyes fixed on the body of her dead husband. A fresh blanket of snow had fallen, covering him in its icy powder.

'You could always wait and worry about it once spring comes....'

She rolled her eyes, not liking the ghost's humor; she could already feel herself reaching the point of panic.

"Not funny."

She walked back into her house, making a left into the kitchen and taking hold of the receiver of the black cordless.

The kitchen was dark, save for the light from a tiny white tea candle in a silver tray, the blue of the moon reflecting on the stainless steel counter of the island. She dialed the only person that she could think of, not knowing how to put into context what had happened.

"Hello?" It was Queen Mab, her voice raspy from sleep, though music could be heard playing loudly in the background.

"Mabel, it's Kathryn; I need your help with something...."

"Yeah, he's dead, all right," Mabel said to her niece, the two of them staring at the cold, blue-gray body of the person who in life had been Tom Preston.

Kathryn rolled her eyes, both women holding a glass of merlot in their hands.

"Well, thank you; though I think that was already concluded before you got here."

Mabel chuckled and took another sip. Her face looked deader than the corpse, and she was dressed as if she were going to her own funeral. Her eyes were shadowed in a metallic blue, and her lips were bright red. Her frail body was clothed in a black silk slip and a blue satin theater cape; her feet clicking with blue stilettos when she walked.

"Are you sure it was self-defense? I mean, I could understand why you did it, and neither I nor anyone else in the family would hold it against you."

Kathryn rolled her eyes and Mabel shrugged, her gaze still focused on the dead man.

"No, it really was self-defense. I mean, I wanted him to suffer, but I had given up on killing him a couple of nights ago."

Ever since Trevor had interrupted her spell, she hadn't bothered to go back and try again; she had had time to cool off, and had decided that to make him live with everything that he had lost would be a much greater punishment.

"So, then, what do you want to do with the body?" Mabel asked her, sensing the nearby presence of Jonathan Marker: a spirit that her niece had neglected to tell her about, but knew existed nonetheless.

"I don't know...."

Kathryn's voice trailed off, feeling as if for a moment she were not really there, that in fact she was nothing more than the wind.

The feeling passed.

"And you say you pushed him over that railing all on your own?"

She did not like the suspicion in her aunt's voice.

"That's what I'm saying."

Again Mabel nodded.

"The carriage-house?" she suggested, and Kathryn shrugged, staring at her secret temple through the distortion of her wine glass.

"Let's get the garbage bags!"

The two women inhaled the rest of their wine, turning around and heading back into the kitchen, which was now lit with many candles and the light from above the stove. Neither woman seemed the least bit bothered by their casualness with the situation, and if either one of them had noticed, it would have most likely been shrugged off anyways—considered nothing more than passing remorse.

"Jesus, Tom, you really should have gone on that diet that I had suggested to you last year!"

Kathryn was lifting him by the neck as she slipped the black durable lawn bag over his body, using all of her muscles to support the dead weight.

"But then again, you always had to make things difficult, didn't you?"

Mabel looked at her and laughed, her aged body finding no issue with getting his legs and waist wrapped up.

In order to get his middle half concealed they had to cut a hole in the bottom of the second bag and slip it on him like a skirt, followed with the third bag at the bottom. The women then secured the openings with duct tape so that no part of him would be visible; she was grateful then that her son did not go into the carriage-house.

"Where do we put him?" Mabel asked, staring about the space, smelling the herbs and seeing the plaster saints illuminated only by the light that spilled in from the crack in the partially-opened door.

"Jesus... um, what about up in the rafters?" Dust came at them in all directions as Kathryn climbed the ladder, throwing a piece of rope around one of the wood beams and letting the other end drop to Queen Mab, who then took it and tied the piece around the dead man's neck, making sure that it was secure enough to support him.

"Now for his feet!" Mabel commanded.

Kathryn stepped off the ladder and went immediately for another piece of rope, repeating the same action three rafters back, throwing it over and allowing her aunt to tie the other end around the ankles; oblivious to how much noise they were actually making.

Finally they both climbed up to the ends.

Kathryn went to the head via the ladder, and Mabel grabbed the piece of rope at the feet by way of step stool. Once up there they silently counted to three and hopped off, making the ten-foot descent while the body rose into the air, the women's skirts inflated by the air. When they touched ground the body slammed against the rafters, millions of particles of dust billowing in the winter air.

To complete the task, the women wrapped each end around the banisters until they felt secure enough to be left alone. Kathryn knew that within a couple of days, she would forget that Tom Preston was even out there: a sinner amongst her saints.

FOURTEEN

He wanted to go home and sleep, but he was too tired to argue with Jonathan about the phone conversation that he must have obviously had with Braxton the night before. Besides; his mother ordered him to stay away till the morning.

It explains why he was next to the phone in my room last night, he said to himself, desperate to make sense out of what was happening around him.

The walk down Seventeenth Street was filled with eerie silence. Great houses that were as familiar to him as his own stood decorated for the holidays, crowning their mammoth lawns in Technicolor glow.

He hadn't dared Seventeenth Street in two years and now suddenly here he was: going to the only other place that still made sense to him; the home of Lila and Emanuel Vasquez. Trevor had only seen it once after its remodeling, and now here he was standing before it, praying that Christian's parents weren't home or else he didn't know what he would do.

"Well, here goes nothing."

The pain in his heart was immense and he was uncertain how to quell it. After all, it involved one person whom he loved more than anything else in the world, and yet because of his determination to be the good guy he could not act on it.

He had given himself to Christian, and that was who he belonged to until the Universe saw fit to make it otherwise. Besides, he loved Christian as well.

He pressed his fingers into the doorbell and listened as it chimed, praying that his boyfriend would wake up and come to him—rescuing him and keeping him safe—just as he had when they were kids.

Nothing.

The hall was dark and no lights came on. He decided to give it one more try before calling it quits; he needed to give himself that much courage to brave his own insecurities and do what he felt that he needed to do.

It rang again and this time a door opened.

A door one floor above him.

"Hello?" Christian called out sleepily.

Trevor walked backwards onto the walk and looked up, seeing Christian on a balcony that must have been off of his bedroom. He was shirtless; that much he could tell, and his dark eyes looked endless in the moonlight.

"Hi...." His voice immediately caught the tears in his throat.

"Trevor?"

He nodded.

"I'll be down in a second."

Trevor nodded again, and watched as Christian disappeared into the house.

He walked back up to the front door, just in time to see the lights in the grand hall light up and his boyfriend stumble towards him, dressed in those same gray boxer-briefs as earlier in the field.

He suddenly remembered the events of the morning and the tears just came out from him again, just as Christian opened his front door, catching Trevor as he collided with his bare chest.

"Shh... baby, what is it?"

He rocked him gently, running his fingers through his damp, dark red hair, feeling the firmness of Trevor's body against him.

"What is it?" he asked again.

"I fucked up so bad," he let out in great belts, struggling for air.

"When? Today?" Christian asked, shaking his head.

"With everything; I'm just so fucked-up, Christian, so fucked up...."

Again Christian shook his head, trying to quell his boyfriend's silence.

"No, you're not fucked-up, I am... I'm fucked-up for ever leaving you."

In that moment, Christian realized that he could not go through with this awful scheme; he was too in love with Trevor and was willing to risk it all for his childhood friend—even the bounties of high school popularity.

Nothing mattered but holding Trevor and tasting the sweet salt of his skin between his lips. To look him in the eyes and know that all the mysteries of the universe resided within him—and though they may never be revealed, they were still there; a secret promise of a land outside of the limitations of South Hill.

"Let's go to bed," Christian suggested with a yawn; taking Trevor's hands and kissing them before allowing them to linger on his fingers while they made their way up the grand steps, turning out the lights in the hall.

Christian's room was immense, with purple walls with silver swirls, and two chairs and a couch made of crushed velvet the color of plum. There was a fireplace made of marble that was unlit, and Christian's trophies sat along the mantle and on the shelves, representing a world that was so different from his own.

They spoke not a word as Christian removed Trevor's shirt. Running his hands along his firm body, just as taut and fit as his own, and this time Trevor gave no objection when he went to unfasten his pants.

There was only a brief pause before going the rest of the way, revealing his thick, hard cock.

They were soon beneath the sheets, following with the rhythm of each other's bodies, the sweat glistening on their backsides. The moment was made in silence: Christian removed a condom from his nightstand and slipped it on, careful as he guided himself inside of Trevor, who only winced before loosening his muscle to allow him entry.

For nearly an hour they rocked back and forth; Christian guiding his lips along Trevor's neck and shoulders, their eyes meeting and both boys sighing while Christian reached down and worked him from underneath, not caring about the sheets. The winds began to howl, and if any attention had been paid, then Trevor would have realized that it was Jonathan mourning the final loss of his young Blackmoore, who was now drifting in a sea of forbidden ecstasy.

And the snow continued to fall.

They had fallen asleep in the parlor, having drunk two more bottles of wine after they had taken care of Tom's body, and even as the daylight began to slip through the windows and cast blue light on the floorboards, Kathryn and Mabel did not move; it appeared nothing could wake them.

Through their drunken slumber they began to stir, rustling as if plagued by a bad dream: a dream that the two women shared, a dream that only they could feel due to their exceptional heritage.

They sat across from each other in two arm chairs, their bodies stirring just a little, and an awful realization came to them, one which thrusted them into the world of the waking.

"Trevor!" they let out in unison, staring at one another wide eyed and full of despair, feeling the dark presence of the Legacy suddenly take fill of the home and shake them with foreboding violence.

"He's done something," Kathryn was saying, suddenly rising and pacing the floor as she had always done when plagued with too many uneasy thoughts and not enough answers.

"Yeah, something he shouldn't have done," Queen Mab responded, watching her niece and fighting back the urge to join her.

"Braxton?" Kathryn asked, wiping the sleep from her eyes.

"No, no... Braxton was supposed to happen. Braxton would be a good thing, but this... this is different—very different."

Kathryn shook her head and walked to the table with the scotch, reaching for the pack of cigarettes next to the glasses, taking one, then offering another to her aunt who took it, both women lighting up and trying to calm their nerves.

"Then Christian...." Kathryn tried to push the impossible from her head.

It wouldn't go that far, she told herself. *He wouldn't go that far....*

"The Vasquez boy?"

Kathryn nodded.

"Jesus, things are off-balance. What could have thrown things so off-course?"

It was too much for the both of them to bear. Things always steered a little off-course, but in the end you got back there; it became right again. But whatever it was that had happened, it was by the influence of others; it was an intervention that would possibly doom them all.

"We have to fix this—"

"We don't even know what *this* is—"

"I think I do." Kathryn concluded. Her steely eyes watching the grayish smoke dance in the air like flittering ballerinas.

There was a pain in his heart when he woke up that morning. The loss of something great began to swell within him, and he feared that there was no turning back.

Braxton knew this feeling well: it was the same feeling that he had had when his mother, Tammy, died of her tumor; it was the same feeling that he had when his father, Eric, suddenly became a living ghost in his own house.

It was a feeling that made him sick.

When he had gotten home last night, his house on the lake appeared empty; desolate; like a barren desert vacant of life.

His heart hung heavy with the events of the night before, and Trevor's lips still seemed to burn on his. It was something that was supposed to work out so right and instead failed miserably. Falling short of destructive.

"What am I going to do?" he asked himself.

His voice was hoarse from crying until the wee hours of the morning, and his clock was already telling him that he was going to be late for school.

"Why bother?"

The one person he loved was with someone else, and for the first time in five years he felt empty. Trevor had filled a void within him, a void left by two dead parents, and now that void returned, no longer filled with the adoration of his friend.

He stood around looking for something to wear when the sudden conclusion dawned on him: he was going to go to the source, the one person who might be able to get through to Trevor.

He was going to go to his mother.

He had only met Kathryn Blackmoore a couple of times, but he knew that she loved her son and despised the Vasquez family. He was going to reveal everything to her and pray that she could intervene, perhaps open her son's eyes and set everything right again.

Quickly he threw on a pair of khakis and a black turtle-neck, the only turtle-neck that he actually owned, and took off out the door, ready to speed over to the two-story manor on Knox Street.

"Morning," Christian whispered, tracing his fingers along Trevor's bare stomach, his erection pressing against his left butt-cheek, the aroma of sex lingering in the air.

"Morning," Trevor responded, feeling warm inside, though there was a slight burning sensation at the bottom of his spine. They were warm and together. Christian no longer feeling empty, and satisfied with what felt like an event that was ten years in the making.

"Shit... we need to get ready for school." Trevor said, finally taking notice of the polished mid-century round gold clock on Christian's wall. The face white and the times in gold Roman numerals.

The mention of school threw them both off, reminding Trevor of what had happened with Braxton, and reinforcing for Christian the plot concocted with Cheri and Greg. Neither one of them wanted to face the day, and yet they both knew that they had to. There was still so much left unraveled and the two boys needed to fix it up.

"Don't worry, it'll be fine," Christian told him, though he knew the doubt that weighed itself on his brain. He knew that the school's social order was about to be broken and there was nothing that he could do about it.

"Well, today's the day," Greg was saying to her, shuffling through the halls of Mariner High School, dressed in loose-fitting jeans and a long-sleeved, collared sweatshirt decorated with blue-and-mustard-yellow horizontal stripes, the letters *A & F* emblazed on his left breast. He wore a white tee underneath, and a navy blue baseball cap on his head; casting a shadow over his cold eyes.

"Yes, it is..." Cheri responded, hearing the sadness in her own voice. She didn't want to do this, knowing that it had gone too far and realizing she really didn't want to hurt Trevor. Her ire was for

Christian—for both of these young men who ruined Trevor and taught her the same would happen to her if she didn't keep up.

In fact, all she wanted was to have him back.

"Greg, am I different?"

He turned and looked at her with confusion; obviously deep conversation wasn't his strong point.

"Never mind."

He shook his head and rolled his eyes, mumbling a "whatever" as they walked, not really knowing what was going on inside of her.

Cheri Hannifin didn't want to be different. She was a senior and soon she would be going away to college, and the thought of looking back on her adolescent years and seeing that all she had been was a bitter, cruel, vicious bitch terrified her. What was worse was the idea of looking back and seeing that she had hurt the one person who had ever seen her for her, and had loved her for it.

It was enough to make her throw up all over the hallway.

"I can't do this," she said, suddenly realizing that the videotape was in Greg's book-bag, knowing that for him that was worth more than gold, which meant that he wouldn't give it to her for anything—not even for a blowjob and a fuck.

"You can't do what?" he asked her, suddenly stopping and demanding an answer.

"This! This plot against Trevor and Christian. I don't want to hurt anyone!"

He curled his fingers into his palms, fighting back the urge to hit her across the face.

"Do I have to remind you that this little plot was your idea in the first place?!" He said it loudly, but not enough to draw attention.

"I know, but I changed my mind." She averted her gaze to the floor and before she knew it, Greg had her by the arm and he was dragging her into the stairwell.

"You listen to me, you little bitch! You have two choices here: you can either go through with this, or I can go ahead and tell everyone what we do together."

She rolled her eyes, not really caring.

"Go ahead and tell, you asshole; no one will believe you. Everybody loves me."

Greg laughed at her response.

"Really, everyone? Why don't you go ask Teri? She's just waiting for you to get out of the way, and then there's Trevor."

His name coming from Greg's mouth made her sick.

"Yeah, that's right; ask Trevor Blackmoore if he still loves you.

"Now, you say no one will believe me? That's fine, but do you really want to take that chance? I mean, I'm a guy; people forgive that. We're supposed to go around fucking the hell out of girls, but you..."—he dug his fingers into her flesh—"You're a girl. Once people find out... once Daddy finds out... you'll be nothing more than a slut, and there's no coming back from that!"

Tears sprang from her eyes. She knew that he was right; there was no coming back from that, not in South Hill and not for all of those students who hated and feared her, and the idea of her father finding out was enough to make her think about killing herself in the girl's bathroom.

She was trapped, and she hated it.

"Now get out of my fucking sight!"

He tossed her towards the hall and watched as Cheri walked away, disappointed in her gutless pleas. He was so close to getting Christian out of the way that nothing was going to stop him, not even the one girl he loved more than anything else.

The skeletal maples that lined Knox Street looked monstrous against the blue-gray morning sky, and the emerald green front door seemed like a glittering jewel within dead white.

Braxton's dark, chocolate-brown eyes were focused on that front door, knowing that Kathryn Blackmoore was most likely home since she had a "thing" about going out in public; at least, that's how Trevor always put it.

The sudden thought of Trevor brought back that same pain, and he wanted so desperately to put a stop to it.

He made his way up the front walk and took a deep breath before knocking, hoping that Kathryn wouldn't be too angry with him showing up so early in the morning. The door quickly swung open and Kathryn stared at him, a cigarette in hand, still dressed in that dark red dress from the night before.

"Braxton?"

He nodded.

"What are you doing here; shouldn't you be at school?" she asked again.

"I'm sorry for dropping by, Mrs. Blackmoore, but I need to talk with you... it's about Trevor."

The mention of her son seemed to register some sort of shock and she stepped aside, allowing him to come in.

He did.

"So, this is Braxton Volaverunt?" Queen Mab said to him, staring with knowing eyes.

"How did you know that?" he asked, having never met the old woman before in his life.

"I know a lot of things."

Her words sent chills down his spine but he shrugged them off, easing himself into the couch.

"But what I'd like to know now is what is going on with my nephew?"

Braxton nodded and began to tell them everything—from what he had found out that morning on the soccer field, to the night previous when he had kissed Trevor, and the strange phone conversation that he apparently didn't have with his best friend.

"... And so that's it. I hope I haven't done any harm here in telling you that Trevor is into guys—"

"Oh, no; you'd be surprised at how many times something like that has happened in this family," Kathryn said, inhaling from her cigarette.

Queen Mab laughed and gave a wink to her niece.

"I'm just so worried about Trevor, and this isn't right. I know I'll probably never get him back," he began to choke up again. "But I don't want him to get hurt, and it's already gone far enough that he will, but I think it would be much better for him if he got the upper hand.

"I'd tell him myself but I know that he wont listen to me, and—"

"Shh... don't give it another thought. Everything will be made right again, I promise."

He nodded at the old woman's response, though it granted him little comfort. He stood and was taken aback by the hug that was given to him by the infamous Kathryn Blackmoore—who didn't hung anybody, let alone show any vulnerability or hint that she comprehended human emotion—and what's more, he could tell that she was as equally as surprised.

He went to the door and had just opened it when the old woman known as Queen Mab called out to him.

"What?" he asked her, suddenly realizing by Kathryn's face that she hadn't heard the old woman.

"You put your mind at ease about this, because you and Trevor are destined for far greater things."

He smiled and walked out the door, closing it behind him and pausing for just a moment before walking back to his car, her words mulling over in his head. He only hoped that the old woman was right.

Christian had been in a state of exhilaration all morning, feeling himself righted again and redeemed; it was a great moment. He tapped his pen against his desk, eager to get out of geometry and meet up with Trevor for lunch, wanting to take him someplace personal and private—someplace where they could once again explore the joys of one another's bodies.

He had managed to avoid Cheri Hannifin and Greg Sheer all day, and now that it was reaching its halfway mark, he hoped that this sudden luck would continue.

He caught a scent.

It was light and sweet, like vanilla, and for a moment he thought that it was a lingering of Trevor, as if his cloud still had its sway over the rest of the world, even if it lacked his physical presence—but a voice in the ear told him otherwise.

"Tick-tock, tick-tock...." He turned to see Cheri behind him, her eyes red from what must have been tears, or possibly because she was high, but Cheri wasn't known to get blazed until lunch or after school.

"Shit, Cheri, what are you doing here?" His black eyes were widened with fear; a fear that he did not want to show his cruel friend.

"Looking for you... we need to talk."

He shook his head, not wanting to have any kind of conversation that involved his boyfriend.

"I'm serious. Come on!" she commanded.

Christian rolled his eyes and stood, slipping out without his teacher's permission; he was too busy catching up on his sleep to take notice anyways.

"All right, what's this all about?" he asked her.

They were standing in the empty hall. A few stray doors opening here and there, and the glimpse of lone students could be seen only briefly, most of them on their way to the bathrooms or to skip out.

"It's about the thing with Trevor—"

"I don't want any part of it anymore. I really, really like him and he likes me. He more than likes me... he loves me, and I love him!"

It felt good to finally be able to say it. To profess his secret to someone who wasn't Trevor or his own confused head and heart—and what surprised him most of all was that Cheri did not seem the least bit shocked.

"That's good and fine, Christian...." She took a deep breath, gazing down the hall as if anticipating someone. "But before you go singing it from high above the mountains, you should remember this love of yours was built on a lie.

"And what's more: if Trevor finds out the truth, do you really think that he'll want to see you again?"

The pain was visible on his face and it made Cheri feel good to see it, to know that he was hurting over Trevor, to get him back for that morning five years previous when he officially shut Trevor out of their circle.

"I don't expect him to find out... not ever!"

She shook her head, knowing that every day more and more of her was falling away, wilted with bitterness and cruelty.

"Well, then, you better get a head start on Greg letting Trevor discover the truth, 'cause as it stands right now... you're sure to lose."

He could feel his heart stop; he was sure of it, and the entire life that he was planning for he and Trevor looked to be funneling down the drain.

"What did you do?"

She shook her head.

"What did you do?!" Christian shouted.

He took hold of her arms and shook her, digging his fingers into the same spot as Greg had. The pain made her suddenly feel alive. She felt like a woman for the first time, and when you knew enough to drive men crazy with self-doubt, when you knew enough secrets to break them, then you could do anything.

"Greg has a video of you with Trevor. In fact, I tried to take it from him this morning. I told him that I had no desire to go through with this. Even though I wanted to humiliate you so badly, though I wanted your trophies broken at your feet because of what you did to Trevor five years ago."

The tears were spilling down her cheeks and her chestnut eyes were suddenly luminous, making her look like an angry girl; angry because she was helpless and alone in a world of men.

"Even after all of that, I couldn't go through with this plan—this plan that I started, no less—and all because I couldn't see you hurt Trevor again.

"Not in front of everyone again. Not like before. Not this time. Not when I would have a truly real part in its send-off!"

He backed away from her, not knowing what he had done, but aware of the fact that it was going to be a repercussion that would last forever, perhaps never forgivable; it all seemed to be ending terribly for him. And in a way, he felt that it was poetic justice.

"Shit, what do I do?"

He was crying now, clutching his fingers to the back of his head, pulling on hairs that were too short to really hold onto.

"Break it off with him the right way. Make up whatever you have to, in whatever way you feel will make him hate you less, but do it."

He looked up at her, seeing the monster that he had created out of his own fear—a monster who, like him, was trying to redeem itself.

"And do it before Greg gets to him. Because if Greg tells him about this plan, it'll be over for you... and what's worse, Greg will push even further to show that video."

He stood and began to walk from her, but after ten paces or so he turned and ran back, taking her face in his hands and gently kissing her on the forehead.

As he walked away, Cheri understood what the kiss meant; it wasn't for friendship and it wasn't a thank-you. It was just a clear, simple message relayed without words, a message which said: "*see you in hell.*"

"You will."

She turned and walked the opposite way, determined to get the video back from Greg, no matter what it took to do it. She had already sold her soul, all she needed to do now was collect payment.

The world felt cold to him, walking between the physical and the mental, trying to alleviate the guilt that he felt inside of his heart.

Trevor had scoured the entire campus trying to find Braxton, wanting to speak with him about the night before, hoping to repair the cord that was severed between them, and wishing that he could fix it all.

He still wore the clothes from the night before, and those clothes smelled of both Christian and Braxton. The scents of the two boys were just as jumbled and intertwined as his feelings.

He sat on a bench between the library and Mariner's little the-ater—the tiny concrete space that had a view of the parking lot, hoping that he would spot Braxton's car, but to his disappointment his car was not there. So he decided to wait, missing his classes but not really caring; if Braxton showed up, then he wanted to be the first to see him.

"Trevor...."

He heard Christian's voice and turned around, seeing him standing there at the foot of the paved steps, his eyes red and his cheeks streaked with tears.

"Hey... what's wrong?" He could feel his heart begin to pound as Christian came closer, and his stomach began to fill with the most sickening feeling.

"I have to tell you something... but if you talk I'll lose my nerve. I'll lose myself in you, and I just can't do that!" He sniffled, and the tears came again.

Trevor wanted to go to him and comfort him, but he knew that Christian had suddenly drawn an invisible line between them; a line that he could not cross.

"Christian you're worrying me."

He put his hand up to protest.

"Please, just don't, okay? Let me do what I have to do."

Trevor nodded and took a deep breath, knowing that he wasn't going to be prepared for whatever Christian had to say.

"This is just so hard; I never thought that it would be this hard."

He didn't want to cry, but he couldn't stop the tears from com-ing.

"Are you breaking up with me?"

His words caught in his throat and he stood, though he didn't mean to. It was reflexive, and he was offended to see Christian avert his gaze from his own.

"Shit, Trevor... you need to be with someone who can hold hands with you in public. You need to be with a guy that can be everything that you need him to be."

He hated this. Hated knowing that he was hurting Trevor again, and this time it was to protect him not to shun him; but what did it matter? The effect was still the same, and in the end Trevor would be the one left broken.

"Do you have any idea what I had to give up for you? The people who I hurt by being with you? Does that even register in your head?" Trevor was shaking.

"Baby, I'm sorry—"

"Don't! Your words mean nothing to me."

He was sniffling now and he didn't bother to wipe away the tears that were running down his face, the tears that stained his flushed cheeks and hung on his lips. The cold air was a comfort now, and the snow that was freezing up and becoming like rock, felt like a physical manifestation of his embittered heart.

"Please Trevor...."

He knew that something inside of him was dying; he could feel the poison within and he knew that he could never get it out in time. He was slipping, and now no one would be there to catch his fall.

"Don't say my name; why do you have to say my name?" He was walking towards Christian now, and then past him, but he could get no further than his shoulder when Christian stepped over to block his path.

"Now, stop... just stop!" He held tight to his arms, refusing to let go. It seemed that touching Trevor burned his fingers; it was like fire, the feel of his body too intense to be controlled.

"Let me go, Christian."

He shook his head.

"No. Look, I understand that your hurting; I can see that, but—"

"That's just it, Christian." He pushed him away. "You don't see. You don't see my pain; you don't see the pain that you put me through for the past five years... you don't see anything!"

Trevor felt a great heat rush through every part of his body, much like a fever, and just as quickly as it was there it was gone and so was he.

Suddenly, watching Trevor rush past him down the breezeway and towards the sidewalk that led onto Bill McDonald Parkway, Christian finally let go: his knees buckling before slamming to the ground, the tears spilling down his face and the great heave of his sobs filling the air.

He was empty, and he knew this. Trevor had made him feel alive; his presence had quickened him once more, and now it was over. He could no longer be there for Trevor, he could no longer play the role of the protector, of the guardian angel. That time had passed and he needed to let him go, needed to release him, and he knew just who to release him to.

"It's finished."

Cheri could see by the look on Greg's face that he couldn't accept this, and his steely blue eyes were expressing that anger; the same went for his tightening fists.

"What do you mean, 'it's finished'?" His voice was gruff, like an animal's, and he was becoming hot with rage.

They were standing in the men's restroom in one of the back halls, a restroom that was supposed to be closed for toilet repairs; they both knew that they wouldn't be bothered.

"I had Christian end it with Trevor; I let him do it in his own way."

Cheri had watched the breakup from afar and it had brought a sudden fit of tears to her eyes, tears that for a moment, felt like they would never end.

"Why? I thought we were going to... I mean...." He was pleading now, trying to make sense of it, and the truth was that there was no sense to be made.

"We're monsters, you and I. We became something, something that I don't want to be... something that I know we're going to go to hell for."

She didn't want to be having this conversation. In fact, she only wanted to crawl into a hole and die; to disappear for the remainder of the school year, allowed to repent for five years of growing sin.

"No, this is crazy talking; we're so close to getting what we want. So close to punishing Trevor, so close to getting rid of Christian; I mean, this is what you wanted!"

He began to shed tears, but they were angry tears, tears of utter frustration. Cheri knew that he didn't care what kind of person he was becoming.

"I don't want it anymore."

She began to shake, suddenly afraid of Greg Sheer, knowing what kind of contempt boiled inside of him, just waiting to come to the surface.

"What do you mean, you don't want it anymore?"

He began to knock his fists against his legs, and Cheri Hannifin started to regret every moment that she had ever spent with him.

"Exactly what I said. We can't go around doing this to people, people that we've known our entire lives; it's just—"

"It's just what?"

"It's just wrong," she sighed, feeling a relief that took her by surprise.

To be able to admit the faults in her behavior was freedom, and it really didn't matter to Cheri that it pissed Greg off, or that she stood to experience his wrath.

"You know what, Cheri?"

She shook her head, seeing the stoicism in his eyes, the burning rage that emanated from his pupils.

Before she could think of some clever, snide remark, Greg slammed himself into her, his entire weight colliding with her petite frame, knocking her against the wall and gripping her arms with brute strength.

"You're weak," he growled in her ear. "You're a pathetic little rich girl who suddenly decided to grow a conscience. You think you know where your power is, but it isn't in your mind."

He brought his hand from her arm and trailed it to the place between her legs, her secret space that only Greg had known and was now trespassing.

"It's here. But guess what?" he continued to growl. "It no longer has power over me."

For a moment, before everything went quiet and hazy, Cheri looked at Greg through teary brown eyes and saw him as he truly was: a scared little boy still oblivious to his place in the world.

In that instance of realization, Greg placed his hand on her forehead and smiled before gritting his teeth and slamming her head against the wall; the back of her skull knocking against the tile and bringing her to the ground.

His image became hazy as she laid out on the tile, unable to keep her eyes open or her mind steady.

In that moment of numbness she could only think of one thing: Trevor Blackmoore.

"Bitch," Greg huffed, looking down on her and shaking his head.

He walked towards the wood door and threw it open, leaving the restroom as if nothing had happened. He knew that eventually Cheri would wake up, and he also knew that she wouldn't tell. If she did, questions would be asked and her own sins would then be revealed; it was something Greg knew that she could never risk, and that was security.

For the rest of the day Greg Sheer thought of only one thing: getting Christian. It wouldn't be a difficult task to accomplish; after all, he had the video in his backpack, and that was all anyone could ask for.

FIFTEEN

He hadn't smoked a cigarette since he was twelve, and now Braxton found himself easing through his father's entire pack while sitting out on the deck overlooking the lake, silently saying goodbye to his one love; knowing that Trevor was gone and there was nothing that could be done about it.

The chill felt good to him, and he sat out in nothing but a gray tank and jeans, subconsciously praying that he would catch cold and suddenly take ill, the act concluding with his death.

Dark brown eyes like chocolate gazed out and yet saw nothing, and the bangs of his black hair hung in his lids, giving him the look of a ghost when taken in with the sight of his paling olive skin.

He no longer shivered. That had passed at least twenty minutes ago and now he was comfortably numb, feeling as if he could be here forever.

Braxton looked at his lakeside house, and he quickly realized that sometimes he'd like nothing more than to watch it burn.

The crunching footfalls on the gravel drew his attention back into the present, and the sight of who stood before him stirred the impulse to kill to a fever pitch.

"Braxton...."

It was Christian Vasquez.

He looked like hell, as if he'd been crying for days. His eyes were bloodshot and weary, his stance off-base, and all the confidence that he had possessed was now taken from him; leaving him to be nothing more than an eighteen-year-old boy.

"Christian."

He didn't want to have any conversation about Trevor Blackmoore, especially if it would be Christian gloating about how he got to him first. but upon further inspection, Braxton was able to shove this idea out of his mind.

"Look, we need to talk."

Braxton nodded but stood his ground, refusing to move out of the way. This was not going to be an easy discussion for either one of them.

"Okay; what?"

Christian nodded, as if expecting the sharp tone. He understood what Braxton was saying: *There's no reason to pretend that we're cordial.*

"Look, you don't like me, and, well, I don't like you. I think you're pretty much a welfare whore, though obviously, looking at this place, you're not—"

"Your point?" Braxton interrupted.

"I ended it with Trevor; I told him what I needed to."

Braxton's mouth fell open.

"You told him the truth?"

It was unlikely, and Christian shook his head in response.

"He doesn't need to know the truth. Telling him that it all started out as a cruel game would probably take away the last shred of dignity that he has.

"Besides, it stopped being a game a long time ago...."

His throat choked up and Christian turned away, shaking the tears away.

"The point is that it's over and I can't hurt him anymore, not that I want to."

Braxton still had no words for Christian; he could not deny his joy in seeing the great Christian Vasquez suffer.

"Why are you telling me this?"

He folded his arms across his chest, feeling his heart pumping the blood quickly through his veins.

"Because he needs you, and you need him."

The water lapped against the shore beneath the deck, and yet in this serenity both boys were filled with nothing more than chaos.

"It was wrong for me to step in; it was wrong for me to try to stir up old feelings. I'm not going to lie to you, Braxton, I love Trevor; I love him more than anything, but I know that I need to let him go. I need to give him back to you."

Braxton shook his head, disbelieving what was being said to him.

Is this fucker serious?

"I think that isn't going to happen. I fucked up."

Christian laughed at this proclamation.

"Maybe, but maybe not. How are you going to know unless you try? I mean, I practically ruined his life for the past five years, and yet he let me into his world again. A world that's as intoxicating as any drug... but he let me in.

"If he could forgive me for that, then I'm sure you still have a shot."

Both boys nodded in understanding; a silent reparation was made, and it promised to seal their grudge.

"I don't even know where to start...."

Braxton's words trailed off, suddenly feeling the cold again, and in a way becoming alive with the possibility of still having a chance to make it right with him and Trevor.

"Well, you can start by getting dressed and going to him; I'm sure that he's home by now."

Braxton nodded and grinned, turning to go inside, feeling no need to say goodbye to the one guy who gave away his lease on Trevor's heart.

"But Braxton...."

He turned and gave a tilt with his head.

"Be careful with Trevor; he's not what he seems."

Braxton grinned.

"I know that."

"No, I mean he truly is something else. He's a witch."

Braxton rolled his eyes and tightened his fists.

"God, not this shit again."

Christian shook his head, frustrated with Braxton's refusal to understand.

"I'm serious. I love him, without a doubt, and I always have, but you need to be careful. There are things in his house, things I tried a long time to ignore, but they're there. And Trevor—his whole family—they know things without you telling them ...."

Digging into the past like this was getting a little uncomfortable, but he felt like Braxton should know what he was signing up for.

"We used to have this game, Trevor and I... when we were little. It was like hide-and-seek, but I would hide somewhere in his house and he would stay upstairs in the play room. I would find a place and stay there for five minutes and then I would come back to him.

"He would tell me where I was, and he knew all of the time; he never got it wrong.

"Trevor could also hear the thoughts in my head, and towards the end... well, I would purposely ask him something or tell him something in my mind, and he would answer me."

"What? Should I be afraid of him?"

Christian laughed.

"Look, sharing a different kind of relationship with him, one beyond friendship, is like being drunk. Half the time you're not even sure of who you are anymore, and you're constantly questioning every move you make. I mean, Jesus; he's a ruin to people...."

Braxton nodded and walked towards Christian. He extended his hand and he took it, delivering a firm grip, but it wasn't the grip that took Braxton off-guard.

Through the window of his mind he saw an image. It was quick: A dark Mustang squished into a tree, the trunk tilted down, and the lights of police and EMTs appeared to fill the vision—then it was over. Braxton was unable to comprehend its meaning, which was a natural phenomenon when coming down from one of these flashes.

"What is it?" Christian asked with questioning black eyes. Braxton shook his head and said it was nothing.

He offered a nod and retreated into his home, leaving Christian alone on the porch.

It had started out as a headache as soon as Braxton Volaverunt had returned to his house, and Christian had dismissed it as nothing more than the stress of the day. Quickly, though, his vision began to blur, finding himself squinting as he made his way through Chuckanut Drive, winding around the large pines and Douglas firs.

The snow had ceased but the roads were slick with ice, and now it seemed that even squinting wasn't going to help him.

"What the fuck is going on?" he said, turning down his stereo, while his Mustang raced along the isolated drive. *Everything will be Alright* by the Killers hummed through his car's speakers and his vision was suddenly next to nothing, a splotch of color in a darkening world.

He made one slight turn around a rocky bend and his tires slid atop black ice, and without his sight Christian knew that he was fucked.

He began to let out bleats of tearful frustration as he struggled to regain control of the car, simply enough to bring it to a halt in order to use his cell phone and call for help, but it was no use.

The blue Mustang took out a metal rail guard, tearing up part of the passenger door.

He rolled down a slick, grassy slope before ending against a tree, crashing into it with such force that it ripped through the front of the car, forcing the engine into the front seat and snapping the tree in half, the trunk coming down on top of Christian Vasquez and cracking his skull.

He knew that his death would be painful. The blood was already too much, and yet he felt as if he should have been at peace.

He had experienced what it was to be loved and he felt that he had saved his soul; it really should have been enough.

Fuck that! he thought to himself. *After doing the right thing and sacrificing myself on the altar of love, I get to die?*

That's really fucked-up.

He looked at the irony of everything and was ready to accept death—not because he wanted to, but because he had to.

He was sliding over an engine that had part of itself inside of his body, and he was bleeding from a crack in his skull from a tree that probably weighed over a ton and had most likely fell on him at a speed twice its weight.

While falling into death, he thought of one thing: he hoped that something like heaven existed, and if it did, he hoped that it would be a place that was forever Trevor's backyard and that he could be eleven years old again: Always summer and always with his childhood friends, destined to play hide-and-seek for the rest of eternity.

Trevor walked home with tired strides. The breakup with Christian and the tears that followed had completely worn him out, and all he wanted to do was sleep. He had toiled around for a couple of hours, replaying the situation over and over again, desperate to make sense of it. In fleeting instances he felt as if Christian was there inside of him, a familiarity at the base of his spine and a pressure as if he were still fitted behind him.

These moments were quick to pass, though the passing was always mourned.

He wiped tears from his eyes as the fiery cold snowflakes and the breeze licked his face and stung his eyes. He knew that he would confront him on it later. He'd demand an explanation for his sudden dismissal—and if this breakup had been given much thought, then why did he sleep with him?

Trevor stood on the curb at the edge of his yard, staring down at the bay and the slow movement of the Alaska ferry coming into port. The beauty of winter, the beauty that was normally never lost on him, was nothing more than a gray mess, and he wished for those summers again.

Summers that were spent with kids playing hide-and-seek.

A sudden breeze swept through the naked oaks and the assorted evergreens shook the snow from their limbs as if waking from a long slumber. The breeze caught Trevor's attention instantly, the strangeness of the wind sending a chill to his bones; passing every muscle and every nerve—causing him to question what it was that was in that wind.

There was sadness in it. A message imprinted within its invisible force, and Trevor searched about with frantic eyes.

"Jesus..." he said, slapping his hand over his mouth, as if he had been talking when words were not allowed. He closed his eyes, feeling those snowflakes like tattoo needles on his skin, and the sudden sense of not being alone on the street.

One by one the caws of crows came near, surrounding him and taking up watch in the row of trees along the street. He knew what it must have meant. Crows were bad omens; he had heard them on the day his father had died, had heard them when Darbi's mother, Mona, had gotten in the car accident that killed her. A murder of crows was never good. And now he was in the thick of their murder.

Trevor opened his eyes to find them staring down at him, and to his surprise they were at his feet, as if expecting him to do something.

"Shoo... go away, you dumb birds!" Trevor said, waving his hands and scooting away, nearly walking back on himself.

They came closer to him, pecking and squawking at one another, and yet making no violent advances towards Trevor.

"Go!" He kicked his foot out but they only hopped back once before continuing their approach. In his head he had calculated sixty crows, and memories of scenes from *The Birds* flashed across his brain. He was convinced that at any moment the black things with the sharp beaks would be swooping in for the kill.

He took a quick glance down the alley which led to the back of his aunt's house and spied Christian standing there, a carpet of crows at his feet, taking guard along the lane.

Christian Vasquez looked so strange. A gaping wound seemed to take out part of his stomach and his lower right side. Blood dripped from this, and his head was ebbing with the red bubbly substance; it was like a fount from the center of his skull, and his finger was extended towards Trevor.

He directed his full attention to his former friend and lover, but the apparition was long gone and the crows just stared.

"Christian...?" Trevor whispered to the wind, and the crows responded, opening their wings and taking to the sky, soaring passed him like a great cloud.

Trevor screamed, though it was inaudible through the thick sound of flapping wings, and he ran through them, narrowly avoiding the birds and their sharp beaks.

"Shit!" He fiddled with the lock on the front door and slipped inside, taking comfort in his dark and musty home; safe from the horrors of the outside.

The smell of incense and the light from the small votives lit Kathryn's face and the eyes of the white plaster saints stared back at her from the tallest podiums, as if shocked that she was the only one in the pews.

She rolled the black beads of her rosary between her fingers and whispered silently to herself, ignoring the tears that streaked her face. She hated this place. The Church of the Sacred Heart sat just blocks from her house: a simple white structure with a modest spire.

This place that she had attended as a child, and the school across the street which cost her more than just her sanity: it had also taken her soul.

It was a little more than three decades ago that Kathryn had first killed a man, a man who professed to be a man of God. It was now, in light of what had happened to her ex-husband, that this would be the perfect place to mourn for her soul; knowing that she would surely go to a place called hell once she died.

There was no excusing what she had done, no matter that in her mind both men deserved it.

For once she was wearing pants: black Versace slacks, with a matching jacket, underneath of which she wore a crimson corset with black lace. Her hair was done in loose, curly tendrils and her Marc Jacobs were hurting her ankles slightly as she kneeled.

She knew that it was getting late and that she needed to be home for Trevor, but first she needed to find solace in the things she had done and the crimes that she had committed.

At quick glance she realized that people were coming in, but upon seeing her there, kneeling before the altar, they turned and left—no doubt knowing that it was Kathryn Blackmoore and therefore not daring to disturb her peace, for fear that the devil had come to make a bargain with his jailer.

"Excuse me?"

Kathryn looked up to see a young priest standing before her, his eyes kind and brown. Kathryn could tell by looking at him that he had no idea who she was.

"Yes?" Kathryn asked with her smoky and seductive voice.

"I did not mean to disturb you, but I noticed that you seemed troubled. I just thought I'd let you know that the confessional is open."

There aren't enough Hail Marys in the world for me, Kathryn said to herself, allowing a slight grin.

"Thank you, Father."

The young man nodded and walked away, no doubt to the confessional where he would wait for her.

Kathryn rose to her feet, making the sign of the cross and staring for a moment at the sorrowful face of Jesus with his crowned heart exposed; telling her that he knew her pain.

Father Malady stepped out from the back room, stopping in his place when his eyes caught with hers. Kathryn nodded and walked away, heading back out into the world. She knew the priest would gossip with the young man, but she could care less. Gossip was natural with her, and though it was annoying how it followed, she knew that she could very well forgive it.

The streets were slick with ice that had frozen over, and the daylight was quickly fading. Yet for her, this growing darkness, this impending shadow, was still her favorite time of day: the threshold between the world of light and the temptation of dark.

It was all a blur at first: her head pounding with a thundering migraine; her body aching all over; her skin cold and covered in gooseflesh. She had no idea how long she'd been out.

Her lids fluttered as she surveyed the darkened bathroom, not at all surprised that no one had come in here. After all, it was closed down, and had been since the end of the previous year.

"Jesus...."

Cheri shook her head and smacked the side of her temple with her open palm, trying to stop everything from spinning, wanting the world to just stay in one place, at least long enough for her to get her bearings.

She stood and dusted debris from off her clothes and looked out of the only window in the restroom to see that daylight was fading fast, and the last thing that she wanted was to be locked up in the school for the night.

I guess I'm lucky that I woke up now instead of much later.

She walked to the door and threw it open, grabbing her purse and her book-bag, slightly stumbling as she made her way into the bright hall.

"What time is it?" she asked, searching for the nearest clock.

When she reached the commons with the assorted green blocked benches she caught sight of one of the clocks above the Coke machine, and to her surprise it was a quarter to five.

"Fuck me!" she said, racing to the large fire doors and throwing them open, not realizing that she had set off the alarm.

In a state of panic, Cheri Hannifin raced to the senior parking lot and excitedly climbed into her BMW, desperate to get home before the cops showed up, though they would most likely end up being campus police from neighboring Fairhaven University.

Her car peeled out of Mariner's parking lot, the tires screeching and sliding just a bit on the forming ice. She only hoped that she would be able to make it to Garden Street in one piece.

If Cheri had bothered to turn on the radio, she would have caught the breaking story about a 2007 Mustang convertible that was found just outside of the city along Chuckanut Drive; the young motorist died slowly with a head wound caused by a fallen tree and permanent damage as a result of the car's engine being lodged into his lower right abdominal region.

One of the officers to arrive called it a "really bloody mess." For the moment though, the incident was far away from the South Hill community, and by the time it would reach their doorsteps, nothing could be done.

SIXTEEN

Trevor sat curled up on his bed, long ago out of tears, but still whimpering with despair.

The Tiffany lamp that sat on his bedside table was the only illumination to his large room, casting eerie shadows on papered walls and aged hardwood floors of pine. The mirror on his armoire reflected him, and he realized how child-like he appeared with his knees drawn up to his chest, held secure by his arms.

His mother had come home from church fifteen minutes earlier—but as was custom, if her son was locked away in his room she would not disturb him, knowing that she was silently grateful at having the chance to be relieved of a parental duty.

Jonathan lingered just beyond his door, and yet he did not invite the specter in—knowing that whatever it said would only be lies and complications to his world, which already appeared to be crumbling.

He had fucked up so much already.

He had turned away from Braxton, who was the one person who had stood by him, and in truth, gotten him to his senior year of high school. He was the only other boy that Trevor had desired in such a manner as he had also desired Christian—and yet, with the possibility of gaining his first love, he threw away the one person who he could never truly be without.

"Braxton...."

The name escaped his lips just as the next assault of tears spilled down his face, more than certain that that would be one relationship that could not be mended.

Since he had gotten home, Trevor had spent most of the time evaluating everything in his life. Yet when it came to Christian Vasquez he could not venture too far; afraid that any stirring of memories would invoke the strange occurrence and apparition that had come to him today.

That was too dangerous right now, and for once Trevor wished that he had just blinked out of existence that day years ago when his childhood friends cast him aside for the sake of popularity.

He closed his eyes and thought on the years spent with Braxton Volaverunt, and all of the times that he had felt like a normal person when in in his presence; basking in the kindness that emanated from his actions and words.

Birthdays where he and Braxton would surprise one another early in the morning or late at night, and they would throw parties where they were the only ones to attend—and yet it didn't matter because they had one another, and that was the only thing that had mattered.

The year of their first homecoming, Braxton had taught Trevor how to dance, and for a moment they had shared something more: a buried attraction that had come to the surface.

The two of them standing in Trevor's room, his head nestled on Braxton's shoulder, his eyes closed, while Braxton held one hand on his back and the other on his head, lightly petting his hair and sighing and grinning—while they moved in a tiny circle in front of the bedroom door.

What had made Trevor conclude that his best friend was straight was that Braxton had taken a girl to homecoming and Trevor had stayed home, trying to convince himself that he didn't have a crush on his friend.

The idea of seeing Braxton kiss a girl or hold her on the dance floor like he had held Trevor was enough to make him sick, and in order to avoid throwing up he had just decided to never inquire about homecoming, or his date for the night.

A sturdy knock on his front door roused Trevor from his memories and shocked him into the present, and he raced to the window to see who it was that had arrived.

By the time he pulled the curtain back he found the front stoop empty, and a set of footsteps too heavy to be his mother's making their way to his room.

Again, another knock.

"Who is it?" he asked, choking on his whimper.

"Trevor it's me... can I come in?"

Shit!

It was Braxton: the one person that he had thought would never speak to him again was now outside of his bedroom door.

"Just a minute!" Trevor called out, grabbing Kleenex from his shelf and wiping his eyes softly, trying to blot away the tears.

"Come in!" He watched as the glass knob turned and the wood door jutted open, scraping across the floor.

"Hey..." Braxton said, grinning, though unable to look at him in the eyes. His body appeared to give way to a slight nervous tremor, though if one hadn't been paying close attention, it would have just as easily gone unnoticed.

"Hello," Trevor said, walking back to his bed and sitting down, leaning back against the headboard.

"I hope you don't mind my coming over. I know I'm probably the last person that you want to see right now, but I had to see you."

Trevor nodded and fought back the urge to reach out to his friend, fought the urge to embrace him and kiss his neck; having self-control was one of his greatest assets.

"What is it?" he asked, looking on Braxton with luminous hazel eyes. His heart was pumping the blood quickly in his chest.

"I don't know how to say this, so I'm just going to say it as quickly as possible. I'm in love with you, Trevor... I have been for so long now, and I just don't know what to do anymore."

His eyes were wide and he looked at Trevor as if trying to gauge some kind of response, and slightly upset by the fact that there was none.

"Jesus, Trevor, do you even understand what it is that I'm declaring here?"

Trevor only blinked, feeling as if he no longer knew what to do. It seemed that all of these people had him in their interest, but none seemed to have Trevor's interest in mind. He felt as if he had been in the middle of some great tug-of-war and he was being ripped apart at the seams of his shoulders.

"Understand? Of course I understand, but at the same time I feel as if I don't want to! It's like I'm this thing: this piece of property that can be tossed around and toyed with. By you, by Christian, even by my own goddamned family!

"I don't know if I can do it any longer... I just don't know."

His words stung Braxton. His declaration that he was being used like a puppet on strings for amusement was hurtful; what was more hurtful was that Trevor had accused him amongst those people.

"Trevor, I'm sorry if you feel that way. I'm sorry if it seems that I've been expecting you to do things, but I only wanted to look out for you, and I think I've been doing a good job of that thus far."

Trevor averted his gaze, knowing that if he didn't get a grip he'd be crying again, and losing his resolve was not an option.

"Well then, why couldn't you make me see what kind of person Christian really was? Why couldn't you make me see that he was going to hurt me?"

Braxton sat down on the foot of the bed, knowing that he had no words for his friend—none that could so adequately describe the anger and frustration that he had felt over the entire situation.

"I did, remember? That day when you came for me in the locker room. That day I told you to be careful with Christian, that there was something that I didn't like about him, that I didn't trust him. But you just shrugged it off; you shrugged me off because you had what it was that you had really wanted!"

It was reaching its peak now; they had both stung one another with accusations, and the two of them wondered how far this would go if allowed.

"I did not shrug you off; I went to that party. I was honest about it with Christian because I needed him to know. The only thing I didn't do was tell him that I loved you!"

Trevor reached out and shoved Braxton off the bed, knocking him square on his ass and sending a mild jolt of pain up through his tailbone.

Braxton got to his feet, but not in time before Trevor was on him, slapping him upside the head and punching his chest.

"You hear me? I love you, get-that-through-your-thick-skull!"

Trevor kept hitting him and then he began to cry, letting out great bleats of sobs, feeling himself go automatic as he continued to swing at him, no longer conscious of his actions; allowing all of his built-up frustration and angst come pouring out of him, letting go of the past few years.

"Jesus, Trevor!"

Braxton cupped his hands around Trevor's buttocks, using his strength to lift him off of him, rising with his legs from the floor and throwing him down on the bed, watching as Trevor bounced lightly before laying out on the covers.

Braxton proceeded to sit on him, straddling the boy's waist and holding his hands down at his sides, tightening the grip on his wrists.

"I don't want to hurt you, but goddamn, kid, you've never swung at anyone before, and I'm a little scared of you right now...."

Trevor looked away and Braxton grinned momentarily, amused by his outburst of anger, and yet at the same time his one and only declaration of love.

Trevor grinned, his eyes suddenly the clearest of greens, and his tongue slid across his lips, moistening them seductively. Braxton leaned forward, making his way to Trevor's face, his heart pounding and a mild erection beginning between his legs as his came closer to Trevor, who was looking at him with hungry eyes.

Braxton's lips parted and the breath passed between them silently, his nostrils flaring just a little with each inhale, sensing a change in the air around them. Dressed in a tight black t-shirt and skinny blue jeans, his black bangs were spiked and a chunk of it was electric blue.

When the tips of their noses touched, Trevor leaned over to his friend's ear and parted his lips, bringing it so close that the hot of his breath sent chills through Braxton's body, and his tongue grazed his earlobe.

"You should be," Trevor whispered, grinning at the pressing of Braxton's hard-on.

"God..." Braxton let out, kissing Trevor's neck, his lids closed. "You could kill me without lifting a finger."

He released Trevor's wrists and was shocked when Trevor went to slipping his fingers up underneath the hem of his shirt, rolling it up over his body. Braxton raised his arms to allow it to be removed all of the way. His chains hung just above his firm chest; he felt his nipples harden as Trevor's fingers trailed down his chiseled abs and took hold of the button of his jeans.

Braxton reached down and pulled off Trevor's shirt in the same manner, seeing an equally firm body beckon to him.

Trevor now appeared dreamy, his eyes lethargic with the onset of lust.

In moments their clothes were off—save for their underwear—and their erections were pressing against one another. The friction alone was enough to make them cum, and the pent up want from the past five years drove them without well-thought planning.

It had come and gone in such a blur. There had been no time for reflection and no chance to understand any kind of consequence.

Braxton had worshipped Trevor between his legs and allowed him to spill inside of his mouth, not even concerned with what this could lead to.

Trevor did not even think about the warnings of his mother, who was one floor beneath them, sitting in the kitchen on one of the stools against the island with an aged merlot in her hand, knowing exactly what was happening upstairs in her son's room and knowing that she could not intervene.

Braxton put himself inside of his friend and they rocked with the motion of one another's bodies for an hour, taking it as slow as possible while trying to keep with the fervor of the moment.

This was meant to happen, they both concluded. They seemed to fit in place in a way that he and Christian hadn't. It was as if they were branched from the same tree, grown from the same seed and planted with the same roots, and for once they were at peace.

Now there was no fear inside of Trevor to let someone else take the wheel and drive. With Braxton he was safe, and with Braxton inside of him he knew that he was protected—that all of the horrible monsters, both human and otherwise, could not reach him and nothing was going to change his world.

"I love you..." Braxton hummed in his ear, his hair slick with sweat, a drop of it falling from the bridge of his nose and landed on the nape of Trevor's neck. He didn't notice.

They were both on the same sea, sailing to the same foreign shore, and once again the world was full of possibility.

"Always..." Trevor responded, placing his hands under his pillow and biting down for just a moment before cocking his head back and letting out a great sigh; a great release of all that had been there, silently telling those phantoms to go.

The two of them had found what they were looking for, and Trevor knew that for once he would be able to sleep.

When it was over, when they were too exhausted to continue, the two boys fell asleep in one another's arms, not bothering to turn out the light or lock the door.

That night, Trevor dreamt that he was sitting in the sun room with his family, all of whom were long ago deceased and decayed: his cousin Brighton's father, Carlton, of Savannah, as well as his cousins Mona and Aria, as well as Jeremiah and Nicholas; all of whom had passed before his own mother was born—except for Mona and Aria, who had passed later.

In this dream they drank tea and ate cucumber sandwiches; they whispered something about the Legacy nearing its end and the final curtain being called.

Even with this Trevor felt no fear, and so they continued to drink tea and eat their sandwiches, unafraid of those who had already passed on and those waiting just around the bend.

SEVENTEEN

Lila Vasquez walked into her early morning house, excited to be back home after her excruciating trip in Europe. She was eager to see her son; it was going to be Christmas in a matter of days and this was Christian's favorite holiday, and there was no way that she was going to miss it.

She knew that she should have stayed in Amsterdam a little longer, perhaps a week at the most, but it was the mother's yearning for her child that drove her to catch the red-eye at the last minute, knowing that she would never be able to forgive herself if she came close to missing the twenty-fifth of December.

"Christian, honey I'm home!" Lila called up the grand stairs, her large black eyes following along the banister to the second floor, expecting her son to throw open his bedroom door and come racing down the steps with his arms outstretched for a hug.

She stood there in a black-and-pink Chanel suit, the matching skirt reaching to her knees and the matching heels tapping on the floor, wondering where her son could be at such an early hour.

Lila looked down at her Cartier watch and saw that it was a quarter-to-six, and Christian wasn't known to be up until seven at the earliest—and even that was on a rare occasion.

The idea sparked in her head to check the four-car garage, and so she did, navigating through the large house that, if it wasn't for the flood lights outside, would be entirely too difficult to get through; especially with all of the antiques and sculptures.

The door jutted open and she flipped on the light, watching it flicker for a moment before casting the cold space in a white electric bath, showing Lila what she already knew deep down: the cars were gone and she was alone in the house; her husband gone with the secretary and her son parading around town in the wee hours of dawn.

The problem for Lila was that the longer she stood there the more and more her fear and concern got the better of her. There was a tightening in her chest as she stared at the empty garage and she placed her hand to her heart and began to rub, trying to calm the unease.

The phone rang.

"What...? Who in the hell would be calling this early?"

As she walked towards the black cordless on the console in the hall beneath an ornate seventeenth-century mirror, she began to sense that something was wrong and that it had to do with her son.

"Jesus, stop ringing, I'm coming!"

She thought how silly it was to speak out to a ringing phone when the person on the other line can't even hear you.

"Hello?" she asked, picking up the receiver.

"Yes, is this Mrs. Vasquez?" It was a man's voice, though much younger than she was—perhaps a couple of years older than her son, at the most.

"Speaking... uh, who is this?"

The man grew silent for a second before finally deciding to answer.

"My name is Officer Simpson with the Bellingham Police Department. Um, ma'am, it's about your son...."

He was somber, and Lila felt as if the air was being knocked out of her.

"What's wrong?"

"Well, ma'am—"

"What the fuck has happened to my son?!" she interjected, feeling the acute sense of nausea taking effect, her head beginning to spin.

"I'm sorry to tell you this, Mrs. Vasquez, but Christian is dead.

"He was in a car accident along Chuckanut Drive; it appears that he had slid on some black ice and...."

Lila was sobbing, gripping her heart and shutting her eyes, not wanting to believe it.

"His body's at the county morgue... if you want you can come by later and see him. I know you have a lot of things that you have to do."

Lila could tell that the young cop was uncomfortable, perhaps because he hated doing this job—or worse yet, it was his first time having to make this phone call.

She wished that she could say "I know how you feel," but this was her first phone call too.

"No... not at this time."

She hung up the phone and allowed her knees to buckle, bringing her to the floor, rocking back and fourth as she screamed, damning God and her husband for giving Christian that car in the first place.

She thought about every moment ever spent with her son. Thought about get-togethers at friend's houses and games played at the park. Lila also thought about all the times she was gone from his life. All those times spent traveling the world for her business, all of those months spent abroad and not with her son; it was also in this moment that she realized that she knew nothing about him and what he was doing with his life.

Fuck, she thought to herself, realizing that she had to put everything in the past tense.

For two hours she cried on the floor next to that console beneath the mirror, looking at such a large and empty house.

The laughter of her son—the arguments, all of those things—were never going to be heard again.

Never again would she hear him slam his door or play his music too loud; it was all gone. Death had come and silenced her son's voice, a voice that still had so much to say.

It was in that moment when she could only think of one person to call, and it wasn't her husband. It was a friend that she had not spoken to in five years, and yet was the only person that Lila knew she could speak to without breaking down.

She picked up the phone and dialed.

"Yes?" the raspy female voice answered, the confines of sleep and possible drunkenness not yet gone from her.

"It's me... I need to see you."

Silence. Silence brought on by contemplation.

"Where?"

"*Le Chat Noir*." Again, obvious contemplation.

"All right, Lila."

She sat there, wanting to say more, not quiet ready to give up her familiar voice.

"And Kathryn?"

"Yes?"

She felt the tears catch in her throat.

"It's nice to hear your voice again... I've missed it."

She hung up the phone before Kathryn had a chance to respond, knowing that she couldn't handle any kind of harsh retort, even though she knew she would have deserved it.

Lila got up off of the floor and staggered up the stairs, not really conscious of anything that she was doing. The world was growing bleaker by the second, and she was going to have to learn how to navigate through it unscathed.

Kathryn emerged from her bedroom, stepping out in the darkened hall dressed in a spaghetti-strapped, black silk nightgown with matching robe that dusted the floorboards.

Straight ahead of her was one of two bathrooms in the house, and just before that alongside the wall was her son's room, which was now breathing with a life all of its own.

She felt unsure about the idea of meeting with Lila Vasquez, the woman who had been her best friend throughout high school and college, the woman who had betrayed their friendship and given in to rumors.

Kathryn often wondered if Lila had ever spread any of her own?

As she reached her son's door, preparing to turn the corner and go downstairs to grab her datebook from the office she paused and looked down the hall, seeing the door to the back balcony. For a moment, she thought of Tom Preston and all that had taken place just a few nights ago, wondering about him down in that carriage-house—wondered if he decayed inside of the black lawn bags secured with duct-tape, or did the lack of oxygen keep him from decomposing?

Part of her wanted to go and take a look, but she also knew that disturbing the dead could have grave consequence.

She shook the thought from her head and prepared to make her way to the stairs, when suddenly her son's door creaked open slowly, just enough for the young man inside to slip out.

"Mrs. Blackmoore!" Braxton let out with a whispered gasp, his soft lips parted slightly.

Kathryn felt the mild tinge of lust make itself known between her legs as she looked at this young man. His broad shoulders and firm chest, his flesh olive and soft, his nipples erect and much more brown than pink; expressing the Spanish in his blood.

Her eyes widened at the sight of his abs and the thin line of hair that moved from his navel and made it's way to the semi-bulge beneath his tiny black boxer-briefs, the band reading: *2(X)ist* in white.

His strong, muscular thighs and calves were enticing to Kathryn, who could not deny the attraction that she was feeling towards the young Volaverunt.

"Braxton..." she said, staring at him with cold and calculating ice-blue eyes.

She searched his body and smirked, noticing the band of black stars tattooed around his forearm; making him appear even older than his age of eighteen.

"Nice ink."

She reached out and traced her finger gently along the design, daring to step closer to the young man, pressing her body firmly against his, the bulge between his legs growing, digging into her thigh.

Kathryn closed her eyes and parted her lips, allowing her tongue to slip out, testing Braxton's resolve and commitment to her son—though, deep down, a part of her hoped that this young man would want her, taking her in her arms and telling her that she was far from an old woman—a dried up shrew twice widowed.

Their tongues met and Braxton closed his eyes, going with the flow. He placed a firm grip on her arm and Kathryn could sense a mild kinetic surge pass between them—a feeling that she hadn't known in quite a long time, and she knew then that he was reading her.

He released her, and gently moved Kathryn away from him.

"If I were just some dumb and horny teenage boy, I would have assumed that you actually wanted me."

He looked back briefly to Trevor's door; relieved when he still heard silence from within.

"But I'm not dumb."

Kathryn smiled and held his gaze.

"You don't need to test my loyalty to your son. I love Trevor with all of my heart, and I couldn't be without him even if I tried.

"I'm under his spell."

"Good."

She turned, pivoting on her heel and preparing to make her way down the steps, when she quickly stopped and turned around; her lips spread in a devilish grin.

"But Braxton... you're wrong."

"About what?"

He folded his arms across his chest, his muscles bulking with the movement of his arms.

"About me not wanting you."

His lips curled into a nervous smirk.

"Because I did."

Kathryn winked and made her way down the steps, leaving the dumbstruck young man in the early morning hall; feeling as if he had just been properly initiated into the Blackmoore clan.

Le Chat Noir was located inside of Sycamore Square on the third floor. The inside lobby had a grand fountain and a wrap of ornate stairs led to the top of the brick structure. At the end of the nineteenth century, the building was a series of apartments, and due to a tragic fire a young woman had died—and ever since, her apparition has been spotted wandering the halls and restaurant kitchens ever since.

Kathryn stepped out of the elevator and made a left, walking towards the restaurant's entrance. A series of French paintings hung from the brick walls, and the many windows that faced out to the bay and the rest of Fairhaven were the establishment's only lighting.

She looked about and immediately spied the mahogany bar with its row of stools and large mirror on the wall behind it. Several clear wine glasses hung from the racks over-head, and though the bar was tempting, she had other business to attend to.

Lila Vasquez sat at the table across from the entrance, the white curtains kept closed. Fixed to these windows outside along the ancient brick was a light post with the famous image of the restaurant's namesake, staring out onto the street with its slightly curled tail and lean frame perched on a ledge.

As Kathryn approached, she saw that her former friend was drinking a mimosa—and she had the sudden thought that it was the wrong season to be drinking one of these—but by the heaviness with which she moved her hands, Kathryn realized that she had been drinking more than one.

"Lila..." Kathryn said, staring at her in her formal suit.

Kathryn had just slipped on a pair of Manolo Blahniks and an ankle-length suede coat with mink collar, not bothering to change out of her night gown.

"Kathryn..." Lila responded, motioning to the chair in front of her.

Kathryn nodded and sat down, placing her Burberry handbag on the table, watching in silence as Lila motioned for the waiter.

"How's Trevor?" she asked, downing the last of her mimosa, waving the empty glass around in her hand.

"He's fine. I mean, you know how it is with the anticipation of college, and, well... trying to get along with people in high school."

Kathryn averted her gaze for just a moment.

"You know how it is." She finished. Already bored.

Lila shook her head and watched impatiently as the waiter arrived.

"How's Christian?"

Though Kathryn could care less about the boy who had hurt her son, she knew that it was the polite thing to do.

At that moment the waiter arrived, staring at the two women. The first thing Kathryn noticed was that he looked a lot like the young server Parker from Nimbus, but instead of brown hair, his was blond and a little longer in length.

"Another mimosa, please," Lila asked him, her lids heavy and her eyes bloodshot.

"And you?" he asked, turning to Kathryn.

"An Irish coffee, please."

The waiter nodded and began to turn.

"Christian's dead."

Kathryn looked at Lila and felt her heart stop, calling out to the waiter.

"Change that. Just give me a scotch."

The young man nodded and made his way back to the bar, leaving the two mothers to begin a conversation that was years in the making.

Cheri Hannifin awoke that morning feeling as if she had slept for the first time in five years. The process of redeeming her soul lifting many a weight off her shoulder—weights that she hadn't even realized were there.

The gray morning light shone through the bay windows of the turret room, casting a cold glow on the oak floors, the air brisk and refreshing as it came through her open window.

She sat there in her baby-blue tee and tiny cotton shorts, rubbing her hands through her hair and wondering if Christian had felt the same way, if doing the right thing had made him sleep better?

She knew that she would have to ask him later, perhaps when they returned in January from winter break.

Lazily, she reached over for her remote control and flipped on her new plasma TV, watching as the crisp screen lit up with images of a crushed blue Mustang convertible, the name *Christian Vasquez* displayed across the screen.

Cheri felt her heart race and her body begin to shake with slight tremors as the tears welled in her eyes and spilled down her face, dripping off her cheeks and landing on the soft white linen of her bedspread.

Her mind raced with what to do, and she quickly grabbed the phone and dialed the first number that came to mind, and the only voice that she had wished to hear at the moment.

"You're not going anywhere!" Braxton said, reaching his hands under Trevor's legs and gripping his thighs, flipping him on his back.

The two boys rolled around on his bed in nothing more than their underwear, Braxton's tongue gently trailing down Trevor's abs and rolling over his crotch, his hot breath on his boyfriend's groin.

The phone rang, causing them both to roll their eyes, but Trevor knew that he needed to answer it.

"Hello?"

"Trevor."

His eyes grew wide and his heart began to pump at an alarming rate.

"Cheri...."

Braxton's head perked up and his eyes widened in response to hearing who it was on the other end.

"Turn on your TV."

Instinctively Trevor stood, and Cheri could hear his bare feet padding across the floorboards and thud down the steps as he made his way into the quiet entertainment room.

"What's wrong?" His voice was already beginning to quiver with unease.

"Just... change it to Channel Four, okay?"

He could hear her voice breaking with what sounded like sobs.

Cheri listened as the television set lifted from its secret compartment and then the sudden sound of the television as Trevor changed it to the appropriate channel, unprepared for the feeling of his heart stopping in mid-beat.

"What...?"

The tears spilled down his face as he stared at the screen.

Christian's senior picture stared back at him and a paragraph listing his accomplishments and a brief history of his life came on the screen, and he suddenly heard Cheri break down too.

"No!"

His knees gave way, bringing him to the floor, his back leaning against the couch. The same couch where he and Cheri had watched late-night creature features; the same couch where he and Christian had slept while Kathryn was at the hospital while his father hemorrhaged to death by a mysterious tumor in his brain. The couch where the head of an eleven-year-old Trevor rested against Christian's chest, lulled by the sound of his heartbeats.

Trevor paid no mind to Braxton racing down the steps at the immediate sound of his best friend's cries, did not budge when he took Trevor by the shoulders and brought him against his chest, allowing his tears to wet his bare flesh.

Braxton took the phone from his hand and placed it to his ear, saying "thank you" before hanging up the line, his eyes focused on the screen.

He tried to stay strong while the realization came to him that he had seen all of this, had shook Christian's hand and had a vision of this newscast, the police like crows scavenging around the crushed sports car—and the onset of guilt, because he had done nothing.

Together they sat, Braxton rocking Trevor back and forth, knowing that there were no words that he could give that would make it right.

"Why does it happen?" Lila asked, attempting her fifth mimosa, staring at Kathryn with pained eyes and speaking with a voice hoarse from crying.

"I don't know. I spent so long trying to figure it out... after the death of my father, later with Sheffield, and yet I came to no conclusion. And I'm no closer to understanding it now than I was five years ago."

Kathryn drank from her glass of scotch, feeling it constrict her throat as it went down.

"He shouldn't have died; I wasn't ready to quit being a mother."

Kathryn nodded, thankful that she hadn't had to bury Trevor—though once, during his sophomore year, she had come close.

The loneliness of being a Blackmoore, the painful shock and realization of who he really was, and the horrible suffering and isolation he had endured from classmates, had pushed him to trying to kill himself. In fact, it had been the first time that she had met Braxton.

She had been woken in the middle of the night by Braxton, his friend whose house he had been staying at for the night. The young man had called and told her that they were at the emergency room because he had found Trevor in the bathroom not breathing, not moving.

A bottle of pain killers and sleeping pills were found next to him on the floor, the bottles close to empty. It had been the scariest moment of her life, and she had started preparing herself for the fact that she would have to be arranging a funeral for her little boy.

"Kathryn..." Lila said, her voice bringing her back into the present.

"Oh, I'm sorry." She took another drink as she waited for Lila to continue.

"I wonder if this is my punishment for not being around more."

The tears came again and in an effort to calm, Kathryn placed her hand over Lila's and shook her head.

"I didn't even know my son, what kind of things he was into, how he was with other people. I just—I deserve to die."

"Listen to me, Lila. We can never know the reasons for things in the moment. Sometimes the pattern of God's plan is open out before us to read, and other times it's a gradual puzzle that takes months, even years, to understand and accept—that's why death is such a mystery."

Lila nodded and looked away, thinking about nothing in particular.

"I just wish I knew something about him."

Kathryn contemplated if she should tell her about Christian and Trevor, if it was her place. After a moments silence and deliberation, she decided that she would.

"I'm going to tell you this now because I don't want it to be gossip later on at the funeral...." She took a deep breath as Lila looked at her with a pressing gaze. "Our sons were together. They had started dating just before he passed away."

Lila looked mildly shocked but then she composed herself with a nod.

"That doesn't surprise me. I had seen the way Christian would close down whenever I would ask him about Trevor and how he was doing.

"In fact, the whole reason that my son had stopped seeing Trevor was because my shit of a husband was afraid that they were becoming too close, and he ordered Christian to stop seeing him."

Kathryn nodded. She had had a feeling that Emanuel had been behind the separation. It made her angry just thinking about it.

"Though I did not understand why your son had reached out to Trevor, I do believe that he loved him with all of his heart. He had shown that while they were growing up, and he began to show it again."

To her own bewilderment, Kathryn began to cry, thinking about the loneliness of her own life, praying that Trevor would no longer know this kind of tragedy.

"Did Trevor love my son?"

It seemed as if a peace were forming within Lila's heart.

"Since they were kids. My son was fiercely devoted to Christian... and he still is, though I don't think he knows yet, and I don't know if I can tell him."

Lila nodded, and the two of them stood, gently kissing one another on the cheek; Kathryn telling the waiter to put it on her tab.

"Please come to the service; I don't think I can do it without you," Lila said, whispering closely.

"I will, and if you need me at all, just call and I'll be there."

The two women parted ways on the street. Lila Vasquez went to wander the shops and Kathryn made her walk up Harris Avenue, preparing herself for what to say to her son and not knowing how.

Death no longer carried any glamour, and the feeling of her body sinking into the earth was very prevalent.

She tried desperately to escape this feeling, but with every step she made along the pavement, the heavier it all became, and she had to fight the urge to give in—to sink into the underground and never again see the light of day.

Kathryn took a deep breath before stepping into her house, unprepared for the sight of Trevor and Braxton clinging to one another on the floor as her son sobbed, the sound of the news broadcast echoing throughout the house.

On instinct she ran to him and placed her hand on Braxton's bare shoulder, letting him know that she would take over. He nodded and got to his feet and watched over them as Kathryn rocked her son back and forth, whispering sweet nothings into his ear.

As she held her son she heard another sound, another cry, and when she turned and looked behind her she saw Braxton sobbing, letting it out in great bleats, his fair face red and his veins visible in his temples.

She reached out to him and he came, pulling him close, running her fingers through their hair, kissing them both on the forehead.

She understood Braxton's tears, understood that his last vestige of innocence had been taken from him—along with every other student at Mariner High School.

Children who had never known Christian would be suffering because death is supposed to be reserved for the world of the grown. Death was an issue that adults were supposed to deal with, not children—and now someone who still had so much to live for was gone; it brought adulthood home a little too early.

It forced children to grow up and it stamped out that last shred of make-believe in all of them. It wasn't fair, but then again it never was.

By 5:30 that evening, Kathryn had left the two boys asleep on the couch, exhausted from crying and wrapped in one another's arms, still bare except for their briefs.

As Kathryn placed the cashmere throw over the two of them, she realized that her son had grown up a long time ago, only she hadn't noticed because she was too busy trying to climb out of her own personal hell.

Kathryn shed a tear.

As she journeyed into the kitchen to drink herself into slumber, Kathryn stared at the faces of dead Blackmoores and wondered if they ever truly learned to live a satisfying life despite the cloud of tragedy that hung over them?

She concluded in the end that they must have had found something to hold onto. Or, perhaps it was simply the promise of hell for the lives they stole that brought them some sort of solace.

It was a Monday.

That was all anyone knew as the wave of bodies dressed in black filled the pews and lined the walls of Sacred Heart, most of them unable to look at the gleaming black coffin that sat at the foot of the altar, knowing what was inside.

Kathryn, Trevor, and Braxton took their place in the back of the church, away from all the eyes that would be focused on their backs, staring at them with bewilderment and contempt for their presence.

Trevor searched the sea of bodies and located Cheri Hannifin dressed in a black skirt-suit and heels, her hair just touching her shoulders, the pain of mourning already taking its toll, making the young woman appear so much older—for a moment, Trevor thought that he was staring at his own mother.

Braxton held tight to Trevor's hand, allowing him to give in to the pain if need be, telling him without words that he would be there to support his weight.

The first person to speak was Coach Peters, who went on and on about Christian as an excellent athlete and role model, not stopping until he was blubbering in hysterics, having to be escorted from the podium by two of his students.

Next was Teri Jules, who was sitting with the cheerleaders, and it was in that moment that Trevor realized that Cheri was by herself. Her parents were on the opposite end of the church and their daughter was in a pew alone, no one appearing to want to sit with her.

It made him sad.

The service continued for two hours and then it led to a procession from the church to Bayview Cemetery. Lila had obviously arranged the service without Emanuel, who was so distant, as if he had better things to do than be at a memorial service for his one and only child.

Limos were waiting along the street, the drivers holding up signs: one was reserved for the family, followed with one that read *Hannifin*, as well as one that was reserved for the Sheers—though it was only his parents in attendance; Greg Sheer was nowhere in sight.

Lastly; there was a car reserved for the Blackmoores: a black Cadillac with a female driver who nodded to them gently; the three of them returned it somberly.

As they shuffled through the snow-caked lawn with its cold tombstones and sloped graves, Trevor felt no unease with being amongst the dead. The only unease he felt was with being so close to Whatcom Falls Park.

It was just beyond the thick of trees that the two boys had shared their first kiss, where they had stood on a bridge and acted on the acceptance of their true nature. And now here they were, one going into the ground, the other preparing to let go of the past several years.

The pallbearers brought the casket that held Christian Vasquez to the dolly that would lower him into the earth, each one of them listening to last rites said by the priest, Father Malady, who took a quick glance at Trevor and his mother, crossed himself briefly before continuing.

Kathryn shook her head and rolled her eyes.

It was then time for the soccer team to approach. This included Braxton; who helped drape the school's banner over the casket, the green and gold silk looking harsh against the snow. Finally, the casket was lowered, descending six feet into the cold earth.

As if driven by something else—something that hovered over them—that lingered like a phantom pulling them to the same place, Cheri and Trevor walked up together, taking hands and scooping up a handful of earth—each of them staring down at their dead friend, knowing exactly what it was that they were doing.

This was the end of their childhood.

There was no hope that down the line when they had all grown up that the four of them would reunite and allow the years of distance to dissolve.

There would be no last game of hide-and-seek; like a candle, that dream had been snuffed out and nothing could bring that back.

Somberly they dumped the earth into the deep rectangle, listening as it tapped on the wood casket, though muffled by the protection of the flag. As others gathered to do the same, Cheri and Trevor embraced, allowing the tears to come.

"I'm so sorry for everything," Cheri managed.

Trevor nodded, glad to have her back and willing to let the past five years go into the earth along with Christian, the both of them now ready to move on.

As they shed their tears for their lost youth, the snow came once again; great goose-feathers fell to the earth and the silence was deafening. As he listened to the sound of his and Cheri's sobs, Trevor realized that he did not hear the dead.

They did not reach out for him or implore him to listen. It was that moment that Trevor smiled, knowing that this meant that Christian had moved on. He was not lingering between the worlds, lost in his confusion.

He was free to begin his next stage of life, and this brought a peace to Trevor, one he had feared would never come. And so he walked away with Cheri in hand, rejoining Braxton and his mother, whispering a silent goodbye.

EIGHTEEN

It took days after the funeral for it to really hit Trevor that Christian Vasquez was dead. That his life and his smile would never shine again. Braxton tried to help him through it, tried to get him to a place where he could begin to live again, but by the third day he had given up.

Trevor lay in his bed unmoving, unflinching, only getting up when he needed to use the bathroom. The days were bleeding into one never-ending stream; the distinguishing signs of night and day did not exist, and Trevor did not sleep.

He stared at photographs long ago buried at the bottom of a shoe-box and stuffed behind old clothes on his shelf inside of his closet, only pulling them out after their five-year stint collecting dust.

Faces so happy, so young, stared back at him as if teasing him, tempting him to try and move on, daring him to forget them once again and put them back in the closet—or more yet, into the garbage can.

The answers to his death were nowhere in sight, Christian's reasons for crashing when they found nothing wrong with the breaks. It was as if Christian had decided to die, though there had been no reason for that either.

Christmas was approaching, which also meant Trevor would soon be eighteen, and yet the idea of growing older was nothing less of a daunting prospect.

Jonathan attempted many a time to rouse him out of his lethargic state, but the phantom could do nothing and Trevor silently asked him to leave him be.

Phone calls came in at all hours: some from Braxton, some from Cheri, and others from his family, who were hoping that he would snap out of it by the time the Blackmoores gathered for the holidays.

He sobbed and ate nothing, knowing that his mother was at her wits' end, finding it impossible to get her son to move or try to move on. He was also aware that he was following his mother's own grieving process and shutting himself from the rest of the world, stubborn in the idea of wading in a pool of self-loathing.

"Trevor...?" Kathryn called out from just beyond his bedroom door, her finger tapping on the old wood.

He stared at the door, refusing to answer.

"Trevor, honey, I know you can hear me... you need to come out. People need you—I need you. Please, Trevor, I can't do this alone!"

Her voice broke into an obvious sob, and yet without his response Kathryn simply made her way back down the stairs, unwilling to have her son hear her cry.

"I can't do this..." Trevor whispered, closing his eyes and allowing exhaustion to take over.

Trevor Blackmoore walked the empty halls of Mariner High School. The lights flickered with white electricity, and the few paper banners announcing the soccer games were hanging on by only single pieces of tape. It was obvious that various students had come by and ripped them off on their way out for the celebration of winter break.

His bare feet shuffled down the tiled hall, ignoring the cold on his soles and the chill that seemed to seep in from the steel walls that faced the outside. The courtyard glistened blue from the light of the full moon, which reflected off of the blanketed snow.

In the distance a door swung open and then shut again, the latch clicking into place. His large, round eyes surveyed the perimeter, and yet he could see nothing—only the sparks of imagery caused by those flickering fluorescent bulbs.

His breath was heavy and his flannel pajama pants and large sea-foam-green t-shirt did little to protect him from the chill, and his skin soon spread with gooseflesh, causing his tiny hairs to stand on end.

It was in this hall alone that Trevor noted how strange it seemed that some walls were plaster while others were brick. It was as if they could never decide what materials they wanted to use when constructing the high school back in the late Sixties.

"Why did I come here?" he asked himself, his breath taking shape in front of him, knowing that he was searching for something ... and yet those details were hidden from him completely.

Trevor took a turn around the bend and found himself in the commons area in the front of the school. Those green-carpeted wood benches placed in one strategic square and the soda machines still buzzing with electric life made it feel all the more foreboding.

"Miss me?" that familiar voice asked just beyond his shoulder.

Trevor turned and smiled, seeing Christian staring at him with the same grin.

"God, I thought something bad had happened to you!" Trevor responded, wrapping his arms around his boyfriend, feeling the joy inside of himself bloom and the relief that everything would be all right, that it was all a nightmare began to wash over him.

"No... I just went to sleep," Christian said, taking Trevor by the hand and leading him to one of those benches, both boys taking a seat next to each other.

"It was so awful... I thought that I would never see you again."

"I'll always be by your side; you know that," he said, rubbing Trevor's hand gently with his fingers.

Trevor nodded and wiped away the tears that danced on the brim of his eyes.

"But I can't stay here."

Trevor looked at him with luminescent eyes, so liquid, much like Christian's pools of black.

"But why? You just got here!"

His voice broke into a slim shriek, and the confusion and the anxiety it caused made him shake with frustration.

"I'm not doing you any good by hanging around." Christian looked so serene in his omission, as if he had come to this decision as casually and nonchalantly as one deciding to put their shoe on the left or right foot first.

"I don't understand...."

He nodded as if expecting this from Trevor, and yet he showed no signs of pain.

"I know, but you will. How can you move on with your life if I'm still seeing you?"

Trevor shook his head and refused to wipe the tears from his eyes.

"Why should I move on? Especially with the way you ended it."

He thought of standing, thought of staring down at Christian and letting out all that was on his mind; but when he looked at those calm black eyes, it was clear to him then that he needed to keep his peace.

"What happened was for your own good, and though I will never leave you, it's time that you let me step out of the limelight, and allow someone else to fill that space."

Trevor shook his head, hating the smile on Christian's face.

"Look... I can't."

"I'm already gone. This is just a dream; I'm not even real, Trevor. Your brain is just hanging on... and now you need to let me go."

Christian leaned forward; placing his lips on Trevor's cheek and ignoring his refusing head-shake, he leaned into Trevor's ear.

"Wake up, Trevor... wake up...."

He opened his eyes and realized that he had really been crying, and the emptiness inside of him grew at the sight of his darkened room, the only light coming from the glow of the moon shining through his window. Those green drapes left open and the shadows on the wall without faces—though Trevor searched desperately with his eyes, trying to find any hint of Christian Vasquez in the dark, but as with most dead things, he was nowhere in sight.

The only things to fill the space were his dressers and the mammoth armoire that sat against his wall between his two closets, opposite his bed.

He ran his hands through his hair, which had gotten longer within the past couple of weeks and would soon need to be cut again, if he decided to go that route.

Trevor shed tears for thinking of things other than Christian, and shed tears for still thinking of him.

He knew that he needed to let him go. That who Christian was no longer existed and that the past would serve as nothing more than a clutch; something to keep him where he was at instead of allowing him to move ahead.

Thinking of his mother, thinking of Cheri, thinking of Braxton; Trevor realized that he needed to move ahead. Too many people were waiting for him on the other side, and if he didn't join them soon they would grow tired of waiting and continue on, leaving him in the dust.

With all of the strength that he could muster, Trevor Blackmoore swung his legs off the mattress and planted them on the floor, and then in a great push he got to his feet and made his way to his door, stepping out into the hall and rejoining the world of the living.

Kathryn wondered how long it could take for the dead to return, and if they had a choice. She thought of Sheffield and wondered why he hadn't come to her after he had passed? Did he know that it had been her fault, that her blood had killed him? She had been so selfish then, wanting a family and friends, and whatever else that it was that constituted a normal life.

It had been her desire to rise above the Legacy, to show it that centuries-old curses and fears could have no hold over her. She was Kathryn Blackmoore, after all: the defiant one, the only woman who could take on the world and win.

That's how it had always been.

But the Legacy won out in the end; it always did. It had worked its dark trick on her and stolen her love from her in order to smite her down and remind her that the Universe was never something that could be made to bow down to you. It was only something that had to be appeased and feared, and in an instant it could take everything away; and, in fact, it often did.

She stared at the glowing tree in the center of the room, casting an eerie glow on the walls and floorboards. Kathryn looked to the hall behind her and thought of her son, knowing that he was up in his room crying—just as she had cried five-and-a-half years ago, not caring about the world or the people closest to her in it.

Trevor had become invisible to her then; he had been the furthest thing from her thoughts, and most of this had to do with the fact that when she looked at her son she could find no trace of Sheffield. Trevor looked more like her, and it made her feel as if he was really gone, that nothing of him existed and never really had.

It was the footfalls on the floor behind her that brought Kathryn out of her sorrowful stupor, and for a moment she had hoped that it would be Sheffield, back from the dead.

"Mom..." Trevor called out, standing behind her in the darkness, looking as he did before puberty: A tiny child helpless—lost in a cruel, adult world.

"Oh, honey... are you feeling better?"

Trevor turned his head, not nodding and not shaking, his eyes searching for just the right answer.

"I think better is still coming... right now, I'm just trying to keep from dying."

Kathryn knew by the bluntness with which he answered that he figured his mother would understand, and he was right. She did understand it; she understood his pain and his darkness. There was no way to get around the shadow that would hover over him, but allowing yourself to continue on seemed to be one's best bet, especially when there were easier ways out.

"Do you want to come sit with me?" she asked.

Trevor nodded, shuffling along the floor to the couch, their eyes focused on the glowing tree, the flakes falling in great chunks as the Vienna Boys' Choir sang from the speakers.

Kathryn draped her arm around her son's shoulders and he nestled against her breast, staring at the collection of presents in gorgeous wrapping, stacks upon stacks. The feeling of their inheritance was so heavy and reality sharp; like a knife that could cut.

They were no longer just mother and son, they were now two grieving widowers, jaded by the loss of loves. If there had ever been some kind of rite of passage for Blackmoores, then this was it—and Trevor had passed.

They stayed like this from night into early morning, drifting to slumber against the warmth of one another, and they dreamt dreams of trees, dinners, gifts, and family: dreams that they shared but would never know it, mother and son attending the same party in the same world.

Mabel Blackmoore sat up in her bed, roused from a deep slumber. The shadowed form of a seventeen-year-old boy stood in front of her, dressed in a black jacket, white shirt, and black breeches; his hand holding the bow of a violin.

'It's happened...' the apparition stated, Mabel knowing that if she flipped on her lamp the specter would vanish.

"The Legacy...."

Her eyes searched her room with its bay windows, papered walls of dark green with muted orange and blue flowers, a collection of antique dolls that sat on shelves and tiny rocking chairs, their glass eyes staring back at her, and for the first time they reminded Mabel of vagabond corpses that could come to life at any moment.

What sounded like a gnarled moan vibrated throughout the house, and she clutched the hem of her covers and brought them to her chest at the same moment the phonograph started.

The scratchy wail of Robert Johnson singing his *Crossroads Blues* traveled from the downstairs music room to the second floor, and the fireplace across from her bedside illuminated with a great flame, while the face of the deceased Michael Donovan came into eerie view.

His round, black eyes, his marble-white skin and attractive face and clothes were expressive of the early 1900s, but it was the look of somber terror that sent a tremor down Mabel's spine.

'It's coming...' he said, Mabel watching his face as Scrooge must have been when beholding the dead Jacob Marley.

"What shall we do?"

She did not move her eyes from his face, though the embers in the hearth began to die down.

'Prepare...'

"For what?"

'To die....'

His image faded, dissipated like mist, and the room was once again dark, the sound of Robert Johnson repeating himself—and, though scared, Mabel knew that she needed to go downstairs and turn the record off.

She stood and walked cautiously towards the door, her bare feet padding across the cold fir floor, and the hall was dark and lifeless save for the large wood bench with the mirror that stood against the banister.

The doors to the other three rooms were closed and the light from the three o'clock world shone through; the early morning sky aglow with slight moonlight trying to break through thick clouds.

She made her way down the stairs with ease, following the call of the musician that was legend to have sold his soul at the cross-roads to be able to play the blues.

She turned the corner into the sitting room and clasped her fingers on the handle of the pocket door, pushing it open, and startled when the music stopped.

To her surprise the phonograph was empty; not a single record on it, the thirty-eights stacked in a wicker basket at the foot of the little table that the music player sat atop of.

She grasped the neckline of her nightgown and held it tight with her fingers, looking from left to right, feeling as if something was out of place and not knowing why.

"Who's here?" she asked calmly, though her heart thundered in her chest. "Michael, are you down here?"

There was no response.

She turned towards the mirror against the wall and gasped when she saw the image of her father Bradley standing behind her, his broad shoulders and dirty blond hair with the round face and sorrowful demeanor staring at her.

There was Jeremiah's doomed wife, Sarah, with her shoulder-length black hair, narrow eyes, and wine-red-and-black plaid gown, her angular face white like Michael and her father.

Nicholas appeared, along with his wife Bethany. Nicholas just short of six feet, his hair a dark red like Trevor's and his face just as innocent.

Bethany was tall and slender, wearing a gray satin dress with blue embroidery stitched at the bottom, which stopped at her knees. Large pearl buttons followed it down and her red hair was a thick wave of brushed-out curls, a navy blue bow visible at the back of her head; all of their faces heavy and mournful.

The last to appear was Sheffield, who looked as he did at seventeen: his dark hair thick, long, and straight, the strands just grazing his cheeks, his bangs parted down the middle, as was the style of the late Seventies and early Eighties. He was lean and dressed in a sky-blue collared shirt, open at the chest with a shell necklace secured around his throat, his long legs accentuated with brown bell-bottom corduroys, a black belt fastened around his waist.

"Daddy...."

With the exception of Nicholas, all of these apparitions had lost their lives to the Legacy and had never come through before. Mabel figured that it was because of her long-ago-dead great grandfather Nicholas that they had found a way.

They did not speak, and their dead eyes only stared. Mabel was quick to catch that they were black, empty, showing no kind of iris, no kind of color.

"Daddy, what is it?"

Still nothing, and she dared not turn around.

The Devil will come. The Devil will come and walk amongst men, claiming souls one by one....

It was Nicholas who spoke, and their mouths moved with his, completely in sync; the voice was a jumble of them all.

For the Devil keeps his witches, and will always come back for them. For the end of the Devil will be at the hand of his own child....

The air was terrifyingly still, and it felt as if the oxygen was evaporating from the room.

"Trevor...." His name escaped her lips without meaning to, and the specters nodded, expressions never changing.

'He is the key....'

Mabel closed her eyes, trying to gather her wits. After a moment, she opened them, and as expected, the home was once again empty, and the paper boy threw her copy of the Bellingham Herald against her door; realizing that time had moved on without her.

"Trevor, are the guest rooms ready?" Kathryn asked, standing at the foot of the stairs, her voice loud and echoing against the walls, the slight paranoia in her voice causing both Trevor and Braxton to grin as they stood in the blue room with its two full beds, sitting opposite each other, while the pillows received one final fluff.

"Yeah, Mom!" he responded, taking a seat at the foot of the bed closest to the window looking out on the side of the house with a view of the bay, the room positioned above the sun room.

"Sounds like your mom's freaking out a little."

Braxton walked over to him, dressed in cargos and a black cashmere sweater, his hair messy. Trevor had called him earlier that morning, asking him to come over. After two days of not hearing anything from him, Braxton was quick to comply, throwing on pants and his sweater, hurrying to his car and racing over; he wasn't even sure if he had locked the door.

"A little? Try a lot."

He smiled and looked around the room, seeing more pictures of dead Blackmoores and period pictures of Bellingham at the end of the nineteenth century.

"Okay, so a lot... why?"

He liked the way Trevor looked in his tight black tee, a Misfits necklace wrapped twice around his throat with a shiny ball chain, his extra-wide jeans nearly hiding his black boots, and the faded grass stains on the knees gave a kind of haphazard charm to his look.

"Because it's been a year since the family's gotten together, and she's afraid that they'll be unimpressed with her.

"If anything, she thinks that they'll be disappointed."

He frowned, and Braxton placed his palm against Trevor's cheek.

"Well, are they like that; does your family not get along or something?"

Trevor furrowed his brows and shook his head.

"No, not at all, we're all very close; there are not a whole lot of us, though. Well, on this side of the ocean."

He nodded and sat himself in the chair across from his boyfriend. "Well, how many Blackmoores are there? Alive, I mean?"

Trevor smiled and thought for a moment, grabbing the soft blue pillow and fiddled with its case. "Well, here in America there's Magdalene; she's Queen Mab's daughter and lives in New Orleans. Then there's my cousin Darbi, who lives in El Paso. He's a year older than me, though he's a senior too... his mom Mona died a few years ago.

"Let's see... my great-grandmother Fiona is coming, and so is my cousin Marcel; he's three years younger than me and lives in San Francisco with his dad Jeffery. There's my cousin Brighton; he's in his early eighties.

"There's Mitchell; he's twenty-eight and owns a winery in the Napa valley... Maria, who lives in Tacoma and is Brighton's daughter. Her son Jason died a few years ago due to a drug deal gone bad; it happened the same time my dad passed, actually...."

He averted his gaze, and Braxton reached out for his hand and took it into his own, reminding him that he knew his pain.

"Anyone in Europe?"

Trevor nodded.

"There's Natalie and Mary-Margaret, twins that live in Dublin. They're known as dueling violinists and are really famous over there. Actually, there's a whole other branch of the family in Ireland; but we don't know them. Well, at least I don't. I think my mom and a few other people do. They don't really want anything to do with us.

"Then there's Adamo; he's a priest and works at the Vatican—"

Braxton interjected, his face visibly stunned:

"Wait, wait you have a cousin who's a priest?" Trevor grinned and nodded. "And works in the Vatican?"

"Yeah. Crazy, huh?"

Braxton nodded.

"Well, what does he do there; is he Italian?"

"Yeah; well his dad is the twin's uncle and he married this woman Margarita, who gave birth to Adamo and his younger sister by three years, Francesca.

"She was a beautiful woman who lived in Rome and before she died, she requested that Adamo become an altar boy and eventually a priest."

This history was astounding to Braxton, who knew little of his own family.

"In terms of what he does in the Vatican... well, he investigates possessions, demonology, sightings, and stigmatas, basically all of the weird shit.

"I don't know, you can ask him yourself."

Braxton looked at him inquisitively.

"He's coming for Christmas... in fact, he'll be arriving tonight. He and his sister are the only ones from Europe that are coming; the twins can't make it because they're playing some holiday thing at the Royal Albert Hall in London... plus, you know, they hate us, so...."

"Why would anyone in your family be a priest? It just seems, well...."

Trevor chuckled.

"You mean, with everything you've heard about us and what we do, how is it possible that one of us can work for the Vatican?"

Braxton grinned sheepishly and nodded.

"Well, that's why...."

He shook his head.

"My mom was involved in an... incident... related to a priest like twenty-five or thirty years ago, and the church got curious... so Adamo's dad informed him why he had to abide by his dead mother's wishes and become a priest. He didn't want to do it; he was Catholic, yes, but he wanted to play football for Italy—but family dedication came first."

Braxton sat attentively and let out a long sigh from his grinning lips, captivated by the story.

"Shit, it's like the Mafia."

Trevor's left brow rose and he shook his head.

"Not quite. My family just likes its privacy and doesn't want a bunch of robe-wearers poking their heads in where they don't belong.

"Plus, the priest here, Father Malady; he was the one who reported the incident involving my mom, and he must have told them that the devil was involved or something, because it's the group that Adamo works for that began looking into what happened.

"They questioned my mom's classmates and knocked on doors; I guess it was really scary.

"Anyway, with Adamo there they can't investigate us....

"So, honey, there's my whole fucked-up family in a nutshell."

Braxton averted his gaze and scoffed, putting Trevor off.

"What is it with this town and people thinking all this weird shit about you guys?"

Trevor sighed.

"Braxton, what people say is true... kind of."

His eyes locked with Trevor's and his mouth dropped open.

"Um...."

"My great-great-grandmother Aria used to run the spiritualist church here in Bellingham back in the early 1900s. In fact, she ran séances from her house, which was only two houses across the street, near Dianaca Castle—you know, the big purple mansion at the end of the block?"

Braxton nodded, waiting for him to continue.

"Her grandfather Tristan moved to Bellingham from New Orleans in the 1890's and was offered the house down the alley—where Queen Mab now lives—by the Donovans in 1910, after their son Michael disappeared.

"The old house was destroyed in a fire, and Aria had gotten pregnant by someone who still remains unknown and gave birth to my great-grandmother Fiona, who carried on the séances with her mother and continued to do so even after she died.

"She had two children with her husband Bradley: Annaline and Queen Mab.

"Annaline met my grandfather Trevor Mayland, whom I'm named for.

He lived in this house, and his family had been here for as long as my family had—actually, longer—and they weren't happy with him marrying my grandmother.

Queen Mab got the house and still runs the séances as well as the spiritualist church in downtown. There are other churches now, but the original Church of Light still looks and acts just as it did a hundred years ago and its congregation is still standing firm."

Trevor looked winded from his history lesson, and Braxton could not help but try and wrap his thoughts around it and finding that he was coming up short.

"And the whole 'witch' thing?"

Trevor rolled his eyes and gave a chuckle.

"The Blackmoores were involved in some traditions back in Ireland. After arriving in New Orleans, Sarafeene Blackmoore and her husband Malachey were initiated into New Orleans Vodou and were often found dancing in Congo Square.

"My cousin Magdalene is actually a priestess in Louisiana; you'll be meeting her, too."

"I don't know if I should be interested, run for the hills, or call the insane asylum." Trevor flashed him a grin and stood, approaching him slowly.

"Are you afraid of me now, Braxton Volaverunt?"

He shook his head.

"No, I'm not. Why, do you think I should be?"

Trevor frowned and gave a shrug.

"I don't know anymore...."

"Close your eyes."

Trevor complied and Braxton did the same, accessing that part of himself that he rarely ever reached out to on command, part of him not even sure if he would know how to do it at will.

Trevor felt a slightly electrical sensation, as if he had just placed his hands on an electric fence—though the jolt was not as fierce; it was more in tiny pulsing waves, and it made Trevor giggle.

He opened his eyes and saw Braxton staring at him, tears spilling down his cheeks.

"Braxton, what is it?"

He reached out and gripped his shoulder, trying to bring comfort to his boyfriend.

"I saw you... I saw through you, felt what you felt."

Trevor's mouth hung open slightly, as if he was going to ask a question but couldn't think of how.

"I saw how you've seen me for the past five years. Every moment in the halls, in class, how you felt when you discovered that I was going to homecoming with a girl... how you sat in your room crying and wishing that you could just disappear instead of feel the way that you felt at the moment."

Trevor shook his head and stood, not knowing what to make of any of it.

"I don't understand... how can you do that?"

Braxton shrugged.

"My whole life, really... I don't know where it comes from; I've never talked to *the living dead* about it."

Trevor knew that he was referring to his father Eric.

"This is amazing—oh, wow...."

Braxton laughed and stood, now towering an inch and a half above Trevor.

"No, it's not...."

"Oh, please," Trevor interjected. "That was, too, but I am kinda like you. I'm a clairvoyant medium. You know I can see, feel, and talk to dead people... though that's not as cool as being able to know people just by touching them!"

For the first time Braxton felt good about his gift—as if he was no longer the only freak in town.

For the first time, he felt as if he belonged.

They grinned at one another and Braxton walked towards the door and out into the hall, telling Trevor that he was going to grab a soda from downstairs.

He nodded and stayed behind, the telling of his family's history forcing him to look into those passed-away faces—seeing Nicholas and Tristan, Jeremiah and his wife Sarah, as well as their two children Sarafeene and Aria.

The curtains in front of him began to curl, and a wisp of cold air circulated through the room. Trevor closed his eyes, anticipating his approach and possible displeasure.

'You told him... you told him....'

Trevor opened his eyes and turned to face the door, seeing the hazy apparition of Jonathan Marker in the corner next to the closet, and to his utter amazement the spirit slowly but surely became all the more solid.

His black tweed jacket and white shirt, as well as the black tie, the collar of the shirt, small and turned up, covering his neck. His face was smooth and flesh like marble, his brown hair reflecting the light.

"That was my prerogative, spirit, not yours!"

Jonathan shook his head. The movement felt outside of reality, and yet at the same time he was existing within the present space.

'You've made me unhappy, Trevor.'

He did not move from where he was standing, and looking at the specter, it seemed that for the fist time in his life since he was a child he feared the entity.

"How have I made you unhappy, Jonathan?"

The specter shook its head, and Trevor rolled his eyes, trying to keep his resolve—though he knew that the spirit could see his fear as clearly as it could see and know everything else.

'You've gone from one mortal to the other, and exposed them both to your world without even thinking of the consequence.'

"What are you threatening Jonathan? What is it that you're trying to scare me with?"

The specter moved towards him without ever really moving, and Trevor backed up, the back of his knee knocking against the arm of the chair.

'I'm threatening nothing. I want you to be happy, Trevor, truly I do. I just think you should be careful who you allow into this world

of yours; it may end up hurting more than just you in the end, and it could determine the entire fate of your family.'

Trevor furrowed his brows and reached for a tiny snow globe on the curved console, with its many photos. He picked it up and hurled it at the phantom, seeing in known dismay as it slipped through his ectoplasm, smashing against the floor, its liquid slipping into the cracks and knots.

"Now, you listen to me, Jonathan—"

"Trevor?" his mother called out, her feet running up the steps.

"Trevor, baby you okay?" Braxton asked—the both of them on the other side of the room wanting to come in.

"You come near my family, spirit, or anyone else that I love, and I will find a way to own you forever; I promise you that one!"

The spirit began to fade, its form becoming smoky.

'Not me Trevor, not me....'

Jonathan vanished entirely, and the door was thrown open. Braxton and his mother looked at him, completely bewildered by the broken globe.

"Is everything all right?" Kathryn asked, her voice soft and husky as usual.

"Yeah, Mom, just a little stressed about everyone coming, that's all."

She nodded, though it was obvious that she doubted his words. Her eyes searched the room for another presence, and it was then—once again—that Trevor was left to wonder how much Kathryn really knew but left unsaid.

"I'm sure everything will be fine. It'll be fun, and much needed," Braxton reassured him with a smile, wrapping his arms around his own and giving him a peck on the cheek.

"Yeah... me too, me too."

His gaze became distant as he began to contemplate the ghost's words, the meaning... and all he could think of was the Legacy and its legend about that Dark God of the Wood—that ominous deity that would one day come for the family once the Legacy was conquered. He could not see how it could have been, and he wasn't ready to try and figure it out.

He smiled at the little boy with the bulbous blue eyes who stared at the white of his cleric's collar, knowing on instinct that if a man had this around his neck with the black shirt, then he must be a good man.

In a few years, the kid would know better.

He stared at the separate door, left open for first class passengers, his crisp aqua eyes observing the tinted black windows—knowing that he wasn't going to have any more security issues. In fact, he was never once hassled or searched, all on account of the fact that he was a priest.

Though forty-two, he hardly looked it; in fact, most people mistook him for thirty-five—sometimes thirty-seven, but never any older. He was always thankful for the good genetics. The flight from Rome to New York had been an exhausting endeavor, namely due to a case of a possessed little boy in the middle of Vatican City; in fact, it had occurred during one of the Pope's many appearances.

This new pope, Pope Benedict, was a man greatly disliked, though it was rarely ever mentioned—but this was no greater felt than especially by his order. It seemed that this man, this Doberman of the Catholic Church, threatened more than just the few rights that most people in his country held onto. Ever since his rise to power there had been more reports of possession and other strange phenomenon in one month than in an entire year under Pope John Paul.

He ran his hands through his black hair, now just turning silver at the roots, and a great yawn escaped his lips, stretching his body out and draping the long coat over him, desperate to get on the plane.

He smiled when he heard the young flight attendant announce that they were going to start seating the airline's first class passengers.

Finally, he thought to himself, waiting for the seat numbers to be called.

"Seats four and five."

He stood and walked towards the young woman, removing his passport.

"Oh, thank you, Father Blackmoore."

He nodded to the young woman, who was obviously from Brooklyn.

"And might I say that Adamo is an awfully handsome name."

She winked and Adamo grinned sheepishly, knowing once again he was going to have to fight against the temptations that were before him now that he was away from the suffocations of Vatican City.

He clutched his black, squared-off suitcase and moved to his row, feeling a sense of relief when looking upon the extra-wide, blue upholstered seats, the complimentary fleece blanket and fluffed pillow already warmed and toasty. It made the idea of flying out of New York's haze of snow all the more possible.

"Grand," he let out with a sigh, the Irish blending with the Italian, smirking at the fact that even to him it sounded funny. He stretched and plopped himself down in his seat, the little port hole window moist and fogged, the harsh cool seeping through the windows only briefly felt across Adamo's face before it mixed with the warmth of the plane's heater.

His skin was olive in color, and hindered by only a few wrinkles. He knew that if he hadn't become a priest, if he hadn't been born a Blackmoore, he would have gone to Hollywood and become a film star, or played football for Italy.

He would have married and had hundreds of women and men on the side, and he would have been ignorant to the world of the dead—like the majority of the world, which only sees it as something to talk about over firelight or throughout the entire month of October.

That little boy came by and took a seat next to him, dressed in a blue suit and matching tie, a blue gingham shirt beneath it; his plump peach face scattered with light brown freckles.

They smiled at one another, and for just a moment the boy only blinked—as if apprehensive, recalling the parental warning about talking to strangers.

They watched more people filing into the plane, the first class now completely seated and those in coach passing by and by, all of them in a cluster of pushing and heaving suitcases.

"What's your name?" the little boy asked him, with a sharp curiosity accompanied with cautious innocence.

"Adamo. Adamo Blackmoore." T

he boy smiled and his eyes gleamed. For a moment the kid reminded Adamo of his cousin, Trevor, who was going to be eighteen. It shocked him to realize how fast the years pass by.

"I'm Alex Baker."

The boy stuck out his hand and Adamo took it, giving the boy a firm yet gentle handshake.

"It's a pleasure to meet you, Alex. So, where are your parents?"

The boy shrugged.

"I don't know. I lived in a foster home, but I just met my family last week; they live in Seattle and they want to give me a home." His voice grew sullen. "I just hope that they still like me. I don't want to go back to the people that I've been living with; they've been the worst of all the people that I've lived with."

There was a maturity in the young boy's words, a maturity that no one his age should have.

"And why's that?" Adamo asked him with genuine interest and concern.

"You'll just think I'm making things up—"

"No, I won't, I promise." Adamo leaned in and brought down the decibel of his voice. "You'd be surprised what things I believe in."

He appeared to gain some sort of hope from Adamo's words, as if no one had given him this sort of confidence before this very moment.

"Well, things happen when I'm around...."

Adamo knew where this was going. In fact, it was a normal thing that was said by the people that he and his order interviewed.

"What kind of things?"

The hairs on the back of his neck began to stand on end, and as if by clockwork the plane's engines began to hum.

"When I get upset things fly around the room; sometimes windows and mirrors will break...."

His voice was beginning to quiver and his blue orbs for eyes began to fill with tears.

"I don't mean to do it; I really don't, but I can't control it. The people I stay with always end up getting rid of me.

"I've been going from foster home to foster home for so long, and I'm only eleven!"

Adamo frowned. He knew that it was hard for people to come to grips with psychic phenomenon—especially when coming from a child—but to just throw a kid away like that, only to be recycled to another family and thrown away again, broke his heart.

"I do believe you, Alex."

The boy's eyes grew wide and the look of bewilderment was evident on his face.

"Really, I do. In fact, I'm just like you."

Alex Baker shook his head, unable to comprehend what was being said to him.

During the erratic confession of Alex, the flight attendants had begun and completed their routine of safety instructions, and the plane was now speeding down the runway, picking up pace and lifting into the snowy nighttime air.

Adamo felt the usual lift in his gut and could tell by the slight grimace on the boy's face that he was feeling it too.

"But... but how? I mean, you're a priest; isn't that stuff like evil to you?"

Adamo smiled and winked, giving him reassurance.

"It's true, I am a priest; that I cannot deny. The thing is, though—now bear with me, here—I serve an order within the church that investigate things like possessions, psychic persons, and hauntings.

"But it is also true that I am like you; in fact, I was born into a family that is just like you.

"So no; I don't think that it is evil."

Alex took a deep breath and shook his head, his eyes moving around the plane, checking to see if anyone was listening in on them or staring.

"Prove it."

As if expecting this, Adamo removed a pen from his coat pocket and placed it in his open palm, aware of Alex's attentive and slightly confused stare. He took a deep breath, closed his eyes and then opened them, keeping his eyes steady on the pen in his hand, refusing to blink, zoning out and welcoming that familiar pulsating buzz—the tiny, heated pin-pricks on the back of his skull and the familiar weightlessness that took hold.

Within seconds, the sleek ball-point twitched slightly before lifting three inches from his palm and spinning clockwise four times, before stopping and drifting back down into his open hand.

Adamo gave a slight shake of his head, bringing himself back out of his trance, and smiled at the young Baker with his jaw gaped open.

"Oh my God!"

There was no sign of apprehension or fear in this reaction; it was more of a gentle and amazed recognition.

"I could have made it rise up above my head, but I don't want to draw attention."

For some strange reason, a sudden thought of his sister Francesca flashed into his head, and he knew that she was thinking of him.

"And you can control it?"

Adamo nodded.

"How?"

"Well, I was fortunate enough, as I said before, to be raised in a family where everyone has some form of psychic ability. But if I hadn't, I'd imagine that it would still be out of control. It's very easy to control once you understand the method."

Alex was going to respond when he was suddenly stopped by the young flight attendant. Her name-tag read: *Michelle*, and she was slender, with slightly curled blonde hair and adequately-applied makeup. Her nails were perfectly manicured and she looked as if she belonged on *QVC*, and not minding to the comforts of airplane passengers.

"What can I get you two to drink?"

Alex told her that he would like a coke, and Adamo responded with an order for a Bellini.

"All right, I'll be back with those, and I'm going to leave you with a menu; we'll be taking orders in the next twenty minutes." And with that Michelle made her way down the rest of the aisle.

"So, you're riding first class, Alex; I'm assuming your real family paid for this?"

The boy shrugged and looked to his hands, which were resting in his lap.

"I'm not sure. I just got the ticket and sat where the ticket said my seat was."

Adamo nodded and saw the slight despair in his eyes.

"I really don't know much about them; I don't even know if they're going to like me."

A curious thought was beginning to take its place at the forefront of Adamo's brain, a thought that he needed to press casually.

"Well I'm sure they will, especially if they know what's good for them."

He gave Alex a reassuring grin.

"Have you met any of them?"

Alex looked up at the light above his head and reached out for it, though his brows were furrowed in thought, and Adamo watched with mild humor as the light suddenly flipped on before Alex had a chance to press the button—followed with every other light in the first class compartment, and the mildly startled passengers began to look about in confusion.

"Sorry...." Alex gave a defeated shrug. "I didn't mean for that to happen. It's just... well, I was remembering the first and only time I met anyone in my family.

"They're from my mom's side; I don't think the Bakers even know that I exist, or that their son even had a child."

Adamo could hear the heartache in the boy's voice, but he knew that it was not the time to speak.

"I was in my room with the Hardings—they're the foster family that I was living with—anyways, I was folding the laundry in my room—which was actually a really large walk-in closet or something, but it was to the backside of the house, and that's where they liked to keep me."

His eyes became somewhat vacant, and Adamo knew that Alex was drifting back into recollection.

"Anywhoo... um, like I was saying, I was folding clothes when from the window I saw this really fancy black car pull up at the side of the house. It looked like an old car from, like, the Thirties or Forties.

"For some reason I knew that they were there for me, and so I stopped folding and just watched them.

"First the driver stepped out, and he was wearing a really nice dark blue suit and he opened the back door. Two people stepped out and they looked nice, but also kinda scary, ya know?

"Like they had something about them that was different from other people."

"Here you go," Michelle said, interrupting Alex's story, "one Coke and one Bellini. And I'll be back in ten minutes to take your order."

They both nodded and watched her walk away, and without missing a beat Alex continued with his story.

"Anyways, it was a guy and a girl. Well, not really a girl. She was probably in her mid-thirties or early forties, and the guy was probably in his late twenties.

"He was tall and wore a really nice gray suit. He had short black hair and large eyes. The woman had long black hair, like to her elbows, and she was wearing this tight black skirt that had, like, a sheen to it.

"She wore a matching jacket, and it was obvious that she was wearing one of those corset thingies underneath.

"She was really pretty and she had a long necklace with pearl beads and a big gothic-looking cross hanging from it."

Alex stopped to catch his breath before continuing.

"Well, they began to walk around the house and then the woman just stopped and turned to look at the window and she saw me! She saw me and she had the prettiest eyes ever. They were bright green, like a jewel; it's like they glittered, and then she smiled and nodded as if I had asked her a question.

"Soon there was a knock on the front door and then Mrs. Harding opened it, and I ran to the door to my room and listened. She asked if she could see me and Mrs. Harding told her no, and that's when she said that her name was Elisabeth... um, something; I can't really remember the last name, and then she said that the guy that was with her was her brother Joshua.

"She told Mrs. Harding that I was their nephew and that they wanted to see me.

"When I heard her say that she was my aunt I ran out into the living room, and it was so weird, Father—"

He chuckled.

"Please, just call me Adamo."

"Okay, Adamo. Well, anyways, it was like I knew them, like we all had the exact same freckles in our eyes or something, ya know?"

He nodded.

"They told me that they recently found out about me upon trying to track down what happened to my parents: their sister Lisa and her husband Rupert Baker. They said that they wanted to take me out to lunch.

"Mrs. Harding kept trying to stop me from going, but I wasn't afraid. I knew that I could trust them; I don't really know why, but I did, and so I went. And this was in upstate New York.

"Anyways, I went with them and we went into that fancy car, and we drove all of the way to New York City. I'd never been before, and it was so cool. We went to this big fancy store called Barney's and they bought me bags and bags full of clothes, which the driver just threw in the car, then we went to the restaurant at the store and I ate the best food ever.

"They told me that they lived in Seattle, Washington, in a penthouse apartment and that they wanted me to come live with them. They said that I could go to the best schools if I wanted to, or I could have a private tutor.

"They said that I have tons and tons of relatives and that everyone in their family is shown tons of love and is never ignored, and that they really wanted me to come live with them."

"Obviously, you said yes."

Alex nodded.

"Yeah, I told them that I would and so they said that I could keep two bags of my new stuff but that the rest would be sent to Seattle, and they told me that they have a big room waiting for me with a view of downtown and the water."

Adamo nodded, and again the thought of his raven-haired sister flashed into his thoughts.

"Well, what did your foster parents say?"

Alex frowned for a brief instant, and then continued in his excited tone.

"When we got back Elisabeth and Joshua told Mr. and Mrs. Harding that they were going to be taking care of me and that I would be flying out on the twenty-first of December; this was like a week ago. They said that everything was all set and my flight was already booked.

"Mr. and Mrs. Harding shook their heads and said no, which was really weird because they didn't like me, but they did keep me around for the monthly check, so I got scared, but Joshua at spoke up.

"He said, 'He is my nephew and I want him home; I do not appreciate the fact that you've kept him home to do all your housework, and that you keep him in that back closet.'

"Mrs. Harding got upset, and Mr. Harding was denying it and looking at me all angrily. But Joshua said, 'He didn't tell us these things. We've had people watching you, people that you would never know about, and they've told us.

"Now, we're taking him and that's final.'"

It was like listening to some great soap opera.

"Have you all decided?" Michelle asked. She was holding a pen and notepad.

"Yes, I'll have the salmon spread." Alex answered.

Michelle smiled and then turned to look at Adamo.

"And can I have the steak sandwich with the garden salad and ranch dressing?'" Michelle nodded and walked away, permitting Alex to conclude his story.

"So Elisabeth and Joshua hugged me really, really tight and told me that they loved me and that they'd see me in a week, and if anything went wrong, if the Hardings tried to stop me, they'd know.

"It was really strange but really cool, and now here I am talking to you.

"I just hope that they'll still love me after they find out the truth about me."

Adamo gave another reassuring smile. He could read between the lines of what it was that his relatives were like. He knew it because his family was the same way, and behaved in the same bewildering manner. It was certain to him that this family of Alex's were psychic—or 'witches,' as the church would call them.

Though the American Blackmoores were extremely entwined with the occult, the European Blackmoores were engrained with Catholicism—though the shadows of their pagan roots were still greatly evident.

The fact of the matter was that Irish Catholicism was so different from any form of the faith that existed. The church had been unable to completely extinguish the traditions and the mythos of the Celts, and with the Blackmoores, who were from a Spanish Romani background, having arrived in Ireland and making a home along its Black Moors in 1066, this blended Christianity had become the family's norm.

Whenever instances of psychic phenomenon occurred (and were proven), the church believed that his order should look at it from the conviction that the families or persons had somehow made a pact with the devil—but Adamo could not do this, and ordered everyone in his organization to refute this idea as well.

For the remainder of their plane ride from New York to their three-hour layover in Idaho, they talked about everything that seemed to be on Alex Baker's mind, and Adamo was more than willing to share his insights and information. He told him about Rome and the order that he worked for, willing to do whatever he could to put the boy's mind at ease.

He promised that when they got off the plane in Idaho, he would coach him on some simple exercises to control his emotional responses that his powers were reacting from, and how to focus his energies towards specific goals for his abilities—so that they were moving one or two things picked out at a time instead of just affecting everything in his immediate vicinity.

They walked beneath the rusted green metal breezeway of El Paso International Airport, the wheels of the two suitcases scratching along the pavement. It was the first time in five years that Darbi Blackmoore was traveling, and the prospect of seeing his family served as an adrenaline that not only made him excited but kept him focused, despite his grandfather's protests.

John Blackmoore was deeply opposed to his grandson traveling to Bellingham, but seeing that Darbi was now nineteen and would be entering into university next year, he could no longer make decisions for him.

Besides, at ten in the morning it was too early to put up a fight.

Darbi was a stable six foot in height, with a solid build and broad shoulders. He had been an accomplished Lacrosse and football player with an aggressiveness that made itself known in whatever task he was involved in.

He wore a forest-green wool ribbed sweater, which zipped from the chest up to the neck, and a navy blue Hollister baseball cap on his head.

He had light brown hair, which was shaved down to just three inches, and his jawline was defined and protruded. A patch of hair rested beneath his rather pouty lips, and his eyes were wide and green with hints of blue and yellow like glittering glass shards set in the irises.

"C'mon, Grandpa John," Darbi mumbled in a rather deep and steady tone, his white sneakers tapping on the sidewalk as they made their final approach to the automatic doors of the airport.

"I don't see why you have to do this!" John Blackmoore responded, secretly hoping that his grandson would miss his plane. John was rather rotund. His hair was a shock of silver and receding at the sides; his voice was showing the cracked signs of his sixty-three years, but nothing else about him was. His weight appeared to obliterate what could have been a great amount of wrinkles, and he chewed lightly on the cigar that hung from his mouth.

"I'm not going to go through this with you again. Trevor is going to be eighteen; just because you don't love him doesn't mean that I don't."

They reached the inside of the airport and began to make their way to the row of airlines that occupied the left side of the airport.

Though it was the desert, it was still winter, and so the ground was dry and the air was chilled and slightly painful to breathe in. Darbi was relieved to be indoors.

"I didn't say I don't love him. Of course I love him; there's no question about that. It's just that there are things about this family that you do not understand, that your mother was blinded by, and I don't want the same thing happening to you."

Darbi shook his head and allowed the comment about his dead mother to roll off his shoulders.

He tried to make it a point not to discuss Mona Blackmoore with anyone, not even his own grandfather.

"Not this again...."

They reached the American Airlines ticket counter, John having tossed his cigar on the walkway outside of the door with little regard of where it landed, and the quickening of his pulse was evident beneath the flesh of his throat.

"Just be careful. There's so much more to that town; it has an air, a sort of soul that can suck you in if you're not careful. I should know; that's why I left."

Darbi rolled his eyes and set through the mundane task of presenting his identification and registering his luggage.

When it was all done, they stood outside the first security check-point and said their final goodbyes, both Blackmoores satisfied with a simple handshake and slightly distant farewells, John delivering a somewhat inaudible blessing for a safe journey.

While scaling up the escalator, Darbi caught a glimpse of a woman in a period of dress that was more akin to those worn in the 1920s. Her long, red hair draped over her shoulders, and a three-stringed amber necklace caught the light of the white fluorescents above the airport.

It only lasted for a second before wisping away into nothingness, and a strange prickle attacked the back of his neck.

Darbi knew that it was a spirit, and he knew somehow (though without any real knowledge) that this apparition was meant for him and that he was somehow connected to her. Knew that their blood was the same, and he left with a strange unease.

This is going to be interesting, he thought, *interesting indeed.*

"We will be making our final descent into Seattle in ten minutes. Please make sure that your tray tables are secure and your seats are in their upright position. On behalf of the crew we thank you for flying Alaska Airlines, and we wish you a happy holiday."

Magdalene Blackmoore rubbed the crusty sleep from her brilliant amber eyes and gave a yawn, seeing the gray of clouds and the shower of snowflakes cast the world in a confusing blur. The rumble of the jet engines tickled the heels of her knee-high black leather Pradas, tucked under her tight denim Versace hip huggers.

"Jesus..." she let out, trying to regain her senses. Her thick auburn hair hung an inch past her shoulders in loose, curly tendrils, and her face held an exotic beauty which was intensified by the olive tone of her flesh. She wore a tight ribbed turtleneck with a knitted midnight-blue shawl, knotted at her left shoulder.

She turned to see her Grandmother Fiona staring at her. Though now one-hundred-and-sixteen, she was in no way out of sorts—and aside from the arthritis, which left her to the resources of a polished oak cane, she was absolutely healthy.

"Did you sleep well, dear?" Fiona asked her, holding the glass that had been her champagne, obviously waiting for one of the flight attendants to come and relieve her of it.

"I guess I had too much merlot."

Fiona gave an agreeing nod and looked about the first class cabin with crisp gray eyes. Her thick hair, which had remained red for so long, was now a dirty white and wrapped in a bun.

She wore a wine-red slip dress which came to her ankles, and her skin—though aged and heavily wrinkled—could not hide her uncompromising beauty.

"Where in the hell are those damn flight attendants? I'm about ready to just throw this goddamn glass on the aisle!"

Magdalene gave a chuckle and looked back out on the falling snow, the fertile green earth beneath them only now coming into distorted view.

For a couple of minutes they said nothing, Magdalene thinking of her mother Mabel and her cousins Kathryn and Trevor, hoping that they were both doing much better from the last time that she had seen them. It was when she was slowly drifting back into sleep that she heard her grandmother cry out, and the glass that she had been holding only moments before crashed to the floor, forcing Magdalene turned around.

"Grandma, what is it?"

Fiona's eyes were wide and filled with terror, focused on the front of the plane.

"Grandma?"

Fiona's boney fingers gripped her arm, and she slowly turned her eyes towards her granddaughter.

"He's here... don't you see him? He's here!"

Magdalene looked ahead of her, and it took her moment in all of the confusion, but at last she did.

Standing there in the front of the cabin, completely oblivious to the rest of the passengers, was a young man no more that twenty-seven years of age.

He was dressed in a black jacket and matching trousers, a white collared shirt looking formal on his body, and a silk black tie around his neck.

His face was the coldest whites, and his eyes were black and empty.

His dirty blond hair was combed neatly and parted at the hairline, and Magdalene felt what could have only been described as the coldest winter fill the cabin.

"Who... who is it?"

It took Fiona several seconds before she could muster the words.

"It...it's my husband!"

She couldn't believe it. Bradley Foster had materialized at his own will inside of the Boeing, and he looked as solid as ever.

Slowly he lifted his arm and extended his finger, pointing it at his still-living wife and granddaughter, before suddenly becoming hazy and evaporating before them.

"But, Grandma what does it mean?"

She reached for her black-and-red wood beads, which hung round her neck, and rubbed them between her fingers, chanting the god Legba's invocation, hoping for some sort of divine answer.

"It's happened."

The confusion was evident, and Magdalene had no idea how to put together what her grandmother was saying.

"But Grandma..." she began, with her voice quivering in her throat. "What has happened? I don't understand."

Fiona's eyes began to mist with tears, and they spilled down her creviced cheeks. Magdalene's heart ached for her grandmother.

"The Legacy of our family...." Her heart seemed to stop for just a moment, and her breath halted in her chest. "It's been conquered."

She couldn't believe it; in no way could she comprehend such a thing as being true.

"But... but...."

"It's been conquered, and we're all doomed!"

The plane touched down and the wheels of the airline screeched on the slightly-frozen runway, burning off the ice.

They unfastened their seatbelts and began to gather their purses. Fiona was clutching to her cane and trying desperately to keep calm. Magdalene knew that her grandmother's body wanted to give out on her, to just stop and keep her in place on that plane, but she couldn't do it. She had to move.

They stood and filed out.

People were polite enough to allow Fiona Blackmoore seniority in this endeavor, and it was good for them because it meant the quicker that they could slip out, meet with the limo driver in baggage claim, and begin making the hour-and-a-half journey up north to Bellingham. The world before them ink-blue and spotted with falling white; it made them both look at each other with reassuring smiles. It didn't matter what was happening, it didn't matter what awaited all of them; they would face it and they would survive it.

They were Blackmoores. There was no other way to be.

"Darbi...? Darbi Blackmoore, look at you!"

Darbi looked weary and tired, as he stood in the lower baggage claim of SeaTac International Airport. The first class flight had been comfortable enough, but the anxiety he was feeling at the prospect of seeing everyone had been too much to allow him any actual rest.

He nodded and smiled at the tall woman with the shock of black hair that rode down her back and her dark olive skin was scattered with tiny moles.

She was dressed in a black skirt and black turtleneck. To complete the ensemble, she had a long knitted sweater-jacket protecting her from the cold. The Italian in her was very prominent, but so was the Irish blue of her eyes.

"Cousin Francesca?"

She nodded, and they hugged. Her perfume was faint and smelled of vanilla and jasmine, and it was a great comfort to Darbi to no longer be alone on the last leg of his journey.

"God, look at ya; ye'r so handsome."

Darbi smirked at the blended Italian and Irish of her voice.

Francesca motioned to the young and classically handsome man in the black suit and a formal black-billed hat on his head. He walked over and grasped Darbi's luggage with hands sheathed in leather gloves, and directed them out to the pick-up and drop-off lanes of the mammoth airport, a black Rolls Royce limousine was waiting for them beneath the orange flood lights.

It was a quarter-past-five, and the world was falling into a quickening darkness. Their breath formed in front of them and the cold bit their cheeks. They were both relieved to be in the limo's confines.

"Why, the last time I saw ya...."

Francesca stopped herself. She was going to say *"was at your mother's funeral,"* but she didn't.

"Well, it's been quite a while."

Darbi suffered a polite grin but it hurt him too much, and he hoped that the shadow of death would not damper their holiday.

He could not begrudge his cousin because she had suffered the same pain, as all Blackmoores do. Death was an essential part of being a member of this family, and he had learned to accept that. The trouble was that he had lost his father at the age of eleven, and not more than a year later he had to bury his mother.

Yes, death was essential to this family, and he hated it.

"So, what are you doing now? Grandpa John says that you're a curator at the *Louvre* and that you're engaged."

Francesca gave a grin that seemed to be married with a frown and she thought for a moment before continuing.

"It's true, I do work at the Louvre, and I was engaged—"

Darbi interjected: "*Was*... what happened?"

Francesca reached for the bottle of Cristal that sat in the iced bucket and poured herself a glass.

"How much do you know about this family, Darbi?"

He seemed perplexed by the question, but did not see any reason in not answering it.

"Well, I know that everyone who loves us ends up dead."

Francesca looked away.

"I know that we came to America from Ireland, and that we have more secrets it seems than the government."

She laughed at this and nodded, downing her champagne and pouring herself another glass as well as one for him.

"Trust me, you're going to need this."

She handed him the glass and looked out the tinted windows. They had just passed the city of Everett and were now passing fields covered in white and rivers flowing black while the limo's speakers hummed Christmas carols calmly.

"Have you ever been able to do things that you couldn't explain? When you're angry, do objects seem to move or light bulbs implode?

"Have you been able to know when people were lying and what they were lying about, hear their thoughts, or know their secrets?"

Darbi's heart began to pound within the cavity of his chest and he gave a slight nod.

"I can hear people's thoughts, but more than that, Francesca.

"Sometimes I can go into people's heads and tell them what to do and say, or see things that aren't really there."

She nodded and smiled. It wasn't a smile of pride, but of understanding.

"We all can do things in this family. I don't really know why; it's never fully been explained, and everything is so shrouded in mystery that I don't think we'll ever truly know the truth.

"But we can.

"Some can speak with and see and hear spirits. Some, like my brother and I, are telekinetic: we can move objects with our minds.

"It really just depends on how close you are to the immediate bloodline that determines how strong you are, I suppose."

Darbi's eyes grew wide as he threw back the Cristal and poured himself another glass. His cousin had been right; he was going to need it.

"I still don't understand."

"I know, and to tell you the truth I really don't either.

"You see, Darbi, we're not the only family out there that is like this. There are families all over the world that are like we are. Adamo tells me how the church calls families like ours 'witches,' but really we're not."

Darbi thought on this and remembered something his mother had told him. "What about Vodou, and the pagan traditions of the family from Ireland?"

Francesca looked at him and grinned.

"When Sarafeene and Malachey Blackmoore came to New Orleans from Ireland, they did get involved in the practice of Vodou with the Free People of Color along the swamplands of the Irish Channel. And some—like Magdalene, Kathryn, and Queen Mab—practice the faith still, as it is mixed with Catholicism and whatever Sarafeene and Malachey came over here with.

"I think it's a very American thing; I myself have never practiced."

Darbi nodded, and feeling more at ease with the conversation, simply sipped his champagne.

"So you don't practice magic?"

Francesca gave another grin.

"Now, I didn't say that either. I can do a love spell or two, and if you need some quick cash or help finding your keys... well, I'm the girl to come to—but no, not like the rest of them.

"Your mother did more than me."

Darbi looked at her, confused, and Francesca suddenly seemed to reflect this confusion.

"What?"

"Didn't you know?"

Darbi shook his head and averted his gaze to the road, glimsping fields covered in snow and barren of cattle.

"The point is, Darbi, this family has an interesting heritage, but it is not one that is unique to us alone. And though sometimes it may seem strange, scary, or silly, it holds great power—just as your blood holds power."

Darbi looked into those compassionate blue eyes and felt the pain in him grow.

"Yeah, the power to kill."

He thought of his father, his grandmother. His cousins Sheffield and Emma, Marcel's mother. This was a family whose blood brought death, whose love created destruction.

"It's true; that's our Legacy, a Legacy that has plagued us for over two hundred years. But our blood has the power to help if only you let it."

Darbi scoffed, and Francesca could not hold it against him. It had taken her a long time to come to that revelation herself.

"So why didn't you marry? Was it because of the Legacy, as it's called?"

Francesca shook her head.

"There are people out there, as I've said—families and individuals like us, and when we cross paths it's not always good. Bad people who can do the things that we can do attacked me and my fiancé. They had been stalking us for some time and one of them—a woman who was a 'psychic vampire,' so to speak—put her hands on my fiancé and drained him of his energy, his health.

"Before I could do anything, the woman's husband struck me over the head and knocked me out. When I woke up, my fiancé and I were both in the hospital; in the end, he didn't make it."

Francesca's eyes were now dripping with tears.

"What did you do?"

"I found them both at the Eiffel Tower one afternoon, about a week after my fiancé's funeral. I didn't even give them a chance to respond. I focused all of my strength, all of my power on the husband and I threw him off the tower.

"The woman looked at me, horrified, and tried to run. I used my power to throw her repeatedly into the metal beams. A lot of people thought that she was going crazy and purposefully trying to hurt herself.

"There was so much blood.

"Before anyone could get a hold of her, I threw her off the top just as I had done with her husband. I didn't even bother to learn their identities or why they had attacked us in the first place."

Darbi wasn't sure if there was any guilt on his cousin's part, and he could understand if there wasn't. Hell was private and it was real; if this was now where she was, it was Francesca's hell alone and he could not intervene in her saving.

"Does being us get any easier?" he asked.

Francesca looked at him and shrugged.

"Honestly, Darbi, I don't know. I think that it's not about *it* getting easier, but us getting stronger—and sometimes strength is the only way to make it through our days."

He nodded and finished his champagne, opting not to have another glass. In a defeated state of mind, feeling as if there was nothing left to say, he looked out of the window and an ominous feeling took hold.

They were curving around jagged cliffs, which looked fierce with dominant evergreens which appeared like armed guards. The limo wound around this and navigated cautiously through the falling snow. From Francesca's window he spied a dropping valley filled with more trees, and he knew that somehow they were at the edge of the world.

Like Jonathan Harker making his final round to Dracula's castle, they neared the city of Bellingham, and as if both tuned into the forces of the unseen, Francesca and Darbi looked at one another. The car growing all the more dark, a dark that was so different from any that Darbi had ever known before, and the world of the living and the dead suddenly existed as one.

NINETEEN

"Cheri...baby?" Her heart seemed to stop, and her words caught in her throat as Cheri listened to Greg's voice on the other end of the line. The strained voice sounded as if it were ten.

"Greg?"

She was standing in her living room, the walls painted cream and bordered by old pine wainscoting, the twelve-foot windows bringing in the winter darkness.

"I've seen him, Cheri, I've seen him." His voice was so vacant, as if he were slowly losing his mind. At this point, she didn't doubt it.

"Seen who, Greg; what are you talking about?"

She felt as if her legs were going to give out, and she walked over to the large candy-striped sofa, seating herself atop the cushions.

"Christian. He's alive. That's why I didn't go to the funeral; I knew that it wasn't real." She swallowed her tears; there was no reason to give him that kind of power.

"Greg, you've totally lost it. God, that's not even funny; why would you say something like that?"

She expected him to laugh, to tell her that she was a fucking cunt, but it never happened.

"Cheri, it's true; he's alive. He came to see me and he told me things, things that you really should hear."

She didn't want to deal with this; she wasn't going to deal with it.

"Goodbye, Greg."

Cheri hung up the phone before he could say more. Feeling more alone than ever before, Cheri collected her knees against her chest and wrapped her arms around them.

297

Her parents wouldn't be back until Christmas Eve, and she was home alone; left to deal with all of the bad things, all of the guilt that harbored along the shores of her heart.

She cried then. She cried fast and she cried hard, feeling for the first time in a long time that it was okay. She was alone and there was no one to hear her sobs.

She was completely alone.

"Fucking bitch!" Greg Sheer yelled at the phone.

He was standing in his bedroom, made barren by his frustration over the news of Christian's death. But he was relieved when he came home from driving around the block of Fifteenth Street after the news first broke, to find Christian Vasquez standing in his room with a smile on his face, a gaping wound on the side of his stomach and crusted blood on the top of his head.

He had asked Greg if he wanted to touch it, and he did. It felt squishy and wet between his fingers and he licked the bloody goop off of his hands and felt happy for the first time in his life to see that his best friend was alive, but no longer without blemish.

'I told you they won't believe you if you told them the truth, if you told them that I'm alive.'

Greg looked at Christian, who was standing there with his arms folded across his chest, his black eyes red with the blood that had dripped inside.

"But why? You're here; I thought that she'd be happy."

Christian laughed and shook his head. Greg didn't get the humor, but he still liked the joke; if only he were in on it.

'It doesn't work like that....'

He sat down on Greg's bed.

'But they will, soon enough.'

Greg rubbed his face, made scratchy by the days gone by without shaving. He was standing in the same pair of navy blue boxer-briefs that he had worn for the past three days, and he walked over to Christian, grinning.

"Do that thing you did to Trevor, that thing in the video."

Christian smiled and lifted his hands, slipping one behind Greg's buttocks and another into his underwear, massaging Greg's growing erection.

'You mean this?'

Christian pulled it out and opened his mouth, letting Greg inside.

"Yeah... that," Greg growled.

He brought his hands up and placed them on top of Christian's bloodied skull, sifting his fingers through the crimson mess. He laughed while Christian sucked him off and looked at his fingers. They were caked in blood and membrane and he smiled, sticking his fingers in his mouth and tasting the mess.

Finally, he had Christian where he wanted him. Finally, he was right where he was always meant to be: worshipping his masculinity, using his mouth to admit that Greg Sheer was the better man—and as a result of this generosity, he would do whatever his best friend asked him to do.

The first car to arrive was Francesca's and Darbi's.

Braxton could feel the excitement in the house; in fact, it seemed so thick that it could have been cut cleanly with a knife. He and Trevor had been lying out on his bed not five minutes before, making out and grinding against one another over their clothes, while Kathryn presided over the hired chefs in the kitchen.

Earlier that day, in one of the guest rooms, Braxton had used his gift to look inside of Trevor and ever since then, whenever they touched for long periods of time visions came against his will.

"Oh, man..." Braxton said, with a huff between his lips.

Trevor looked at him curiously and Braxton just shrugged it off, telling him that it was nothing. It went on like this for over forty minutes, the boys fighting against their own temptations to tear off one another's clothes and explore each other once again with their tongues.

It had driven him crazy.

He had seen visions of Trevor as a happy little boy with a mom and a dad, blowing out birthday candles and wearing a paper hat. He caught visions of Trevor sitting in an adjacent room and writing in a trance-like state, with hazel eyes void of any real thought.

With each kiss—each massaging press of tongue and each play-ful touch of wandering fingers—Braxton glimpsed through more and more of the windows into Trevor's world, and it was increas-ingly addicting.

When the limo's horn gave a honk, the two teenagers sat up and ran their hands through their disheveled hair and grinned sheepishly as they tried to hide away their hard-ons.

And now here they were in the front foyer, Braxton shaking hands with people he had never met but knew nonetheless, and Trevor smiling in a way he had never seen before.

"What an attractive young man..." the beautiful woman named Francesca said, her bright blue eyes—so unlike Kathryn's—focused on Braxton Volaverunt.

"Yes, he is..." Kathryn began, looking at him and sharing a se-cret grin. "And completely devoted to your cousin."

Francesca looked slightly stunned, and blinked twice before nodding and turning her attentions to Trevor.

"And you, my sweet boy! You're going to be eighteen in three days!"

Trevor blushed and looked away, while Francesca grinned and pulled her cousin to her, giving him a tight and loving hug.

"And might I also add," Francesca whispered, but loud enough for everyone to hear, "that you have great taste in men."

Trevor smiled and stepped away, looking at his cousin Darbi.

"Hey, buddy..." Darbi said with a grin.

He opened his arms and Trevor fell into his embrace.

For Darbi, seeing Trevor was like coming home. It was like everything in life would be okay, and he was proud once again to carry the name Blackmoore.

"Hi, Darbi," he responded, and they glimpsed Kathryn wipe a tear from her eye.

"I feel like I have my boys home at last!"

Darbi grinned gently and hugged his cousin lovingly.

"You do, cousin... you do," Darbi said to her.

For a moment, Braxton didn't know what to do. He had his hands tucked in his pockets and focused his gaze on Trevor, who was grinning dumbly.

"Hey, man, what's up? I'm Darbi."

He extended his hand and jerked his head in a slight nod. Braxton returned the handshake and nodded back.

"Braxton... Braxton Volaverunt."

If he had been paying attention, he would have seen the knowing glances shared between Kathryn and Francesca. The strange thing was that with Darbi, Braxton felt as if he was with J.T. or something, because his demeanor became what Trevor would later say "was a little more butch."

"Here, let me get that for you."

Braxton grabbed their luggage and began to make his way towards the stairs. He stopped only briefly to give Trevor a peck on the cheek, and Darbi was quick to follow him upstairs offering to help with the suitcases.

"So, how long have you known Trevor?" Darbi asked Braxton, following it up with a yawn. They were now in the guest room nearest to the back balcony. The lone full looked comfortable and sleek between the sharp end-tables.

"Um, well, for five years."

Braxton threw the luggage on the bed and they stepped out, making their way to the room with the two fulls—where Darbi would be sharing space with Adamo, who would be arriving later in the evening.

Darbi nodded and adjusted the baseball cap on his head, knowing that there was no point in trying to use his physicality to intimidate, because Braxton's strength was evident by the black tee that stretched across his strong frame.

"You play sports?" Darbi asked him.

Braxton looked at him with those large brown eyes and grinned.

"Soccer, though occasionally I wrestle.

"You?"

Darbi nodded.

"Lacrosse and football."

Braxton grinned, but showed no signs of awkwardness.

"So, how long have you been fucking him?"

Braxton looked at Darbi and had to fight back every urge to strike him across the face.

"That wouldn't be a good idea."

Braxton smiled when he remembered what Trevor had told him about all of the Blackmoores having powers.

"Just answer the question."

"Two weeks."

Darbi nodded, but showed no signs of displeasure or approval. "And do you love him?"

Braxton smiled widely and sheepishly. This was the easiest question to answer.

"With all of my heart. I've loved him since the first day I laid eyes on him, and I know I always will."

Darbi smirked only briefly and nodded.

"Good."

They made their way to the door and Braxton stopped him, gripping tightly to Darbi's hand. The flash was brief, just enough to get what he needed.

"And Darbi,"—he leaned in really close, close enough to smell his cologne mixed with perspiration—"I won't tell anyone that you pissed in the chalice at your school's chapel."

Darbi stepped back and looked at him, bewildered.

"Wait... how did you...?"

Braxton grinned and winked.

"Just because I'm not a Blackmoore doesn't mean I'm not special too."

Darbi nodded and laughed. The both of them made their way back down the steps to rejoin everyone else in the kitchen.

"God, this is good... is this Mitchell's stuff?" Francesca asked, sipping the thick merlot. Kathryn nodded.

"Yeah, he sends it to me at least once a week."

The girls laughed, and Trevor stood with his soda, his elbows pressed on the island's counter.

"Lucky bitch."

They chuckled, and Trevor rolled his eyes. His home had never felt so warm, so inviting, no longer feeling like a tomb. It was vibrant and pulsating. It was full of life, and greatly needed. It had been so long since the house was full of people that he had forgotten what a home filled with laughter was like.

"I only get my bottles from Mitchell once a month."

Kathryn laughed again; that great, deep laugh that bellowed. She leaned back and her thick hair with its slight wave moved from side to side, and her usual three-tiered pearl necklace glistened in the tract lights.

"Yeah, but I know damn well he sends it to you by the crateful. It's not my fault if your greedy, drunk, Italian ass guzzles it all down in one night."

The women laughed, and Francesca had to wipe the tears from her eyes.

"It's not gone in a day...."

Kathryn looked at her, doubtful.

"It's gone in a week!"

And with this, the women were howling and pouring more wine from Mitchell's Napa winery. The Blackmoore name was advertised with impressive type and bordered in gold.

"Hello, ladies..." Darbi said.

He and Braxton were strutting into the kitchen, and it was strangely off-putting to Trevor. He felt as if he were at school and seeing another Braxton. The Braxton who played in a band and got hit on by all of the girls, the Braxton who played soccer and won trophies for the honor of Mariner High School. He knew that there was no reason to feel so out of place, but suddenly he did.

They were talking about things that he couldn't relate to. They were talking about sports and cars and even fraternities. These were things that Trevor Blackmoore knew nothing about. He wasn't any of these things. He wasn't popular; he didn't have tons of friends or take part in after-school activities.

Quietly Trevor slipped out of the kitchen and wandered down the darkened hall. With the threat of tears, he twisted the knob and entered the large office, still filled with Tom's things. He stepped inside and closed the door behind him. The light splashed in from the adjoining sun room, and the tiers of crystal which cried from the chandelier glittered above him.

He felt as if he could not really relate to Braxton, if a person really took an objective look at their relationship. They had become friends in the first place because Braxton had felt sorry for him, and from there that pity had grown into confused love.

"God, I'm such an idiot."

The polished floorboards creaked beneath his steps and the long drapes billowed ever so slightly. Sullenly Trevor walked over to the large French doors and threw them open. The paint seemed to fight just a little, but soon Trevor was standing out on the darkened sun porch.

The windows lined the upper-half and the white wood walls were decorated with pictures and side-tables. There were rows of wicker chairs painted the same crisp white, and the brick was cold beneath his sock-covered feet.

"Daddy, I don't know what to do... I wish you were here."

The brims of his eyes lined with tears, and Trevor fell into one of those wicker chairs, folding his legs into the seat.

This time of the year was always the hardest with his father gone. Sheffield had been the stable voice; he had always been the one to tell Trevor what to do, and how to handle whatever dilemma seemed to present itself to his son. But now he was gone, and so was a part of Trevor.

'Trevor....'

He looked up to see the figure of his father standing in the shadows at the opposite end of the sun porch, his face white and his lips curved into a half-smile. Trevor couldn't see his eyes. Those eyes of his were black and empty, but he didn't feel threatened.

"Trevor?"

He turned to see Francesca staring at him from the door frame. He looked back, but the apparition of his father had vanished, just as he knew it would.

"Oh, hi, Francesca."

He wiped the tears from his eyes and looked towards the window.

"The last time I was out here, it was your mother crying in that chair."

She walked over and took a seat in the neighboring chair, her heels tapping on the brick. She reached out for him and placed her hand gently on his knee.

"I remember."

He swallowed, and the orange fluorescent shone through the icy panes of glass from across the street.

"You don't mind if I smoke, do you?"

Trevor shook his head and watched in mild fascination as Francesca pulled a silver cigarette case from her purse, which he hadn't even realized she brought in with her.

The glow from the lighter sparked in her eyes and she took a long drag from the cigarette.

"So, why are you out here?"

Trevor shrugged.

"Well, this is my guess... it has to do with the very attractive young man in there laughing it up with your cousin?"

Again, Trevor only shrugged.

"And they're talking about things that you couldn't possibly relate to, and in fact, I bet he's acting completely different from when it's just the two of you."

The tears made his eyes luminescent, and Trevor was quick to wipe them away.

"It's just that I forgot what kind of person he is when he's around other guys."

Francesca looked at him perplexed.

"But, Trevor, you're a guy... I should know; I changed you on more than one occasion when you were a baby."

She tried to coax a grin out of him, but it wasn't working.

"But I'm not like them. I don't play sports, I'm not macho; in fact, I'm pretty much a sissy. When he's with other guys its all 'dudes' and 'what's ups'—you know, guy talk, and I don't do that."

His cousin grinned shortly and sighed.

"I should hope not."

The snow fell silently against the glass, and Francesca smiled. She thought of her dead fiancé; she thought of the blood spilt in his name, and it made her feel empty inside.

There's no point to any of it, is there? she questioned.

"No, there isn't."

By the passive look on Trevor's face, it was obvious to her that he hadn't the slightest clue that he had just answered her thoughts, and she knew to keep it that way.

For several minutes they sat in this silence. There were no words that Francesca could deliver for comfort, and she knew that it wasn't her responsibility to do so. This was something that Trevor needed to figure out on his own, and this was also something that Braxton Volaverunt needed to vindicate.

God, a Volaverunt....

"Well, my love," she said, standing, "I think I'm going to go back into the kitchen. Your mother laid out a prosciutto and cheese plate, and if I don't get in there now those two strapping young men are going to consume it all in a matter of seconds."

Trevor nodded and smiled as Francesca bent to kiss him on the head. Her thick black hair grazed his face gently and was richly perfumed.

He watched her walk back into the office with steady eyes, and he felt the knot in his stomach tighten once again as he thought about how well Darbi and Braxton were getting along, and he wondered if he would ever find common ground to relate to Braxton again.

"You're in a band... that's tight!" Darbi said to Braxton, sticking a ball of cantaloupe wrapped in prosciutto Di Parma into his mouth, the sweet fruit dancing well with the saltiness of the Italian ham.

"Yeah, the Spit Monkeys."

He felt somewhat strange, as if he were bragging—though it was Kathryn who had mentioned it, but nonetheless it was still awkward.

"My friend J.T. and I started it. You really should ask Trevor about it... he's our biggest fan, after all."

It was then that he took notice of the fact that his boyfriend was no longer in the kitchen, and the feeling of his insides dropping in his gut took hold.

"Where is he, by the way?"

Kathryn shrugged.

It was then that Francesca walked back into the room with a knowing look on her face, and her eyes immediately fell on the young Volaverunt.

"He's in the sun room... I think you should go talk to him."

He nodded and made silent pardon as he slipped by her and walked out into the house, maneuvering through the darkened hall and slipping through the opened office door, the lights from outside casting on the floorboards.

The immense French doors were wide open, beckoning him to the later-added room.

He stood still for a moment just beyond the door's frame, feeling his heart sink ever-so-slightly at the sight that presented itself before him.

There, in one of the many polished wicker chairs, sat Trevor, his face directed towards the windows above him watching the flakes fall. His large eyes were like liquid, and the tears that fell were staining his cheeks and sparkled like glass.

Braxton's lips parted, though he could find no words to speak. His chocolate eyes were wide and innocent, though they mirrored a kind of pain and understanding that most people would never know—but that Trevor understood all too well.

He sighed, and this seemed to garner Trevor's attention, but he looked only briefly before turning his focus back to the window.

Cautiously, Braxton made his way to the chair that Francesca had been occupying not five minutes earlier, but he did not sit. Instead he crouched in front of Trevor and looked him in the face. He was attempting to find some reason for this sadness, but there was none that he could deduce, and he knew that it would be an invasion of privacy to lay his hands on him and uncover the truth.

"Hey," Trevor said to him, only briefly acknowledging his presence with his eyes.

The image of Braxton kneeling before him in those tight fitting denim boot-cuts that he had changed into earlier in the day, and the black tee which stretched across his muscular chest and torso, was torturous. His tattoo was partially visible beneath the tee's sleeve.

But it was that other-worldly beautiful face with those enormously soulful brown eyes that forced him to avert his gaze.

"Hey back."

For the first time in their lives, the silence between them was uncomfortable, and Braxton didn't like it. It was as if within a matter of thirty minutes a great wall had been constructed between them, and he hadn't the slightest clue as how to tear it down.

He put his hand on Trevor's knee and quite quickly he felt a jarring pain in the back of his skull, and sharp, brutally bright shades of red filled his mind.

He clutched the back of his head and fell back, writhing in silent agony. Trevor pulled back and looked at Braxton with fear and guilt in his eyes, finding it impossible to react.

In an instant it was over, and Braxton looked up from the cold brick with tears clouding his vision, and the vessels in his eyes felt like they were going to burst.

He did not move, and neither did Trevor. They both sat staring at one another, and for the first time Trevor seemed like a predator in wait. A lion on the prowl, innocent enough until it was ready to pounce.

I don't understand... he said to himself.

Braxton wiped the tears from his eyes and stood, grasping the arm of the nearby chair, and throwing himself into it. His face was red and his breath erratic. For a moment he could not look at anything, it was all too hard and too confusing.

Braxton placed his head in his hands and struggled to regain control of his senses, to relax his head and ease himself into one cohesive calm.

"I'm... I'm sorry," Trevor offered, and it was sincere.

Braxton wanted to scream at him. He wanted to tell him how horrible and irresponsible he was. In truth, he wanted to hit him.

"I wouldn't blame you if you did," said Trevor, obviously reading his thoughts.

Braxton looked up at him and felt sick and awful.

Here was this boy that he loved more than anything else in the world, a boy who had been played with and ostracized, and abandoned either by death or social status, and he wanted to hit him.

"It's not right... it's not right..." Braxton repeated over and over again, more for himself than for Trevor.

"I didn't mean...."

Braxton looked up at him, the pain still evident on his face.

"What I mean is... look, I'm sorry."

Trevor could find no excuses, and Braxton didn't want him to. There was something going on, and he wondered if Trevor had wanted to keep him out of his head. Trevor looked away.

"That's it, isn't it? You thought that I was going to read you."

Trevor's tears spilled down his face and glistened in the orange streetlight. Here was a power in Trevor, one that the young Blackmoore didn't even realize he had, and suddenly Braxton wondered what else it was he could do.

"Baby, I'm sorry," Braxton found himself saying, without truly meaning to.

He didn't really understand why he was apologizing, but in all of that jarring confusion he caught the sense that he had inadvertently hurt Trevor in some way, and now he needed to know how.

"It's stupid; really it is," Trevor was pleading. He needed Braxton to understand, but he hadn't the slightest idea of how to do it without feeling extremely selfish.

"But why...? What did I do?"

Trevor shook his head and bowed it in shame.

"Please, Trevor, help me understand why you're so sad."

Trevor's lips quivered, but no words came out. To Braxton it felt like this wall was only growing stronger, and he knew that if Trevor didn't allow him to break through now, then it would never come down.

"You'll just hate me."

This declaration hurt him. He could not understand how Trevor could ever think that he could hate him. Even when they had fallen out after that doomed kiss at J.T.'s party, he had never been angry with Trevor—hurt, yes, but never angry.

"When have I ever done that?"

Trevor did not answer, and Braxton was at his wits' end.

"Do you trust me?"

Trevor shrugged, and Braxton began to reach out his hand.

"Trust me...."

His fingers walked across Trevor's knee and began to grip Trevor's hand.

"Trust me."

Their fingers connected, and that familiar heat pulsated through his palm and fingers, the sensation of being filled through his veins once again, and he opened himself to the visions.

He felt the pain and slight envy of Trevor watching boys run around on a field; the want of needing to belong, to be like everyone else.

He felt the frustration in Trevor's heart as two boys sat around talking about sports cars in a cafeteria, and the sensation of knowing that he could never enter into a conversation like this and come off convincingly that he actually enjoyed the discussion.

Though Braxton was just as queer as Trevor, he could pull off a heterosexual façade. It was never intentional; it was just assumed by most that Braxton liked girls, though he was more than willing to tell otherwise if only asked.

The problem was that he rarely ever was.

Trevor didn't play sports except for swimming; in fact, he didn't like them.

He wasn't into cars and racing. He didn't know how to build things or work on engines. He was a boy who kept to himself. He liked to read and write and watch movies. He enjoyed cooking and going out to good restaurants.

He didn't lift weights or work out as consistently as the other boys, including Braxton. He was different; completely the opposite of Braxton.

But that had been one of the first things that he had liked about Trevor Blackmoore.

He was innocent in ways that so many teenage boys weren't, and he was wise about things that most adults could never be. Braxton had wanted to protect him. He had wanted to shelter his historically enriched world from those who would want to tear it down, and he wouldn't trade in Trevor Blackmoore for anyone.

"Baby..." Braxton let out.

The tears dripped from his eyes, and he sniffled casually as he looked at his boyfriend. He could not even come close to understanding the separation that Trevor felt every day of his life—until now, that is.

"I'd never leave you for someone like that."

He began to reevaluate those images and he realized that the boys on the field were his soccer team, and that Trevor had been watching him. He understood that the two boys in the cafeteria were he and J.T.

It was making so much sense now, and all of it strung into a web that told Braxton that Trevor felt as if he could never be like him. That they would always be separated by the way in which they expressed their sex.

"I know, it's stupid."

Trevor lifted his fingers to his eyes and discarded the salty tears.

"It's just that I saw how well you were getting along with Darbi, and I wondered if you ever wanted someone like that... someone more like you."

Braxton shook his head and brought Trevor's hands to his lips, kissing each knuckle.

"Never."

Trevor looked at him and seemed to frown.

"I mean it. Trevor, you're all I've ever wanted. If I could show that to you I would, but I don't think I can make my power work in reverse."

He grinned and Trevor chuckled, though he was quick to stop.

"Don't hold onto it, just let it out... I love you, and you can tell me anything. You can tell me your hopes and your fears. We can dance in circles for no reason if you want to, and I will always be more than happy to oblige.

"We can lie out on your bed and rest in each other's arms, listening to our heartbeats. We can do whatever you want to, and you can say whatever you want to, and I will always listen and I will always love you."

Trevor nodded in acceptance, and Braxton wrapped his arms around him, pulling the young Blackmoore from off the chair and crushing him gently to his chest.

They stood there for countless minutes, taking in the comfort of each other's warmth and the scent of their skin mixed with cologne. There was nowhere else that Braxton would rather be, and no one else he'd rather be with.

They had spent their layover in Idaho practicing how to control his power. Alex Baker had been a patient study, and after two hours of trying, he finally was able to lift selected items on command, while Adamo stood proud.

It wasn't easy.

Within those first one hundred and twenty minutes, Alex had managed to affect all the trash cans within a one-hundred-foot radius, the garbage within erupting and billowing in the air, causing airport patrons to shriek out in fear.

He caused many suitcases the fly across the airport and hit many passengers in the face and legs.

Adamo was going to suggest they stop when Alex finally concentrated on a chair and made it lift without the others moving—then, setting it down, he tried it with two with the same pleasing outcome.

Now they were riding down the packed elevator towards the great carousels of the SeaTac baggage claim. Alex visibly nervous, and Adamo wanting to tell him that he had nothing to worry about, but the further they descended the more doubtful he became.

They hit ground and Adamo walked beside Alex, his long cleric's coat skirting across the floor, and people about him mumbled apologies as they rushed by in desperation to meet with family and friends.

He spotted the limo driver holding up the big white sign with his last name advertised in big black letters, but he was not yet ready to meet with the woman until he had made sure that Alex was situated.

"There they are!" Alex cried.

He was pointing at a smiling and exquisite-looking woman. Her face was gorgeous and her eyes were sharp. She looked so commanding, and Adamo thought of Kathryn and the air of dominance that his cousin projected.

The young man standing with her was classically handsome and his suit was elegant and yet subdued, as if he was above attracting attention.

"Alex, how are you; was your flight safe?" the woman asked her nephew.

She was dressed in a lilac skirt with a matching jacket; luminescent ivy vines crawled up the fabric, and beneath this she wore a white oxford, opened at the neckline, and that pearled cross was strung twice around her neck.

The brother stood *en garde* at the sight of Adamo, but remained cordial. The woman looked at him for a moment as if she might know him, but she seemed to shake it away and extend her hand which Adamo received.

"Elisabeth Dianaca, and this is my brother, Joshua Dianaca."

Dianaca—the name set off an alarm, but he was quick to disarm this from becoming a real, tangible thought... one thought that perhaps could be read.

"Adamo."

He omitted his last name for his own protection. Though he doubted a public spectacle, he knew that it was too much to risk.

She grinned and nodded, pointing out his accent and telling him it was nice.

"*Grazie.*"

Joshua extended his hand to Adamo, but he took it only gently, sensing the intention behind those eyes.

"I accompanied your nephew on the plane, kept him company... you know?"

Elisabeth nodded and smiled.

"Your accent... do you have Irish in there as well?"

He nodded and placed his hand gently on Alex's shoulder, but only for a moment.

"Do you know any Irish?" he asked, only now hearing the slight English of her words.

Elisabeth and Joshua looked at one another before she answered.

"Only one family, really...but they were very arrogant people."

Adamo nodded and played himself ignorant to her words. He was quite certain that at this point the siblings had not put two and two together, but he wasn't willing to risk it.

"Well, I need to gather my luggage. I hope you all have a pleasant holiday, and Alex...."

The boy looked up at him; the innocence and adoration that resided in his face was not sure to last, and Adamo felt his heart breaking.

"Take care to be good. Study hard, and remember that no matter what you do in life, no matter how confused or alone you may get, remember that God is listening..." he glanced quickly at the boy's aunt and uncle and then back at Alex, "and so am I."

He slipped his card to the young boy, and Alex looked at it quickly and tucked it in his pocket. With his thoughts Adamo told the young boy not to show it in case of emergency, but he couldn't be sure if Alex had any sort of telepathy. And in the end, it probably wouldn't matter.

"Happy Christmas!" Elisabeth called out.

"*Buon Natale!*"

Father Adamo Blackmoore made his way over to the female limo driver and directed her to follow him to gather his luggage. He knew that Alex's world was going to change forever. He was a member of a great family that had been at odds with the Blackmoores since the family had first moved to Bellingham and into the posh neighborhood of South Hill.

The family had been at the crest of the occult scene of the Victorian city, but by the late Seventies the family had been run out of their ornate purple Victorian down the street from the Blackmoore homes.

Though the feuding had started long before that, including the killings; but it was this Blackmoore domination that had set the stage for a war that had yet to come, but had been brewing for years.

Alex was going to be taught by them, educated in their traditions, and would inherit their hate for the Blackmoore name, and Adamo prayed that he would never have to see the young man again.

Once more he caught a flash of his sister in his thoughts, and he wondered what it could all mean.

Would he ever get the answers?

By nine o'clock, the house on Knox Street was filled with jumbled conversation. Adamo had arrived and was now chatting it up with Francesca and Kathryn, while Queen Mab sat in a corner chair, looking at all of them in silence with a glass of scotch.

Darbi and Braxton conversed about their schools and most importantly their schools' sports teams. Though Braxton was now more than mindful of Trevor and his inclusion.

Magdalene and Fiona had arrived shortly after Adamo, and Fiona, for all her energy, was already passed out in a chair neighboring that of her daughter Mabel's.

"We need another platter..." Magdalene said to her cousin Trevor, downing the rest of her merlot in its glass, and Trevor smiled at her.

Like Adamo and Francesca, she was alluring with her beautiful golden skin and amber eyes, which sparkled like the necklace around his aunt's neck.

"All right." Trevor took her glass and walked into the kitchen.

He smiled affectionately at Braxton before wandering down the darkened corridor, ignoring the faces of dead Blackmoores, Burgeses, and Maylands who seemed to be eyeing his every step.

The kitchen was blessedly empty. The hired chefs had slipped out as soon as they finished the dinner, and had set them secure in heated basins and covered the food in tin foil. Dinner had been as routine as everything else, and now the family was working through an after-dinner assortment of wines and cheeses.

The window that looked out on the alley at the side of the house was glistening blue with snow, and the kitchen, usually so sterile, appeared warm and inviting.

"There they are," he said, smiling.

He walked over to the island and looked at the gourmet cheeses, all lined up and waiting to be eaten.

There were two jars of *Boilie's* goat's milk cheese from Ryefield Farm on the shores of *Lough Ramour*, which was forty-five miles northwest of Dublin. The creamy, hand-rolled balls of cheese the size of golf balls sat in a mixture of sunflower oil, herbs, and garlic, keeping it fresh and young. The cheese spread easily and had a smooth, slightly tangy flavor like a French chèvre.

Trevor unscrewed the jars and stuck a tiny metal pick inside, removing the cheese and placing them neatly on the white platter.

With a sharp cheese knife he began to cut the vintage Irish cheddar, which was secured in black wax. This cheese was aged two years before being sold, and therefore earned the title of a vintage cheese. The flavor was rich and rounded with a firm, smooth body. It was probably one of his favorites.

Next, he cut into the block of Carrigaline. A farmhouse cheese from County Cork, it was named for the town from where it came, derived from the Gaelic *Carraig-Ui-Leeighin*, which meant "Rock of the Lynes," and was wrapped in a spring grass-green wax.

He had just moved to the last of the cheeses when the lights above him began to flicker before going out, and the curtains about the windows began to rustle.

"Hello?" he called out.

His heart was thundering in his chest, and he could not help but feel the certain malice that filled the air around him. In fact, it was all-consuming. It was thick and tainted and yet strangely familiar.

"Who's there?"

His eyes moved erratically around the darkened kitchen, and to his surprise this darkness only seemed to grow, and he knew that it was not natural.

"I'm not afraid of you."

His voice was hushed and his breath took form in front of his face, and he realized then how cold the kitchen had become.

"Shit!"

He clutched the collar of his shirt and backed up slowly against the sink, suddenly fearful for his life.

'And you shouldn't be, Trevor Blackmoore.'

The voice was Jonathan's, but at the same time it wasn't. He had never heard this decay in the spirit's tone, and for the first time in his life he feared it.

"Jonathan, what are you doing... why don't you show yourself?"

He felt the spirit laugh, and he realized what was true about the specter, something the spirit was going to verify.

'I am... for the first time since my years as flesh and blood, I am.'

This was evil, complete and utterly. Jonathan was no longer the needy phantom that clung to Trevor or this house; he was something else, something more entirely.

'Correct. I am so much more!'

Trevor closed his eyes and struggled to take command of his environment, to reclaim his home and make it his own.

"Get thee behind me, Satan...."

The spirit laughed once again.

'You dare! You dare invoke such a prayer, when you yourself know that such a being as Satan does not exist? How foolish.'

Trevor could feel a strange, whirling tingle inside of himself. It was a power that was circulating throughout his body, but he hadn't the slightest idea of how to use it. He couldn't tap into it and make it move. It just stayed inside of him, restless and waiting.

'I will give you one chance... be with me, help me.... You don't want to be alone with the things that are about to come....'

Trevor dared not try to make sense of his words, and there seemed no reason to.

"No, spirit.... I denounce you!"

He could feel the hurt and resentful anger of the specter, but he would not budge, not for anything—especially when it felt like this.

'Fine. Then you will die with the rest of them; your kith and kin. You shall rot beneath the earth and your blood will continue no more... you shall know no peace even after death!'

Trevor shook his head, and everything around him was frosting over, ice forming on every corner hinge and from every drop of water from the faucet of the sink.

He shut his eyes tight as he began to hear the cracking sound of ice and the cold numbing of his fingers. He thought then that he was going to die, but just as quickly as this had come, the kitchen was once again warm and bright and when he opened his eyes he found Magdalene standing in the doorframe with her fingers twirling around her beads.

"Everything okay?" she asked knowingly. Her eyes were steady and compassionate.

Trevor nodded and searched casually around the kitchen.

"Um, yeah... I just got a little of the oil from those jars in my eyes, that's all."

Unconvincingly, he began to rub his eyes as if they were irritated, and Magdalene nodded.

"Well, I was just wondering what was taking so long with my drink."

She gripped the bottle that stood on the island and held it up.

"And here it is! So, well... yeah, okay, I'm going to go now, and... yeah."

Trevor watched her turn and make her way back out the door when she suddenly stopped, turned, and looked on her twenty-three-year-younger cousin.

"Be careful of what they tell you. Just because they're dead doesn't mean they don't lie."

He gave her a peculiar look, but Magdalene only winked and disappeared back through the hall.

TWENTY

She had spent so many hours here on the floor of her son's room, trying to piece together the story of his life and who he was to the rest of the world. Through all of his trophies and various awards and certificates, she was no closer to understanding him than when she was first delivered the news of his death.

Lila Vasquez had lost a tremendous amount of weight in the past week, and her already-petite frame appeared sickly, and she thought the dark circles under her eyes made her look like an addict. The world felt as if it had caved in on itself, suffocating and extreme, spilling into her lungs and drowning her from the inside, gathering like a giant weight over her life.

Emanuel had not been home, save for the few minutes that he stopped by to check in before leaving again—before he made up some stupid excuse as to why he could not be with her to comfort her, to remind her that she was not alone in this and that she was loved.

Her son's face stared back at her through glossy photographs. Faces of friends and lips curled in grins and clumsy smiles, eyes bright, some red-eyed from the camera's flash. Times on beaches and on soccer fields, parties where the look of alcohol was evident on teenage faces, hands gripping to red and blue plastic cups.

She wanted so desperately to be able to reach through and touch her son, to slip into his world and know his soft face and smiling eyes, to hear him tell her once more that he loved her, to hear him call her 'Mother' one last time. It had all fallen apart; it was chipping away and she did not know how much longer she could hold on.

In the silent darkness of her home she heard the knock on her front door, and then the chime of her doorbell echo off the walls and carry up to her ears on the second floor.

"What...?"

Her voice was hoarse and almost gone. Wearily she rose from the floor and padded barefoot down the hall and down the steps of the opulent stairs, seeing the shadowed silhouette of a man on the other side of the glass.

I forgot to turn on the porch lights.

With a great amount of fatigue, Lila opened her front door and switched on the lights, the man's face coming into harsh view.

He was tall, perhaps 6'5, his eyes dark, brown hair combed back and slightly greasy. A hardness in his face and the way in which he stood told her that he was a cop.

"Mrs. Vasquez?"

She nodded.

"I'm detective Randy Kit, Homicide Division. I need to ask you questions about your son."

Lila nodded, and yet did not step aside. No way in hell was she going to let this man into her home.

"What about?"

He closed his eyes for just a moment, telling her that he expected the question.

"Well, it's routine to investigate things like suicide or fatal car accidents as possible foul play. I just want to know if on the day of his death, did Christian go see any of his friends?"

Lila shook her head.

"I couldn't tell you. You see, Detective, I was out of the country on business... but he was best friends with Greg Sheer. He only lives up the block ... same street. Address is 1718... you can't miss it."

"Anyone else?"

Lila nodded.

"Cheri Hannifin... you can find her on North Garden."

At first she was going to omit his name, but she knew that he could answer any and all questions. In a way, he knew her son the most.

"And Trevor Blackmoore."

At the mention of the boy's name, Detective Randy Kit appeared to come to life, eyes wide with interest.

"Well, thank you, Mrs. Vasquez. Like I said, this is just routine."

He pivoted on his heel and began to make his way down the front walk, when Lila called out for his attention.

"Detective!"

He turned and watched as she ran out to him.

"Let me give you some advice."

He nodded.

"If you're looking for murder, I suggest you stop. And if you're hoping to find it here... if you're hoping to find your answers here, well, you should probably stop that as well."

He looked slightly amused.

"And why's that?"

"Because this is South Hill, it's not just another Bellingham neighborhood. It's another world entirely, and we like our silence."

He nodded and turned to go, but Lila took hold of his arm.

"Mrs. Vasquez—"

"Don't question the Blackmoores; in fact, stay away from them entirely. Better men than you have tried and failed. I may be friends with Kathryn, but I'm not stupid... there are far worse things than what is seen by the eyes of man."

He chuckled and looked to her hand before gently, yet forcefully, removing it from his arm.

"I know the stories... but I don't believe in goblins or ghosts... certainly not witches."

Now it was Lila's turn to chuckle.

"Then take my advice and leave them at peace. Because if you don't... you soon will."

Lila watched Detective Randy Kit climb into his car and drive away in the icy darkness, dipping down the sloping hill towards North Garden, knowing that he would be paying Cheri a visit, and the emptiness inside only seemed to grow.

Cheri was curled up on the couch in the T.V. room. The 1951 version of *A Christmas Carol* played on the screen; its dark, bluish glow illuminated her otherwise darkened home, the light brightening on her mournful face.

The phone call from Greg played over and over again in her mind, not understanding what had happened and knowing that there was nothing that she could do for him. In her mind, he had officially lost it.

He's alive....

It made her cringe, and she wished so desperately for it to be true, but knew that it wasn't, and tonight's absence of her parents made her loneliness all the more noticeable.

She had just begun to doze when the sudden buzzing of her doorbell brought Cheri to her feet and to her front door.

"Yes?"

An off-putting man in his mid-thirties stood on her porch staring down at her. The smile he attempted made him only seem the more suspicious.

"Are you Cheri Hannifin?"

She nodded.

"I'm detective Randy Kit." He flashed his badge. "I'm investigating the death of your friend Christian Vasquez."

Hearing a stranger say his name felt like a kick in the gut.

"Come in."

She stepped aside and the detective nodded as he crossed the threshold into her home.

"I'd offer you something to drink, but you're obviously on the clock."

It was sharp, this response, trying to see how far she could push him.

"Your parents allow you to drink... even though you're under-age?"

Cheri grinned.

"Look where you are... what do you think?"

There was a strange superiority to her tone when she said this; he had found it in Lila Vasquez' voice as well.

"I don't know anymore."

She toasted him and took a swig from a bottle of wine.

"I do need to ask some questions about Christian, though."

"Shoot."

"Well, the day he died, did you see him at all?"

Moments in the hallway came across her mind, watching him break up with Trevor, the joy in seeing him fall.

"No, I didn't."

He nodded, though his face was cast in doubt.

"Anyone you know of seen him?"

She shrugged.

"Greg Sheer, maybe?"

She shrugged again.

"Possibly... I couldn't tell you."

"But I thought you were all close."

Cheri sat the bottle down and stared at him coldly; her brown eyes digging into him.

"We were once... but not so much... near the end."

He moved closer towards her, his body casting her in shadow.

"Why?"

"Don't act like a fool, Detective. You're about to walk off a cliff and you can't even see it."

She knew that she shouldn't be smarting off to a cop like this, but somehow she knew he'd take it.

"And what about Trevor Blackmoore?"

A rage quickened inside of her and Randy took notice, stepping two paces back.

"He was Christian's boyfriend, Detective...." She looked away.

"But?"

She knew that she shouldn't; it was best to leave him out of it, but if she didn't say something now, it would be a lot worse for him if the cop got his information from Greg Sheer.

"They broke up that morning. Christian just wasn't ready to come out... there was a lot of stress."

"So he was gay?"

Again, she shrugged.

"Was he in love with Trevor Blackmoore? Ever since we were little. Was he gay? Well, that I can't answer."

Randy looked at her, confused.

"Well, if he was in love with Trevor Blackmoore, then obviously...."

Cheri scoffed at this.

"His loving Trevor had nothing to do with gender or sexual orientation. It was Trevor Blackmoore... he couldn't help himself."

She began to walk the detective back towards the door, letting him know without words that the conversation was over.

"One more thing, Detective Kit."

He nodded.

"If you know this town and know anything about the Blackmoores, then you know that it's best to stay away from them.

"I'm assuming that you've already spoken with Lila... and if you inquired about the Blackmoores, then I'm sure she told you the same thing."

He nodded.

"If you come at Trevor, if you try to get to him or upset him, you'll live to regret it. The family won't let you get near him, and what's more, you may find yourself driven mad—or worse yet; dead.

"If you're smart, you'll stay away from them."

"If they try to harm me, they'll wind up in jail. If they lay a hand on me—"

"They don't need to touch you to kill you, Detective. In fact, they don't even need to be in the same state... they just have to know your name."

And with that she shut the door in his face, returning to the couch in tears.

"I should probably get home... though I doubt that my dad even noticed I was gone."

Trevor nodded and held tight to the midnight blue knitted blanket that he had wrapped around his body. They were standing out on the front walk, watching the snowflakes fall around them, twinkling in the streetlamp.

"Yeah... just to be safe," Trevor responded, feeling strange now that the reality of Braxton not sharing his bed with him was becoming much more tangible.

Though they had long ago worked out the problems that had plagued them earlier in the night, it still felt to him as if it was going unfinished, as if they were parting on the wrong note.

"I'm going to miss you, though." Braxton reached out for his friend, wrapping his arms securely around his shoulders.

"I'll see you tomorrow, though, right?"

Braxton sighed. His face was made ruddy by the cold, flushed cheeks, and his big dark eyes seemed to encompass everything, including Trevor's future.

"I don't think so... I should probably hang around the house tomorrow and make sure that my dad's okay. This time of year is always the weirdest."

Trevor nodded, understanding it but not liking it. Though for once he would not be alone in his home, it still seemed as if without Braxton his world was lacking, and he needed to find something to fill that void.

He felt the pull of Christian while they stood there.

It was faint, and as he looked at Braxton he thought that he had glimpsed a form over his shoulder and across the street, sheltered by thick shadow—though upon a more substantial glance, he realized that the sidewalk was barren.

"Will you be around on my birthday?"

Braxton heard that slightly mournful tone and grinned.

"You know I wouldn't miss that for the world!"

Trevor smiled and they drew close together, their eyes closing as they kissed gently and sweetly.

It still felt too short.

Before going, Braxton tilted his head down, gripping Trevor's cheeks, placing his lips on his forehead and sighing before letting go and disappearing in his car.

"I love you."

Trevor watched him go and knew that there would be nothing to distract him from all of the darkness that filled his world. With Braxton he was permitted temporary relief, but now, with the young Volaverunt gone, all he had for company were those same demons.

"Will he be back tomorrow?" Kathryn asked. She stood in the kitchen with Magdalene and Francesca. Their wise eyes focused on him, perhaps seeing through him.

"No. He has to hang around the house with his dad tomorrow, since it's just the two of them."

The women nodded and sipped from mugs of hot tea.

"Well, he was very sweet.... Is he your first boyfriend?" Magdalene asked.

Trevor looked to his mother, whose eyes were wide and sorrowful.

"You can fill them in, Mom... I'm going to bed."

He waved to them and began to make his way out of the hall and towards the stairs.

"What did I say?" she asked, and then there was only the muffled sound of Kathryn's voice as he made his ascent into the quiet of the second floor.

"Is it always this hard?" he questioned.

The tears were filling in his eyes and the sobs were catching in his throat. There was no escaping the darkness. It followed him, and he knew this. It lingered above him and refused to give him peace.

When Christian had come to him in the dream, it was to bring him peace and comfort—still, somehow there was an ominous foreshadowing that underlined his words. There was no reassurance, no finale; in fact, it only left him with more questions and more doubt.

"Enough of this!" Trevor declared as he stepped inside his bedroom.

The adjacent playroom that had been left alone for years seemed to beckon to him, and he could not deny it. This had been the place where he had used his powers in games with Christian;

this had been where, at the age of six, he had discovered to spirit of Jonathan Marker.

He sighed and cautiously placed his hand on the aged knob of glass, giving it a twist and forcing it open, the door skirting across the floorboards and jutting open. The sight before him took the breath right out of him.

Afternoon sun shone through the partings of satin drapes, thick in royal green and accented with golden tassels, painting dim light on the hardwood floors and reflecting yellow hues on mahogany panels with inlaid shelves and tattered books—titles obscure and lost to time.

A squared room occupied with polished furniture of cherrywood, satin, and white doilies of lace, breathing with formality and antiquity.

In the room a child sat: petite and silent as all children can be—a little boy with parted hair—wine-red—dressed in khaki shorts and a t-shirt of blue and white horizontal stripes. His skin was fair and slightly pinked, hazel eyes stared blank, empty, lids unmoving.

The only motion from the boy came from a frantic left hand. A pencil secure in his curled fingers, moving along the surface of large news print, disregarding the marginal blue lines, delivering an unconscious message.

He moved closer to the boy.

The walls moaned and could have been passed off as century age, the home attempting to settle as all homes often do. But Trevor knew that it was not.

Figured shadows moved along the paneled walls, moving as if surveying, watching as if in curiosity, much like he was doing.

The boy did not move, save for his hand on the paper.

His lips quivered slightly, and the writing ceased.

The hand of the boy came to a stop; his lids fell together, meeting in the way that closed lids meet. The boy's head fell back, rolling just a little; his hands fell limp at his sides and marked the conclusion of the task.

The child did not know, was not aware of the message relayed, the one scribbled in another's hand. Writ on news print. But Trevor knew, and as he approached he read that paper and shuddered.

Jonathan Marker.

1885. 23.

Hi.

He reached out for that paper, but no sooner had his fingers connected with the print that a great distortion was felt and he shut his eyes. Trevor gave a deep sigh and when he opened his eyes again, he was not at all surprised to find the room dark and empty, smelling of damp and the string of cobwebs.

He had closed the door to this room at the end of his friendship with Cheri, Greg, and Christian. He felt that the memories of them, combined with those of his father playing Peter Pan, would be too much to bear, so he had said goodbye to it all.

Until now.

"Let's go."

Trevor walked to the large round table and cleared it off, not bothering to dust it. He gathered candles left neglected and yellowed from those old shelves, setting them about the table in a sparse cluster.

He wasn't certain exactly what it was that he was doing, but he was aware that he could do it.

"This is my birthright, after all."

He stopped for a moment and tried to weigh what it was that he was doing, but knew that in the end he had to do it and all damnable warnings could go to hell.

"Hocus pocus..." he chuckled with unease as he went back into his room and collected those things which he thought might be of use.

"Little Christian... the Hispanic boy?" Magdalene asked, and Kathryn nodded. She had yet to mention the young man's death.

"The very same. They were together, for a short time ... officially, but their love had existed long before they had even really known what sex was."

The women nodded, and Kathryn began to dread the inevitable.

"So, what happened?" Francesca asked.

The time had come, and she had no choice but to answer.

"He died."

"What?" she responded.

"You're shitting me!"

Kathryn looked at Magdalene and shook her head.

"No, cousin, I am not. It only happened a week ago. He was in a car accident and his wheels slid on some ice; he was killed instantly."

She sat down her mug of tea and looked out to the hall, thinking of her husband.

"And Braxton?" Francesca asked.

"He came into the picture five or six years ago. Trevor loved them both, but for a while Christian wasn't around."

The women grew sullen.

"You don't think Trevor would—no, he wouldn't...."

They looked at Francesca peculiarly.

"What?" Kathryn asked.

"Nothing."

"What are you thinking, cousin?" Magdalene added.

"Only... you don't think he'd try to..." she averted her gaze, "raise the dead?"

Their minds began to wrap around the question.

"He wouldn't..." said Magdalene.

"He doesn't know how. I haven't taught him anything, and he doesn't have any...." Kathryn stood at full attention and shuddered, "spell books!"

The cousins rose and followed Kathryn out of the kitchen and towards the stairs as fast as they could move.

He lit the candles about him and closed his eyes, taking a deep breath, allowing himself to feel the familiar buzz of energy, that tingling that pricked every limb, every nerve from the inside out. It was thrilling and left him strangely weightless as he allowed it to course freely from within.

He opened his eyes and looked down at the tattered brown book that had resided on the shelf within this room. The book that had been left there one afternoon by Queen Mab years ago, before he could ride a two-wheel bicycle.

A book that he had always remembered.

In dingy gold it read: *Conjure!* in big bold letters. It had beckoned to him and with the book open he raised its yellowed pages and began to read.

"I place this charm down beside you, subterranean gods," he laid out that fleece sweatshirt of Christian's on the table between the candles, followed with a picture of the deceased Vasquez.

"Mighty and all-powerful and all controlling—mother of Gods and Man, of angels and Daemons—Mother of Witches—Hekate. Kore, Persephone, Ereschigal and Adonis, Hermes, the subterranean. Thoth and the strong Anubis, who holds the keys of those in Hades."

"We can't wake anyone! If they even knew what could possibly be going on, Adamo would have a fit and Darbi would probably take off!" Kathryn commanded.

She had long ago abandoned her heels, and though the matter was pressing, she was relieved to be standing on level feet.

"Agreed... but what's going on? Why are we barging in on Trevor like this?" Magdalene asked, clutching to her red and black beads and spinning them in her fingers, feeling the strange power that was rising in the house.

"Because years ago, when Trevor was only four, your mother left one of her books in the playroom after she had gone home from babysitting him while I was at the office. I meant to take it back to her, but stupidly I left it."

She was punishing herself now, and the two cousins had no idea how to reassure her.

"But you think that he has found it? That he's even looked?"

Kathryn frowned and rapped her fingers against the door.

"Trevor, open up!"

Francesca and Magdalene were quick to join in.

"Trevor!"

Kathryn reached down for the door's knob and was not surprised to find it locked.

"Move out of the way."

They stepped aside and Francesca stared down at the door, but did not really see it. She began to drift, to empty her thoughts, holding on to one desire: her one need to get into the room.

As if being kicked open, the door drew inward, its knob slamming into the wall and they walked in, only to find it empty.

"Shit!" Kathryn exclaimed.

They heard him calling out beyond the door to the playroom. The dread she felt at the thought of her son in there raising hell and not knowing what he was doing, of summoning things that he knew nothing about, things that he could not comprehend.

"Trevor, open up!'" Magdalene began to call out, her body pressed against the aged door. "The dead can't give you anything that they couldn't in life... Trevor, don't do this!"

The three of them began to fight with the door, sensing that something was going to unravel.

"The gods of the underworld and the demons, those untimely carried off: Men, women, youths and maidens, year by year, month by month, day by day, hour by hour!"

The house began to stir, and shadows on walls and floorboards seemed to spark with life, a will of their own.

"I conjure you, all demons assembled here, to assist me, and awaken *him* at my command. Whoever you may be, male or female. Betake yourself to *that* place and *that* street and *that* house and bring *him* hither, and bind *him* here! Bind him to *me!*"

"No!"

Trevor turned and faced the door behind him, just as the candles on the table snuffed out.

"Mom?"

It was then that what looked like a bright flash—a light so strong and physical—knocked him to the ground and race through him, moving through him and spreading out about him in one great, electric rush.

"Trev—"

As if hit hard in the face and chest, Kathryn, Magdalene, and Francesca were thrown from the door and across the room, their bodies colliding with the bed and floor. A bright, hot, white light filled the room—and the entire house it seemed—for just a moment before it was gone, as if it had never been there in the first place.

"Jesus fucking Christ!"

Francesca rubbed the side of her head and helped her cousins up off the floor. They shook their heads and knew that the damage was done, and whatever they found on the other side of the door, they would just have to accept.

"Honey..." Kathryn let out, opening the door and finding her son on the floor clutching a black sweatshirt and sobbing, gasping for breath—for relief—and not finding any.

"I just wanted to see him again... I just wanted answers. I wanted to know how...."

She bent down to him and collected her son's head in her lap, caressing his hair and telling him to calm down. She could not help her own tears—and neither could Francesca and Magdalene, who were holding one another and thinking of the loves that they had lost.

And the house remained silent.

He moved like a funnel, racing down a blackened hole—a tunnel—and now he was nearing the end. A mass of connected particles, still separate and unchanging in a whole, yet somehow different: changed. Powerful.

From the darkness he existed in, to the darkness he found when he opened his eyes and took his first breath of air, and finding that he had none. It was all different, new; it was his chance.

He searched with his fingers, found himself bound by the tight and sticky heat of plastic, the confines of what must have been duct tape and rope, and the sudden sensation that he was above ground.

"Bitch!"

He pulled his arms, felt the muscles stretch and loosen, felt his force as he struggled without breaking a sweat. Slowly but surely, the plastic tore and he pulled himself up and out, gripping to wood beams. In this moonlit darkness he jumped to the ground beneath him and hit stone, though he did not feel the impact.

Saints cast in shadow stared at him and though he felt a presence emanate from within their plaster bodies, he ignored them and made his way to the carriage-house doors.

With a grin on his decaying face, he pulled them open and stepped outside. The house was dark, save for the glow of kitchen light, and though naked and barefoot, he could not feel the cold on his body; he was unhindered.

Tom Preston was home.

Flowers on trees blossomed and the brick felt warm beneath his bare feet, grinning at the warm glow of springtime sunlight, seeing it shine green through paper-thin leaves of maple, knowing that he was in a dream, yet embracing its comfort.

Birds chirped and the salty perfume of the bay mixed with the scent of floral made him smile as he made his way to one of those wrought-iron tables.

He sat down and looked towards the carriage house, finding himself sighing as he saw lively candlelight move from beneath the crack of the wood doors, and though he was dressed only in his little gray briefs, he was warm and the breeze that moved about him was soothing.

He could have very easily questioned the state of this universe, but found it better to enjoy its peace, knowing that at any moment, even the safest of dreams can become nightmares.

'I wish sometimes you could let me go.'

He turned towards the back gate near the kitchen to see Christian standing in front of him, unblemished and kind.

"I do too. It's different now, though Christian; I just wish I understood how it happened. How did you die?"

The specter shook his head and made his way towards Trevor.

'The truth is sometimes better left to mystery. It can cause more harm than one ever needs, and I want you protected.'

Christian smiled warmly and took his place next to Trevor, cupping his hands in his and letting out a great sigh.

'You have Braxton, and I'm already gone. I'm not coming back, Trevor... I can't come back, not like you'd want.'

Trevor averted his gaze and realized quite suddenly that he was crying.

"I love Braxton... I do, but he's not you, Christian. He'll never be you... and I can't let you go."

Christian reached out and drew his face towards him, looking into Trevor's eyes and placing his thumb quickly and lightly on his lip.

'The truth of me would be too awful for you to know... and then I would know no peace. Death is not as terrible as it seems for those still on earth.'

Trevor stood, feeling defeated but not yet ready to give up. It wasn't right that Christian could be so at peace when all Trevor could feel was a growing darkness.

"Then why are you still here?"

Christian looked up at him with a stunned stare.

'What?'

"Why are you still here? If you've truly moved on and found peace, then why are you still hanging around? Why haven't you let go and moved on? You're not making any sense!"

He threw his arms up in the air and stared down at the spirit who in life had been his friend and lover, the one who opened him up to the truth of his sexual nature.

'Careful, Trevor... you're asking questions that the living are not permitted to ask—'

Trevor interjected with a chuckle: "I'm not like any other 'person,' I'm a fucking Blackmoore! I can see and commune with the dead; my will makes things happen, and my words have power!"

Christian averted his gaze and stared at a black beetle skirting across the brick.

'Yes, they do....'

His tone became mournful, and the sky began to change; the sun fading as if being dimmed by a switch, the breeze slowly growing stronger and becoming colder.

"What does that mean?" he questioned, but Christian shook his head.

'You're not ready to know, and you shouldn't.'

This was going nowhere, and Trevor knew it; Christian wasn't going to tell him anything.

"Goddamn it! Why are you doing this to me, Christian? I can't fucking let you go because you won't let me! I can't live my life like this. I'm constantly questioning everything, trying to understand why you died... how it could have happened when they couldn't find any visible reason on your car as to why you went off the road.

"And I don't believe that you had been speeding."

The world about them was darkening and the leaves, once so rich and green, were withering rapidly before his eyes, turning brown and drying before being ripped from the limbs.

Christian stood now, nodding and walking to him, his arms outstretched, and closing them around Trevor's body, holding him close and kissing the side of his neck.

'God, I miss kissing you... I miss the taste of your skin on my lips. Now there's nothing, and I can't even feel you.'

He was sad now, his tone mournful, and Trevor could feel his pain from within and without.

"What happened, Christian? What's going on; why are you still here?"

Christian began to sob, the tears running down his face and onto Trevor's bare shoulders and down his back, hot and red.

'I can't!' he let out, and the sky went black and the leaves moved about them in a cyclone, the air cold and crisp, Trevor's breath taking shape in front of him.

"Can't what?"

He pulled back from Christian and saw the blood seep out from his eyes like tears, and Trevor found it staining the right side of his shoulder and his chest, painting his nipples.

"Blood... Jesus... blood!"

'You're in danger, Trevor. All of you are in danger!'

Trevor reached out for his dead lover and found him pulling away.

"Danger? What do you mean, danger? From whom?"

Christian shook his head and wiped the blood from his face, Trevor seeing as it caked his hands.

'From those who want your blood: the dark one of the Moors. It's stirring, and it wants you, Trevor... it wants all of you!'

Trevor looked towards the heavens, seeing past the stars, seeing planets and meteors, clusters of light within the cosmos, the universe forming above his head.

"But who?"

Christian shook his head and began to point to the carriage-house, its wood doors now open and moving quickly in and out.

'Jonathan is not the worst, and he will not be the last. The dead and those beyond it crave Blackmoore blood... they crave the line and the one who overcame the Legacy....'

Trevor drew his arms around his bare chest and shook his head, screaming over the wind.

"But who, Christian? Who overcame the Legacy?"

The specter shook his head.

"In the carriage-house?" Trevor asked, and Christian said nothing.

"Christian!" he called out, even as the phantom began to fade, and Trevor was already making his way to the little house of secrets.

He took a deep breath and stepped across the threshold, finding it alit with candles of all sizes and shapes. Statues of saints no bigger than Barbie dolls, and others as tall as he was, stared down at him from raised planks of wood. Bodies about him beat on drums, their faces concealed by black shawls.

"I don't understand...."

He looked down at his body and found it naked and covered in symbols that began to bleed, seeping out with blood and stinging hot.

"Shit!" he called out, falling to the stone floor and placing his hand on the largest marking on his chest.

Others moved about him, dancing in precise circles, paying no mind, though he lay suffering on the floor.

'The Devil comes for his witches.'

He turned and found Christian standing behind him, looking as if he were alive, regret on his face.

"What did you say?"

Christian said nothing, only staring with black eyes absorbing the light of the candles, and Trevor noted how much like those plaster saints he seemed.

'I never wanted this for you. I thought when we were younger that if I kept you close, if I was with you and looked out for you then you wouldn't end up like the rest of your family.

'I thought that maybe I could keep you from the rumors and fears of this town.'

Trevor lifted himself up from off the ground, seeing that as soon as he did the masked patrons vanished and the wounds on his body were gone, and so was the blood.

"You did what you could, and so did I."

Christian began to whimper and shed tears that were real: tears that were not blood, simply saline.

Trevor raised his hand and cupped the dead boy's face.

"I could never escape the darkness of my name, as long as I remained in this town."

Christian shook his head.

'I should have never abandoned you.... I shouldn't have turned my back on you like I did; I sealed your fate and left you to a ghost.'

Trevor expressed a sympathetic smile.

"The ghost was there before the flesh of us even existed. He had been waiting for me, just as my fate with this family was waiting for me.

"You couldn't keep me from that."

There was no sound; it was silent and warm, like a day from their youth, and the candles burned without malice.

'There's so much darkness in your future, Trevor Blackmoore... so much heartache, and I don't know how to keep you from it. But I know I can't leave you; I can't let you go.'

"So, then, I'll have two phantoms haunting me?"

Christian gripped Trevor's hand and brought it to his stomach.

'I can't find peace, Trevor... and I can't move on. I don't know if it's the truth that keeps me here, or if it's my love for you. All I know is that I'm not leaving.'

Trevor sighed and drew him close, placing his lips on Christian's, missing the touch of his childhood god.

"But I'm with Braxton and I love him. Not like I love you, but I do love him, and the idea of something else getting in the way of that—"

'I don't want to get in the way of that; you need to be with him. I just wish we could let each other go.'

He nodded, and felt a part of him detaching from Christian Vasquez.

"Then perhaps, Christian... the truth will set you free."

He brought Christian to him and placed his lips against his ear.

"I'm sorry."

Christian looked at him, confused.

'Why?'

"Dead, obey my words henceforth... deny me nothing and loosen your tongue—a"

'Trevor!'

Christian gripped him and tried to stop him.

"By my blood and by my name I command you, I compel you!"

Christian's grip loosened and his hands fell to his side, helpless, staring at Trevor with tears slipping gently down his face.

'Trevor...'

His plea was weak, and though it pained Trevor, he needed to know.

"Tell me, Christian, what happened? Why did you die?"

Christian shook his head, and Trevor could see him struggle with the words in his throat, but he knew that he could not be denied.

'You!'

Trevor felt what must have been his heart stopping for just a moment, his stomach dropping; it was something that he hadn't felt since he had been informed of Christian's death.

"No...."

'You told me... you told me!'

There was anger in Christian's voice, a boiling rage that he was still trying to oppress.

"Told you what?"

Trevor was shaking, his knees threatening to buckle and force him to the floor.

'That I couldn't see. You said, "That's just it... you don't see. You don't see anything."'

The voice that came out of Christian's mouth was Trevor's, an exact duplicate of tone, and soon it was all coming back to the young Blackmoore.

"What are you saying?"

The tears began to slip down his face.

'You told me that I couldn't see and I went blind. By the time I got on Chuckanut, everything was a collection of white and dark blurs, and then it was black... all I could do was listen to the world around me and panic.

"All I could do was listen helplessly as I lost control of my car... and then there was the crash and the engine inside of me, and the impact of the tree slamming down on the hood of the car and splitting my head open.'

The top of his skull suddenly cracked open like an egg, and the blood began to ebb down his face and the right side of his body began to split open, rotting away and seeping out its contents.

"What's happening?"

Trevor's lip began to quiver, and he placed his hand over his gaping mouth.

'That's your power, Trevor... that's your gift: death.'

He shook his head in disbelief and felt as if he would vomit.

'You give it when you don't even know it, and your blood is cursed... Until now.'

Trevor looked at Christian, dumbfounded.

'You overcame the Legacy, you were the one that was prophesized centuries ago... you're the one they want.'

"Enough!"

Trevor flung his arm out and Christian hit the ground, gasping for breath he did not have in the real world.

'Why did you make me tell you? Why did you have to know?' Christian pleaded with desperation and pain in his voice, the tears once again slipping down his face.

"I don't know, but I did... I did!"

Trevor sat himself helplessly on the ground and tucked his head into his arms and sobbed.

'Listen to me, Trevor.'

He shook his head.

'Trevor, listen!'

He placed his hands on Trevor's shoulders, forcing the young Blackmoore to look at him.

'Now that you know, now that you're aware of the truth, I need to tell you that's there's so much more to you than death. You never gave it on purpose; you've never cursed to cause pain. You're okay, Trevor... you're okay, and you're good and powerful.

'The truth from spirits is interwoven with bitterness and angst... what you forced me to say came from a dark place. It's not what I believe, nor is it the truth.'

Trevor looked up at him and wiped the snot from his nose.

"Then what is the truth? From where I'm sitting, it's everything that you said."

Christian shook his head and brought Trevor's head against his chest, wishing so desperately that he could feel the young Blackmoore one more time.

'The truth is that you're a good person. One of those few lights in the world that exists in true innocence. You never showed a flash of

*anger towards us, even after we abandoned you, and you forgave me
and loved me even though I probably didn't deserve it. You crave love
and desire to give it; you just want others to like you and know how
special you are... that's the truth.*

*'Not death. Not witchcraft, ghosts, phantoms; not gay or straight,
not good or evil... just love!'*

Trevor shook his head.

"I just wish that I knew what to do! There are all of these things
that seem to be happening, and all I want to do is crawl under my
bed and not come out."

Christian chuckled, and his laughter reverberated in his chest,
vibrating in Trevor's ear.

*'You'll know what to do when it's time... and I'll be there watch-
ing.'*

Trevor looked up at him and smiled, his eyes glassy with tears.
"Promise?"

Christian smiled and leaned in.

'I wouldn't miss it for the world.'

TWENTY-ONE

Trevor woke to find his room empty and the gray morning light brightening his room. Voices could be heard downstairs, and he knew that the house was up and alive—and though the dream of the night before seemed to be slipping from him, only being able to recall snippets like snapshots here and there, he knew that it had involved Christian and his truths.

"God... I feel so fucked-up."

He placed his hand to his head and gave his hair a rough rub, looking about his room, seeing it cast in cold gray while the snow still fell in large goose feathers, covering the dead earth in soft white.

He walked over to his mammoth dresser, dating back to Paris in the eighteenth century, opening the top drawer and removing a thin white tee, then he pulled open the drawer beneath it and removed a pair of black-and-red plaid flannel pants; ready to go downstairs and greet the day with the rest of his family.

His door creaked, announcing his emergence. As Trevor made his way down the empty hall, hearing laughter and joyful conversation, he wondered if everyone had caught wind of the events from the night before.

He concluded that in the end his attempt at raising Christian must have worked. Aside from that slightly odd and dreamlike light show, Christian had indeed come to him, but it wasn't like the book had implied he would.

His feet touched down on the cool floorboards for just a moment before he moved onto the long runner, his footfalls were made in silence as he neared the front door, turning the corner, through the entertainment room to his left and finally to the closed pocket doors of the dining room.

He hesitated for just a moment before going in, opting instead to lean his ear against the doors and listen to what was being discussed.

"Trevor... we haven't eaten yet, so I would make a suggestion that you come in here," his mother called out, stopping his heart for just a moment.

He shook his head in defeat and slid one of the doors open, finding Kathryn and his cousins Adamo, Darbi, Francesca, and Magdalene sitting around the table, Adamo and Darbi giving him affectionate grins—and though they tried, his mother, along with Francesca and Magdalene, were exchanging worried glances.

"Morning, Trevor," Darbi said.

Trevor turned to him and offered a nod, taking his place at the opposite end of the table, his eyes connecting with his mother's.

"Yeah, did you sleep well?" Adamo asked him.

Trevor gave another nod and reached for the silver pot, pouring himself a hot stream in a white porcelain cup.

"I slept fine; interesting dream, though... but other than that it was fine."

He looked directly at his mother, Francesca and Magdalene, challenging them to inquire. They didn't.

"Oh, really... what about?"

Trevor looked to Darbi and smiled.

"Nothing important, just weird; you know how dreams are."

Darbi nodded, and they all watched as Kathryn and Adamo stood, making their way into the kitchen, seconds later returning with a basket of warm scones, plates of eggs benedict with warm hollandaise sauce, Belgian waffles and crêpes.

"Now, that's much better," Kathryn said when taking her seat, her eyes knowing and keenly aware of everything.

A little too keenly, as far as Trevor was concerned.

"Well what's planned for today?" Adamo asked, wiping his mouth discreetly with his cloth napkin.

"I don't know, as far as the boys are concerned. As for me... I still have some Christmas gifts to take care of." She stared at her son. "And a few birthday gifts."

They laughed, and Trevor buried his face in the mouth of his cup, hiding the look of disgust on his face.

After the events of this month, the last thing that he wanted to do was celebrate his birthday, especially when it appeared that all of their lives were in danger.

"Oh, that's nice...." He said with a yawn.

Trevor suddenly caught sight of an object of some mass out in the alley next to the house and covered with a water-proof black tarp.

"Um, Mom, what's that?"

Kathryn sat down her cup and shook her head.

"What's what, honey?"

There were grins spreading on all of their faces, and it was making Trevor uncomfortable.

"Outside of the window there... behind you."

Kathryn turned in her chair and looked out of the window, her auburn hair glossy in the winter light.

"Oh, that. I don't know... maybe you should go out there and see for yourself."

Trevor shook his head, though already to his feet, and his family followed him as he made his way through the kitchen and out into the back courtyard.

It was wet and cold but he didn't care; soon he would be made numb by the snow and he'd worry about it then, but for now he wanted to know what was hidden at the side of his house.

"It looks like a car!"

Trevor declared. He pushed open the wood gate and had his hand resting on the wood post, which was overtaken by leafless and brittle vines of Virginia creeper.

"Huh...."

Kathryn grinned and held onto her cup of coffee, its steam rising up in the December morning. As he approached it, curling his fingers under the tarp, he paid no mind to his cousins standing about with the knowing smirks on their faces, and he was too absorbed to notice the slick of drying blood only a few feet from the mysterious vehicle.

With a little hesitation Trevor pulled the tarp off quickly, nearly losing his balance as he realized what it was before him.

Smooth and black, with seating for two and a leather interior the color of lightened coffee, was a 1956 Jaguar Roadster, sparkling where it sat, even though there was no sun in sight.

"Whose is this?" he asked his mother. Logically, he knew the answer to his own question, but he needed to hear it, needed to have it confirmed so he could believe it and not think himself dreaming.

"Whose do you think, sweetie? It's yours!"

He shook his head in disbelief, knowing that it wasn't new. He had seen it before, though memory seemed hidden, and recalling it seemed to be inoperable.

"I know it," he ran his fingers along its body. "Why do I know it?"

Kathryn frowned slightly and walked to him, wrapping her arms around his shoulders. She was dressed in her black slip with long silk robe, her feet in black bedroom heels.

"Because, Trevor, it was your father's."

He turned and looked at his mother with tears welling in his eyes and a disbelieving chuckle.

"My dad's?"

Kathryn nodded and kissed him on the cheek.

"He always wanted you to have it. Take care of it, okay?"

He nodded.

"Your father used to take you out for rides when you were little. When he decided to give it to you, he locked it up in one of the warehouses along the waterfront."

Trevor nodded, knowing that they owned more than one storage unit around the city. "I will, Mom, I will. I won't let anything happen to it."

He patted her hand and threw the tarp back over the car, following his clan back into the house.

"Hey, can we take it out?" Darbi asked as they took to their seats back in the dining room.

Trevor looked to his mother, who simply nodded.

"Yeah, we can go to the mall; I want to buy some things anyways." He said to his cousin with a beaming grin.

There was a strange sense in knowing that he was about to drive his father's car, knowing that he would be touching and turning a steering wheel that his father had, and he would be driving on roads that his father had driven years before.

"Cool," Darbi responded, giving a grin to his younger cousin and taking a couple of scones. Kathryn chuckled at something Adamo had said, though Trevor had missed it and wasn't too concerned with what it was.

"Little Marcel and Jeffery will be arriving today... I think they'll be staying with Queen Mab, though, because God knows where I would put them."

Trevor looked at his mother and nodded, excited in seeing his fourteen-year-old cousin from San Francisco.

Marcel's father, Jeffery, ran a funeral parlor in an old Beaux-Arts townhouse in Pacific Heights. Trevor was always curious what it would be like to grow up so close to death, in a completely different manner from all the other Blackmoores.

For the next two hours they all ate, laughed, and talked, though Trevor heard none of it. He could sense the unease that was taking over the house—this indescribable cloud of darkness that was making its way through every crevice, through the doorways, passing through the panes of glass.

Hell was coming, and it was going to make the house on Knox Street its breeding ground.

It was only a matter of time.

He watched from across the street, checking his watch every five minutes as the manor appeared to wake up, the many Blackmoores that were residing in the house moving from window to window, floor to floor, all preparing for their day.

Randy Kit wondered what secrets existed behind its walls and what kind of people the Blackmoores were—and more importantly, how dangerous?

After an hour of observation, trying to stay out of sight behind a large maple, the front door opened. The clan of six emerged from the house, wrapped in warm coats of wool and fur, the two young men dressed in brand name clothes too fashionable in his opinion, and the adults were dressed in conservative attire that was obviously designer.

He was going to make a smooth exit when he locked eyes with the striking Kathryn Blackmoore. Her steely eyes fixed with his and a destructive grin spread across her immaculate face, her tall stature clothed in a simple black dress with a cashmere cardigan sweater of the same color, a black coat of rabbit draped across her left arm.

"Detective Kit... no need to hide behind that tree!" she called out.

His palms broke out into a sweat as he began to make his way across the quiet street, the family becoming more distinguishable as he approached.

"Ms. Blackmoore...."

The warnings of the previous night began to play again, filling his brain with cautious thoughts and suspicions. The family looked at him with sharp and knowing eyes, eyes that he did not like but knew he could not avoid.

Trevor Blackmoore, with his hazel eyes and dark red hair, drew close to his mother and quietly took the coat from her arm.

"How can I help you this morning, Detective?"

Though she asked, Randy knew that she was already aware of the reason for his presence.

"Well," he began, kicking his feet against the red brick path, "I'm investigating the death of Christian Vasquez. I believe you knew him, Trevor."

He looked at the kid and smiled.

Trevor said nothing.

"Investigating his death? Wasn't it an accident?" the unknown woman with the thick curled auburn hair asked; her golden eyes looking at him with great suspicion.

"And you are?"

The woman smiled.

"Magdalene Blackmoore, of New Orleans."

He held out his hand to shake it, but she only stared at it.

"Well, Ms. Blackmoore... that's what we're trying to determine."

Trevor rolled his eyes and shook his head.

"The strange thing is, Trevor's name kept coming up in connection to Christian—and, well, let's just say it got my mind working overtime."

At that moment they all turned to him. The other young man, the one with the football player build and the Irish face with the hallmarks of other races and ethnicities—the most prominent being Spanish and Middle Eastern—turned to him and glared. His eyes looked preternaturally dangerous with their blend of green, blue, and yellow; much like a church window.

"Careful, Detective; your implications could take you places you don't want to go," the young man said to him with a solid and stern tone.

"And your name?" he asked.

A devious smirk spread across his face as he thought about the idea of arresting one of these people.

"Darbi... and you know my last name."

At that moment Darbi reached out and pulled Trevor behind him, only allowing Trevor to see what he could from over his cousin's shoulder.

"I don't take kindly to threats, kid... so watch it!"

There was something in his tone that sparked alarm in the family, and soon they had all lined up along the lawn with the exception of Trevor, who stayed behind them.

"Leave, Detective. Things can become very difficult for you, this I can promise," Kathryn said to him.

Detective Kit stood his ground, refusing to move.

"I'm not afraid of you people. Everyone else thinks that you have real power; they fear you and your name, but I know its just parlor tricks!"

Kathryn shook her head, and the other woman with the olive skin and black hair stifled a laugh.

"Turn back now, Detective. Do not pursue us, and furthermore do not pursue my son. If you come near him, I will make your life hell, and you can count on that!"

The family turned and made their way across the lawn towards the alley, moving past the green hedge.

In anger and without thinking, Randy reached out and took hold of Trevor's arm, pulling him towards him.

"Let me go!" Trevor yelled, catching the attention of the family and forcing them to make their way close to him.

"Shut up, kid. Now I want to talk to you and if I have to come back here with a warrant, I will. You're the main suspect in an open investigation, and you will talk to me—"

"Detective!" Kathryn commanded. "Detective, release my son this instant."

He shook his head and began to twist his fingers into Trevor's arm.

"Stop it, you're hurting me!" Trevor called out.

"Detective!"

He turned to see the one named Darbi staring at him with eyes that did not blink, eyes that held him in place with a silent ferocity that had no end.

"Let him go," Darbi at last commanded. His decibel dropping and his voice becoming the only thing that Randy could hear.

As if lacking any will of his own, his fingers grew lax and released their hold on Trevor, who pushed him away and returned to his family. Detective Kit did not move, could not move, his eyes still locked with Darbi's.

"Goodbye, Detective," Darbi responded, and the family turned to the alley, making their way to the Jaguar along the house, Detective Kit still standing in the snow-covered front lawn.

As if waking from a fog, Randy Kit watched as a classic black limo pulled out from the house, the window rolled down and the grinning face of Kathryn Blackmoore staring at him. He could see next to her and across from her the faces of Magdalene, the older gentleman with the calm face, and the woman—who, he realized for the first time, looked much like the other gentlemen.

Trevor and Darbi were nowhere in sight.

"What the hell happened?" he questioned, rubbing his open hand against his head.

The last thing he could recall was Darbi's voice commanding his attention, and then there was nothing. He thought that perhaps he was losing his mind, which at the moment seemed as acceptable as any answer.

"The car!"

He rushed to the alley, only to find it empty of the classic roadster—but a curious stain garnered his attention.

Looking around the alley, Detective Kit moved cautiously, his loafers tapping on the iced concrete, the sound echoing through the alley. The closer he approached, the more he began to recognize the dark pool. Hundreds of murder cases had prepared him for it, the most recent being the one which involved the Murphy girl in Bayview Cemetery, dead and gutted—though everyone else had known her as Andy Stone, the daughter of notorious serial killer John Murphy, also known as The Nightime Man, who had terrorized the city throughout the early Nineties.

"Jesus."

The pool was spilt blood, blood that had to have come from a major artery, like one found in the throat or chest. He knew he needed to call for backup. The crime scene investigators needed to get in here and secure the area; the fact that it was in the vicinity of the Blackmoore home gave him a sense of delight. It was a joy he could not describe.

Within an hour a crowd had gathered in the alley, watching as the police went to work investigating the area. Shortly before backup had arrived, Randy had looked around the bushes along the carriage house, and to his disgust he found what would have been a human heart—that is, if it hadn't been withered, as if sucked dry.

This was now an official crime scene, and the Blackmoores were the prime suspects.

"What's going on here?" an older woman called out.

She was tall and thin, dressed in black pants and a forest green turtleneck, a long three-tiered amber necklace hanging from her neck, her graying blonde hair pulled up in a loose bun. Her presence appeared to demand respect, and the rest of the neighbors stepped out of the way with their heads bowed as she made her way through them and towards Randy Kit.

"Ma'am, this is a crime scene; I'm going to have to ask you to stay back and let us do our—"

"Excuse me, but you've just secured my niece's home. I demand to know what's going on!"

Randy looked at the old woman and shook his head.

"Your niece's?"

She nodded and stared at him coldly.

"That's right. I'm Mabel Blackmoore. Now, who are you and what the hell is going on here?"

Randy clutched her arm gently but applied force, bringing her out of the way and drawing near to the covered window of the carriage-house.

"I'm Detective Kit, Homicide." He flashed his badge. "I'm sorry to inform you, miss, but you and your family are suspects."

She shook her head and laughed.

"For what?"

"Murder, Mrs. Blackmoore."

She laughed again.

It was angering him—this disregard—as if they were somehow above the law.

"Murder... of who?"

He shook his head.

"That has yet to be determined, but I'm going to have to place you under arrest."

He reached for his cuffs and attempted to slip them on her, but Mabel yanked her arm away.

"You cannot arrest me."

She turned from him and began to walk away, moving back through the crowd.

"Arrest her!" Randy ordered, and one of the two officers moved towards her, only to stop in mid-stance.

"Keep your distance!" she commanded, and the officers complied. The crowd watched on and said nothing, and no one moved to help in her capture.

Defiantly, Mabel Blackmoore moved further down the alley until she made a sharp left, disappearing through a back gate.

"What in the hell is going on?" Mabel huffed. She slammed the back door behind her and made her way through the hall and into the kitchen, where her mother Fiona was sitting at the breakfast table, drinking hot coffee in a porcelain mug.

"Let me guess... some stranger turned up dead?"

Mabel looked at her mother and nodded; she did not appear to be the least bit surprised.

"Looks that way, and now Kathryn's home is surrounded by police tape; does this have to do with the Legacy?"

Fiona cocked her head to the side and frowned, her aged face revealing her wisdom and insight.

"Maybe."

Mabel furrowed her brows and poured herself a cup of hot coffee as well, staring out of the widow above the sink. The fence, though covered by naked ivy, looked beautiful with its fresh blanket of snow.

"Well, how?"

Her mother sighed and took another drink, closing her eyes briefly and taking in the wonderful quiet of the morning.

"I don't know, but I feel as if something has gone terribly wrong, something that has nothing to do with the Legacy—or us—not in the beginning—but with the house down the block."

Mabel knew that her mother was referring to Kathryn and Trevor, and the only thing that came to mind was the death of Tom Preston.

"That's it, but he's not dead."

Mabel hated it when her mother read her thoughts, but as with the rest of the Blackmoores, this event was usually never intentional.

"He's dead; I helped hide the body."

Fiona frowned and stood up, walking over to her daughter and placing her aged hands on her shoulders.

Standing there, Fiona thought of the fact that people could pass she and Mabel as sisters, as close in age they looked now—even though they were twenty-eight years apart.

"Oh, honey, why didn't you do it right? Instead you put him in that damned carriage-house?"

Mabel kept her mother's gaze and refused to show any regret.

"We were drunk, Mother; it happens, but he was dead."

That word meant nothing in their world and Mabel knew it, though she prayed that this time it did hold some value.

"*Dead* being the word in question.

"Honey, whatever state he was in, it was only temporary. Now Tom is most likely walking amongst us, and not the man he was."

Mabel nodded and brought her cup of coffee to the table, taking a seat across from her mother.

She could hear the muffled pacing of Michael Donovan above their heads, and she knew that her mother heard them too. Her mother had known Michael when she resided in the great house, and yet they made no mention of it. There were now much more pressing matters that they were going to have to attend to, the most urgent being that a dead man now walked the earth with a breath of fresh air in his lugs.

TWENTY-TWO

The Bellis Fair Mall was a kaleidoscope of neon. Built in the Eighties, it still retained its Day-Glo look. It split in four wings, and the ceiling of the mall was covered with reflective strips of brass, and the noise of hundreds of patrons bounced off of white tiled walls.

Darbi and Trevor had just stepped out of Abercrombie & Fitch, adding to their collection of shopping bags, when his cousin decided to inquire about what had taken place earlier that morning on the front lawn of the Blackmoore home.

"So, why was that guy accusing you of having anything to do with Christian Vasquez?"

It stopped Trevor in his tracks and his first instinct was to dismiss his cousin, but it was the fact that it was his cousin that he decided to answer him.

"Because Christian was my boyfriend—well, only for a short time; it's kind of a blur—but I guess he's trying to connect me with his death."

He began to replay that fateful call from Cheri, and the sudden numbness followed with the inevitable sense of doom he had felt when first laying his eyes on the local news and its announcement of Christian's passing.

"That's so fucking shady; I'm sorry."

Trevor nodded and could see the regret in Darbi's face, the way his eyes dropped to the ground, the tightening of his grip around the handle of his shopping bag.

You wanted to know, he thought.

"I know, but I still shouldn't have asked you."

It startled him that his cousin had picked up his thoughts, but he said nothing about it; instead, they continued to walk.

"Don't worry about it, Darbi. Look at it this way: how am I ever supposed to move on from it if I never talk about it?"

The truth was that he didn't want to move on from it. A part of him wanted to wallow in it, to savor the suffering, though he wasn't certain why.

He wondered if this need to take responsibility had something to do with what Christian had told him in his dream from the night before, though he could not recall its details.

"So, Braxton seems cool."

Trevor smirked at Darbi's attempt to change the subject, but it all seemed to be related to the late Vasquez, and no matter what they discussed or what they did, Christian would be lingering somewhere beneath the surface.

They were just about to step inside of the GAP when a familiar face stepped out, gripping blue bags with the company's logo on it, and Trevor wondered how much more awkward this day could get.

"Trevor!" Cheri let out.

Though she was dressed in tight corduroys, a tight black sweater with a V-neck, a white tee underneath and a long Burberry scarf around her neck, she still appeared to be amiss.

Perhaps it was the fact that her hair wasn't brushed, or the big black Dolce & Gabbana sunglasses on her face that hid her eyes from the world... but she wasn't immaculate, as was her usual appearance.

"Hey, Cheri, how you doing?"

She nodded and gave a slight shrug.

"Hanging in there, I guess. How are you?"

Should he tell the truth, he wondered, or should he lie? In the end he picked for somewhere in between.

"Fine, I think, though I guess some moments are better than others...."

There was a pause, and it was in this moment that Darbi purposefully cleared his throat. "Oh, Cheri, this is my cousin Darbi—"

"I remember," she interjected, sticking her hand out and shaking his.

This was getting slightly more uncomfortable the longer they stood here. He knew that he and Cheri had cleared the air between them—but five years was still five years, and the past doesn't just go away so quickly.

He knew that they still had a long way to go.

"It's nice to see you again," Darbi responded.

Trevor felt something cruel and out of place just beyond his shoulder. It was cold and angry, and when he turned he caught the unmistakable face of his stepfather staring back at him—though when a cluster of teens moved in front of him, Tom Preston was suddenly gone, as if he had never been there to begin with.

His heart quickened, his blood began to race, and his palms started to sweat. He knew that Tom was gone, that he must have left the house and his mother the night of J.T.'s party, but now he wasn't so sure. He knew that he would have to mention it to his mother. Something else was off, something that only now he could recall:

Tom's face had been different. Grayed and sunken in. is cheek bones protruding, and it was only now that he could recall those eyes: like that of a blind person. A pale, misted blue lacking a pupil, only the blue iris staring out from those somewhat-hollow sockets.

"Trevor... Trevor?"

His attention came back, and he found Cheri and Darbi staring at him, confusion all over their faces.

"Huh?"

Cheri smirked before going on.

"I asked you if you were going to go to midnight mass this year."

It was such a mundane question—yet at this moment, filled with the befuddlement of Tom Preston, it became one of the hardest to answer.

"Oh, yeah, of course; we go every year."

Cheri nodded and told him that she would see him there. Then, with only the lightest of hugs, she went her way and the two young Blackmoores stared at one another, Trevor trying to figure out what he should tell his cousin, and Darbi trying to understand what had suddenly stolen Trevor's attention.

The four of them sat at Nimbus with their eyes focused on the snow which fell to the city beneath them, silent and lonely, bringing a chill to the glass and making the wine that they drank all the more warming.

Kathryn was too busy thinking of her son and the things that had come to pass in his own life, in such a short period of time.

She thought about the night before: his need to raise the freshly dead; to quicken the soul of Christian Vasquez and learn his secrets. How could she have been so stupid, she asked herself, pouring another glass of merlot and throwing it back quickly while her cousins discussed the visit of Detective Kit, and the Legacy.

"Well, Grandma Fiona knew it was the Legacy when we were on that plane. She saw Grandpa Bradley, and so did I."

Adamo shook his head.

"But Magdalene, it's not like the dead haven't come to us before; it happens all of the time!"

She shook her head, her curly auburn tendrils barely moving as she did.

"No, Adamo. Blackmoores have come through to us time and again, but not those who lost their lives to the Legacy. My mother told me years ago that only when the Legacy was conquered could those who died by our blood come through, 'and be it that they would hearken prophecies of doom to the Blackmoore line.'

"That's what she told me."

He scoffed and shook his head, taking another sip of wine, allowing it to warm his cheeks.

"Well, forgive me, cousin, but Queen Mab can be a little eccentric at times. Besides, who would have conquered it? We've all lost people to it, even Trevor."

Kathryn cocked her head to the side and gave a cynical laugh, forcing her cousins to look at her in confusion.

"He only lost someone once, and it was in a car accident; we have no idea if he would have died.

"Also, there's Braxton Volaverunt."

At the mention of his name, their faces appeared to lose all color.

"That's his name?" Adamo asked, and Kathryn nodded.

"Jesu—"

They were cut short by the news being broadcasted on the television set behind the bar: a picture of Kathryn's home guarded off with yellow police tape caught their eyes, and they all stood and began to inch closer to the screen.

"The stately manor of the Blackmoores was closed off by police this morning, shortly after a large amount of blood—along with what was apparently a heart—were found in the vicinity of the home. No confirmation if the heart was human," the young news broadcaster was saying, standing at the edge of their lawn.

A crowd could be seen beyond her, as well as a flock of reporters snapping pictures of the house.

"So far there haven't been any arrests, but the Bellingham Police Department issued a statement, saying that 'they will treat the Black-

moores as they would every other citizen, and grant them the same rights, but that no special exceptions would be made for them either.'

"*The home is occupied by Kathryn Blackmoore and her son whose name we cannot make public at this time as he is still a minor. Also residing in the home is Kathryn's husband, Thomas Preston—though so far police haven't been able to locate him.*"

Kathryn felt as if her world were about to collapse.

It wasn't a far-fetched idea, after all, since lesser things had come close to bringing about her ruin. But with this, this news which would surely be announced all over the country, the companies might surely suffer.

"The devil comes for his witches..." Kathryn said without really thinking about it. She needed to get home; she needed to get back to Trevor, make sure she was home before her was.

Francesca gripped her hand, and the four Blackmoores slipped out of the restaurant. Outside, the limo was waiting for them. Quickly, they slipped in and closed the door before anyone could notice them.

They moved up the steep hill of Fourteenth Street and leaves began to shower the limo, and the snow collected even thicker than it had been. Through tinted windows Kathryn, Magdalene, Francesca, and Adamo spied the various news reporters waiting for them, flashing their cameras in rapid recession and trying in desperation to get a good shot of the family.

The car pulled up in front of the house and Miles made a quick gesture towards the door, just as the locust-like reporters moved in on them, ready to pick Kathryn apart.

"Mrs. Blackmoore, do you have any comments?" one reporter asked as soon as Adamo stepped outside, standing patiently as his three cousins emerged, bulbs flashing violently. "What about the rumors that you practice devil worship and human sacrifice?" another asked, trying to push her into reacting.

Kathryn still said nothing.

Stoically she ripped the police tape from off of her trees and moved into her yard, followed by eager reporters.

"Mrs. Blackmoore, please!"

They were begging her now, but she would not give them the satisfaction. She stepped onto the stoop of her door and removed her keys, slipping it into the lock and giving it a turn, allowing her three cousins to go in first.

"Mrs. Blackmoore, does this have any connection with the sudden disappearance of your husband Tom Preston, or the rumored connection of your son to the death of Christian Vasquez?"

That was the thing to do it; that was the thing that stopped Kathryn in her tracks and forced her to make a statement.

"Who told you that thing about my son?" she asked the young male reporter with the somewhat terrified look on his face.

"I overheard one of the detectives mention it to one of the officers."

She knew he was speaking of Randy Kit, and her rage only increased.

"Now, you listen to me, all of you!" Kathryn began, bringing the reporters and on-lookers alike to a halt. "You have spread lies and rumors about my family for over a hundred years now. You want me to tell you something about this? Well, I wont give you the satisfaction.

"All you'll do is twist my words and create lies out of them. You'll try to ruin the lives of me and my family, and I will not let you do it!"

The cameras were flashing again, and reporters were holding up tape recorders to catch every word Kathryn uttered.

"And Detective Kit, if you're listening, which I'm sure you are since you seem like the kind of man that likes to breathe in the scent of your own shit...."

The crowd erupted in muffled laughter.

"If you ever come at my son again—if you ever attack him again as you did this morning, I will ruin you; you can take that as a guarantee.

"You wanted a war; well, now you've got one! But remember: you're not the first person to try and take us down, and you won't be the last. You're just a pathetic man with penis envy, and you don't want anyone to know it.

"I know all of your secrets, Detective Kit. All of them. Are you sure you want to do this?"

Kathryn Blackmoore turned her back to them and stepped inside her home, slamming the door behind her and locking it tightly, realizing only now that she was shaking.

Her cousins stood staring at her in the hall, concerned looks on their faces, and for the fourth time in her life Kathryn felt as if she were losing control. Not since the death of her husband had she felt this way—all of her anxieties returning to her, creeping on her slowly. Her paranoia; her regret; her suffering. It was now as real as anything, and she wasn't sure that she would survive it—especially when she came out nearly broken the first time.

Braxton walked empty halls, passing pictures of relatives who were like strangers to him. Even this house, this house he had grown up in his entire life, was nothing more than a tomb.

The snow had died down, once again falling in specks, so light and tiny that they could be missed if no one was paying attention. He couldn't help but think about Trevor and what he must be doing, surrounded by all of his family—something that he himself hadn't known in years.

Not since his mother's death had he known that kind of kinship, that kind of bond that comes with being in that kind of clan. But last night, surrounded by all of the Blackmoores, he had felt something, had felt as if he belonged. And now, this place, this still-life of a house, meant nothing to him, and he hated his father for letting it get this way.

Dressed in his usual frayed and baggy Jnco's and a tight black chenille sweater, Braxton slipped through the living room and moved to the front hall, passing those white walls and paintings and photographs of historic Bellingham, seeing the cold gray of the lake outside of the row of picture windows.

His father's office was at the very end of this hall: a place that Braxton hadn't been to in months.

"Dad?" he called through the polished cedar door, waiting for a response, only to find that there was none.

"Dad, I'm coming in!" he called again, and just as promised Braxton gave the sleek stainless steel handle a turn, and the door opened.

The sight before him caused Braxton to shudder.

His dad sat there motionless, staring at the walls; staring at a growing collage of pictures of his wife Tammy. She was seeing everything. A thousand Tammy eyes watched the room, watched her husband, and now, with him standing in the doorframe, she was watching her son.

"Jesus Christ... Dad...." It slipped his lips in a whisper, but still his dad said nothing.

The room held with it the strong sense of decay—of rot. It was the smell of things left to mold: food gone bad and grooming that was left unattended.

This was not the place he wanted to be.

One lonely turmeric-colored candle burned on the old wood desk, stately in his mother's time—but as with all things, in her passing, this too fell into disarray. The curtains were drawn, leaving this room with its bright vanilla walls in darkness, and the weariness and fatigue of Eric Volaverunt made him look like a corpse.

"Dad, its Braxton!" he called out, and yet Eric did not budge.

Braxton sighed and walked over to his father, found life in his eyes, but that life was distant, and his face was worn and thin. Though only forty-four, he looked to be sixty-seven.

"Dad?" he asked again.

At last, Eric jerked his head from the wall to his son's concerned face—yet it was as if he were in a dream.

"Oh, hello, son... do you like what I've done for your mother?"

He directed his weary hand to the wall. Braxton said nothing.

"She does; she says it's beautiful...."

"When did you do this?" he asked his father, gripping his arm and attempting to pull him up from that chair.

"Oh, about three weeks ago. I had all of these pictures of your mother just lying around in photo albums and in picture frames, but still I didn't know what to do with them, and that's when it happened!"

He got his father to his feet and slipped his arm under his shoulders, only to catch sight of the excrement on the black leather desk chair. His father had been soiling himself for days.

"What happened?" Braxton asked his father, trying to ignore the mess on the chair.

"Your mother, she came. She walked up to my desk. She was so beautiful. She told me that soon we would join her—you and I—we would be with her shortly; we needed to only prepare for it."

Braxton gasped and looked at his father, his dark eyes trying to understand his father's words and falling short.

"Dad, Mom is gone. She's dead, and she's not coming back.... I know you miss her, but you can't be doing this to yourself. Jesus, I mean, you haven't showered in weeks. There's shit all over you and the chair in the office! What the hell?!"

His father looked up at him with anger in his eyes, an anger that he had never shown his son before.

"You bastard! How dare you talk to me this way. How dare you talk about your mother like this!"

He attempted to hit his son, but Braxton blocked it without the slightest effort.

"She comes to me all of the time; she tells me about what you're doing. She says she's happy at how big and strong you've become, and that I've done a wonderful job raising you."

Braxton let go of his father and looked at him with an offended glimmer in his eyes, a sparked resentment in his irises.

"You didn't raise me, you disappeared as soon as Mom died! I've had to raise myself, you psychotic shit! You're lucky I didn't go ahead and off myself! Though I'm sure you wouldn't even have noticed!"

Eric Volaverunt seemed unable to compute what his son was saying to him. His face became dreamy once again, and it was as if someone were whispering in his ear. He tilted his head and looked to the window. His thickened beard was awful and had bits of food in it. His skin looked as if it were crawling with microscopic bacterium.

It made Braxton sick.

"Well, I'm sure that witch, that Trevor Blackmoore, has treated you well these past few years!"

It was as if his father had punched him across the face: the cruelty in his words, the anger with which he said Trevor's name.

"Leave him out of this, Dad!"

Eric laughed, untying his blue robe and allowing it to drop to the floor, his emaciated body clothed in white silk pajamas, which were now too big for him—and, to Braxton's disgust, were stained with urine and shit.

"I'm not too old to take you!"

He wasn't going to fight his father. The added fact that he had been soiling himself only furthered this anti-violent decision.

"Dad, we're not going to fight."

"Why not? C'mon, faggot!"

He had never heard this word come out of his father's mouth; it was alien to him. Strange and completely unnatural.

"Dad, stop it!"

Braxton was curling his fists, tightening his fingers into his palms, trying to get a grip on his anger.

"C'mon, you fucking cocksucker. Yeah, that's right, I know. Your mother told me all about what you've done with that witch! She's told me about how you've shared his bed; it's sick!"

He couldn't believe this: was it really his mother, was she really returning from the afterlife? It was making his head spin.

"Stop it..." Braxton demanded, but still his father persisted.

"No. Your mother tells me everything. She tells me about how you've been infected, poisoned by that witch—that murderer—how you get on your knees and put him in your mouth!

"She is ashamed of you!"

Braxton felt the tears well in his eyes, knew that they were spilling down his face and dripping from his jaw to the floor.

"Dad, I'm warning you, you had better stop...."

Eric laughed and walked closer to his son—challenging him—daring him to make a move against him.

Braxton only stood there.

"You warn me? Oh, that's rich; that's funny. Let me tell you, faggot! I created you. I provided a roof over your head, and this is how you thank me? By becoming a faggot? By getting bewitched by Trevor Blackmoore.

"This isn't the son I raised, the son I created!"

"You didn't have a choice!" he huffed under his breath, and Eric squinted his eyes and looked at his son, dissecting him, seeing where to make his next incision.

"I didn't have a choice? I wanted to get rid of you, to abort you or give you up. But no, Tammy wanted to keep you; she wanted to raise you and love you and have her family.

"Well, I could smell the poison inside of you—the sickness—the evil in your veins! I knew it was there; I could see it."

He felt a strange sensation, different from what he felt when getting a premonition. This was like a humming inside of his body, like a cyclone swirling in the shell of his flesh, running the electrical course of his nerves.

He felt as if he were about to fly.

"Stop...."

"I didn't have a choice, Braxton? Well, let me tell you, your mother, the person you tried so hard to please... well, she's sickened by you; she regrets you."

It was coming on stronger, manifesting his hurt—his rage—all of these things that had been beneath the surface for so long, and now his father's words brought it life.

"She says she should have flushed you out of her like the sick parasite that you are!"

"No!" Braxton yelled, and it was as if all of that energy were being rushed out of his body, spilling out into the air.

The hall of windows burst, glass shattering everywhere, shards falling to the ground outside. Those picture frames that lined the wall broke into thousands of pieces, and like stars they twinkled on the polished wood floorboards.

"You've got it in you!" Eric Volaverunt said, pointing an unsteady finger at his son. "You got it in you! I tried to keep it out; I could see it in your eyes, the evil that was in your blood—my blood!"

Braxton stepped closer to his father.

"Shut the fuck up!" he screamed, and his dad was scared; for the first time in a long time, Eric Volaverunt looked terrified.

"Witch!" Eric cried out and attempted to run from his son, run back into the shelter of his office.

"Stop!" Braxton called out after his father, wiping the tears that now blurred his vision. There was so much going on, so many things happening in his world. His life was changing; he was changing, and he could feel it.

"Dad, stop!"

Again the great rush was felt, and as if hit hard, Eric fell the ground, his nose hitting the floor and breaking.

"Why...?" he asked, the blood pouring from his damaged nose, dripping in his mouth and onto the floor, his eyes steady on his son who was coming closer and closer, closing the distance between them.

Braxton felt different to him; looked different. His dark eyes appeared to have a shimmer to them; his skin lighter, it was as if his body were glowing with a bright red light.

It took Eric a moment to realize that he was seeing something he hadn't seen since childhood, something his father Michael Volaverunt had warned him against.

He was seeing his son's aura.

"I should have drowned you when you took your first bath! My father could see it; he told me that you would be the one to give in to your evil!

"He told me to drown you. He told me to kill you!"

Eric looked to his left and was relieved to see that he was only inches away from his old wood cabinet, the contents of which would be able to put an end to his son's growing evil.

"Dad, stop talking like this, please...."

Eric shook his head and dragged his body over to the cabinet; still, when he looked at his son he saw that terrifying bright light.

"I will not let you bring the evil out of me; I will not let you infect me too!"

Eric gripped the cabinet door and pulled out the old loaded pistol he kept beneath an aging cloth.

"I will send you to hell myself!"

He lifted the gun to his son's head, feeling himself hesitate only briefly before beginning to pull the trigger back.

"Goodbye, Braxton."

"No!"

It left Braxton again: that rush—that force—and Eric began to convulse, dropping the pistol and gasping for air. His eyes looked hard on his son, and the pressure seemed to build in his veins, the veins beginning to protrude from his skull.

"Dad?" Braxton asked helplessly as the blood suddenly slipped from his father's ears and trailed down his neck, his face red and strained.

There was no sound to accompany his passing: Eric Volaverunt fell to the floor. Dead. Unmoving and lacking any sign of life. Gone, just like his mother.

Braxton ran to his father and lifted that dead hand gently, sobbing and asking himself why, trying to understand what had happened. Never mind the glass on the floor, or the fact that the windows had suddenly imploded. His father was dead; he had no one. No family, and he was alone, terribly alone.

"Jesus, Dad, I'm sorry... please, Dad, forgive me...."

He sniffled and wiped the tears from his eyes when his cell phone began to ring in his pocket.

At first he wasn't going to answer it, but something told him that he'd better.

"Hello?"

"Dude!"

It was J.T.

"Hey, uh, what's up?"

The world outside was growing darker, and he could not understand where the day had gone.

"Have you been watching the news?"

His voice sounded panicked.

"No."

"Well, go turn it on right now; our little man is in a lot of trouble."

He knew that J.T. was referring to Trevor; J.T. had a tendency to call Trevor "little man."

He stood without even bothering to take another look at his father; instead, he moved back out through the family room and through another door into the living room, gripping the little black remote and turning on the large television.

There was a young reporter standing outside of Trevor's home, updating the viewers on the investigation.

He mentioned something about the trash having been collected earlier that morning and that when workers had searched through the bags at the city dump, they had discovered the mangled and torn up body of a twenty-three-year-old girl who lived two blocks from the Blackmoore home. She was folded in what was considered "an inhuman position," and her heart had been "removed from her chest", as the field reporter said.

"Oh, shit!" His dad no longer seemed to exist. He wasn't real, just a phantom lying out on the floor; a mirage caused by heat and light. Nothing else mattered to him at the moment but Trevor.

"Yeah, you need to get over to him right away; they've mentioned something about connecting him to Christian's death."

Braxton couldn't believe it. Trevor had nothing to do with it; if anything, Braxton did, because he had seen it and didn't warn him. He had known what was going to happen to the young Vasquez, and still he had said nothing.

He hung up his phone and grabbed his keys from off the kitchen counter, not even bothering to look at the lifeless corpse of his father, paying it no mind as he slipped out the front door and ran up the white graveled path to the drive.

He took a deep breath and opened the door of his Acura, switching off the radio and pulling out rather quickly, praying that he wouldn't be foiled by black ice. His world was changing. Things inside of him were changing. He was evolving, and it took the death of his father to realize this and become this... whatever it was that he was becoming; or had been all along.

TWENTY-THREE

They were sitting in the T.V. room watching the news, even though it was being broadcast from right outside the front door.

Kathryn couldn't believe it; they had found the owner of the heart, and Kathryn recognized her immediately: It was Betty from Abigail's Garden.

They showed a photo of her with her mop of soft brown hair, her bright green eyes and sweet smile. She couldn't believe that Betty was dead, and that she was being accused of having something to do with it.

"Kathryn, what are we going to do? We've all been here; we're all suspects. We could call John."

Kathryn shook her head.

"No, John wouldn't help us, even if we asked. Besides, they won't trust a lawyer with the Blackmoore name... we're going to have to see who else we have on retainer."

The sky was darkening; the streetlights flickered on outside. The only light that was on was in the kitchen, and from the Christmas tree in the formal sitting room. The rest of the house was bathed in darkness, save for the glow of the television set.

"Adamo, do you think this has reached the ears of the Vatican?" Francesca asked.

He looked at his sister and shrugged.

"I couldn't tell you, but with Father Malady over there..." he cocked his head in the direction of Scared Heart Cathedral, "I wouldn't doubt it."

Kathryn sighed and stood, making her way into the kitchen, moving through the front hall, hoping not to be seen through any of the windows.

In the kitchen she poured herself some scotch and looked out into the back, seeing the carriage house and knowing that something was off. She could feel it; there was an absence—a vacancy.

Like a bolt of lightning, it struck her hard and fast.

"Tom."

They had driven around the block and seen in horror that the house was swamped with reporters and spectators, people trying to satisfy their own morbid curiosity about his family.

They had driven to the back of his aunt's house, turning off the engine and rolling in quietly, so as not to catch the attention of anyone down the way. He couldn't understand what was going on, hadn't heard anything on the radio; but now, in the front parlor of Queen Mab's home, sitting there with his great-grandmother Fiona and watching the news intently, he felt a chill pour down his spine.

"What's going on, Aunt Mabel?" Darbi asked. His eyes were wide and intense, but she shook her head.

"You know what's going on; it's right there on the news." She said this without the slightest bit of irritation.

"No, he means what's *really* going on," Trevor added, and his aunt grinned at him dispassionately.

"The trumpets of our ruin... the heralding of our extinction."

Fiona nodded sullenly, and Trevor understood. It was the Legacy—the prophecy. It was coming to its close; they were in their final hours. Whether it be weeks, months, or years, this was truly the setting of their era.

The telephone rang and Mabel stood, walking into the music room and closing the pocket door behind her, knowing that it was Kathryn.

"Yes, dear?" she asked as soon as she lifted the receiver.

"How are Trevor and Darbi?" Kathryn asked numbly.

"Fine, dear." She paused for a moment before continuing. "It's Tom."

Kathryn sighed.

"I know. I felt it just now when I looked over at the carriage-house; I knew he was no longer in there."

Mabel could hear the sound of people outside of the house in the alley, most likely trying to look through the windows.

"That's exactly what's going on," Kathryn replied.

"Are you okay; is everyone okay?"

Kathryn chuckled.

"As good as we can be, but Jeffery and Marcel are already on their way; they're flying in with Mitchell. Maria is driving down with Brighton; in fact, I think they've already left Tacoma, which means that they're going to get here anytime now."

Mabel could hear the panic in Kathryn's voice, and knew that there was nothing that she could do to ease her niece's suffering.

"What's worse, I think we need a lawyer," Kathryn concluded.

Mabel already knew this, and knew who they would have to call.

"Well, then, get John on the phone."

She could hear Kathryn's cynical chuckle.

"That bastard wouldn't help us even if we paid him."

Mabel didn't like that her niece had suddenly lost faith in family in a time of crisis. She understood where it came from, but still it made her sad.

"Then I'll call him. It's that simple, darling: we need him. We have too many secrets not to ask for his help.

"Besides, he's part of those secrets, remember?"

She could feel Michael's dead eyes staring at her from the dark-ened corner of the music room, right next to the window. The night was setting in, and swiftly she switched on a little Tiffany lamp in the corner, her face becoming illuminated in its glow.

"Yes, but still...."

Mabel didn't want to hear this disagreement.

"Look, he needs to be called, plain and simple—and we need to find Tom as quickly as possible."

"Don't worry, I know my husband; he'll come for me soon enough."

Kathryn hung up the line, and Mabel glimpsed the dead Donovan's reflection in the window pane.

"That's what I'm afraid of."

TWENTY-FOUR

They were everywhere—these reporters—and Braxton felt himself twist and turn inside. He knew that something was going on, something that went way beyond him, something that was much more than just a dead girl without a heart. There was an unseen evil in the world, an evil that was taking shape and gathering over the city—over the Blackmoore home—infecting everyone and everything around them slowly.

The night was heavy.

He parked along the curb and stepped outside, locking the door behind him and switching on the alarm. He approached the house slowly and watched in fear as the reporters turned their attentions and cameras towards him, shining those bright lights in his face and hurling him with questions.

Kathryn, Magdalene—someone please open the door, he thought to himself as he stepped up on the curb and moved past the maples, keeping his eyes focused on the dark green of the front door.

"Do you know the Blackmoores?" one reporter asked him.

"Hey, kid, are you a Blackmoore?" another one asked—in fact, it was the young reporter from the earlier broadcast. This didn't feel real to Braxton, but he knew that it was; that this media storm was real and damning.

He stepped up onto the front stoop without any acknowledgment of the press, and before he could knock, the knob turned and the door swung open, Braxton instantly feeling relief at the sight of Magdalene's smiling face.

"Shit, what in the hell is going on?" he asked, while Magdalene closed the door behind him, the shouting of the reporters becoming muffled pleas behind the manor's walls.

"Well, we're Public Enemy Number One, apparently," She responded, brushing her hair over her shoulders.

"Where's Kathryn?" he asked, looking down the hall.

"I'm right here, Braxton." she said, emerging from the T.V. room. She opened her arms and hugged the young man, feeling the presence of fresh death about him, but deciding to keep it to herself.

"Where's Trevor?"

Kathryn grinned and nodded, as if she had been expecting that to be his first question.

"He's at Queen Mab's with my grandmother Fiona; he's with Darbi, and he's safe."

He nodded, and the three of them moved back into the T.V. room to watch the unfolding story and wait to see what was going to happen.

"Are they going to arrest you?" he asked, and Francesca shrugged.

"We don't know; we came home to this. The house was taped off, but we came in anyways. They haven't come to take us away, but now, with the discovery of this girl... they just might."

Braxton looked around the home and into these faces and realized how awful his life would be if the Blackmoores were arrested. This was now the only family he had; without them he'd be alone.

If that were to happen, he concluded, *then there would be no point in living.*

Kathryn reached out and clasped his hand.

"Don't worry, that's not going to happen. We're not going anywhere. Remember, we're Blackmoores. We may not be the largest family in the country, but we are one of the most powerful."

He tried to find reassurance in her words, but still he found none. Even the Blackmoores had to have their limits. Yes, they helped make Bellingham into what it is, but outside of this town their grip must wear thin.

"Don't forget, Braxton, we're everywhere."

She kissed him on the cheek and walked over to the sleek, black cordless sitting on one of the end tables. Picking it up, she called her aunt's home to tell Trevor that Braxton was over.

She had just hung up the phone when it rang again, and upon picking it up she was greeted by a voice that she had not expected to hear.

"Kathryn, what in the hell is going on up there?"

It was John.

The same man who had vowed to stay away from the family and ensure that Darbi had no connection with the rest of the American Blackmoores, was now calling her home after five years.

"Well, hello, John."

"Don't give me that, Kathryn; it's all over the news!"

She chuckled and looked to the corner of the home, seeing what she thought was the silhouette of Sheffield but knew it to be a lie; a creation by the evil that was threatening to take over the family and wipe them out.

"Wow, our little town has reached the media in El Paso? How nice."

John mumbled some sort of swear word, but seemed to shrug it off.

"Kathryn, Amy came to see me last night. She told me that we were all going to die."

Amy had been John's wife, but as with the rest of the people who gave themselves to the Blackmoores, she lost her life to the Legacy.

"You can't escape the Legacy, John. You know that, and you know what will happen if the Legacy is conquered...."

He gasped. It was loud and rather startled; she knew that she had struck a nerve.

"Who?"

She contemplated lying to him, but she knew that if he was reaching out, then she shouldn't give reason to push him away.

"Trevor."

"But how?"

She looked over her shoulder, saw them all looking at her, and she knew she couldn't say.

"I don't know how, really, but I do know that he did, and now we're in our last days." John knew the prophecy as much as anyone else in the family. Once the Legacy was conquered, then the extinction of their family was imminent.

In the end it would fall on Trevor's shoulders. In the end, it would be up to him if the family would continue on or be lost forever to the thick of time.

"I'm flying up; you need help; legal help. I'll fly private."

Suddenly this wave of gratefulness took hold and it brought tears to Kathryn's eyes.

"Thank you, John...."

"And Kathryn, no matter what, don't you talk to anyone. If they try to arrest you, tell them that your attorney's on the way. Also, I'm going to call Judge Holden right now and see if he can put a stay on your arrest—if they try to, that is."

They agreed, and Kathryn hung up the line feeling slightly more relieved. Still, there was a fear lining all of those thoughts—a fear that Trevor's future was going to be ruined and none of them would come out of this unscathed.

The jet had just taken to the sky and was climbing above the city of El Paso when John Blackmoore called Richard Holden from the phone, feeling the knot in his stomach over what he was coming back to.

"Hello?" the gruff voice answered.

"Richard, it's John Blackmoore, long time...."

"You could say that, couldn't you?"

John sipped on a martini and looked out of the window, seeing the limitless stars overhead—watching him—protecting him—letting him know that he would get home safely.

"Yeah, look I need a favor."

He heard the laugh in the man's voice.

"I knew that was coming; what is it?"

"Well, you know, I'm sure."

Richard Holden chuckled once again.

"If you're referring to the dead girl... you're right; I do."

John could feel the tension begin to build inside of his head and the anger attempt to creep up on him.

"I need you to block any attempt at arresting my family."

Richard cleared his throat in a purposeful way, as if trying to tell him that it wouldn't happen.

"John, you know damn well I can't do that. The evidence points to your family. And let's face it, most of the people in this city have been waiting for something just like this.

"In the minds of Bellingham's citizens, your family is already guilty."

This was truth and he knew it; it was this kind of behavior that had driven him away in the first place—that and the Legacy. At twenty years old, John left El Paso and moved to Bellingham to begin learning the ropes of Blackmoore World Corp. while attending Fairhaven University. His mother, Oona, had emigrated from the family home in Ireland to live in the border city when she was eighteen years old; obsessed with the American West. Shortly after, she married Hernesto Lechuga of neighboring Juarez, and as with all in the family, John's father passed three days before his twelfth birthday.

His mother had warned him about the American Blackmoores, and their embrace of the family's witchcraft. She had also warned him of the reception he would receive in Bellingham once people found out who was. At the time he had simplified all of it as the over-exaggerations of his side of the family's Catholic superstitions, but not too long after arriving in Bellingham, John quickly learned that all of Oona Blackmoore's warnings had been true.

"Look, I know; I just need you to buy me time until I can get there. I'm on a jet right now. Please, I just need a few hours—a head start—please!"

John Blackmoore didn't beg; that was something he thought he could never do, but now here he was, and he knew that this would sway his old colleague.

"All right John, I'll see what I can do. But you need to be careful. Your family is under fire, and you're gonna get burned."

They hung up, and he tried so desperately to focus on other things—seeing his family, the coming holiday—but none of it would work. He was returning to a place that he had no desire to see and to a family he all but abandoned years ago. But it seemed as if it was all coming around full circle and he had no choice but to give in; he had no choice but to return to its source.

And the plane flew on.

That bitch thinks she can challenge me; let's see what she'll think once I put her behind bars! Randy thought to himself as he stalked up the front walk of Kathryn's home, ignoring the reporters and accompanied by two uniforms; a pleased grin on his face.

"Detective—Detective Kit, what are you doing here?" one of the nameless reporters asked.

Though he wanted so desperately to gloat, he knew that it was not the time. He would get enough validation when they strapped cuffs around all of them, especially Kathryn Blackmoore.

He pounded on the door and didn't have to wait long. Through the window he could see Kathryn Blackmoore approach the door, her eyes cold and harsh like the falling winter, and her face showed visible anger at the sight of him.

"Detective," she said, paying no mind to everyone beyond him.

"Kathryn Blackmoore, I have arrest warrants for every member of your family."

She grinned.

It was a grin that angered him: a grin of the smug; the rich; those who think that they're above the law.

He wanted to slap that grin off of her face.

"I don't recommend slapping me, Detective; it might not look too good."

It threw him off, but he wasn't going to show it. The tables had turned, and now he had all of the Blackmoores in the palm of his hand.

"Inside!" he said to the two officers.

They hesitated for just a moment before proceeding inside, saying "excuse me" to Kathryn as they passed.

"You won't be arresting us, Randy. Not tonight."

It was then that his cell phone rang.

"Captain, what is it?" he asked, looking at the smile on Kathryn's face. "What; are you fucking serious?" He began to shake his head in frustration and disbelief. "Not enough evidence?! But the heart was found in their fucking yard!"

The more he was being told "no," the angrier he became.

"Yeah, okay, so we don't know whose trash the body was found in, but that's not the point. They did it. We have enough evidence to make an arrest!" Still he was refused, and Randy had no choice but to comply.

"Merry Christmas, Detective," Kathryn said.

He had walked up to this door victorious and was going to leave it completely humiliated. He had half-a-mind to pull his gun out and shoot Kathryn Blackmoore between the eyes.

"You evil fucking bitch; I don't know what you did—how you did it—but this isn't over!"

She winked at him and stepped aside to let the officers out. The anger simmered, began to boil as he walked back to his car empty-handed, enraged and embarrassed. The cameras flashed in his eyes and the reporters began to turn the tide, asking him if he had screwed up; worse yet, many were already accusing him of being wrong.

As he opened the door to his car he looked back at the Blackmoore home, and saw Kathryn standing there in the doorframe, staring at him with that satisfied grin. Randy vowed that he would watch her suffer if it was the last thing he did.

"I don't understand why we have to wait. Why we can't get Trevor now?!" Greg Sheer was saying, pacing his room and staring at Christian. He hadn't slept in days, his body was fatigued, his eyes a little heavy, his movements erratic.

'Because it's not time yet. I told you all of the American Blackmoores need to be there—all of them, or else it won't work. This has been planned for a very long time, and you can't just go in there and fuck it all up.'

Christian was now much more decayed: his face wasting away, cheekbones protruding, eyes black—no whites, no irises—just black and empty.

"I just hate waiting; I want him. I want to kill him. Him, and everyone that he loves!"

The spirit grinned at this desperation, liked seeing Greg's frustration, his rage. He could feed off of this, in the end he could make them all suffer.

'I know, dude, but fucking chill....'

He stood and walked to Greg, placing his hand on his shoulders, easing him back gently, pressing the boy's body against the door.

"Do that thing again; it calms me down. Please, Christian do that thing...."

He eased his hand on his crotch and began to rub it, to pull, placing his head on the sticky membrane mess of Christian's head, pushing the dead boy to his knees.

"Yeah, that's it...."

Brighton Blackmoore held his daughter's arm tightly, clutching his polished cane in his other hand as they walked up the steps to Queen Mab's home, grinning as they looked at the light glowing from behind the windows, hearing the familial voices as the came closer to the door.

Maria Blackmoore-Taylor stood no more than four inches past five foot, her curvy frame much like Marilyn Monroe's. Her chin-length, honey-blonde hair was pulled back and held by a black clip. Her black heels tapped on the old wood steps, helping her father gently, easing him one step at a time, and approaching the front door at their own pace.

They knocked, and to her surprise Darbi answered the door.

He looked much older than the last time she saw him, and the few pictures of him she did receive did him little justice.

"Oh my God, Kathryn told me you were flying up!"

Darbi grinned and hugged her while Trevor assisted Brighton into the house. Fiona stood and placed her lips on her second cousin's cheek, telling him that he looked well.

"Oh, I could be better, my dear..." he struggled, and they laughed.

"Well, I think in this case we all could," Fiona responded, scooting out of the way and allowing him to take a seat next to her.

"So, if you don't mind me asking, what in the hell has been happening up here?"

Maria looked at Mabel, who only shook her head.

"Much more than you could possibly imagine, my dear."

Maria walked over to one of the arm chairs and took a seat, scanning the opulent home. "And is there an end in sight?"

Trevor looked up, startled and turning to Fiona, whose eyes were fixed firmly on him. The look on her face was ominous, as if she were expecting something from him.

"We should hope not, but at this point we don't know anything. For the first time, we Blackmoores are utterly oblivious to any and everything."

Maria knew that Fiona was referring to the Legacy. She had seen her own husband just the night before, and her father had told her of the visit from his wife Amanda.

They all knew that this was the sign that the power of the Legacy had been broken—when those killed by it could finally come through, when the curse that chained their souls was overcome.

It was a sign they all had dreaded.

Suddenly, there was another knock at the door, and cautiously Trevor went to open it, relieved to find Jeffery and Marcel staring at him.

Jeffery looked weary and startled, his black hair unkempt and longer than usual, his green eyes distant, cold—like his mother's, but more so.

He was stocky, broad shoulders but in no way husky. The grin on his face looked like it took effort. He was a man overcome by the grief of his wife's passing. It had only occurred two years previous, and so he could understand that it still held power.

"Trevor!"

Marcel was thin and nearly as tall as Trevor, though he was lacking four inches. Like his father, his hair was black and short, his eyes large and the deepest shade of blue that Trevor had ever seen: like nighttime waters. His ears were sharp like an elf's, and his smile was infectious.

"Hey, Marcel, how you doing?" Darbi asked, stretching his arms out wide and embracing the San Franciscan Blackmoore.

"Darbi!"

They hugged and Trevor grinned, warmed to see his family together—though he understood that this held a darker meaning, one that wasn't being discussed but at the same time was known by everyone.

"Jeffery, how are you?" Maria asked, and he shrugged, letting go of a long sigh.

"Tired, and a little scared."

Mabel stood and walked over to him, gripping his shoulders and kissing him on the cheek.

"You saw Emma, didn't you?"

Jeffery nodded dumbly, the tears filling his eyes and slipping down his face.

"I know, darling... I know...."

She brought him in close, petting his hair and singing to him softly.

Trevor noticed the weariness in all of them, the strain of death. This was whom the bells tolled for. This family. This family, that, until now, had suffered constant and immense grief; but with the conquering of the Legacy did this mean that it would end, no matter how brief their time left?

He hoped so.

"Well, now that we're all here, I think we should head over to Kathryn's. The crowd has died down—I think—and Trevor, Braxton's there; I forgot to tell you."

Trevor grinned at Queen Mab, but another feeling crept in: a feeling of suspicion. Braxton had told him that he would be staying home, that he needed to be with his father. Something had happened, he knew it; he only questioned whether or not Braxton would tell him.

"Wait, where's Mitchell?" Trevor asked, worried about his older cousin, afraid for him suddenly.

"Oh, he'll be up; he rented a separate car. He also said that he needed a special gift for a certain birthday boy..." Jeffery responded, sounding like his old, teasing self.

It wouldn't last; Trevor knew it. He could see the darkness wash over Jeffery just as quickly as it had passed.

TWENTY-FIVE

"Cheri, what in the hell is wrong with you?" Teri Jules asked. She was walking along Eighteenth Street, making her way back home in the snowy dark, grateful that she had the street lights and Christmas glow to keep her company.

"Nothing, Teri, I just need some time...."

Teri frowned. Wearing white sneakers and boot-cut jeans, warmed by her wool pea coat, she continued to walk. She played with the pink-and-white striped scarf that hung from her neck, and she grinned at the fact that it would be Christmas soon and she knew she would be getting a brand new BMW.

"Well, whatever; call me when you've come back to your senses!"

She hung up and stuck her cell back into her pocket, trying to keep her hands warm inside. She wondered when next she would see Greg, and if he was doing okay. She hoped that a new car might sway him into asking her out. All she wanted was Greg Sheer, and with the apparent separation of their circle since Christian's death, she feared that she wouldn't even have a chance.

She began to sing *Temptation Waits* by Garbage; it was one of her favorite songs, and something she liked to sing when walking alone at night.

Before her the lights began to blink out, one by one, closing the inky pitch all around her.

"What's going on?"

She looked behind her to see the lights do the same thing and her heart began to pound as she searched the streets frantically. Porch lights went out; Christmas lights flickered off. Within moments Teri Jules was standing alone, helpless and afraid under the light of a single lamp post, its orange beam affording her her only sense of security.

"All alone..." a voice whispered, making her yelp and forcing Teri to turn around.

"Whoever you are, I'm calling the police; I mean it, motherfucker!"

She reached into her pocket and retrieved her cell phone, shaking while she held it. The sweat began to bead down her terrified face, her lip quivering, the tears slipping down her cheeks.

"All alone...." It came again, and the lamp above her went out.

She screamed and dropped her phone, hearing it break in two. It was one of those moments, those times when you just knew how the story was going to end, and she knew that she was going to die. Her time had come; she had no place to go and she was too scared to run.

"Please, God...."

It was like a tree limb had ripped into her, tearing through her back, clutching her heart and ripping it out, removing it from the crater that was made.

She gasped, and then nothing. Her body fell to the pavement. Blood washed out from the wound, pooling around her lifeless body, changing the color of her hair. Tomorrow, people were going to think that she was a redhead.

Tom Preston stepped forward, sucking on her heart, treating it like a juice box, feeling it wither as he sucked out all of its nutrients. He could feel this restoring him, could feel his face fill out, his cheeks expanding and his body becoming thick.

Just as had happened with the girl who had been walking down the alley when he had first emerged from the carriage house the night before.

Whatever it was that fueled him—this force that gave him strength—he understood it. He understood what it wanted: it wanted the Blackmoores dead, and he would deliver.

Wearing clothes that he had taken from a homeless man earlier in the day, Tom Preston walked down the street, whistling, his hands in his pockets, feeling no cold, no discomfort.

Above him the lights came back on one by one, brightening the street as Christmas lights sparked back to life. He left Teri Jules there to be found. He had no reason to hide her. He was a God amongst sheep. He feared nothing, and they could never arrest a dead man.

Once again, the Blackmoore home was filled with life. Laughter and joyous conversation could be heard through every part of the house, clinking glasses of fine crystal, and old Christmas tunes from the 1930s and '40s played from the numerous speakers. For a while, at least, they could pretend that they were normal; they could pretend that they were just like every other family in the world.

This was exactly how Trevor had wanted it.

"Hey, baby, you doing good?" Braxton asked, purring in Trevor's ear.

Trevor turned and nodded, placing his head against his boyfriend's chest.

"Yeah, just a little tired, that's all."

Braxton nodded and kissed him on the cheek. They stood there in silence, Trevor looking at him intensely, trying to decipher what it was that he was hiding, what it was that had taken him from his father.

"And you, Braxton, are you doing okay?"

He nodded, but his gaze became heavy, distant, as if the weight of the world were now suddenly on his shoulders and his alone.

Trevor understood this feeling all too well.

"I just... I don't know...."

Trevor nodded and led Braxton into the kitchen, snatching a bottle of wine before going back out into the hallway. They stopped at a bookshelf in the hall across from the staircase. Braxton had never noticed it before, and it was obvious to Trevor that he was trying to understand why they were looking at it.

"I'll show you what I do when I have a problem that I just want to scream out."

Trevor's eyes scanned the books and with his fingers ran it along the tops of the pages before finally settling on a copy of *The Old Man and the Sea*. He looked at Braxton before giving it a pull. It drew back from the shelf only slightly and they both heard a *click*, as if a latch had released, and Trevor pulled the shelf back, revealing a narrow and pitch black abyss with a winding stairwell.

"What are we...?"

Braxton's words trailed off as he gripped Trevor's hand, following him down these narrow, cold, steps, maneuvering in utter darkness as the shelf-door drew in on them.

"Hold tight to me Braxton." Trevor felt his way through, dragging his fingers on the slightly moist wall of marble, winding their way down.

"Here we are..." Trevor's voice rang out, bouncing off wide walls. Braxton hadn't the slightest clue of where they were.

"Any light?" Braxton asked.

"Yeah." He heard a sharp snap, and suddenly the space was lit by a collection of ornate sconces made to look like torches. "There we go." His breath caught in his throat as his eyes took in what was before him.

Walls of polished white marble and blue trim, cool granite floors, and before them in the middle of the floor was an enormous swimming pool. Its water glistening, the bright white lights beneath the surface reflecting off of the mother-of-pearl floor, creating rainbows under the water's surface.

"Jesus Christ!"

Trevor looked at him and smirked.

It ran the entire length of the property; starting at a wading of three feet before slowly dipping into a smooth twelve feet.

Braxton placed his hand to the wall and caught quick images, erratic: children playing; music humming; laughter; swimming suits from decades ago; Eton crops and cigarette smoke.

He pulled away.

"What did you see?" Trevor asked, just as hypnotized by the place as Braxton was.

"Happiness."

"Yeah, well, it started out like that anyways.

"My grandfather, Trevor, was born in this house; his family had built it.

"In 1922 they began construction on this place. Originally this was a shelter; I'm not really sure for what, but that's what my mom told me.

"Anyways, I guess the threat was over and so they converted it into a giant indoor spa. They imported all of the marble from Venice, and the sconces were the first electrical light fixtures in this house; they wired everything else afterwards."

Trevor walked over to an old wood bench and took a seat; Braxton followed.

"After my grandmother, Annaline, married Grandpa Trevor in 1959, this place became really popular with the family, but, sadly, while swimming his laps as he did every morning, my grandpa Trevor died. My mom was in junior high."

Braxton's eyes fell on the pool's glittering surface and gasped.

"How?"

"A brain tumor. There was no chance, and even if there had been, it wouldn't have done any good; he drowned in there."

Trevor's eyes caught the light on the water, and for a moment, it looked like they were on fire; two bright emerald sparks in the dark.

"Anyways, my grandmother found him floating there, dead; so she closed it off. She sealed it up and thought that that would be the end of it.

"In 1990 my grandmother had a stroke or something and came to stay with us. She kept looking at the bookshelf and I couldn't understand why; at the time I didn't know about the pool. But she kept telling me that she could hear my grandfather calling her name at the shelf, telling her to come see him.

"Personally, I couldn't figure out why Grandpa wanted her to read so much, but I just ignored it."

"So what happened?"

"Well, apparently she came down here and committed suicide. I guess she blamed herself for his death; we don't know for sure.

"All I *do* know is that my dad was carrying me downstairs for breakfast when we saw the shelf opened, and my dad got this scared look on his face. He screamed for my mother, who came running down the stairs in her nightgown yelling 'Mom' over and over again, and both she and my dad disappeared in the darkness.

"My mom was screaming, and I went down after her. When I got to the steps, my mother jumped into the water trying to get to Grandma. My dad freaked out and jumped in after her, pulling her back and then getting my grandmother's body; he eased it out of the water.

"I don't think my mom even noticed that I was standing there. She just held onto Grandma Annaline and cried, whispering that she would bring her back.

"I didn't get it at the time, but I do now."

Braxton didn't know what to say, so he didn't. He reached into his pocket and fished out a pack of Camels, offering one to

Trevor—who took it, not bothering to admit that he'd never smoked before.

"That's intense...."

Trevor chuckled.

"But why would she blame herself for a tumor?"

Here it was: the subject Trevor had hoped to avoid, the subject he had feared above all else, but there was no escaping it.

"Because brain tumors happen a lot in my family... to everyone...."

Braxton looked at him, worried.

"Everyone?"

Trevor shook his head and sighed.

"No, just everyone who has sex with us or gets our fluids in their bodies someway or another."

Braxton stood and looked down at Trevor, running every moment of intimacy they had ever shared, ever known—and now it was revealed that it was all a death sentence.

"You mean I'm going to die?"

Trevor stood and shook his head.

"No, it's over; our Legacy is over."

Braxton could not understand what was being said to him; he wanted Trevor to pick which one. He said they all die, but then he said that it wasn't going to happen. He was growing all the more confused.

"Well, who knows? Maybe I deserve to die."

Trevor couldn't believe what he had just heard. It didn't make any sense: this sudden acceptance of death, the possibility of being taken from him. It was obvious to him that he was right to suspect that Braxton was hiding something.

"Why would you say that?"

Braxton's eyes began to fill with tears; gently they fell down his face, his bottom lip quivering.

"What happened?"

"I killed my father."

Trevor shook his head. He couldn't have heard what he just heard; he tried to convince himself that it was a mistake, but he knew that he had heard him right.

"What do you mean?"

"Today; before I came over. My father was such a mess, Trevor. Covered in shit—in a daze—talking about how he'd seen my dead mother, calling me names, calling you names. I just... I don't know.

"I felt this, like, power, and the next thing I knew all of the windows and pictures in the front hall blew up; I don't know how else to describe it.

"He pulled out a pistol and was going to shoot me, calling me a witch. I just snapped. Something came out of me and he died, like he had a seizure, and all of this blood came out of his ears, and nose, and fucking anywhere else you could think of!"

Trevor couldn't believe it, couldn't understand it. Braxton had killed; though he hadn't meant to, he still did it, and there was no escaping that fact.

"What did you do?"

Braxton sobbed and sat back down on the bench, swigging back from the wine bottle as if it held the elixir of truth.

"I left him there on the floor. J.T. called and told me what was going on with you, and I raced right over. I don't know... I'm just so scared."

Trevor nodded and gripped his hands, kissing his knuckles lightly and telling him that everything would be all right—though much like his own mother, he wasn't so sure about anything anymore.

"Merry Christmas!" They all turned to see twenty-eight-year-old Mitchell Blackmoore stumble through the front door, clutching bags upon bags of gifts, his luggage sitting neatly on the stoop behind him.

"Well, look at you!" Kathryn said, walking up to her cousin and taking him in for just a moment before kissing him on the cheek.

He was 6'2, short blond hair and bright blue eyes on a cleanly-shaven and gorgeous face, dressed in a black ribbed turtleneck and dark denim carpenter jeans. His pale face was flushed from the cold, but he didn't mind it.

"Look at me? Well, what about you, Kathryn? You're stunning as always."

She blushed and threw her hair back out of her eyes. The clan was gathering, coming together, and they could all feel it: the surge, the force of being together, and they all tried desperately to push aside the darkening cloud that was casting shadow over them.

"Oh, thank you—here, um, Adamo, grab his luggage."

Her cousin nodded and slipped behind them, grabbing the two suitcases and bringing them inside.

"You're going to have to stay at Queen Mab's, is that okay?"

Mitchell grinned at Kathryn and nodded, telling her not to worry.

"So, where in the hell is Trevor?"

Kathryn cocked her head and drew her gaze to the bookcase, feeling the apprehension, but she pushed it aside with a wry grin.

"Trevor!" she called out. "Mitchell's here...."

Within a matter of moments the commotion of footfalls could be heard, and Trevor and Braxton appeared in the hall, Braxton closing the bookcase behind him.

"Oh my God, Mitchell!"

He ran to him and Mitchell opened his arms, wrapping them around his cousin and lifting him off the ground.

"I missed you," he whispered, eyes closed, taking in the warmth of one another.

"I missed you too," Trevor mused, smiling uncontrollably.

For a moment, the dark revelation of Eric Volaverunt's death was nowhere near him; that was, until Mitchell put him back down and he once again saw the darkness cast on Braxton's face, the red of his eyes and the weight on his shoulders.

"Um, Mom?"

Kathryn turned and looked at her son.

"Yes?"

"Braxton needs to talk to you in the office."

Kathryn turned just in time to see the startled look on Braxton's face.

"Come with me, darling."

She moved to him and took Braxton by the hands, leading him down the dimly lit hall, Trevor watching as his mother and his boyfriend disappeared in the quiet room.

"So, who's that?" Mitchell asked, watching the same door, knowing that he was referring to Braxton.

He didn't know how to tell him; confessing something like this to Mitchell felt like a betrayal. He had always had a big-brother/little-brother relationship with Mitchell, and confessing his relationship to Mitchell meant confessing that he was getting older, that he was growing up.

"That's Braxton... my boyfriend."

His heart began to pound as he watched for any sign of letdown or sorrow, or even disgust, on his older cousin's face.

There was none.

"Oh, that's cool... but don't worry, you'll always be six years old to me."

Mitchell winked and messed his hands through Trevor's hair.

"Well, I wouldn't say that, Mitchell..." Francesca began. "Trevor's got the Jag."

Mitchell laughed and moved on into the sitting room, carrying the bags of gifts, and began unloading them under the tree, which was already overflowing.

As the rest of the family went on talking and enjoying their togetherness, Trevor stood in the foyer and felt a chill sweep through the hall. It was dark, unfeeling, and yet very much aware; Trevor knew that it was a sign that things were about to get very messy.

TWENTY-SIX

The morning of Trevor's birthday was hindered to say the least, the events of the day before creeping in on him and reminding him that there was no time for celebration. The sky was still that deep inky blue of early morning, long before the dawn would ever come, and the snow had returned once again, filling the city with thick white ice feathers.

He turned and grinned sullenly at the sleeping body of Braxton, whose bare backside and muscular shoulders told its own story of suffering. John had arrived twelve-past-eleven the night before and was immediately filled in on the events at hand—including the death of Eric Volaverunt.

He agreed to represent Braxton, and set out right away in obtaining the will and making sure that any investigation into Eric's death was deferred immediately—which meant not reporting it until the next day.

It had been strange for all of them to have John back in the house, back in Bellingham, a town that he had amply declared he would never return to. Aside from the twins and the rest of the Irish Blackmoores, the family was together, and their dead were screaming to get in.

The floorboards creaked outside of his door, and he watched with bated breath as the knob turned and his mother's face peeked in, a look of concerned horror on her face.

"Mom, what is it?"

She shook her head and ushered for her son to come out into the hall.

"On the news, honey; you need to see this."

He nodded and tried to ignore the beating of his own heart as he followed his mother down the darkened steps and into the television room. His cousins Darbi, Magdalene, Adamo, and Francesca were already awake and standing, each holding a cup of coffee and staring at the glowing screen with terror in their eyes.

"Not even five blocks away from the sight of the first killing, another just as tragic and grisly crime has taken place," the same young reporter from the day before began, standing only three streets up from the Blackmoore home, police and onlookers filling the lane.

Trevor's breath caught in his throat as last year's school photo of Teri Jules flashed on the screen.

"Teri Jules, the seventeen-year-old daughter of St. Joseph Hospital's Chief-of-Staff, Scott Jules, was found dead this morning. Right behind me is the site where she was discovered. The official details are still unknown, but observers stated that she had been found lying in a pool of her own blood, her heart only a few away. One neighbor described it as being withered—as if dried out."

Trevor thought he was going to vomit and yet he couldn't move, and he was silently relieved when his mother switched off the television.

"It's happening, and there's nothing we can do about it."

They looked at Adamo and frowned, dismayed by what he was saying, though they were all thinking it.

"You see, Trevor," Kathryn began, walking to her son and drawing him close, her hands unsteady on his forearms.

He had never seen his mother this terrified.

"This is what we're up against," she continued. "This is the prophecy, the great evil for which we have to fight—you have to fight."

Trevor shook his head, staring at his family in the dark home, seeing all of their eyes black, seeing them all stare at him.

"Me? I'm just... me... why are you saying this?"

Kathryn sighed and directed Trevor to the couch, forcing him to sit with her as they all gathered round.

"You conquered the Legacy; you brought its end, which means only you can stop what's coming."

They all agreed, and for the first time Trevor felt inferior when compared to his family; he also felt betrayed.

"What is coming? The great evil, I know, but what? I mean, am I going to have it out with this thing, like right here and now?"

Magdalene sighed, and they all shook their heads; all but Darbi, who was visibly shaken by all of this.

"No. There will be signs, agents—fulfillers of this great evil. How long this may go on, we don't know. This being, this Dark God, is not strong enough yet, but it will be, and what form it will take we don't know.

"But it will come, and you have to be ready; we all do. They're going to try and take us out until only you're left standing, then *it* will come."

Trevor stood and shook his head, feeling the world begin to cave, and the border between this world and the next was shifting, thinning—and Trevor knew that soon it would be spilling in and taking over.

"I can't deal with this; you've got the wrong person, Mom, all of you... I'm not this savior, I'm just some stupid kid who can talk to dead people."

He moved from them, slowly at first—then he began to move faster, moving through the hall and up the steps to his room. He needed to talk to Braxton, needed some sense of comfort, some voice of sanity and reason; but now, the question became how was he going to tell this to Braxton?

He slammed the door behind him, forgetting that Braxton might be asleep, trying to wipe away the tears.

"Trevor, babe what's wrong?"

He looked to see Braxton staring at him, his dark eyes large and his handsome face a wash of concern. He propped his knees and balanced his arms on them, waiting for Trevor to fill him in.

"Everything. I'm wrong; I'm screwed-up...."

He made his way to the bed, climbing on the mattress while staring into Braxton's deep gaze.

"What are you talking about?"

Trevor sniffled and wiped his nose.

"The murder of the girl in the alley, and now Teri Jules; it's all my fault!"

At the mention of Teri's name, Braxton's mouth fell open and he stared at Trevor, dumbfounded.

"What are you talking about?"

Trevor sighed, praying silently to those Blackmoores who had gone before him, praying that they would protect him.

"They found her dead this morning, only three blocks away. She was lying in a pool of her own blood and her heart was apparently ripped out of her, just like the first victim."

Braxton placed his hands to his temples and began to rub, closing his eyes and taking it all in.

"Jesus Christ, and why is this your fault?"

Trevor sighed.

"My family's cursed.

"Thousands of years ago, back in Ireland, my family lived in an area known as the Black Moors. There they worshiped a goddess and a god, like all of the people of pre-Christian Ireland. Anyways, this god—this being—was evil and took over at night, demanding human blood sacrifice.

"For generations they sacrificed innocent people to this thing once a month, until finally they moved away, forgetting about him, but adopting the name Blackmoore to remind them of their darkness.

"Our blood was cursed and anyone who came into contact with our fluids, our DNA, was destined to die. It was our Legacy—until me, that is."

Braxton looked at him, unblinking, unmoving, trying to process what was being told to him.

"Why you?" he asked, his words in a hushed whisper, as if it was dangerous for anyone else to hear.

"Because, like I told you last night in the spa, I overcame the Legacy. I don't know how, but I did. And when this happened, the great evil—this thing—would be released and the devil would return for us... his witches."

Braxton looked at him with question, struggling to grasp the tale.

"It's what the curse states: the devil will come. The devil will come and walk amongst men, claiming souls one by one... for the devil keeps his witches, and will always come back for them....

"For the end of the devil will be at the hand of his own child."

An eerie silence feel over the room and Braxton instinctively reached out for Trevor, drawing him near to his own body, kissing his forehead gently.

"But do you all honestly believe that it's *the* devil?"

"No, that's just how it goes. I guess it's just supposed to mean the ultimate evil or some shit like that."

Braxton nodded and thought for a moment before responding.

"And you, you're this child that will bring about its end?"

Trevor looked at him and nodded, chuckling at the rather absurd sound of it, though he knew that it was very much a reality.

"Yeah, I'm the chosen one. I'm the one who gets to decide the fate of my family, possibly the world—and all I want to do is crawl under the covers and never come out."

His face grew dark once again, and once again Braxton could see the strange loneliness of Trevor's life.

"Well, if it's any consolation, I think if anyone can save the world it's you, and I don't think there's anyone more qualified to fight for your family than you."

Trevor looked around his dim room—lit by a single bedside lamp—looked at the furniture, the antiquity of the walls themselves, and he shrugged, closing his eyes and letting more tears to fall.

"What if I'm not strong enough; what if I fail?"

Braxton placed his finger under his chin and drew Trevor's gaze to meet his.

"You won't, because I won't let you fail, and if you fall... you won't fall alone."

They kissed and Trevor pushed the darkness aside, slipping back down into the thick blanket, drawing his body close to Braxton's. He would have crawled beneath his skin if he could.

Cheri sat on the stool in her kitchen, smoking her tenth cigarette of the morning and staring at the report of Teri's death, which was front page news of the Bellingham Herald's Christmas Eve edition.

She couldn't believe it: her friend Teri was dead. Someone had murdered her, ripped her to pieces, and she was left with more questions.

"Everyone around me is dying; everyone I know is being taken from me. What's going on; what have I done?"

Cheri had no answers, and she was further confounded by the fact that her parents would not be returning home until late into the night.

It didn't seem right that at this time of year, it would become a season of death. Lives so young, lives terribly unlived, were being taken, as if God were harvesting his human garden for the winter's hibernation.

If this was the cost, if this was the price of her redemption, then she didn't want it—not if it meant the loss of so many lives. She sighed, just as the house creaked and the steps of a stranger could be heard behind her.

"Hello?" she called out, her brown eyes searching the kitchen and entryways, attempting to discern the source of the sudden footfalls.

Again it happened.

"Who's there? Motherfucker, you had better answer me!"

Her heart was pounding now, slamming in the cavity of her chest, her breathing becoming erratic.

"Stop it!"

The cabinet doors began to fly open, drawers beginning to slam and hinges beginning to rattle.

"Shit!"

Cheri jumped from the stool and fell to the floor, throwing herself between some drawers and the fridge.

"Stop it!" she screamed louder, clutching her hands to her ears, attempting to block out the noise, her eyes filling with tears.

'Cheri....'

She looked up to see Christian staring at her.

Her voice was dead in her throat as she looked at the sight before her: Christian with his face gray and decaying, withered, bones visible; blood ebbed and membrane caked on falling skin, his sockets empty.

Cheri Hannifin fainted without a chance to question the phantom's reason.

Amongst candles burning and the scent of patchouli and tobacco Mabel stood, her eyes closed and chanting, grounding herself amongst the silent eyes of plaster saints, feeling the familiar sensation of floating; as if she were lifting off the very floor.

She began to chant, to call out, summoning the strongest gods she knew and praying for their guidance.

"Legba, I call to thee; Damballah, I call to thee; Baron-Samedi, keeper of the lost souls, those of the damned, I beseech thee...."

The windows of her basement were covered in black plastic, and the walls were painted with the various *vèvès* of the *Loas*.

"From the darkest depths the souls stir and grow restless, those lost to our curse, our Legacy. I seek thine aid, great god Samedi; I ask that you keep them at bay. Legba, I call to thee, I plead with you, close the gates, most powerful one.

"Keep the gates closed; do not let them through!"

She was desperate, sensing the presence of suffered Blackmoores, those who had joined with their blood, those who had fallen victim. She felt them in her home; in the halls and streets they were gathering, as if in restless anticipation of the clan's demise.

"Great Damballah, protect this family, protect us, and most of all protect Trevor and Braxton. Prepare them and ready them for what is to come, for the war that is already here, for the blood that has already been spilt."

In the shadows cast by candlelight she could see the formations, could see what lived within the darkness, the evils that were waiting. And she knew then, as if being struck a powerful blow to the head, that tonight the first wave of destruction would come to their doorstep, would come like a hungry beast for their blood.

When she had finished, when she had closed her ceremony and paid her respects, Mabel returned to her family, returned to their anxious faces as they watched the news and John spoke excitedly on the phone to Kathryn.

"What's happened?"

Brighton, Maria, Jeffery, Marcel, and Mitchell all pointed to the screen; her mother Fiona was on the couch knitting and looking at her daughter with a knowing gaze.

"Another death... another sacrifice."

Fiona's voice was sullen yet matter-of-fact. She knew that her mother was keenly aware that tonight was the night; that war was imminent.

"I know; *they* told me."

They all knew that she was speaking of their doomed loved ones, generations past, those who craved the spilling of Blackmoore blood just as the great evil was.

"Well," John began, placing the phone back on the receiver. "Kathryn has informed Trevor of his role in all of this, his destiny. I wouldn't have wanted to believe it myself; in El Paso I was able to deny it, brush it off as family superstition."

They all nodded.

"I know, John..." Mabel said to him sympathetically.

"But now—now that I'm here, now that I'm watching this unfold—I can't deny it any longer, and I also know that I am not prepared for it. I'm not prepared to die."

They all thought of Marcel, looking at him and questioning if he could handle this, if he should not be sent to the other room, but the look on his face told them no. He was going to stay right where he was. He was fourteen, and old enough to know the truth. There was no denying that; it was his unfortunate birthright.

"How did he take it?" Mitchell asked. The look of concern on his face was heartbreaking. They all knew that they couldn't protect Trevor, and that there were still many more truths to be told, many more secrets still lying in wait.

"He became upset and ran back up into his room, and he's been in there since," John responded, his aged eyes weary.

"There is no way for us to escape this and in this world, this new world that has been created by the merging of two, Trevor will be all alone."

Brighton's aged voice came out almost as a whisper, and Maria, the ever-loving daughter, gripped his arm and fought back tears.

"There's more..." John began, his voice becoming just as sullen as the rest of them, just as weary. "Much more."

"Please, Detective sit down." He wasn't going to fall for her calculated hospitality any longer; he wasn't going to wait for her to say something witty and demeaning. He had them all where he wanted them.

"You know what? I think I'm fine standing right here."

He had been accompanied by four officers, all of them reluctant and yet prepared to take them all away in cuffs.

"You know, Kathryn, I find it very interesting that at the same time your little clan arrives, two girls wind up dead."

She shook her head and sighed.

"Don't try to rile me up, Detective; it's not going to work."

Bing Crosby sang Christmas carols through the speakers, and five other Blackmoores—including Trevor, who was still in pajama pants—stared at the detective with the same cold hate in their eyes.

"And you know, I don't recognize this kid in your family photos." He cocked his head towards Braxton, who had just emerged from the kitchen carrying a tray of coffee and china mugs.

"Well, that's because you wouldn't. This is Braxton Volaverunt; he's Trevor's boyfriend."

Magdalene chuckled, throwing her head back seductively, her eyes catching with the bashful glance of one of the younger male officers.

"Well, isn't that nice?" He moved closer to Trevor, rubbing his unshaven face. "Your boyfriend Christian not dead a month, and you've already got someone else. Interesting... you must have found closure quickly."

They all stood. The family gathering, moving closer to him. He felt like a zebra surrounded by a pride of lions.

"How dare you!"

Trevor stood and looked Randy in the eyes; they were a smokey green that appeared to be clearing at that very second.

"You think that you can just walk into this house—*my* house—and start whatever shit you feel like starting?"

Randy grinned, entertaining the idea of being able to justifiably strike this spoiled kid.

"Sit down!"

Randy's lips curled and he brought his hand to Trevor's chest, pushing him forcefully to the couch.

It was automatic: The Blackmoores moved fast and hard, surrounding Randy Kit, enclosing him in the vicinity of the couch, the uniformed officers still hesitant to move.

Just as quickly as he had pushed Trevor to the couch, the young Blackmoore was back on his feet and staring at the detective hard.

"You can't fool me, Detective; you can't hide anything from me."

Their eyes locked, and Randy could not pull away.

Trevor's gaze was endless; it was as if it were going on forever, reaching into him, exploring him; opening him up like a corpse being split in two.

"I see all of your secrets, all of your insecurities, those things you don't want anyone to know about."

Randy was becoming nervous, the sweat beading down his face as he struggled to pull away from Trevor's gaze.

"What are you...?"

Trevor shook his head and grinned.

"I know about how you once copped a feel on a corpse you had found in a dumpster behind the Royal; I know all about your drunken stupors and your frequent pick-up of hookers for your own pleasure; I know about all of it."

Nothing existed now but Trevor's eyes and his hypnotic and accusing voice—his ability to remove every secret, every shame, and lay it out on the table for everyone to see.

"You think that as long a there's no witnesses, you're safe. No one can get you, no one can touch you... well, I'm here to tell you otherwise."

He felt a sense of dread then, an indescribable weight that was being pressed on him, like Giles Corey of Salem in 1692.

"Oh, and here comes the rest of my family."

Whatever it was that had happened, whatever hold that had been on him broke with Kathryn's announcement.

The Blackmoores moved away as a parade of people in fine clothes came across the lawn, making their way to the front door.

Randy watched as they moved inside: three elderly, one no more than thirteen or fourteen years old, a middle-aged guy in his early forties who looked like the boy's father, an attractive twenty-something with short blond hair and a strong build in black jeans and an emerald green sweater, another middle-aged woman with blond hair—very attractive in his opinion. The only one in a suit was the gentleman that he assumed was their lawyer.

"Detective Kit, I presume?" John Blackmoore asked.

His gaze was just as penetrating and cold as the rest of them, and he was very much aware of the fact that by the mild confidence in John's voice that he was in for a battle.

"Yes. And now that you are all here, I've come to let you know that you are all under arrest for murder—"

"Murder?" John asked calmly.

"Yeah, double homicides. I'm afraid you are all going to have to come with me."

Randy looked over to the four officers and gave a nod, signaling them to proceed.

"I don't think so, Detective."

John's voice was stern and commanding. The look on all of their faces told him that they indeed weren't going anywhere.

"Excuse me; I have a warrant for your arrest."

John shook his head, and Kathryn snickered.

"Really, and what evidence, if any, do you have linking any one of us to these crimes?"

John Blackmoore was going to play hardball, and he knew it. As Randy looked around him, he was suddenly aware of the fact that he was outnumbered by twelve Blackmoores and Braxton, making it a total of thirteen people ready to oppose him.

"The scene of the first murder was right in your alleyway, and the second victim was a known acquaintance of Trevor's!"

John laughed and shook his head.

"So I take it you arrested the elderly couple that live in the house that Teri Jules was found lying in front of?"

Randy dropped his gaze and frowned, curling his fingers into the palms of his hands, digging them in.

"I didn't think so. If this is the route you're going, Detective, then I suggest you stop, because you have enough evidence to arrest that old couple, if not more.

"With them you found a body; as far as I'm aware, the body wasn't even here... it was at the dump."

Randy's head was spinning. He was able to present enough of a connection to obtain a warrant, but even the D.A. and his captain told him that it still wasn't going to be enough to bring them in if they had a lawyer smart enough to run it into the ground. And as it just so happened, not only did they have a good lawyer, but he was also a Blackmoore.

"Well, I think that settles it," Kathryn began, walking to Randy and looking him coolly in the eyes. "I would say that it was nice seeing you, Detective, but that would be a lie, and I don't like to lie."

She walked over to the front door and pulled it open, standing there in the grand foyer with a bemused grin on her face as the police officers moved past her, tipping their caps and mumbling apologies.

"This isn't over with; I will nail you...."

Kathryn smirked and shook her head.

"Not on your life."

It wasn't until after she had slammed the door behind him that Randy looked at his hands and realized that he had been pressing his nails in so tightly that he was bleeding, the red crimson seeping out of crescent moon incisions.

From across the street, Tom Preston watched it all take place and grinned. His bitch of a wife was being accused of his killings, and for his own personal amusement he wanted to do more—but the power that facilitated his return was telling him that it was time: that tonight was the night. Soon he could feast on the life he really wanted to.

He could devour the Blackmoores.

TWENTY-SEVEN

She had no real sense of time. Cheri woke up lying there on the kitchen floor, her head pounding and her eyes popping open as she tried to take in the scene around her. The kitchen was dark, her cup of coffee still sitting on the island's granite top, the liquid inside now ice cold.

Cheri struggled to her feet, trying to make sense of what she had seen, the unbelievable apparition that had taken shape in front of her very eyes.

"Christian...."

She tried to forget it, but she couldn't; and his rotting face was now forever burned on her brain. She was trying to understand it, this thing, and now she knew that Greg had been right—Christian was here, but he wasn't alive like he had thought.

Her home did not feel like hers anymore, and for the first time she began to ponder the souls that might still roam the halls of her immense Victorian, feeling suddenly as if she weren't alone, that a thousand invisible eyes were on her, watching her all of the time.

She thought she was going to pass out again.

"Trevor!"

Cheri raced down the long hall and turned up the grand staircase, knowing that she needed to get ready: she needed to get to his house as quickly as possible; there was no delaying it. The dead were waking and walking in Bellingham; they were stirring and coming to life in the prominent lanes of South Hill.

Whatever these deaths were, she knew that they were all connected to Trevor. She also knew without a doubt (and contrary to what the news was saying), that he was not the reason for them.

By now Christian Vasquez was all but bones, rotting before Greg Sheer with a permanent grin due to the nearly disintegrated face, the ivory of the skeleton beneath entirely visible.

They stood in his bedroom staring at one another. Greg was restless, eyes bloodshot, and a full beard now formed. He hadn't eaten since Christian had first come to him, and as a result his body was devouring itself.

He understood what today meant: it was Trevor's birthday. Little Trevor was eighteen; he had come of age, and Greg was to send him quickly into death's arms.

He also knew that after tonight, he and Christian would never see each other again.

'Are you ready?' Christian asked, his voice hauntingly detached like the soft whistle of wind.

"Yes..." he managed.

Greg felt so weak, felt as if he were going to fall asleep at any moment, yet the charge of Christian's presence gave him strength. It brought him to his feet and encouraged him to get dressed.

As if being told what to do, Greg walked to his closet and undressed, pulling out clothes haphazardly and throwing on a sweater and a fresh pair of jeans, struggling with the button as his sight was now hazy, and clumsily he forced his feet into his boots.

'Now, close your eyes...' Christian said to him, and without hesitation he obeyed.

As if he were out in the middle of a storm the air stirred, followed with the sense of invasion—of being taken over.

It was as if a powerful hand had stuck itself inside of him and began to push his soul to the lower depths of his body, and someone else was working his machine. He knew it to was Christian.

"That's better," Greg said, though the new vitality and spirit within was not Greg. "Flesh... I love it."

Greg walked to the glass cabinet which housed his various firearms and gripped a double barrel shotgun, yanking it from its slot and giving it a powerful cock.

"All right, Trevor, it's time to deliver you to the angels of hell.... For there are many waiting for you."

Confidently, Greg Sheer walked out of his room, gun in hand, prepared to put an end to it once and for all.

"So we're just supposed to sit here and wait?" Trevor asked, gripping tightly to Braxton's hand. They were all sitting in the formal room, the doors to the office open, the doors to the sun room open, every light in the great house now on.

"Well, what else can we do?" Francesca asked him rhetorically. "Look, Trevor, there's no training for this, no preparation. Death is coming for us, and we have to be ready."

They all looked nervously at each other, Kathryn occasionally peeking out through the thick satin curtains, trying to detect any sense of Tom.

"Jesus... I just don't know. I don't understand how this happened, how I conquered the Legacy."

Kathryn looked to Mabel, her eyes telling her everything she needed to know: that it was time to tell him the truth.

"Trevor, honey... there's something else, something that puts you in the center of this... something that involves Braxton."

They looked at her, confusion on both of their faces, a tightening in Braxton's stomach. Sitting there, both boys in jeans and black t-shirts, neither one prepared for the gravity of what they were about to be told, the fate that was about to be revealed to them.

"Me?"

Braxton pressed his finger into his chest and watched uneasily as Kathryn nodded.

"The Legacy's end was predicted centuries ago; it's in the family history. I believe, Trevor, that you read part of it at Queen Mab's house...."

He said nothing.

"The darkest of evils will rise amongst men, and amongst these men he will walk, tempting all those and claiming their souls; feeding on their fear.

"Upon this earth he will come, seeking out the one who holds the key, searching without exhaustion till he's gone through them all, testing each until the one is found."

Kathryn paused and Mabel continued:

"Upon the tenth generation this evil will come, and the Blackmoore blood may cease to exist; the key to this evil rising will be the Blackmoores who conquer the Legacy, and it will be these same Blackmoores who can bring about evil's end."

Mabel looked back to Kathryn, telling her without words that it was her duty to reveal the most crucial element.

"Of disbanded clans they'll come, sharing the same blood. They will be known by their initials, which will hold the answer to the mysteries and the revelations of our fate.

"The ones to come will hold the initials T. and B."

Braxton and Trevor looked at one another and shook their heads, either not understanding or not wanting to.

"You see, darling," Fiona began in her aged voice, "Tristan's daughter Katy denounced the family and our curse. She wanted no part of it, and in the winter of 1845 she left New Orleans for Spain, wanting to see the cathedrals and to just simply get away. That following winter of 1845 she returned, married and pregnant to a young aristocrat named Antonio Volaverunt."

A silence swept through the room and as their destiny, the well-versed plan of the family, began to unravel, both boys felt sick to their stomachs.

Mabel finished the tale for her mother.

"She returned an extremely wealthy woman who had previously grown up in the poor and squalor of what is now known as the Irish Channel. As a plea bargain to be left alone by her family, she gave them an amount equivalent to five million dollars today.

"In 1880 the family moved west, some stopping along the way and making homes in various states, but knowing that they would keep the bond strong. Once the majority of the family took up residence here in Bellingham—well, Fairhaven—Katy made her son Alexandre promise that he would never seek us out, that he should never come to Bellingham and find us.

"In 1866, at the age of twenty, Alexandre Volaverunt married his wife Margaret and they gave birth to a little girl named Jaime. They imposed the same precedence on Jaime not to seek out her family and to not move north, just as this vow had been demanded of him by his dying mother.

"They told her enough horror stories to ensure that, let me tell ya.

"However, in 1890 Jaime married James Richter, who was a prominent lawyer with a great firm which had just acquired the Donovan accounts, including the mill and shipping yard." Trevor understood now, slowly piecing the puzzle together in his head; knowing that Braxton was still putting the story together in his own troubled mind.

"As a result of this account, James was sent to handle the properties here in Bellingham, and though she did not want to come, Jaime loved her husband and agreed. So close to the estranged family, who by now had grown their fortune through development and real estate, Jaime felt trapped. Yet, she knew that as long as she stayed away from the Blackmoores, she would be okay.

"In 1910 Mr. and Mrs. Donovan, grieving over the loss of their son Michael, put their home and other properties for sale, all of which was handled by James and sold to Tristan Blackmoore, Katy's father, who was an astounding one hundred-and-twenty-years old, and being taken care of by his grandson Jeremiah and his wife Sarah, as well as his granddaughter Aria and her daughter Fiona.

"Well, James knew nothing of the connection, and so could not understand his wife's anger when he had told her of his selling the mill and shipping yard to the Blackmoores.

"Oddly enough, he was found dead the next day: sudden cardiac arrest."

This part of the story Trevor knew, but elected to keep his mouth shut.

"Well, they moved into the Donovan home—my home—and Fiona, my mother, gave birth to my sister Annaline and I. Annaline had a lifelong love with Trevor Mayland, who grew up in this house. They married in the spring of 1959, gave birth to Kathryn two years later, and that was that; for us, anyways."

"As for Jaime Volaverunt—well, she had a son named Michael, who by all reports was a telekinetic, but Katy beat him whenever she suspected him of using his gifts and told him to never use them... that it was evil, from the devil. Michael Jr. married Julia Brown in 1963 and she gave birth to Braxton's father Eric; and, well, here we are."

Their heads were swimming, trying to absorb all that had been revealed to them—most importantly Braxton, who was just taking in the knowledge that he had a family, this family, and that he and Trevor were related.

"But that would mean that Braxton and I are cousins...."

Now Trevor really felt sick; it gave him chills to think about, and he wondered what to do now that this news was given.

"Oh, honey, nowhere near close, now; only enough to make him a Blackmoore by blood, but that line is very thin."

"It still had enough power to end the Legacy," Braxton said.

He hadn't spoken at all throughout this tale, and now they were all looking at him, gauging him—especially Trevor—who was terrified of his reaction.

"Yes, this is true. But don't you see? This was meant to be; this was what was meant to happen. Your union, your joining. It had to happen in the tenth line: the only blood that could not be infected by the curse of the Legacy had to be between two Blackmoores, and it was set to happen when the line had no possibility of continuing through this union!"

Braxton moved his hand back to Trevor's and squeezed his hand tightly.

"But what does this mean?"

Kathryn sighed, feeling as if she were delivering these two boys their death sentences, that she was condemning her own son—and in truth, she was.

"That it lies with the both of you... our existence. It's going to be your power, your strength that will save this family. You two conquered the Legacy, which means that the two of you are the only ones with the power to save us all."

"How touching." A voice growled.

They turned to see a disheveled Greg Sheer standing in the foyer, the front door open, shotgun in hand, the barrels pointed at them all.

"Greg... what the fuck happened to you... what are you doing?" Braxton asked.

He moved in, laughing, grinning psychotically, more together than one should have been in his condition.

"Shut up, witch!" Greg screamed. His voice was maniacal, detached.

Kathryn stood and began to move towards Greg's weary stance.

"This isn't right... he's not the one...."

"Sit down, whore!"

He smacked her hard across the face with the back of his hand, knocking her to the ground.

"Don't you fucking touch my mother!" Trevor screamed with tears in his eyes.

Greg swung the gun around the room and pointed it at Trevor. "Don't."

Braxton stood up and quickly took hold of Trevor's arm, pulling him back to him.

They were sitting ducks and they knew it. Greg Sheer had them all lined up, ripe for the picking.

They looked at one another, scared, all of them taking a moment, trying to process what was going on and what they were going to do.

"Okay, okay... now, Greg, why don't you put that gun down?" Braxton was saying, moving Trevor behind him protectively and walking towards the distraught teenager slowly.

"Keep your mouth shut, faggot! God, you know what gets me?" Greg began, knocking the shotgun against his leg and pacing erratically, his boots stomping on the hardwood. "What gets me is that Trevor murdered Christian and he doesn't even feel remorse about it!"

Braxton shook his head, his brain throbbing, thinking of that far-away day when he had a chance to save Christian but didn't.

"No, he didn't...."

Trevor stood there, his mind drifting to dreams, to that moment in the carriage-house, the one in his dreams, where amongst candles and saints Christian told him the truth.

"Wait... he's right. I did... Christian told me I did."

They looked at him with their mouths gaped open—all except for Greg, who was grinning insanely.

"What are you talking about?" Braxton questioned, looking into Trevor's eyes with desperation.

"I told him the day that he died, the day that he broke up with me, that he couldn't see the pain he caused, that he couldn't see anything—and he couldn't.

"He lost his vision and drove off the road. I did it; I killed him."

Braxton shook his head, trying to denounce what Trevor was saying, but knew that he couldn't, and somewhere deep down inside he knew that what he said was true—just as he knew that he had killed his own father.

"Finally," he sighed. "And now you can go be with him."

Greg lifted the gun and pointed it at Trevor.

"Get over here!" Greg snarled, a thin stream of saliva flying out of his mouth.

They looked startled, unmoving, all of them trying to understand what was going on, trying to comprehend what was about to happen. This wasn't supposed to happen, this thing with Greg, his arrival; it wasn't part of the destiny and they knew it. This was something else, something else entirely.

"No, no, not my son!" Kathryn shouted, rising to her feet, hellfire in her eyes.

"Sit down, whore!"

Kathryn shook her head and began walking towards him, knowing full well that she may be walking to her death.

"No. This is my house, little boy. This is my house, and you will not—I mean, will not—threaten my son!"

Greg began to laugh, began to wail in humor, and he cocked the gun and pointed it at Kathryn's chest.

"Your house; your house?!" He wiped sweat from his brow. "I was here long before you were. This was my house before your brood came along and took it over!"

They all looked at one another, perplexed, trying to understand what he was saying.

"That's it, bitch!"

He put his finger on the trigger and began to pull.

"No!" Brighton called out, and without hesitation Greg spun around and fired two rounds into Brighton Blackmoore's chest. It exploded blood and tissue everywhere, spraying the home, covering the now-screaming Maria Blackmoore, looking horrified at her dead father.

"You fucker, you motherfucking bastard, I'll kill you!"

Maria was gripping her father's hand, staring at Greg with hate in her eyes, the deepest vengeance burning in her heart.

"Don't," he said to her as she stood, wiping the blood of her father off of her face. She feared nothing: not his gun, not his power to pull the trigger and put a hole in her body.

"Oh, please; you think I'm afraid of you?!" she shouted, and Greg stumbled back as if being slapped across the face. "I've lost my husband, my only son, and now, now I've lost my father... I've got nothing left to lose!"

Greg shook his head and lifted the firearm again, pointing it at the sudden force that was Maria Blackmoore.

"I said, don't move!"

Maria chuckled and shook her head and stepped forward.

"I moved."

As if a collection of arms had hold of him, Greg was tossed across the room, moving through the passage of the office and landing on top of the desk before tumbling down behind it.

"Still alive?" Maria questioned, looking at the desk only briefly before throwing her head to the left and tossing the desk across the room, hearing it crash through the French doors that led to the sun room.

"Not even close." Greg snickered, bits of blood and glass all over him, his breath labored and his lip bloody.

Cheri Hannifin was running down Fifteenth Street when she heard the second round of gunfire.

Shit!

She picked up the pace, her heart pounding, knowing that the sound, the clap of shots going off, was coming from Trevor's house. She also knew without a doubt that Greg was there.

It as if the snow had moved in much harder now, its force strengthened by the sudden anger of wind that was ripping branches from off of trees and tearing chimes and Christmas lights of off porches.

The world was growing darker, as if it were being consumed by night, and it took her a moment to realize that one by one the streets lights were going out, along with lights inside of homes and on doorsteps.

I have to get to Trevor!

Greg Sheer was dead and Tom Preston was standing over him, the house now dark, and the world outside just as ominous.

Greg had stood up and cocked his shotgun once again, preparing to put a lug through Maria, but to their horror the power blinked out and an awful choking sound could be heard coming from Greg just as the shotgun went off in the ceiling, blowing a hole into Kathryn's room, his now glassy eyes staring at the fist that was protruding out of his chest and the fingers clutching his heart.

"Hi, honey, I'm home," he had said as soon as he ripped his hand back out of Greg, allowing his corpse to fall to the floor.

It was at that same moment that Trevor and Kathryn both saw the form of Jonathan Marker detach itself from Greg's body.

"Holy shit..." Maria said, backing away and racing back to her family at the front of the room.

"Well, not holy...." Tom moved towards them, looking just as he had in life: a fully-functioning heart and lungs beneath his skin.

"Tom... you've come for us. I take it you're the first?"

Tom grinned and nodded at his wife.

"Oh, Kathryn, you thought you could kill me; you thought that you could just throw me in a plastic bag and be rid of me.

"Did you really think it would be that easy?"

His voice moved in a growl, and his eyes looked from them to the corpse of Brighton Blackmoore.

"I'm glad I got here now before that little shit had all my fun."

They said nothing, the remaining Blackmoores preparing, trying to predict his next move.

"Fuck you..." Maria said wearily.

Tom laughed.

"Look at you, all of you... you're not a coven of witches, you're a coven of widows; all of you!"

He paced the room, looking at them, dressed in the clothes of the homeless man he had robbed.

"Jesus, Tom, shut up."

He turned to Trevor, who was staring at him coldly.

"And you, my glorious stepson, the boy who never minded me, the kid who just wanted to be loved, the boy who didn't know who he was...."

Trevor shook his head and took to his feet.

"And who are you now, Trevor?"

Trevor looked at his mother, feeling a strength rise within him, a power, a confidence that he had been struggling for years to find and had never known existed.

"I'm the person that's going to kill you."

Tom frowned and shook his head.

"You can't kill me, Trevor; I'm already dead!"

He began to laugh and shake his head, feeling like he had finally put Trevor in his place, feeling as if now Trevor was truly helpless.

That was until Trevor started laughing.

Tom looked at Trevor and began to grow nervous. The laughter coming out of Trevor was dark, almost manic, and hinting at something much deeper, something that had been waiting a long time to surface.

"You'd be surprised how many times a soul can die."

Braxton placed his hand on Trevor's shoulder assuredly, telling him without words that he was prepared to go down fighting.

"Okay, you know what? I'm done with this... can we just get to the part where I'm killing you?"

Kathryn looked to all of them, her icy eyes connecting with the gaze of her entire family, staring at the young Marcel, calming him and his tears.

When I give the sign to run, I want you all to run, except for Mabel and Grandma Fiona. You two stay here; he won't go after you....

They all heard her. They had become one great collective conscious, connected by blood, blood that had power, blood that could not be severed. They all nodded, and Tom seemed befuddled, attempting to understand but not even coming close.

"Tom!"

Kathryn directed her gaze to her now resurrected husband, feeling that power, that anger, thinking of their last confrontation, thinking of the time he hit her and she did nothing. All of those moments were now released from her and he went flying across the room, his body crashing to the ground and knocking against the corpse of Greg Sheer, who was now lying in a deep pool of crimson.

"You bitch!"

He struggled to his feet just as the family, save for Mabel and Fiona, shot out of his sight, moving through the home, their sounds fading quickly in the darkness and growing faint.

"Where are you?"

He looked to the couch, seeing nothing, not seeing the forms of the two old women, completely unaware of their presence.

"When I find you, Kathryn, I'll kill you! I'm going to rip you open after I do it to your son first, and I'll make you watch!"

"What are we going to do?" John asked, his face red from Brighton's blood.

All of them—save for Kathryn, who had been furthest from the impact—had Brighton Blackmoore's blood on their bodies.

They were standing in the spa beneath the house, the only light coming from the white shimmer beneath the water's surface.

"I don't know. He might be strong, he might even be something other than human, but he's alive; there's no doubt about that. He's alive, and that means that he can be killed."

Kathryn looked at her huddled family, prayed that her aunt and her grandmother would be safe, and then she asked for forgiveness.

"Mom, what is it?"

Trevor reached out for the tears that were now spilling down her face, her lip quivering as she looked at her son, knowing that she had no choice but to deliver him to his destiny.

"All I ever wanted for you, Trevor, was a normal life, to be spared the darkness of this family. I prayed so often that it wouldn't be you, that you would not be touched."

She looked to Braxton and reached her hand out to his face, caressing it gently.

"But I know that I can't change fate; it will always have its way, and the Universe will always have its sacrifice."

Trevor looked at his family, seeing for the first time what they saw when they looked at him.

They saw hope, they saw the proof of a higher power, something beyond the darkness that had touched the Blackmoore name for thousands of years: they saw salvation.

"Mom, I understand what I have to do...."

She frowned helplessly and shook her head.

"It's not just you; I'm afraid one of the biggest crimes is that Braxton finally has a family, and now he's being asked to die for them."

Braxton's dark eyes filled with tears and he shook his head slowly, almost without control.

"No. Kathryn you're not asking me to die for my family; you're asking me to *save* my family! To *save* me; that's not some horrible thing, it's an honor."

"Jesus, the both of you are acting as if this isn't some big deal!"

Darbi was speaking now, his voice steady.

"Trevor, you're not going out there; neither are you."

He directed his gaze to Braxton, but the two of them were adamant.

"You were lucky, Darbi; you got to be spared from years of this. John protected you from it, but this is the reality!" Kathryn whispered.

He looked to John as the voice of reason, but there was no backup that he could give his grandson.

"Listen to me," Magdalene said, stepping forward and placing her hands on their cheeks. "Tom needs to be in contact with you. Whatever he is, he doesn't appear to have any kind of power outside of that. That book of conjure, that spell you did, Trevor—that's what brought Tom back!"

Trevor felt as if he had been kicked hard in the stomach.

"I did this?"

The tears sprung to his eyes and he looked up to the ceiling, knowing that Tom was one floor above them and time was running out.

"It was meant to happen. Remember that, Trevor, just like you need to remember that you and Braxton are meant to win this. You're meant to go against the source of all of this, which means in order for that to happen, you have to beat Tom.

"Just remember that. The both of you!"

Braxton tightened his grip on Trevor's hand and they looked at one another, seeing the power of their relationship, the trust that moved through them both—and Trevor knew then that they would win.

"You're going to be calling on some powerful magic," Kathryn said to the both of them, gripping their forearms and taking a deep breath, allowing her strength—her love—to go with them.

"Don't discredit those who have gone before us. Remember that though those who died by our curse, including your father, are waiting for you—even with that, remember that our spirits are strong and our power is great.

"And I'm always with you."

"Trevor!"

Her voice brought his heart to a stop, his breath to a standstill. Cheri was in the house. Cheri was there looking for him; Cheri was in danger.

"Trevor!"

Her call was followed with a scream; a shrill and terrifying cry.

"Gotta go!"

Braxton moved ahead of him up that stairwell, and Trevor was quick to follow, pushing his fear aside, pushing back all of his doubts, his loneliness. He was meant for something greater now. No longer was he the scared little boy at the stairs, watching his father die in his mother's arms; no longer was he the kid without any friends, and wondering when he'd be something more.

That time had come; that time was now.

"Trevor!" Kathryn called out, and he turned to her once more.

"Yeah?"

"Kick Tom's ass."

He nodded and ran up the steps, meeting Braxton at the bookcase, kissing once more, long and deep, the both of them tasting one another's tears—knowing that with each other they'd be okay.

TWENTY-EIGHT

The house was quiet as they stepped out into the hall, pushing the bookcase back into place and spotting the stairs, knowing that they had to be quick but careful, aware that Tom could be around the corner at any moment, ready to kill them the same way that he killed Greg Sheer and Teri Jules.

"Shh...."

Braxton placed his finger to his lips and Trevor nodded, their hands still gripped as they began to creep up the steps. Those pictures of Blackmoores watched them, watched them from their paper-life, watched them behind the glass of their picture frames.

"Where is he?" Trevor asked.

They were now on the second floor, seeing that the wind had blown the French doors wide open, hurling snow in from off the back balcony.

"Where's this book?" Braxton asked his boyfriend, eyes darting around and searching the darkness.

"It's in the playroom adjoining my room."

Braxton nodded, and they began to walk towards his door, the floorboards creaking beneath their steps.

They reached his room and Braxton lifted his hand to the knob, closing his eyes and allowing the images to come, allowing them to fill his mind.

In quick flashes he saw Tom gripping Cheri over his shoulders. He could feel her fear, her manic prayers for help. It caused his knees to buckle and he gripped tightly to Trevor's shoulders, using his boyfriend's weight to steady him.

"They went inside...."

Trevor nodded, and they took a deep breath before pushing the door open and going in. The room was as dark as every other room in the house, and the windows were wide open. The snow was coming in with the wind, billowing papers and knocking things to the ground.

"They must be in the playroom."

They looked at the door and it was suddenly more to them that a simple piece of wood: it was the end; it was the doorway to hell itself.

"Trevor, son, is that you?"

Tom's unmistakable voice called out from beyond the door, sensing them and giving them no choice but to go in.

They looked at one another, eyes wide, and they each took a deep breath, prepared for the first of many fights of their lives.

He was there, standing against the round-cherry wood table, a sick grin on his face, his eyes penetrating—as if glowing, even in this dark. Cheri was on the table, his right hand on her chest, pressing down, the tears streaming down her face, her brown eyes wide and filled with terror.

"No... please...."

Her voice was weak, and it took Trevor a moment to realize that she was bleeding from a contusion on her head. Books lay scattered about, used candles thrown on the ground, and Christian's fleece sweatshirt splayed out on the floor.

"Oh, hush, now, my dear." He looked from her to Trevor, and smirked. "It'll all be over soon enough."

There was nothing stopping Tom Preston from shoving his fist through her chest, just as he had done with the rest of his victims; there was nothing stopping him from ripping out Cheri's heart and sucking it dry.

"Let her go, Tom; it's me you want." Trevor commanded.

Braxton curled his fists and stared stoically at Tom, waiting for the moment when he would have to react.

"Oh, Trevor, you selfish, spoiled little brat, it's not *just* you... it's your whole family. They want your blood spilt; they want the bay to run red with Blackmoore blood... most importantly, *WE* want him."

He cocked his head towards Braxton and drew his lips back, his teeth gleaming.

"Braxton?"

Trevor turned and looked at his boyfriend, feeling as if he had just led him into a trap.

"That's right, Trevor, we want your boyfriend too. The two of you, you're a package deal; you're the Holy Grail. I bet the blood in your guys' hearts tastes like God itself!"

This constant referral to "we" gave Trevor the chills. Tom was admitting to the force that brought him back, the force that had come forth and cast its shadow over his entire future.

"Tom... I took you out of hell; it was me. And now... now it's time to put you back."

Tom's face contorted, grew dark, and his mouth dropped into a frown.

"You little shit, how dare you?!"

He moved from Cheri, knocking her to the ground, charging at Trevor, moving quickly with his arms extended and desperate to get his deadly grip on him.

"Hey!"

Braxton shoved Trevor out of the way and lunged at Tom Preston, striking him hard across the face.

Through terror-filled eyes, Trevor watched Tom take hold of Braxton by the throat and lift him off his feet.

"What have we here?" Tom questioned, staring deep into Braxton's eyes. "A little boy?"

Trevor prepared for what was next, prepared for Tom to strike him, to tear his fist through Braxton's chest, but instead he tossed him across the room.

"Braxton!" Trevor shouted, his tears catching in his throat, not even bothering to see Tom Preston, not paying attention to the force of him.

"You're mine now, little Blackmoore!"

Tom gripped Trevor hard on the throat, his fingers pressing into his trachea, threatening to crush it. The world was going dark as the oxygen was being cut from his brain.

He could feel it: the sleepiness, and the waves that seemed to engulf him. It was as if Trevor was on a ship, a gentle ship rocking on an endless sea.

You're meant to win this; don't forget that.

It was the voice of a hundred Blackmoores; it was his bloodline calling out to him, stirring him, reminding him.

He opened his eyes and looked to the ceiling, saw past the ceiling, saw the planets and stars, saw a million suns, a million lights shining down on him. He could feel it, rushing through his hair, rushing through his head.

It was time.

He heard nothing, saw nothing but those endless lights and felt the humming of his own power, the cyclone of his own soul.

"No!" he shouted, and the house itself began to shake, the floorboards loosening beneath their feet, the bookshelves trembling, the books on those shelves flying across the room, moving about them—papers and pencils, all of it swimming around the room, the windows slamming into one another over and over again.

"What the...?" Tom questioned, looking around him, the objects moving about the room, trying to keep his balance on the shaking floorboards.

"Get off of me!"

It felt as if he had been ripped from Trevor by hands stronger than his own, throwing Tom across the playroom.

"Trevor!" Cheri and Braxton called out in unison.

They ran to him, maneuvering around the still-airborne objects, struggling on those floorboards. They each took an arm and lifted him off the ground, knowing that they had only seconds before Tom was up off the floor and charging at them once again.

"Cheri, get out of this room right now!" Trevor ordered, though his throat still hurt.

She was crying and shaking her head.

"No, I'm not leaving you!"

He looked to Braxton for support.

"Cheri, you have to leave now; you can't stay here!" He echoed.

She looked at them, saw the conviction in their eyes, and sighed, kissing Trevor on the cheek without really thinking about it, and left. Braxton watched as she closed the door behind her, and their attentions were once again directed at Tom Preston, who was on his feet once again, ready to attack.

"The book!"

Trevor spotted it lying there on the floor, not three feet away from them.

"Got it."

Braxton lunged for it, sliding on the floor and gripping it tightly and holding his other hand out for Trevor.

He didn't have time to think about it. Trevor jumped towards Braxton and they moved under the table, Trevor flipping through the pages, desperate to find the incantation.

"Here!" There, written in faded ink, was the name *Exorcism of Demons.* "We have to chant this together!" he was screaming over the wind, looking into Braxton's fearful eyes, eyes that also told him that no matter what, they were in it till the end.

"Lofaham, Solomon, Iyouel, Iyosenaoui," they began, staring only at each other, holding tight to each others hands. "Lofaham, Solomon, Iyouel, Iyosenaoui...."

The floorboards came to a halt, returning once again to the way in which they had been laid, giving no hint to their sudden life.

"I can hear you!" Tom began, walking towards the table. They could hear him, as well, his footfalls getting closer, becoming louder.

"Lofaham, Solomon, Iyouel, Iyosenaoui!"

Braxton and Trevor began to scream it, keeping their eyes locked on each other.

"Don't you get it? WE are many; WE are one, and WE are hell on earth!"

Tom gripped the edge of the table and hurled it into the bookcase with such force that it broke the shelves and the table split into pieces.

"There you are." He was staring down at them, but they continued chanting, not looking at him, not moving.

"Cute." Tom snickered.

He attempted to move forward, attempted to grip them both by the hair, but something was stopping him; he couldn't move. Tom was helpless. No matter how much he willed his body, he couldn't move any closer to the boys; they were protected.

"What are you doing to me?" he struggled, muscles tightening, veins constricting. He could feel himself losing his grip on his body. He was becoming light; his sense of presence was fading quickly, his vision blurring.

"Lofaham, Solomon, Iyouel, Iyosenaoui!"

Tom hit the floor, helpless but still very much conscious, trying to make sense of it, trying to keep his hold on his body.

"Goodbye, Tom."

Trevor and Braxton broke from their trance and saw Kathryn standing there with one hand on her hip, another gripping a shovel.

"Kathryn...." He reached out for her, but she stepped back and grinned.

"You're just a man now, Tom." Kathryn lifted the shovel. "And men can be killed; husbands can be killed.

"Take it from me... I know."

Kathryn brought the shovel down into the back of his neck, splitting the flesh and severing the spinal cord, detaching head from bone and pulling it back out, the fount of blood spurting out from the wound and pooling around them.

Trevor and Braxton looked at one another for just a moment before embracing each other forcefully, the tears streaming down their faces, their sobs heavy and loud.

Kathryn looked at her home, saw the bloodshed and destruction. She saw the lives lost, and knew that this was only the beginning. It would come again, worse than Tom Preston, and it would come for others in her family. All over the world it would come, and it wouldn't stop until there were no Blackmoores left.

'What have you done?'

The voice was familiar, carried in a whisper, and they looked back to the shelves to see the form of Jonathan Marker present, as solid as they were.

"You!"

Trevor moved closer to the spirit, knowing that he couldn't actually cause it any physical harm.

'I tried to bring it to an end. I tried to give you all a fitting farewell before this happened, before Tom killed more.'

The spirit's tone was steady, as if talking about the weather.

"You were behind all of this, weren't you?"

Jonathan's face moved into what must have been a grin.

'From the very beginning. I took the form of Trevor Mayland and led your grandmother into the pool; I did it, to see if I could....'

Kathryn could feel her anger begin to stir: the remembrance of Annaline floating dead in the pool, her crying and her loss.

'I called Braxton pretending to be you... to try and separate the two of you, to keep you from coming together. It was me who then took the form of Christian once he died. I went to Greg and began to wear him thin, knowing that I was going to have to use him, that he was going to be my vessel to end your line.'

"No, you couldn't have been Christian... the dreams...."

Trevor could feel the growing deceit of the spirit.

'I wasn't. If Christian did come to you, Trevor, then it wasn't me... I would never do that to you.'

It was more lies. He had been working on this for years, plotting, manipulating them, and bending the Blackmoores to his will.

For his own selfish means he had concocted this, and yet it had still managed to blow up in his face.

"Yet you could try to kill me?"

Jonathan frowned.

'Only to protect you from yourself, to protect the world from the evil that you and Braxton's union has created.'

Kathryn tried to recall those years when she had first summoned the spirit, tried to remember his history, but she couldn't.

"But why did you want to wipe us out?"

Jonathan laughed and they all stared at it, Braxton unable to understand any of it. This was all new to him; this was foreign territory. He knew nothing about spirits. Before Trevor, he hadn't really even believed that ghosts were real.

'Because I was here first. I was a tutor to the Mayland child, but in the end I was murdered, bound to this home before it was my time. And then your family moved in and their power was strong, but your mother would not help me—'

"You're the tutor who had murdered my father's older brother in a ritual sacrifice... you're the tutor that Gregory Mayland had murdered!"

Jonathan's grin became devilish and confident.

'He also cut off my limbs and buried me in the walls....'

Again, that overwhelming feeling that the family had been played from the very beginning began to creep in on them all.

'It was Aria Blackmoore who bound me to the home, to suffer between the worlds for the rest of time. It was Aria who agreed to inflict this punishment on the request and payment of Martha Mayland....'

The puzzle began to solve itself more and more, the pieces continuing to come together and fit into place.

'It was I who secured your position in the Donovan home. It was I, along with others who brought fire to your home on the vacant lot across the street, forcing Tristan to buy that house.'

"How?"

The phantom shook its head.

'It was planned from the very beginning, and even then, there were devotees willing to see it through...'

"How?" Kathryn questioned again.

'My secret.'

Kathryn was growing angry and tired of Jonathan's gloating. There was nothing else that he could tell them, nothing else that he would share. Their mystery was far from being solved.

"By the mysteries of the deep, by the flames of Banal...."

Kathryn's eyes closed, recalling the binding that she had been tempted to use before against Jonathan Marker, but in thinking him nothing more than a troubled soul, had bound him within the walls instead.

'What are you doing...?'

Jonathan's voice was growing panicked, something that Trevor had never heard from him before.

"By the power of the east, by the Holy rites of Hecate, I conjure and exorcise thee, spirit."

Trevor's eyes widened as he watched the form of Jonathan become hazy, thin, fading like mist. Trevor knew what was going with it. He finally understood that with this banishing, his life before this night was really gone, its traces fading with him.

'No, stop... you need me. There are far worse things coming... things that you cannot even begin to comprehend!'

The spirit's voice grew dim—drifting—now nothing more than a fading whisper.

"Into the darkest depths I send thee, into the forever land I banish thee; into the arms of your hellish brethren I condemn thee!"

A howling was heard, ringing out through the home itself and then nothing.

They stood there, knowing that everything was different now, that they had all been set up from the very beginning, to the very last detail: this was their end.

TWENTY-NINE

"Is it over?" Darbi asked as they stood in the sitting room, staring at the chaos.

Maria was standing next to her father, staring at his bloodied body, which she had covered with a sheet—though it did little to stop the blood from seeping through. Cheri Hannifin was standing next to the corpse of Greg Sheer, and sobbing. It was another piece of her childhood gone, another thread to the necklace of her past unraveled.

"For now..." Kathryn responded, looking at her family. "For now."

The tears slipped down her face; it was the first time in God knew how long that she had allowed herself to be seen crying in front of anyone.

"What in the hell is this?" Randy Kit asked, looking at the mess that he had just walked into.

"This is your killer, Detective: my fuck-of-a-husband who had mysteriously vanished."

They had dragged his corpse back downstairs, mopping up the bloody mess before calling the police.

"But..." Randy was doubtful, namely because he didn't want to believe it.

"It's true."

He turned to see Cheri Hannifin coming towards him, holding an ice pack to a growing wound.

"I came here looking for Trevor and he grabbed me and beat me."

She looked down at the decapitated corpse.

"He tried to kill me."

"And what about that kid over there?"

Randy looked to Kathryn, who sighed.

"He grew crazed, spouting out that Trevor had murdered his best friend."

Randy's mouth dropped open.

"No doubt influenced by what he saw on the news... the mess you caused!"

She stared him down hard before pivoting on her heels and walking from him.

"Because of you and your accusations, my cousin, Brighton—Maria's father—an innocent man... is dead!"

There was guilt to be had and Randy knew it, could feel it, though he didn't want to own up to it.

"I'm sorry...."

She stopped and glanced back at him over her shoulder, her hair parting and only now revealing the bruise that Greg had given her.

"I'll make you pay for this."

Randy's heart began to pound, and for the first time he was feeling fear, genuine fear and he knew then that the great Kathryn Blackmoore would ruin him.

They would have a funeral for a great man, a cousin that Braxton had never had the chance to know. Greg would be committed in a peaceful, unknown ceremony, and once again Cheri and Trevor would drop earth into the grave, allowing the ash of their childhood to go down into hell with the dead Sheer.

Just like the rest of it, just like Christian Vasquez, they knew that their fates were sealed and their pasts were forever stained with childhood blood: a massacre of the innocent grown tainted.

But that was all to come, as well as the growing and impending darkness, the great evil that was moving, gaining strength. If they stood quietly in the still of the night, they could all feel it. Creeping up on them, it was there.

"Hey, Trevor...?"

He turned and looked at Braxton, saw the weariness in his eyes and the longing on his face.

"Yeah?"

Braxton leaned in and Trevor closed his eyes, smiling as Braxton's lips touched his lightly.

"I forgot to tell you...."

"Yeah?"

"Happy birthday."

It was then that Trevor sobbed. His body fell against Braxton, who in turn placed his hand on the back of his head, bracing him and sustaining his balance.

Things were changing for Trevor; his world was no longer the same, moving from conversations with Jonathan Marker and the mystery of his family, to the knowledge that he and Braxton were their family's only hope.

In the end it would all come down to them, and they had better be prepared. He was growing older now; he was of age; an adult.

He didn't notice that that game of hide-and-seek with his three best friends in a yard that was always sunny and green was nothing more than a failed and distant dream, one he would never know again.

Soon it would come, and he had to be ready. They had to be ready so the Blackmoores could carry on through the generations, as they always had. Battling their darkness; battling their demons.

Look for the first book, of a two-part Blackmoore prequel:

Rise of the Nephilim coming July, 2017
And the conclusion; *Fall of the Nephilim*
coming Autumn, 2017
From Candiano Books

ABOUT THE AUTHOR

Marcus James is the award-winning author of five novels, including
The Blackmoore Legacy series. He lives in Seattle, Washington and
is 32 years old.
Discover more at: marcusjamesbooks.com
And connect with him on social media:
Facebook: @MJameswriter
Twitter: @MJamesbooks
Instagram: @marcusjamesauthor

Made in the USA
Middletown, DE
23 October 2022

13290763R00272